The Chosen

"I am very disappointed in our new doctor," Finoa said as Dr. Shona Taylor and her family left the room.

"Did you expect she would understand right away?" Laren asked. "You were much too hard on her."

"What if she doesn't understand at all? What if she never comes around to our way of thinking? If she never can accept it at all?"

"She could quit and leave in a huff."

"And take the ottle with her," Baraba said forlornly.

"And take our privacy with her," Robret pointed out. "That's what's important. Our way is the wise way. The best way!"

"Do you think she suspects anything?" Angeta asked.

"Certainly not," Finoa said. "How could she?"

THE LADY AND THE TIGER

JODY LYNN NYE

ACE BOOKS, NEW YORK

This is a work of fiction. Names, characters, places, and incidents either are the product of the author's imagination or are used fictitiously, and any resemblance to actual persons, living or dead, business establishments, events, or locales is entirely coincidental.

THE LADY AND THE TIGER

An Ace Book / published by arrangement with
the author

PRINTING HISTORY
Ace mass market edition / March 2004

Copyright © 2004 by Jody Lynn Nye.
Cover art by Michael Herring.
Cover design by Rita Frangie.
Interior text design by Kristin del Rosario.

For information address: The Berkley Publishing Group,
a division of Penguin Group (USA) Inc.,
375 Hudson Street, New York, New York 10014.

ISBN: 0-441-01148-9

ACE®
Ace Books are published by The Berkley Publishing Group,
a division of Penguin Group (USA) Inc.,
375 Hudson Street, New York, New York 10014.
ACE and the "A" design
are trademarks belonging to Penguin Group (USA) Inc.

PRINTED IN THE UNITED STATES OF AMERICA

10   9   8   7   6   5   4   3   2   1

ONE

Th℮ music continued to cycle over the speakers on the bridge of the merchant ship *Sibyl* as she circled down through landing orbit around the blue and tan planet.

"Welcome, Dr. Shona Taylor!" sang the massed voices. *"We bid welcome to you! We hope you'll feel at home here!"*

Everyone on the bridge was grinning except the subject of the song, a small woman with light brown hair, freckles, and wide hazel eyes. Shona sat in the copilot's seat with her cheeks burning red. "I have never had anything like this happen in my entire life," she said severely.

"You're famous," said Shona's husband Gershom.

"I think it's pretty," said Lani, who dropped her eyes almost as soon as she spoke. The girl, now fifteen, had blossomed from the painfully shy ten-year-old they had adopted to a teenager who still preferred not to call attention to herself. That was growing more difficult by the day, as Lani's dark, exotic beauty drew eyes to her everywhere she went. Shona was glad they had a large dog; even gentle Saffie might act as a deterrent.

"It's embarrassing," Shona said, gesturing at the console. "That's not a computer synthesis. The waveform shows those are real voices. Someone wrote that song and assembled a group to sing it."

"Sounds like the whole Dendebe Interstellar Madrigal Chorus," Gershom said.

"Do you think *they're* down there?" asked Eblich eagerly. The ship's navigator, a slight, shy man, enjoyed classical music.

"No chance," grunted Ivo, the ship's engineer, a big, dark-skinned man. "But they got somebody who knows how to sing harmony. Lots of somebodies."

"Ka-ching," Gershom said, lifting his broad shoulders in a half-apologetic shrug to his wife. "We knew these people were very wealthy. If they choose to spend their credits in an expensive greeting to you, that's their business. Although I'd like it more if they used it to take some of our cargo."

Kai, the storesmaster, just grunted. "Not much chance, since we're confined to the spaceport, except for offloading Shona's module."

"How come they're not singing about me?" Fear of being the cynosure of all eyes was not young Alexander Taylor's problem. At five he was as outgoing as a politician at polling time. Freckled and fair like his mother, he was going to have his father's rangy build, but at the moment he was at the cobby stage that meant he was saving up for another growth spurt.

"They want to welcome your mother because she's the one they hired," Gershom explained to his pouting son. "They didn't mention me, either, did you notice?"

The full lips relaxed a little. "No . . ."

His younger sister, dark-haired and hazel-eyed, was determined not to be left out, either. She climbed up on Shona's lap and made a try for the comm-unit's microphone. Shona beat her to it. "Don't touch, Jilly-flower. Mommy's got to talk to ground control."

Gershom lifted a dark eyebrow at her reluctant tone. "Do you want me to do it?"

"No, thank you, sweetheart," Shona said, steeling herself and hoping the color had faded from her face. "I'm the one who's going to have to face these people daily for six months. And I am grateful that they're so glad to have us. This is Dr. Shona Taylor," she said into the pickup. Ignoring the grins of the rest of the crew, she continued. "Thank you for the wonderful welcome. May we have landing instructions, please?"

"Strap down," Gershom instructed the children. "We're going in."

AFTER the chorus, Shona was surprised that only one person was waiting for her. A young woman with a shy, eager smile approached almost as soon as the airlock door popped open, and grasped Shona's hands.

"You're here!" she exclaimed. She had short brown hair, similar to the color of Shona's own, but her eyes were brown instead of hazel, and she stood about five centimeters taller than Shona's 157. "I'm Dwan Sands. It's so nice to meet you at last! Welcome to Jardindor!"

"Thank you," Shona said, glancing around. The *Sibyl*'s shuttle had come to rest in the small spaceport. Unlike most colonies, Jardindor's landing pad was very close to the living quarters. The landing pad was enclosed in a blast shield so advanced that Mars Dome would have been proud to own it.

On the other side of the clear barrier Shona could see houses. The spaceport, filled with small personal craft and one or two large transports, formed one side of a square. The landscape stretched out into the distance, and if perspective was to be believed, those houses were veritable mansions, covering acres of land. After the constricted quarters of a working starship, and the domes of Mars where she had been brought up, it was an almost ostentatious use of land. Above it all she could see handsome distant mountains in muted bronze and purple. She found the yellowish quality of the light odd, unlikely given Jardindor's blue-white dwarf sun, but she assumed it was a trick of the gravity generators, or the chemicals or biomass that was transforming the rest of the fiercely terraformed planet. The perspective also changed oddly as she turned her head, as though the atmosphere magnified the distance unevenly.

Never in her life had she landed at a spaceport so beautifully landscaped. Topiary evergreens formed a screen along the perimeter, shielding the buildings they'd seen from overhead from view at ground level. Probably gave them some extra relief from the hubbub of a working spaceport. But the plants were more than sound barriers. Not a single twig ruined the outline of birds, animals, even insects carved in a living frieze of green. Along the inner wall someone had planted a string of small gardens that were riotously colorful in their abundance. Shona drank in the vivid reds, oranges, even blues, of the blossoms, all welcome sights after the blackness of space and the sameness of the *Sibyl*'s white enamel interior. She could hardly drag her eyes back to her hostess. "This is a *beautiful* place."

Dwan smiled. "You sound surprised. I know. Some people think we fake the scenery when we send out tridees of the colony, but why would we? It's not as though we're trying to attract anyone's attention."

Shona knew that was true. Once the offer had arrived on her comm-unit asking her to take over as *locum tenens* for Jardindor's vacationing physician, she'd had a hard time locating any information on Jardindor at all. Her dearest friend, Susan MacRoy, had tracked down some data, and suddenly Shona had understood why: Jardindor was one of the wealthiest private colonies in the entire galaxy.

Once EarthGov had started licensing systems that had Earth-type planets, most of the contracts had gone to companies like the Galactic Laboratory Corporation and other megacorporations that were capable of populating whole planets out of their workforce. But some had gone to private concerns, and Jardindor was one of these. Susan's encoded message had given Shona a pretty good idea why they'd been approved. Every family on Jardindor was wealthy enough in its own right to buy a whole planet, let alone settler's rights to a barely viable planet on the far edge of current shipping lanes. They liked their privacy, and kept news of their world hard to get.

"How large is the M-class area here?" Gershom asked Dwan. The summing look on his face told Shona he was estimating how much the colony might need in the way of fertilizers, exotic plants, or ornamental or food crop seed, not to mention building materials or luxury goods to enjoy on those estates. She grinned. Once a merchant, always a merchant.

Dwan's lips tightened for a moment. "That's not really considered a polite question to ask," she said. "It's a good thing you didn't say it in front of the leaders. Governor Hethyr doesn't like to comment on the work in progress."

"Whatever you say," Gershom said, with a friendly smile. "I was just curious. What do you folks do for fun? I have good connections for the latest sports equipment and the best console games. Depends on your tastes."

"You'll have to talk to Hethyr," Dwan said firmly. "Let me show you where you're going to be living. You must have received the innoculations."

"Yes," Shona said, and was again struck how organized this colony appeared to be. "It certainly saved us a great deal of trouble. The children will be able to fit in at once— and thank you for allowing me to include them on this posting—and my animals won't have to be quarantined at all."

"Yes, your animals," Dwan said, her brown eyes lighting up. "You brought *all* of them with you?"

"Of course," Shona replied, surprised by the eagerness of her tone. "Your contract was quite specific. May I ask why?"

"Well . . ." Dwan seemed a bit embarrassed. "We like

animals here. Um, is the ottle still with you? I would love to meet him."

Alien Relations would have had ninety-five fits at Dwan's casual knowledge, but it was hardly a secret that Shona had an ottle in her household. The small extraterrestrials excited comment wherever they went, and the terms of Shona's hosting contract specified that firstly, her visitor was allowed to go wherever he wished, and secondly, she had to accompany him. Given the rarity of ottles and their natural outgoing personalities it was impossible for him not to attract attention, even if there hadn't been galaxy-wide attention drawn to the Taylor ménage over the last few years. Shona, Chirwl, and the rest of her family had been in the tri-dee news during both the scandal over the genocide in GLC colonies that had almost cost her daughter Lani her life, and in Shona's subsequent involvement with renegade scientists on Poxt, the ottle homeworld.

Shona gave a dry chuckle. "You'll hardly be able to avoid Chirwl," she said. "He's looking forward to exploring this settlement. Oh! I'd better let him out of his crash cage. He hates landings."

Dwan followed them into the *Sibyl*. The crew had unstrapped from their own couches and were letting the kids out of theirs. Dwan stopped to kneel beside Alex and Jill. Alex expanded at once in the regard from an interested adult. Jill put her finger in her mouth and went wide-eyed. Lani, as usual, had retreated in the presence of a stranger to the shadows behind the crew. Shona went past them through the narrow metal corridor to the door of her lab.

The white enamel-covered, oblong module fit into any one of the three holds of the ship, and would be left behind when the *Sibyl* launched again. The module had been a gift to her from GLC—a guilt gift, Gershom had pointed out. Maintaining one herself was costly, but Shona felt it made her a more competent physician. As an environmental physician, often by the time she arrived on the scene she found patients needed her immediate attention. There wasn't time to potter around in boxes looking for supplies or equipment. Because the module was made to plunge through atmosphere to the surface on its own where the ship could not land, everything was lined with thin but effective impact foam, and the kennels for her animals were supported by hydraulic gyros to absorb the rigors of landing.

"You won't have a heavy workload," Dwan assured her, following her in. "We're very heathy here. We exercise a lot and we practice natural wellness. There's a hot spring spa, a health club, automasseuse, meditation gardens. We walk, we play tennis, we swim. You're welcome to use our facilities. The children, too."

"I'd enjoy that," Shona said, with pleasure. "It's going to be nice to have a straightforward assignment as a colony doctor. You would be surprised at some of the situations I've had—" She stopped as Dwan chuckled. "Oh, maybe not. We have been all over the tri-dee news. I didn't go looking for notoriety, you know."

"I know," her hostess said, with a rueful smile of understanding. "But it did mean we knew a lot about you in advance. Who's making all that noise?"

Shona sighed and unlatched the first compartment.

Her fox-colored Abyssinian cat, Harry, leaped out of the cage as soon as the crash cushions were out of the way. With an untranslatable comment, he stalked past Dwan to his feeding station, stared at his mistress, and waited.

"Not yet, you greedy brute," Shona said, moving to unlatch the lower compartment, where Saffie waited patiently for liberty. The black dog shook herself thoroughly then came to sniff Dwan's outstretched hand. The Jardindorian woman's face was transformed with joy as she stroked the dog's thick fur.

"She's gorgeous," Dwan breathed. Saffie, hearing a friendly voice, tilted up her great head and slurped the visitor's face with a long pink tongue.

"Thank you," Shona beamed. She loved Saffie so much she enjoyed it when other people adored her on sight.

"She is a genuine Bernese mountain vaccine dog? Pedigreed?" Dwan pressed, looking the dog over carefully.

"Yes," Shona said. She watched her visitor with growing curiosity. "Pedigreed and patented. The Bernese seemed to take the genetic alteration better than some lines."

Dwan seemed on the edge of finishing the phrase with her. "And you never had her spayed, is that right? She's still fertile?"

Shona cocked an eyebrow, wondering if she was going to have to formulate a polite refusal. How awkward when she had just arrived for a long assignment. Saffie's bloodlines were spoken for, and she had no means of negotiating otherwise. "You haven't got a male Bernese here, have you?"

"Oh, no! I couldn't afford a really good pedigreed dog. We just like animals. I go running every morning with my greyhound. If you'd like, she could come with us once in a while. I'd love that." Dwan scratched Saffie's head, making the dog close her big brown eyes and croon. Harry, jealous, came over, smacked Saffie in the nose with a paw, and rubbed against Dwan's leg.

Shona relaxed. Her experiences had made her so jumpy she was seeing challenges and problems where there weren't any. Dwan was just enthusiastic. It'd be nice for Saffie to have someone else to take walks with beside the family.

The Harvard cancer mice and the pair of lop-eared rabbits had withdrawn to the safety of the chewed mass of fluff in the corner of each of their compartments. They ignored Shona as she checked their water dispensers. The last protective enclosure was adapted from the shipping container for a delicate piece of laboratory equipment that was about the size of a medicine ball, leaving plenty of room for the inhabitant and his possessions. Shona flipped back the lid and extracted from it a large leather pouch with a loop on the top. A hook on one wall had been mounted there to accommodate the tree-dwelling alien.

Shona hung up the pouch, flipped back the top flap, and peered in.

"It's safe," she said. "We're down. You don't have to go through that again for six months."

"A mild landing I enjoyed," chittered a high-pitched voice. Chirwl swarmed up out of the opening. "Not rough so the module by itself. Relief." He blinked his round black eyes at her.

"Chirwl, this is Dwan Sands," Shona said, as her new friend stared open-mouthed. Ottles, named by their human discoverers because they were about the same size as Earth otters but with round, flattened bodies like turtles, were still rarely seen anywhere but their homeworld, Poxt. They had sable-brown fur; small, round ears; long vibrissae around their sharp-toothed mouths; clever little hand-paws capable of delicate manipulation; and short, thick tails that ended in a point, suitable for a species that spent as much time in its homeworld's rivers as it did in the forests that flanked them.

Ottles, intelligent and inquiring, were pleased to meet other species. An entirely nontechnological race, they were fascinated by human beings and their symbiosis with machines. They elected to send a few of their number out into human-settled space as observers and ambassadors. Alien Relations, the Galactic Government's department set up to safeguard them, put all potential ottle hosts through a thoroughgoing examination to ensure that they would not exploit their charges, and would allow them the scope to observe human behavior as they saw fit. Shona felt herself privileged to have been chosen for the program, and knew she'd made a friend as well. On Poxt, Chirwl was a philosopher. He had been working for years on his theory of humankind, the notes for which he inscribed with his very sharp claws on an endless series of tiny, round tiles of wood. He must have been working on his thesis during the landing. Some of the rejected chips now littered the inside of his crash couch. Shona scooped them up and put them in the pocket of her tunic. He could sort them later.

"Most pleased," Chirwl said, transfering the blink to Dwan and scanning her up and down with his round black eyes. "Born here were you?"

"Nothing like diving right into personal information," Shona scolded him. "You're losing your grip on your manners."

"No, it's all right," Dwan said. She studied the little alien as closely as he was studying her. "No, I wasn't born here. My parents are on Earth. I live here with my husband and our children. Please come and see your new home," she said, collecting the whole group in a glance. "Do you need help . . . oh," she paused, as Chirwl clambered down the wall. He seemed to be clinging to nothing, but his sharp claws actually were embedded in artificial handholds almost too small for the human eye. There was little in nature that an ottle couldn't climb, but perfectly smooth manmade materials defeated him.

"Carriage is not needed," Chirwl said cheerfully. "My friend Saffie obliges." He swarmed up onto the waiting dog's back. Saffie didn't really like being a pack animal, but she did it patiently for the ottle. Shona gave her a scratch behind the ears for thanks.

Dwan gestured to them to climb into an open four-wheeled car with three bench seats ahead of an open cargo area.

"You don't use flitters?" Gershom asked.

"There's only one here," Dwan said. "It belongs to the governor's son. We prefer to use nonpolluting means of transportation. These carts are comfortable, and I think they harken back to a more gracious age, don't you?"

Gershom held firmly to their two smaller children's hands as they left the spaceport. The landscaping gave them a feeling of cosiness and intimacy. Along the outer edge of the high evergreen wall, little nooks had been carved into the evergreens with benches or pairs of seats, all of them vacant, though on one bench a real paper book had been left open and turned upside down to mark its place as though the reader had stepped away for just a moment.

Shona took a deep breath of the delicious, resin-scented air. "So different from being aboard ship," she said. "I love space travel, but filters can't duplicate a real planetary atmosphere."

"Reminds me of some of the parks on Earth," Gershom mentioned, as Dwan led them over a delicate humpback bridge that crossed a chattering stream.

"How nice of you to notice," Dwan said, happily. "This part is meant to look like Kensington Gardens in old London. That part over there," she pointed toward the other side of the spaceport, "is meant to be like Portland. You can see that the observation tower looks like a lighthouse?" Shona nodded blankly. She'd only seen one part of Earth as a tourist; the rest of her experience had been its ports where they picked up cargo. "The ground drops away into a valley on the far side of the field. It looks *perfect* from the other side."

Shona and Gershom exchanged glances. The plant life in the two gardens were distinctly different, meaning that each group had been imported especially for its location, and probably from the original source. These were, as Susan had put it, seriously rich people.

Saffie, with Chirwl clinging to her back, elected to trot beside Dwan, whose long legs ate up the distance, leaving Shona to chug along behind as best she could with Harry in her arms. Lani stayed close beside her mother, holding Jill, who was goggle-eyed at the scenery. Alex, too, was unwilling to let go of a good listener, and trotted along on Dwan's other side. Though they dropped farther and farther behind, Shona, Gershom, and Lani could still hear Chirwl's shrill piping melded with Alex's insistent soprano as they vied for Dwan's attention. They exchanged grins.

The Taylors were happy to have a chance to take in the scenery without a narrator. The sky was blue with a faint hint of green, and long, narrow clouds scudded overhead. Harry kicked her in the chest with an impatient back foot.

Shona recognized the action as a sign that his sensitive nose was detecting something. She raised her own nose to sniff, and coughed on the mouthful of foul air.

"Do you smell that?" Shona asked. "I *wondered* if I should have brought some filter masks out here."

"Some kind of propylene esters," Gershom said, after a moment. "I wonder where it's coming from."

"Isn't the wild part of the planet rich in those?"

"Yes, but look around you," Gershom said, with a low-key gesture meant to avoid attracting the attention of anyone who might be spying on them from the lush undergrowth. "This section is terraformed to Earth-grade—well above government standards. There should be no trace of toxic atmosphere here."

"Unless someone has breached the force field," Shona said, with alarm. "The entire colony could be poisoned if too many of those compounds are brought in here."

"You can tell them that once you're settled," Gershom said. "It's gone now. I think we're there."

Indeed they were. Dwan waved to them from the top of the steps of a huge building. Its sides gleamed white like finest Earth-Italian marble, which indeed it might have been, and gold glinted from knobs, trim, and window frames. The central peaked roof was at least ten meters high. Flanking it were two smaller wings, bounded by a turretlike structure at each corner. More expensive landscaping framed this small castle, mostly roses. Shona sighed with delight at the vine-covered trellises covered with pink blossoms that ascended to upstairs windows and the neatly trimmed rose trees of every shade blooming in tidy beds.

"Dr. Setve said to make sure to tell you to use this place as your own," Dwan said.

"It's lovely," Shona said. "How many other families live here?"

Dwan frowned, puzzled. "No one else lives here. It's Setve's place."

"This is a one-family house? Never mind," Shona said,

waving her hand, as she recalled Susan's excited messages about the settlers here. "It was a stupid question, really."

"Both of us come from artificial-atmosphere environments," Gershom explained. "To be able to build out in the air like this—well, it's just a dream."

"Ah," Dwan said, nodding. "Let me show you around. You'll love it. Setve has the most wonderful garden!"

"Ahem." A low cough came from the shadows to the side of the verandah. Dwan's mobile face became expressionless.

"Good afternoon, Finoa," she said, stiffly.

"Good afternoon, Dwan," the woman said, coming forward. Tall, with black hair, deep blue eyes, and a hawk's beak nose in a long, narrow face, she offered an austere nod to Dwan. Turning to Shona she smiled pleasantly but formally. "I apologize deeply for intruding. I regret not allowing you time to settle in, but I require your assistance."

She held up her arm. Her hand was wrapped in a cloth.

"Of course!" Shona exclaimed. "What happened?"

Finoa shot a look at Dwan, whose face reddened.

"I will let you have privacy," the young woman said. Gershom cleared his throat. He bent courteously toward their hostess.

"Perhaps you can show me and the children the rest of the house. I like gardens." Lani nodded eagerly.

"Indeed yes!" Chirwl exclaimed. "Plants and wildlife I crave the scent of."

"I want to see my room!" said Alex. Jill just stared with her finger in her mouth.

"I . . . I'm afraid I can't," Dwan said hastily, backing away from them all. "I need to get home. I have a . . . treatment very shortly. But perhaps I may come back early tomorrow and take you around the colony?" She glanced at each of them, almost desperately, Shona thought. "There are so many things I want to show you, and tell you." Shona was surprised at the stern look that Finoa shot her. Some past history, Shona decided. Or, remembering Jardindor's reputation for privacy, some concern that

Dwan was going to reveal personal information. They need not fear. As a doctor Shona was used to keeping confidences.

"We would enjoy having you come back," Shona said warmly, taking Dwan's hand. "Thank you for taking so much time with us."

The young woman flinched as though embarrassed by the contact and retreated hastily down the steps. The moment she was out of sight Finoa seemed to relax, and smiled at Shona.

"I'm sorry to interrupt. I know where Setve's clinic is. May I show you?"

Shona glanced over Finoa's shoulder at Gershom, who shrugged. He sat down on the top step and took a loop of string out of his pocket. Alex and Jill immediately scrambled into his lap to take their turns at cat's cradle. Lani and Saffie sat down beside them. "Yes, thank you."

"I should like to go, too," Chirwl piped up. He scooted forward and looked up at the newcomer. "New laboratory of interest."

"Not yet," Gershom said, grabbing him by his short tail and hauling him back. Shona gave him a grateful look and followed her new patient inside.

"What a wonderful house," Shona said, looking around her as Finoa guided her. "I've never seen so much wood in one place. My husband occasionally gets a shipment of furniture from Earth. This is all so lovely. Rosewood, and oak, and . . . my goodness, is that bird's-eye maple? Wait until Gershom sees that!" Finoa said nothing, but continued to stalk silently onward with purpose. Shona chided herself for gawking when her patient was obviously in pain. She didn't halt again.

They passed down a wide, broad-paneled corridor lit by skylights and shaped bulbs in ornate bronze sconces. Oil paintings lined the wall in between the windows, which gave a view of rolling lawns filled with flowers and discreet glimpses of statuary. "Oh! How delightful! Dwan was right about the garden." Finoa didn't reply.

The next door, to Shona's everlasting relief, opened onto the clinic. Beyond a waiting room with button-back silk-upholstered couches was an examination room that might have been taken straight out of the latest catalogs. Shona recognized the equipment on the stainless-steel tables against the walls as state-of-the-art. Everything looked brand new, including the retorts and glassware. She just knew if she turned on the diagnostic computer beside the white examination couch that it would have every upgrade and all the newest programs. There was even a Nentnor incubator for tissue culturing. Dr. Setve must be able to afford the best. The room had obviously been made ready with Shona in mind. The ultraviolet sanitizer had a knee-pedal that was low enough for her to use, and a shelf filled with boxes of disposable gowns and gloves was placed within easy reach. A second door was set into the wall next to a wide window that overlooked the gardens.

As soon as the door shut behind them Finoa turned to look at her.

"I don't mean to be rude, staring at all the furniture," Shona said apologetically, gesturing Finoa to the white couch. "I hardly know what is considered polite to discuss. Every place I've ever visited is different. Everyone has a 'no-go' area, if you understand what I mean."

"Perfectly," Finoa said, with a sigh that was far removed from the formal stiffness she had displayed outside the clinic walls. She sat down, the expanse of white sterifoam padding compressing comfortably under her weight. "There are a lot of such 'no-gos' here, I am afraid you will find. It comes from our being such a small community."

"Of course." Shona put on a pair of translucent gloves and bent to unwrap Finoa's wrist. The skin was abraded in a large patch on the inside of the arm. It had bled, but Finoa must have washed it before coming to see her. Shona cleaned it again and leaned in for a good look.

"Hmm, this looks nasty, but it's really just a bad scrape.

What were you doing when it happened?" Finoa hesitated. "All right, that's one of those no-go topics. It's inflamed. Did you come in contact with something that you know you're allergic to?"

"No. Definitely not." Finoa was positive.

"All right," Shona said. "I'll give you a general antibiotic against infection." Finoa made a face.

"Must you? I hate to compromise my immune system over a scratch."

The way she said it made Shona raise her eyebrows. "Certainly not, if you prefer. If you would like to assist your immune system in more natural ways, put a lot of onions and garlic in your evening meal, and have some for the next few days. Keep the injury clean, and everything should be all right. Come see me if it becomes hot or puffy."

Finoa seemed relieved. "Thank you. You do understand. Setve did, but we weren't sure his substitute would be flexible enough to recommend natural remedies."

Shona nodded. "I've been in situations where there was nothing else, so believe me, I know there are many I can depend on. So, if I may ask a favor in return, what may we talk about in polite company? You don't confine conversations to the weather and everyone's health, do you? That would get old in the first hour, and I'll be here for six months!"

Finoa laughed, the lines in her long face relaxing. Heavens, no! Philosophy, art, the latest scientific findings, fashion. Politics, sometimes. News. Sports, always. Gardening. Tri-dee videos. *That's* a big topic. Do you watch *Poor Mother McGrew*?"

"It's my favorite show!" Shona exclaimed with delight. "Though I'm pretty sure I missed some of the thirty-sixth season. We get so busy that I forget to check the feeds."

"I have them all," Finoa said.

Shona's eyes lit up. "I would love to catch up. May I borrow them?"

"Of course. It will be my pleasure." With a little smile

Finoa stood up, testing the dressing. "That feels much better. Thank you."

A gong sounded over their heads. Shona's puzzlement must have shown on her face, for Finoa explained, "That is Setve's door signal. I believe you have another patient. I will go out the rear door, if you don't mind."

"As you please," Shona said. "It's been very nice meeting you."

"I enjoyed it, too." As she went out, Finoa's face changed from the pleasant smile to the expressionless mask. The Jardindorians were private, all right, even down to their moods. Shona had only a moment to wonder how difficult it was going to be to fit in when another woman arrived. She was short and plump, her straight, dark hair cut to the nape of her neck. A thread or two of silver told Shona that the newcomer was not as young as her smooth skin suggested. The golden sweater she wore had a green overtone that went well with the hazel eyes set deep under straight dark brows.

"I beg your pardon," the newcomer said, glancing at the open door ahead of her. "Were you busy?"

"I was just finishing," Shona said, easily. She went to close the door, and the visitor relaxed. No one seemed to want to be seen accepting medical treatment. "How may I help you?"

"I was unable to meet you when you landed. I had an off-planet conference call I could not skip. I am Governor Hethyr Candell, the chief administrator here on Jardindor. Are you settling in well?"

"Yes, thank you. I've already seen a patient."

"I know," Hethyr said, her eyes glinting. "I met your husband on the doorstep. I am very glad you are here. I have need of your services, too." She glanced down nervously. "I was . . . I was meditating when I felt unwell. I . . . well, I vomited."

"Did the . . . matter look unusual in any way?" Shona asked tactfully.

Hethyr turned an amused eye to her. "About the same as it went down, I fancy. No."

"Do you think you could be pregnant?"

"No."

"I see," Shona said. "On the way here my husband and I thought we smelled a heavy, cloying scent. If it's what we thought, concentrated exposure could cause gastrointestinal cramping. Did you observe a strong chemical aroma before your stomach became upset?"

Hethyr frowned, eying Shona. "Perhaps I did smell something."

"I can run a blood-gas analysis to see if you were exposed to a large dose," Shona said. Hethyr hesitated. "Or I can get my cat. He'll recognize if it was the same compound."

"No, thank you," Hethyr said. "I really don't want to stay longer than necessary."

"Let me check to see if it might have been good old food poisoning." Shona had seen the swabs behind glass doors in the immaculate cabinets. She smiled at the governor as she leaned forward to take a sample of saliva. "I like your sweater," she said, trying to put the rigid-backed woman at ease. "Real cashmere, isn't it? I don't mean to pry," she added in surprise as Hethyr recoiled. "I love good fabrics. I had a cashmere wrap once."

"Oh," Hethyr said faintly, settling down. "Do you want this one?"

"No!" Shona exclaimed, mortified at the thought. "I was just admiring it."

She swabbed the inside of Hethyr's mouth and ran a quick check for botulism, salmonella, and the usual provocative bacteria. Again, she was impressed by Setve's expansive array, and wished she could afford such fantastically elaborate and accurate equipment. Almost as soon as she had closed the lid of the computerized microscope, a reading rolled up on the screen.

"No unusual levels of any foreign chemicals. I could prescribe something for the stomach upset," Shona began,

and got the same expression of alarm as she had from
Finoa. She changed her suggestion before it was spoken.
"Some tea made with ginger and mint. They'll settle your
stomach. Not too much mint right before bedtime; it's a
stimulant."

"I know that," Hethyr said, with a touch of asperity that
she quickly moderated. "I grow five kinds of mint in my
own garden. I'll use some apple mint. It's nice to see that
you know your job, Dr. Taylor."

"Call me Shona, please. Thank you for the lovely song
that was broadcast to us as I arrived. I didn't get an opportunity to thank the chorus. Is it a community chorale
group? My husband and I love to sing."

Hethyr frowned. "No. Hired singers. As soon as they
were finished we loaded them onto their ship and sent
them off. They'll have broken orbit by now. They were
only contracted to be here until you arrived."

Shona shook her head in amazed disbelief. Wait until
Gershom heard *that*.

"We're glad you have arrived. Your crew will be offered
our hospitality until their departure. When will that be?"

"Most likely tomorrow," Shona said. "Once my module
is offloaded they have no reason to stay, unless there is
something that the Taylor Traveling Medicine Show and
Trading Company can do for you?" she added hopefully.
"We have some fine products you might enjoy browsing
over." Hethyr nodded sharply.

"I've made an appointment with your husband for tomorrow at midday. Join us for lunch. I'll send a car."

"Thank you. I'd enjoy that. We both will."

The door chime sounded again. Hearing it, Hethyr
marched promptly out the rear door. Shona was reminded
of an old-fashioned drawing-room comedy on tri-dee, and
wondered if this happened when the regular doctor was on
duty.

Before she had time to worry about it, her next patient
arrived. A woman with a glorious head of wavy black hair

and dark blue eyes who introduced herself as Shelia came
in towing behind her a child with a fist crammed to his eye.

Shona snapped on a pair of fresh gloves and knelt down
at the boy's level with a swab. She didn't need to put it into
the fancy computer; she'd seen the same ailment a thousand times before. Darrlel had a common eye infection,
one that children contracted often: pinkeye. This time she
was firm, prescribing antibiotic eyedrops.

"Otherwise he will be more miserable, and it will
spread," she told the unhappy mother. She spotted a touch
of red in Shelia's eyes. "You already have it. You'll need to
use this preparation, too. I will give you separate bottles
and sterile eyedroppers. Wash your hands after each treatment."

Shelia seemed dismayed not to be offered an herbal al-
ternative, but she thanked Shona. Once more the patients
hustled out the back when the signal sounded. Shona
stripped her gloves and waited for her next caller.

This visitor was a man about forty. His dark hair had
been streaked with gold over the temples, as though he
couldn't wait long enough to look naturally distinguished.
Without introducing himself he held out a thumb. It bore a
small red wound, which on closer examination Shona
judged to be a pierce-mark.

"Thorn?" Shona asked, looking at the shape with a
scope. "Or a toothmark? A fang?"

"Thorn," the man gritted out. Shona observed a few dif-
ferences in the wound that suggested the man was lying to
her. What on this planet had teeth that long? It didn't matter; she could still treat it. There appeared to be no signs of
infection or inflammation. She cleansed it thoroughly, dotted it with salve, and put a tiny dressing on it.

"It doesn't need to be covered all the time, but the patch
will keep dirt out of it while it heals," she explained.
Though the door chime didn't sound again the man fled as
soon as possible, glancing in the direction of the corridor
as he did.

After he left, Shona waited, almost holding her breath.

She peered out into the waiting room. No one was there. She let out a deep sigh. Impromptu office hours were over for now. She would have to ask someone, maybe Dwan, what Setve's hours were. With the importance people here put on privacy, she couldn't imagine the Jardindorians charging in and out of Setve's house at all hours.

She rejoined Gershom at the front of the house and sank down beside him with a sigh of pleasure. A gentle breeze wafted the scent of vine flowers through the air. The children were playing tag with Saffie on the lawn. Harry and Chirwl were curled up in the window seat enjoying the last rays of sunshine.

"Four callers," Gershom said, "out of a population of only a hundred or so. Dwan said they were healthy."

"They are," Shona said. She picked Harry off the window seat and draped him over her shoulder to stroke his fur with a meditative air. He began to purr, and Shona leaned her cheek against his side. "Most of what was troubling them they could have handled themselves. They were investigating to see whether I am worth the exorbitant fee they are paying us."

"If they are going to keep you this busy, then it isn't exorbitant, not even on a per hour basis," Gershom commented with a wry grin. "There's no industry on this planet. Everything is largely mechanized, including the housecleaning and landscaping. Perhaps visiting the doctor is what they do for a hobby."

"A strange occupation," Chirwl said, lolloping over to sit beside them. "Would you not receive too much medical?"

"With a good doctor, no," Shona said, grinning at the earnest little alien. "One wouldn't overprescribe, especially without knowing their histories. Come on, everybody. Let's see the rest of the house, before someone else shows up." Jill had fallen asleep on Lani's shoulder. Gershom took the limp toddler from her and cuddled her. She sighed, her lips pink and soft in her sleep. Alex sprang up from where he was sitting on the lawn with Saffie.

"Any serious cases?" Gershom asked as they passed into the cool dimness of the house. He knew better than to ask about specifics.

"All trivial problems," Shona assured him, feeling around on the wall near the door for light controls. Suddenly the overhead globes went on by themselves. Shona jumped. Sensors had either detected the fading of the light or the presence of humans who needed illumination. "Nothing they couldn't have taken care of by themselves at home. I was tactful. I just listened in case they had something they wanted to tell me. Their regular doctor's been gone about two weeks."

"They're just taking a close look at you," Gershom said, with a little smile. "I think you'll do very well. You can become the private physician to a tycoon any time."

"They seemed unusually reserved," Shona said, thoughtfully.

"Not surprising! Come along, let's see your new home."

Having been born on a distant colony world and brought up in the domes of Mars, Shona was fascinated by open-air construction. She'd always envied the people of Earth, who could build out or up as far as they liked, and never ran into retaining walls or glass barriers, not having to worry about gas-impermeable fittings. Her uncle's home was spacious by Mars standards, but the entire house could have fit easily into the great room that lay just beyond the foyer.

"What does Dr. Setve use all this space for?" Lani asked, curiously looking at the fresco on the vast ceiling and the carved molding around the six wide windows that ran along the rear of the chamber. Her cabin on the *Sibyl* was eight-feet square.

"Perhaps he entertains a good deal," Shona said.

"There are fewer than a hundred people on the whole planet," Gershom pointed out. "This room could hold two hundred. More."

"They like to spread out?" Shona shrugged. "Everyone has their own ideas about personal space. They have the room to indulge themselves. Chirwl! Get down from there!"

"Inspecting technique of design," the ottle explained, from his vantage point clinging to the plaster molding at the top of the wall. "From below, much more realistic than at eyesight level."

The entire house struck Shona as unreal. She and her family wandered from room to room admiring the décor and enjoying the luxurious feel underfoot of thick, soft carpet or smooth, polished wood. Shona opened a large exterior door leading off the examination room and found herself standing under a portico on a plain, plascrete pad.

"This doesn't look as pretty as the rest of the house," Lani said. "Isn't it finished?"

"It's finished, all right," Gershom said, letting out a long, low whistle. "Look! It's exactly the right size for Shona's lab module. Power ports and disposal ducts in just the right places. They *do* know everything about us. I wonder if they got all this information from our credit history or tri-dee reporters."

"They're very considerate," Shona said firmly. "Now, I want to see that garden!"

At the rear of the house, a clear-paneled door led out into a glass atrium surrounded on three sides by formal gardens. Most of the atrium was taken up by a broad pool with richly colored mosaic tile lining its sides. Shona found the arrangement unusual, since the sides of the pool sloped very gently down into four or five inches of water, then the bottom dipped sharply to several feet in depth. Saffie broke away from the group to smell all around it, her tail wagging enthusiastically. Harry bounded out of Shona's arms to sniff, then backed away. His eyes were huge, and his narrow tail was puffed up to its maximum diameter.

"What's so interesting in there, Harry?" Shona asked, alarmed at the cat's antics.

"Such smells of excitement," Chirwl chittered, translating. "My friend Harry is frightened, but Saffie is enjoying odors in mix."

"Mixed what?" Shona asked, coming forward to take a sniff herself. "Chemicals?" She couldn't smell anything beyond a faint hint of chlorine. Gershom examined the area, too, but shook his head. Shona picked Harry up and deposited him by the pool. The moment she put the cat down, he retreated to the corner, hissing. She could not coax him back. In the meanwhile, the dog was wading back and forth in the shallows, her nose skimming the surface of the water.

"What's wrong? Chirwl, what does she smell?"

"Never have any of us scented of such nature," the ottle said, in great excitement. "Saffie suspects violence."

Shona looked around, but the room was empty. No traces of blood, no damage to the walls, no stains were visible.

"Well, whatever happened, it's over," she said. "Let's go walk around the grounds before the sun is completely gone."

With the setting of the sun, the air cooled significantly, leaving it feeling moist and rich. The broad walks had been turfed with a creeping mint that sent up a heavenly freshness wherever their feet passed. Lani stayed close to her parents, but Chirwl, the children, and the animals ran around the yard, breathing in scents and exploring. The three walked until the big house was out of sight among the trees and shrubs.

"This goes back a long way," Shona said. "I wonder if the land is bounded by fences or markers. I don't want to trespass on anyone else's property. I don't know what's ours and what isn't. I never thought to ask."

"I have a lot of questions for your absent host," Gershom said.

"So do I," said Shona. "I didn't think to ask the Jardindor government why Dr. Setve has taken leave. I am troubled about what Chirwl said, that Saffie scented violence. Has Setve gone away for treatment following an assault? Was he the one who attacked another in the pool house?" She shivered and folded her arms around herself. "There's so much they're not telling me."

She suddenly felt as though she was being watched. Spinning around on her heel, she scanned the thick bushes.

"There," Shona said, pointing. "Do you see that?"

"No," Gershom said, puzzled.

"I saw a glint, like a pair of eyes watching me. I'm almost sure there's someone in there. Hello!" she called. "Who is there?"

There was no answer. Shona started to push into the undergrowth, looking for the spy, but abruptly, Saffie was at Shona's hip, shoving her back with her shoulder against Shona's thigh. Her teeth were bared as she growled low in her throat. Gershom's eyebrows went up, and he felt for his ship-knife, always in an upper pocket of his pants.

"It seems as though you are right," he said, gathering up his family and guiding them back toward the big house. The sky had darkened to a deep blue and he could just barely see the path. "There was someone back there. I'm not sure I like the idea of leaving you here alone anymore."

WHEN they came back inside through the pool house, Saffie lifted her nose to sniff. So did Shona.

"I'm hallucinating," she said. "I smell paprika and onions."

"If you're having a hallucination, so am I," Gershom said. "It smells delicious."

"I'm hungry," Alex said, not unexpectedly. Shona gathered him up in her arms.

"Then let's see where that wonderful aroma is coming from."

They followed their noses a short distance to a swinging door. Behind it was a kitchen over twenty meters long, with every device, bell, and whistle for cooking that Shona had ever seen or heard of. The entire room had been fitted out with roboservers, the most sophisticated but unobtrusive kind, multijointed arms and fine-tuned sensors that could prepare a meal, serve at the table, and clean up, silently and efficiently. But the robotics were idle, folded away against the stainless-steel walls and copper-tiled ceiling. The delicious scent was coming from the broad wooden doors at the far end of the room. Alex wriggled down and dashed ahead, throwing the doors open.

"It's a feast fit for a king," he declared.

Shona smiled. The phrase was from a book she'd been reading the children at bedtime. "That's about Emperor Charles," she said, following her son. "Not us . . . oh, my! How *wonderful*."

"It does look like a feast for a king," Lani said softly.

A long, oval table had been draped with a silky, white damask cloth that made Shona rush to fondle a fold between her fingertips. It was thick and every bit as soft as it looked. Six places at the table were set with silver, china, and crystal that gleamed richly in the soft light from a complicated crystal chandelier. Fruit, candy, nuts, and flowers were arrayed on epergnes set at the foci of the ellipse, and a big basket of bread reposed in the middle of the table, an enticing edible centerpiece. The spicy scent was coming from the big tureen in the center of the table.

As they came closer the chairs moved away from the table.

"The furniture invites us," Chirwl cried, intrigued. He scurried over to examine it minutely. "I see no mechanism, and smell only wood."

"Maglev activators in the feet, responding to a plate under the floor," Gershom explained. "I am very impressed. This is a full-service home. That would explain why the population can remain so low. There is no service class. Everything is electronic. I want to get a look at the whole-house computer."

"It's a little spooky," Shona said. She picked up the tureen lid and inhaled, then tasted a fingertip's worth of sauce. The red paste was delicious. "Mmm. Hungarian goulash. I wonder if it'll choose what we're going to eat for the next six months, or if we get a say? I hate being ruled by technology, even if it is a pretty good cook."

"Enjoy it," Gershom advised her, pushing her chair in once she was seated. "Before you know it, you'll be lugging bed linens from our bunks to the sonic washer and wishing you were here."

AFTER dinner, Alex pleaded to be allowed to watch the roboservers clean up. Shona could tell only excitement was keeping him awake. They sat on the floor at the side of the kitchen. Sure enough, as soon as the hum from the all-water dishwasher filled the room, the little boy swayed against his mother's side. Jill was already drowsing in Gershom's arms. Shona hefted her son and led the way to the stairs.

"My pouch I wish here," Chirwl said, stopping at the mini-office on the landing. "A scholar's suitable vantage point is appropriate."

"If you like," Shona agreed. "We'll hang it up as soon as we put the little ones to bed."

"Exotic," Gershom said, walking into the first bedroom suite in the corridor. "This is obviously meant for Lani."

"I see what you mean," Shona said, pulling the shy girl in to see. Lani stopped on the threshold to stare, her huge, dark eyes wide with astonishment.

Delicate pinks and corals had been chosen as the colors for this suite of rooms. Hangings of sheer cloth muted the warm light from the enameled bronze pendant lamps in the dressing room. A low vanity table loaded with bottles Shona recognized as top-of-the-line cosmetics and perfumes offered an inviting padded seat. All of the bedroom furniture looked comfortable to sit on. Twin armchairs of a squashy, overstuffed, high-backed barrel design were large enough for her to sit in cross-legged. If Lani wanted to be invisible, all she had to do was turn the seat away from the door. A gleaming enameled-wood cabinet nearby, when opened, was full of books and music disks. Silk velvet pil-

lows, some big enough to lounge on, were scattered all
over. Harry immediately claimed the large one on the floor
nearest the window, and settled himself upon it with paws
curled under his breast. The bed itself was draped with
translucent curtains. A tiny lamp beamed from within, and
the lush coverlet was turned down to reveal huge, puffy
pillows covered with shimmering silk.

"It's beautiful," Lani said. She put out a tentative hand
to stroke the nearest pillow. "Soft."

Shona kissed her on the cheek. "We'll let you get settled. Come on, kids," she declared, grabbing Alex before
he could jump on Lani's bed.

The Taylors had no trouble determining which rooms
were intended for the smaller children. Two rooms, side by
side with their own refreshers and a shared playroom,
stood close to the master bedroom. Alex had a blue room
full of roughhouse toys and padded corners, and a light
yellow room furnished with stuffed animals and low play
tables had been set up for Jill. Shona blessed the thought-
fulness of her employers. They put the sleeping toddler in
the bed and raised the padded bumper hanging alongside
the low, padded platform. To Shona's relief, Jill didn't
wake up. After a bedtime story chosen from the tall book-
case beside his spaceship-shaped bed, Alex snuggled down
and didn't protest when Shona turned off the light and
closed the door.

"I've never been so comfortable in my life," she said, as
she and Gershom settled down under a silver silk coverlet
in the enormous master bed. "We couldn't afford to stay in
hotels like this. I almost feel lost in this bed. This room is
larger than a cargo bay. To think I'm being paid to live
here. I could get spoiled."

Gershom looked up at the hangings in the bedroom.
Everything was silk, and the mattress was fantastically
comfortable.

"I wish I could give you all this," he said wistfully.

"You know I'm perfectly happy with the life that we
have," Shona assured him. "The ship is ours, we're not too

far in debt right now, and this contract will put us ahead on Lani's school tuition for next year. We have the life that we want. This"—she gestured at her surroundings—"seems so . . . ostentatious I'm almost afraid of it."

"Well, I don't want to start having feelings of inadequacy," Gershom said, only half kidding.

"Oh, come here," Shona said, playfully. "I'll show you feelings of inadequacy!"

"So long as you don't lose your taste for impecunious space merchants," Gershom said, reaching for her.

"Never," Shona promised, curling gladly into his arms. The familiar aroma of his warm skin mixed with the herb-scented sheets made a homey perfume she couldn't get enough of. Feeling blissfully content, she looked up into his eyes. "I especially like the lanky kind with long black hair and dimples."

Their lips met and melded. His hands started to run up and down along her body, and Shona responded to the caresses like a cat. Her fingers danced up his back and into the thicket of his long hair, pulling his head down beside hers. She enjoyed the feeling of being sandwiched between his warm weight and the silk beneath her. Seven years of marriage had not yet caused their lovemaking to pall. Each still found new delight in pleasing the other. Shona got as much delight from hearing him sigh at her loving attentions as she did from feeling him above, inside, and all around her.

GErShOM dropped back against the luxurious pillows. "Mmm," he said, with a twinkle in his eye. "That was more than adequate."

"That'll have to keep you until you come to visit," Shona said, running a finger down his ribs.

"How could it? But it'll give me something to dream about," Gershom said. He gathered her up in one arm and propped the other behind his head. Shona settled her head on his chest, listening to the familiar rhythm of his heart.

I am safe, she thought contentedly, as she drifted off to sleep.

"Mama!"

The shriek jolted Shona bolt upright. She grabbed for her robe and stumbled out of the huge bed, feeling for the table lamp. The house computer, calculating that of the two people in the room one was still prone, brought up the lights to a low level that gave her enough illumination to find her way out to the hall. Saffie, asleep on the floor outside the door, scrambled to her feet and followed Shona. That was Jill crying. Where was she? How far away was her room? Shona didn't know this house well enough yet. But a sharp line of yellow beneath one of the doors directed her to the right one.

It wouldn't open at first. Shona raised her hands to pound on it, then the security lock clicked off as it seemed to recognize her as an authority, entitling her to enter. She rushed through, only to find the little girl huddled against the wall next to the door, pillow and blanket in a heap under her. Huge eyes wet with tears lifted to hers. Shona dropped to her knees and gathered her daughter in her arms. The dog, always sympathetic, put her great head in Jill's lap.

"I couldn't find you," Jill wept, holding tightly to her mother. "I walked all the way around and around the ship, and no one was there in all of space."

Shona kissed her on the head, rocking her until she calmed down. "It was a nightmare, darling. I think you were sleepwalking. You came all the way across the room. See?" She pointed at the disheveled platform, stuffed animals strewn across its surface. "It wasn't real. We're not on the ship. We're on a planet. The ship is in the spaceport."

"Can I sleep with you?" the child pleaded. "I'll be very small."

"Well . . . all right, but just for tonight," Shona said.

Gershom, with all the instincts of a father, was wrig-

gling back into his sleep shorts when they came in. Jill
stared wide-eyed at the size of the bed, then curled up behind the pillows against the headboard, a neat little nest
that only a three-year-old would find.

"Mama?"

Another little voice, this time from the doorway: Alex.

"Honey, go back to bed."

"Mama, I'm lonely. I want to come in with you and
Papa."

Gershom murmured from his pillow, "It's a strange
place. Let him stay."

"All right," Shona said, making room for him. "But
you'll have to get used to having your own rooms, all
right? All right?" she asked, as Alex burrowed deeply into
the quilt between his parents. He didn't look up, but his
head bobbed in a fierce nod. Shona kissed his dark curls.
He was a courageous little boy. He'd make himself adapt.

Shona was just about to go back to sleep when she saw
a slender silhouette near the door. Lani, clad in her shortie
ship pajamas, clutching the peach-colored coverlet around
her.

"I am sorry," Lani said. "It is too big."

"I think we all feel that way." Shona patted the mattress
beside her. "Come on, sweetheart. There's plenty of room.
I expect the animals will be joining us any time now."

IN the morning a gigantic flatbed transport arrived carrying Shona's laboratory module. Gershom and his crew
oversaw its attachment to the house, using the enormous
crane on the truck. As he had predicted, the portable unit
fit precisely upon the plascrete slab. Once it had been set
down, rollers in the base allowed it to skim gently until it
was snugged securely against the wall of the house. Smart-
valves snaked out from the bottom to connect to the appropriate outlets for water, waste, communications, and
power. Shona got a great deal of satisfaction from seeing
all the systems installed and on green. She really felt then

that she had arrived at her assignment. They went back to the house where breakfast was served for all nine of them, including Chirwl. The house had evidently detected the presence of animals, and provided bowls of some appropriate mashed mess for Harry and Saffie that the animals waded into with good appetite. Shona smelled the food and decided the robot cooks knew a lot more about what tasted good to cats and dogs than she did. Chirwl's smelled much the same, but then he ate cat food when he had the chance.

"How pretty," Lani said, pointing at the center of the table. Shona nodded approvingly. A sheaf of red lilies stood in a painted majolica vase. It went so perfectly with the décor that it seemed as though it had always been there.

"Exquisite," she agreed. "The house brain has been programmed by someone with fabulous taste. But I didn't see any flowers like that in the garden."

"Maybe they came from a greenhouse," Gershom suggested.

"I don't remember seeing one," Shona said. "Just a pool house."

"They might be a gift," Lani said. "People come and go."

"That's it," Shona said, nodding at her husband. "But I wonder why Saffie didn't tell us someone was here?"

Gershom grinned. "She was far too busy supervising us. I'll beef up the house security system before I go."

A royal blue-enameled, four-wheeled open car arrived in front of the house precisely at noon. Leaving the children in Lani's charge, Gershom and Shona climbed aboard.

"Very sweet," Gershom said, bouncing up and down on the padding of the facing bench seats. He looked for a control panel, but found none. "Voice command or wireless control system run by a house computer. Here's a hatch where the weather-dome is stowed. Hmm, nothing in the refreshment compartment, but there's room for plenty. I bet you have a cart just like it tucked away in an outbuilding somewhere."

"I bet Setve has six," Shona said enviously, as they were whisked through the green paths to another mansion, this one made of blocks of ochre-gold stone that made it look cosy and quaint in spite of its size. Hethyr and her partner Dina made the Taylors welcome. A huge glass case full of antique porcelain decorated with the same royal blue as the cart stood in the entry hall. Shona couldn't find words to describe their beauty. Hethyr waved a hand dismissively.

"Just things," she said. "We like to have nice things around."

As Shona expected, the food was produced by roboservers. The Candells chatted blithely while the arms reached down to place servings on every plate. As in the finest restaurants that used human waiters, the arms served from the left and removed dishes from the right. Seeing a mechanical hand reach around her made Shona jump the first couple of times, but thereafter she was able to ignore them as her hostesses did.

"I apologize for not allowing you time to relax after your journey," Hethyr said, sipping wine. "I really did feel unwell yesterday. Thank you for confirming it was nothing to be concerned about. Dina insisted I go see you."

"Hethyr is normally so healthy," Dina said. She was taller than her partner, very thin, with an interesting bony face and expressive hands that had knobbly joints. "So I wanted to be very sure it was nothing serious."

"Not that I could see," Shona said. "If the condition recurs, of course, please come see me at once."

Hethyr turned a stern face toward her. "I don't . . . have to tell you that you may not discuss anything that goes on within the confines of your office? I don't necessarily want it known that I had to consult you."

"Of course not," Shona assured her. "Privacy is guaranteed between doctor and patient. That's only good medical practice, as well as the law."

"Good," Hethyr said shortly. "That might be awkward. You're invited to Friday evening parties. Everyone attends." She turned to stare full-faced at Gershom. "Except you. Your ship's lifting this afternoon, isn't it?"

Shona glanced at her husband, whose eyebrows lifted toward his hairline, then back to the governor. "Speaking of privacy, it surprises me that considering the importance all of you put on it that several patients came marching right through Dr. Setve's house."

"Didn't he tell you about the shingle?" Hethyr asked in surprise. "On the right-hand pillar of your front porch is a flap of wood on a hinge. Very non-tech. When the white side shows, Setve's office is open. When the red side is turned out, it is closed. I'm afraid we all assumed that since the white side was out you were ready to see callers. No one will approach if the red side is showing."

"That's a great relief," Shona said. "I realize that I will be on call for emergencies, but . . . without going into detail . . . little of what I treated yesterday would fall into that category."

"Crossed signals," Dina said, with a grin. She had an engaging smile. A long baying interrupted her. "Oops, got to feed Argent. Don't wait dessert for me."

She pushed back from the table and loped out of the room. Shona wondered what kind of dog they had. It looked as though Saffie would be able to make plenty of new friends. What a difference from their usual assignments, where she was the only dog on a space station or in a bubble colony.

"Good. I won't have to bore her with business," Hethyr said, with a fond look after her partner. She leaned forward on her forearms toward Gershom. "So, tell me more about your proposal. How much can you save us on carriage, if you take away obsolete machines at the same time as you bring us upgrades?"

SHONA was impressed with the governor's firm grasp of trade. By the time they finished lunch her head was spinning with figures, percentages, waivers of tariff, and favorable discounts. Gershom always knew to the hundredth-credit how closely he was cutting their profit, but he was smiling as they left the golden house. When the door closed behind them, he whispered, "Ka-ching!"

"Was that good?" Shona asked, glancing back. Behind the sheer lace curtains Hethyr was watching them walk down the steps toward the waiting car.

"I'll tell you when we have some privacy," he said, seizing her hand and patting it. "Sometimes I am glad you're so notorious."

As Hethyr had said, on the post near the door of her borrowed house was Setve's shingle. It was plain white, to blend with the white trim; small wonder they had not noticed it. Shona promptly flipped it so that the red side was showing, and marched into the house with Gershom in tow.

As they came into the upper hallway Chirwl poked his head out of his pouch, spraying disks of wood over the already cluttered floor of the small office. The position in which his pouch hung on the wall gave him a splendid view out of a picture window facing the side yard. Sunlight pouring in drew auburn highlights from the tips of his whiskers and fur.

"Sss-shona! All is prepared. The house speaks to me. I persuaded to make meals for us. I think we are making friends."

"We have more friends to meet later," Shona said. "We have been invited to a house party later this evening. They especially want you to come."

"With splendid joy," Chirwl said, grooming his whiskers with a foreclaw, looking like a cavalier twirling his mustaches. "My friend Lani has the younger ones behind here playing pick flowers. Once more you are to participate in the human mating ritual departure imminent?" He looked hopeful.

Gershom made a face. "Yes, we are, and no, you can't watch. Some things are not for display, no matter how curious the inquisitor nor for what good and sound research reasons you have."

The ottle let out a long whistle, his version of a sigh. "I had known. But always of hope. I anticipate this later new union of guests." He dived back into his pouch, and Shona could hear him chittering to himself as he made a few notes.

"I'm embarrassed that Hethyr was so rude to you," Shona said. "She all but tossed you off-planet."

"That's all right. My mission is accomplished. I've brought you. Now I ought to blast off."

"*Almost* accomplished," Shona said, with an impish grin. Gershom smiled at her and drew her toward their room.

ThE house party was hosted by the tall woman who'd been Shona's first patient. Finoa and Robret took great pride in introducing the new doctor and her family to the rest of the guests.

"It's so interesting to meet you at last," gushed Angeta, a woman in her fifties with frost-tipped dark blond hair and a dark-skinned triangular face on which the skin seemed stretched too tightly. She gripped Shona's hand with long, slender fingers. "You know, all the stories on tri-dee were fascinating, but I always wonder how different people are from how they seem on screen."

"We were not seeing you at your best, perhaps," Finoa said, rescuing Shona and escorting her to the next person, a man of thirty or so with a shock of black hair. "Ewan." He was seated on the arm of a chair beside a stunning woman with short, carmine hair cut in the latest extreme fashion, most of it shaved close to the scalp with long silky locks sprouting like ferns here and there on her head. Shona glimpsed Lani out of the corner of her eye taking in the woman with great interest.

"Why didn't your husband stay?" the red-haired woman asked. Her name was Baraba.

"Business," Shona said, perhaps more curtly than she intended. Once Gershom had helped her program the whole-house computer, made sure the module was in full working order, and said good-bye to the children there was no real reason for him not to go. She had known all along that he would be leaving, but it was harder than either of them had anticipated. It was not the first time they had been separated for any length of time, nor would it be the last time, but Shona decided she didn't have to like it.

The other woman's eyebrows ascended toward her strange coiffure, and Shona hastened to soften her words. "The governor gave him a commission on behalf of your colony. We have some very good connections with suppliers that you all seem to favor. We have exclusive distribution rights in this sector for Trilliant Textiles."

"Ah," the woman said, appeased. "I adore their silks, especially their damasks. Our entire bedroom is hung in pale blue, woven on the very looms that made the draperies in the royal dining room at the palace of Versailles. I love blue. It goes so well with gold. Though we might change to royal blue next season."

"You must talk to my husband when he returns," Shona said, mentally calculating the cost of covering the walls of a big room in priceless silks.

"Oh, no!" Baraba exclaimed, shocked. "We never deal with tradespeople directly. Hethyr does that for us! Except for . . . I'm sorry," she said, with an appalled look at Shona. "Oh, how tactless of me. Does Setve still have that monochromatic bedroom of his?"

"Pale gray?" Shona asked, smiling in spite of the sting she felt. Tradespeople. Well, she knew she didn't belong in the stratum she currently inhabited.

"Yes. Dull, dull, dull."

"It's really very restful," Shona insisted.

"You mustn't monopolize our new doctor on the first day," Finoa chided Baraba.

The hostess swept Shona away and over to the next couple, a pair of men in their fifties, Laren and Bock Carmody. Then to her final patient from the previous afternoon, whose name was Kely. He gave her a wary look, but she made no reference to his visit. She noticed he was wearing a very elaborate piece of jewelry on his thumb that concealed the small wound. And on to others. By the time she found herself sitting down with a drink in her hand she had lost track of all but the first few names.

"Don't worry," her hostess reassured her. "You'll know everyone's name soon. There are only about a hundred of us."

Shona grinned. "That's smaller than some of the lecture classes I took in medical school," she said. "In fact, this room is larger than the lecture halls themselves. I am enjoying everyone's use of space. It's so . . ."

"Ostentatious?" Bock asked, with a twinkle.

"I was going to say, impressive," Shona said. Finoa's house was only one level, sprawled over an acre or more. The floor plan accomodated the natural curves and rises of the land by inserting rooms a half-level up or down. "On a merchant ship like ours any space that isn't carrying cargo is considered wasted. It's a mental adjustment."

"I hope you'll come to like it," Angeta said.

"Oh, I do!"

"That's Angeta's daughter Clea, Bock's daughter Mona, and Hanya's daughter Zolly over there with your older girl," Finoa said, nodding toward a cluster of chairs close to the entertainment deck. Shona tried to appear casual as she glanced toward the little group of teenaged girls seated in them. As usual, Lani wasn't saying very much, but she looked happy. Shona was pleased that the other girls had taken the initiative to draw Lani into their circle.

The crowd divided itself into several groups. The noisiest part of the party was taking place on the minstrel's gallery that ran along one wall on a half-level above the great room. As they came in the parents sent their young children up behind the Plexiglas half-wall to join their friends. Dwan's three showed Alex and Jill the way. From the joyous shouts echoing down to the adults, some adventure game was being organized up there. Alex's voice could be heard adding his own ideas about monsters to be killed and treasure to be won. Tumi's suddenly cut through them all, and they quieted down. The adults looked at one another anxiously, then laughed.

"I always worry when I can't hear them," Dwan said to Shona. She was warmly friendly to the doctor, and more formal with her neighbors. Obviously some dynamic exempted the local physician from the pecking order. "Usually it means they're breaking something expensive. It helps that we can see what they're up to."

"The invisible force field up there is one of the first things we approved on the house plan when we built," Finoa said, indicating the half-wall. "I don't mind it when Tumi plays inside. It's the safest place to play, and I can keep an eye on him."

"The landscaping is wonderful," Shona said. "But you're right. When the children run off into the back I can't see them at all."

"You have rather a lot to keep track of, don't you?" Baraba asked with arched eyebrows.

"Only three," Shona said.

"Only!"

"We've often thought about having another," Shona admitted. "Both of us were only children. We love the idea of a big family."

"My dear," Angeta said, with a smile, "you'll learn that having more than three children is considered to be ostentatious."

Shona was surprised. "But you have so much room."

Silence fell. She realized she had committed a social gaffe. Again. Too late she remembered what Dwan had said about not discussing the amount of land anyone possessed. She smiled weakly.

"I'd better check on the children." She fled around the corner and up the stairs to the landing. The children, divided into four groups, glanced up briefly at the arrival of an adult, then, when it turned out not to be one of their parents, went back to plotting among themselves. Alex held her gaze the longest, but she shook her head. She spotted Jill in the largest, most giggly group, and decided not to attract her attention.

Gershom had indulged her curiosity before he had departed. Scanning the makeup of the planet, they discovered that the M-class section that had been terraformed was under twenty thousand square miles, most of it an ocean and several inland lakes, sources of oxygen and fresh water for the colony. The terraformers worked in an ever-widening circle. Though progress was slow each family must still own thousands of acres. The force field holding back the toxic atmosphere of the outer reaches was an expensive and power-hungry model, but as efficient as anything like it could be.

Conditions must have been horrible on Jardindor during the initial stages. Workers would have had to live in a protective dome or series of interconnected modules that vibrated constantly with the grinding of the terraformers. A spectrographic reading of the atmosphere outside the force field revealed that it was breathable—barely—but profuse with unpleasant-smelling esters and poisonous compounds in low concentration.

The machines penetrated deep into the crust of the planet, weeding out toxic chemicals and rendering them inert. Valuable ones were gathered from the aggregate and stored in tanks for use or shipment. Sensors would also have identified and benchmarked any useful minerals, although until it was bid on by the Jardindor collective the planet had been considered virtually worthless. To compare the pastoral calm of the finished product with the original biosphere was to compare not just apples to oranges, but chocolate to rocks.

"So, Shona, Finoa tells me you're a fan of the tri-dees?" Laren said from the other side of the big room, as she came back looking for an empty seat. He turned aside to hide a cough, not for the first time that night, and Shona wondered whether he would come to see her about it.

"Would you like some tea with lemon for that cough?" Finoa asked.

"It's not a cough!" Laren protested. "Shelia, how are those young gingkos doing in your yard?"

"Very well," Shelia said. "I've started making my own tea. I had to grab the robogardener this morning. I misprogrammed it a little. It took all the leaves off one branch. I thought I told it just to pick one here and there, but I didn't define 'here and there' well enough."

"Moronic geniuses," opined Dwan's husband, a mild man with graying brown hair. "They only do what you tell them."

"I know, I know," Shelia said, tossing her thick hair. "It was me. I'm terrible with machines. But the tea is far superior to the freeze-dried stuff I've been drinking."

"May we try some?" Laren asked politely.

"Oh, yes," Shelia said, with a smile. "It tastes awful, though."

"I'll put some extracts in it, then. And lots of stevia," Laren said, looking defiantly around at the others. "It's good for everything, including dry throat, which is all that I've got."

Shona found everyone's eyes on her. She cleared her throat.

"Everyone does seem to be very healthy," she said. "Whatever you're doing is very good for you. As long as you aren't taking anything your bodies don't need."

That seemed to be exactly the right thing to say. Everyone burst out about the combination of vitamins they were taking and the virtuous dietary regimens they followed.

"And I run five miles every day, along with tai chi and yoga and I take vitamin supplements, not that our diet is lacking, and of course—" Baraba paused abruptly. "And I think you'd be surprised at how much a balanced lifestyle can do for you. Look at Finoa," she added, hastily. "She's the healthiest of us all." Shona took a critical glance at her hostess. "How old do you think she is?"

"Oh, I don't think I should . . ."

"Never mind," Finoa said, with a modest smile. "She could look it up in my records, Bar. I'm fifty-eight."

Shona gasped. "Really? I thought you were my age!" Apart from a few sun-lines at the corners of her eyes, the tall woman could have been thirty. She had taut, youthful skin, clear eyes, and thick hair.

"We live well," Finoa said, with smug complacence.

"I think I'd better study your lifestyle while I'm here," Shona said. "All of humanity will want to know your secret."

There was an embarrassed silence. "I'm sorry," she said. "I just can't seem to say the right things tonight."

"It's all right," Baraba said. "I ought to be able to resist bragging. You can tell we don't have a lot of outside contact. Manners go right out the airlock!"

Shona heard Chirwl's high-pitched chitter break through the buzz of conversation. She glanced over toward the sound. He was virtually holding court at his end of the room—small wonder, since so few ottles were abroad in human space.

The research that had provided every comfort for Shona and her family had also deduced the sort of furniture Chirwl liked best for lounging in company. Shona wondered which newscast or tri-dee clip the idea had come from. The ottle was enthroned on an elevated, circular padded platform with raised sides, like a big birdbath made of red velvet, that showed off his fur to great advantage. Chirwl rolled from one side to another of his couch, responding to questions, but mostly asking them. The Jardindorians appeared to take the greatest pleasure in answering him, though they were smiling as if speaking to a very small child. Shona shook her head. They would be surprised how intelligent he was, in spite of his comically bent grasp of Standard.

"He's a very interesting being, isn't he?" Baraba said to Shona.

"Yes, I've enjoyed hosting him. He's got a philosophy about humans that I find it difficult to dispute," Shona said.

"He thinks we're too attached to technology, in almost a symbiotic relationship. I'm trying to disprove it, but the more I do, the more I think I'm helping him prove his thesis."

"What do *you* think, Finoa?" Laren asked, watching the ottle with hungry eyes.

"Possible," Finoa said casually. "Definitely possible. I hope you'll let him visit us all while you're busy, Dr. Shona," the tall woman added. "He's fascinating. And all of us would like to help him with his research."

"He'll do most of the talking," Shona said with a grin, though she was wary of the silent byplay between the two Jardindorians. She promised herself she would accompany Chirwl on any visits he made for a while. "By the way, Chirwl said that he smelled an aroma today that he associates with predators. And yesterday my dog was behaving as if she had found a strong animal scent. Are there any dangerous species on the planet? Any natural predators left over from before the terraforming began?"

"Native animals?" Hethyr said, overhearing the last sentence. "Of course not. We would never allow ourselves to be responsible for the extinction of a species. Far from it: we are committed to preserving species. I think you will find that we are all very ecologically minded." But they all looked uneasy. Perhaps, Shona thought, there had been something that the terraforming association had come across late in the process and not admitted to EarthGov lest they be forbidden to use the planet. It was not unknown for colonies to be evacuated, even after several years' occupancy, if it could be proved that they had willingly contributed to the demise of an evolving bioculture.

A wild whoop rang off the ceiling. Finoa rose majestically and stalked toward the ramp leading to the children's domain.

"What kind of educational program are you using for your children?" Dwan piped up.

"Oh, we're using Home Tutor," Shona said. "Alex is just starting level 7, and Jill is on level 4. Since my assignments are often so short-term, we never could enroll any of them in local schools. It would be too disruptive. How about you?"

"We have Home Tutor, too," Dwan said, happily. "And Dougie is on level 7. I'd love it if you would bring them over and let them work on the same console. They'd get so much out of sharing lessons with peers."

"And my Zolly is about the same age as your Lani," said Hanya. "Is she doing level 20?"

"Yes," Shona said. "Is Zolly?"

"Sure is. Our elder daughter is off-planet at school. Zolly's been going crazy by herself. She doesn't go off until next year. She'd love to have a study-buddy."

"We're hoping to send Lani to an academy next year, too," Shona said. "She's been getting brochures aplenty. If they want to work together, I would be delighted. They could help one another decide where to go. Lani's very quiet. She's smart and she has her own mind, but she needs to be drawn out."

"Well, that's the opposite of my Zolly," Hanya said proudly. "I think she's the most outgoing child who ever lived. I'll ask her."

The two girls were excited at the idea of taking lessons together. They started making plans at once. They implored their respective parents to let them meet early the next day. Shona looked at the ornate wall chronometer.

"Good heavens," she said. "I'd better get us all home. Is our cart still out front?"

"It's in our shelter," Robret said. "Hazel!"

"Working," said the disembodied voice of the house computer. Shona looked at him curiously.

"We named it after a two-dee program my mother used to watch when I was a kid," he admitted sheepishly. "All our machines have names. Hazel, bring Dr. Shona's cart around. Good night. We look forward to seeing you again next Friday. But please visit us in the meantime."

"Thank you so much for the hospitality," Shona said, shaking hands all around. "Come by to see us, too. Not just when you need my professional skills. We want very much to be part of this community." She was careful not to meet anyone's eyes in particular, for which Laren, Hethyr, Finoa, and Kely looked very grateful. "Chirwl, it's time!"

"So early ready?" the ottle said, reluctant to give up his audience. Over his protests, Shona bundled him into his pouch and slung it onto her back.

She gathered up the yawning children and herded them outside into the waiting cart. She couldn't see its dark-green enamel in the dark, but a glowing "S" on the door panel let her know it was the right one. The children huddled together. Lani put her head on Shona's shoulder. Shona breathed in a delicious lungful of air. The night was cool, moist, and fragrant.

"Home, James," she said, and chuckled to herself. "Say, Robret is right. It is fun."

"You find it cheering to call things by names?" Chirwl asked, sticking his head up out of the pouch and putting it over her shoulder.

"Don't do that; your whiskers tickle," Shona said, pushing his nose out of her ear. "It's just nice to know these people have little foibles. I think it's endearing to name your house systems after your mother's favorite vids. It makes people more . . . approachable. More human."

Chirwl twitched his whiskers. "When all the person is human, how can he-she be more so?"

"It's just an expression! Hmm. Well, I mean that they don't seem like such lofty beings. They are all very wealthy, and they live such reclusive lives. I found that intimidating. I thought they might be very different from us. I was nervous what they might think of me, but I see they are just as nervous. Did you observe the way they kept stopping so they wouldn't blurt something out? At first I wondered if there was anything sinister, the way they kept glancing at one another, but it was probably nothing more than all of them wondering when I would find out about their quirks. They probably thought I was going to make fun of their diets. Most of the ones they're on are fads, but can do little harm."

"Strange that these who may have what they like tell themselves not to."

"True," Shona said. "But when you're brought up to have no limits I suppose you start setting your own. I don't know. If you get to know any of these people well enough to ask them, please tell me."

BATHTIME was uneventful, but the moment Shona tried to put Jill to bed in the big yellow room all by herself, the toddler started whimpering.

"Don't go, Mama," Jill begged. "I couldn't find you."

"Oh, sweetheart, I'm just down the hall."

"The mechanomen are up there!" The child pointed at the ceiling. Shona glanced up.

"Those are just roboservers, honey. Don't pay any attention to them. They're just machines. They clean the bathroom for you. They fold your clothes and put them away for you."

The toddler's eyes widened. "They're in the closet? I want to come with you!" She wrapped her arms around Shona and wouldn't let go. Shona shook her head. She had accidentally triggered Jill's most terrifying monster association, closet monsters. A tousled little head peeked around the corner. Alex was waiting to hear what Shona decided. He didn't want to be the one who said first that he was scared.

"Papa's not here to protect us," Jill said, her face buried in Shona's sleeve.

"But Saffie's here. And Chirwl is very brave. He loves you. I bet he'd stay here with you if you wanted. He's not scared. He'll tell you all about the mechanomen. He tells good stories about them. *Long* ones." Jill giggled in spite of herself. Getting Chirwl to tell them bedtime stories was one of the children's favorite ploys for staying up late. His stories tended to ramble on because he would get so interested in what he was talking about that he would go off on tangents. By the time he got back to the main plot it was usually a good twenty or thirty minutes past their usual lights-out.

"Please, Mama? I too little."

Shona relented. "All right. This is a very big house. I feel very little in here, too. Let's go make some beds for everyone in my room. You can stay there for a few days, until you get used to it. But everyone has to use their own bathroom. All right? This is the first time I have a tub all to myself, and I don't want forty-five Convertible Babies in it with me. All right?"

"Okay," Jill said.

"Yay!" Alex said, forgetting to be invisible and jumping up and down in the hall.

Lani must have been within earshot, too. When Shona went to her room to tell her the plan, the girl already had her arms full of quilts and pillows. She gave her mother a shy grin.

The pale gray chamber took on the air of a dormitory. Once the children were in, Chirwl insisted that he wished to be a member of the party. Shona hung his pouch up on a hook on the huge breakfront that was meant for holding hangers or a bathrobe. Saffie and Harry nosed their way in and settled on whatever makeshift mattress offered the most comfortable spot. Despite having all her family around her, the huge room still felt empty to Shona. She drifted off to sleep missing Gershom.

TWO

"ARE you certain this will be all right?" Shona asked, watching through a one-way transparent wall into the Sands family playroom as Alex and Jill sized up Dwan's three youngsters and were evaluated in their turn. Dougie was Alex's size. Ginny and Nell were four-year-old fraternal twins: one red-haired and one dark. The room was full of expensive toys and electronic devices, but the five ignored them, instead creating a complicated make-believe involving a discarded plastic packing crate from the hold of the *Sibyl* and several lengths of flex cable. "I can hook up an auto-tutor program in Dr. Setve's house. My children have all used them before."

Dwan patted her arm. "I'm sure. In fact, it will be nice to give the children contact with people from somewhere else. There aren't any other five-year-olds. I'm afraid Dougie might grow up spoiled if he doesn't have anybody to learn to share with. That's so important. I meant what I said last night."

Shona smiled and sipped her tea. She was pleased by the casual contact of pats on the arms, handshakes, and so on. She'd been afraid that the colonists' obsession with natural medicine might mean they stood off from personal contact.

"It's so generous of you to let me help myself to plant cuttings," Shona said. "It would cost me a fortune for even a small quantity of any of these. I usually end up season-ing with extracts because it costs me credits per gram for cooking herbs."

Dwan waved a hand. "Take all you want. Indulge your-self. This is one of the joys of Jardindor. I love to cook with herbs, and I like to take baths with handfuls of mint and rosemary."

"Thank you so much," Shona said happily. "Fresh is so much better for you. It's rare that I have access even to a small amount. I feel . . . shamelessly self-indulgent even *thinking* about bathing with handfuls of rosemary. Mmm," she hummed, picturing fragrant clouds of steam rising around her body. "And the chance to cook anything I like. I don't know where to start."

Dwan stretched out her legs. "I'm like you: I was born in a bubble colony. I love having land to wander around on. It . . . it feeds my soul. My husband likes it because it's quiet."

Shona glanced around. "Will I see him?"

"Captain Code? Not until afternoon, at the earliest. He'll be in front of his console until I absolutely drive him away from it. You were lucky to meet him yesterday. Come on, let's go sit on the terrace." She picked up the tea tray and led the way. Shona struggled to catch up with Dwan's long stride.

Saffie and Dwan's lithe greyhound/shepherd mix, Lark, bolted out of the door ahead of their mistresses. Shona was just in time to see both dogs disappear into the under-growth. She heard the yelping and crashing associated with two large animals trampling possibly valuable plants. Alarmed, she started to call after them.

"Don't worry," Dwan said. "Lark knows her way home.

They'll want to smell every centimeter, but they'll come home when they're hungry."

"Are there any dangerous life-forms here?" Shona had asked the question the night before but had been put off by the reaction from her hostess and the other guests. Dwan seemed more open. Shona hoped she would get an answer, and she was rewarded for her perserverance.

"You mean indigenous species? Nothing larger than microbes. This was such an in-between place when they started terraforming. Almost as though it couldn't make up its mind whether to have an atmosphere or not, so very little local fauna, let alone flora, evolved. It might have happened in a few billion more years, but nothing was imminent in the next million or so. It made the decision for the board much easier than it's been on a lot of other planets."

"I can imagine." Shona said. Dwan dumped the cold tea into the bushes and poured fresh cups. "The results are fantastic."

"We like it," Dwan said complacently. "Where's the ottle today?"

"Exploring the trees on Setve's property. His species evolved in trees. When they formed a civilization they started living in pouches, but they've always been arboreal. I've promised him I'll take him down to that big round lake tomorrow."

"Better ask Laren," Dwan warned her. "It's on their property."

"The whole lake?" Shona asked, wide-eyed.

"Yes. But the ocean is community property, just like the spaceport."

The terraformed part of Jardindor had turned out to be smaller than Shona would ever have guessed, looking out at the forests and fields from Dwan's patio. Their expanse lay in clever use of perspective, intended to fool the eye. Most of the conifers ran from normal trees at the rear of the property to smaller species further out. She suspected the most distant ones were dwarf trees. With six months in her tenure she had plenty of time to find out.

"What's that?" Shona asked, pointing at a wing of Dwan's house that extended into a garden lined with thick evergreens.

"Just a part of the house," Dwan said hastily. "Nothing important."

"Setve has a conservatory that looks a lot like that," Shona said, eyeing it. "There's a swimming pool in it. Do you have a pool?"

"Everyone has a pool," Dwan said, clearly wanting to change the subject. Shona wondered if she knew about the odor that Saffie had detected in Setve's house, the one Chirwl called violent, and decided that it was none of her business.

"What a treat to talk to someone in person," she said. "The time lag between ships is enough to make me lose the thread of a conversation a dozen times! By the way, perhaps you can help me solve a mystery. Yesterday morning someone left us a glorious bouquet of red lilies, but no note. And today there was a cluster of the most delicious-smelling muguet in the examination room. Gorgeous, but they didn't come from Setve's garden. I'm sure of that."

Dwan handed her a cup of tea. "Everyone likes to be generous."

"It's funny," Shona said, looking out at the landscape as she took a sip, "Saffie went insane when she smelled the vase. It had a scent that intrigued her. I couldn't smell a thing, of course. Her nose is phenomenal. But I think it must have been the scent of the person who left the flowers, not a chemical compound. Harry wasn't interested except to eat the leaves. And throw them up. Of course." Shona sighed. "It's his hobby. Do you have any other pets beside Lark?"

"Oh, yes," Dwan said, rising suddenly. She glanced at her sleeve chronometer. "Is that the time? The kids will be chewing the walls. Join us for lunch?"

Shona spent the rest of the day with her new friend. She

felt a trifle guilty skipping office hours, but decided she would open for business after dinner. Using Dwan's console to call Hanya's house, she checked in with Lani. The teenager didn't want to come home. She was having so much fun with Zolly that they decided to make a night of it. Hanya assured her it was all right. Feeling very content, Shona decided she was going to enjoy the posting.

The isolated quality of Jardindor might have been why the families there chose it in the first place, but Shona began to notice a desperation among her patients to spend time simply talking. Few of the thirty families interacted, outside of the Friday parties—to those everyone came, almost as though there was mandatory attendance being taken. Shona began to understand the need for great rooms. A hundred people, all sitting at maximum distance from one another, made a large party chamber a virtual necessity. She began to see that while Hethyr was the governor of the colony, Finoa seemed to be the real leader. The parties did not seem to begin until she and her husband arrived. Some of the younger women and a few of the men appeared to be openly afraid or in awe of her, though she was always polite, even warm, to Shona. She and Robret were genetic researchers, though she never discussed her work, but that did not explain Finoa's clear preeminence. Her fellows were all captains of industry, owners of important financial concerns, inventors, and artists, but they all tried to curry favor with her, deferring to her wishes in everything.

She observed, too, that the Jardindorians might as well have been living on spaceships. The fabulous gardens were empty, more often than not. Shona discovered that she was a rarity, taking advantage of the blissful scents and sunshine. Except for Dwan, she seldom saw anyone else hiking or riding out in the voice-operated carts. They rarely gardened for themselves, and no living support workers lived on the planet. There were gardening robots that took care of the outside, as the housekeeping robots minded the inside. Jardindorian pets, at least one cat or dog per household, seemed to enjoy their beautiful land more than the humans did.

Her own animals adapted to Jardindor as if they had always been there. Saffie dashed out every morning to sniff favorite trees and rocks before doing her business. Harry sauntered in and out at a more leisurely, catlike pace, chewing plants and leaves only for the pleasure of throwing them up later.

As for her patients' health regimens, Shona approved of most of what they were doing. There was no harm in herbalism and aromatherapy, so long as they didn't use toxic plants, or ingest too much of what they didn't need. On the whole they had little requirement for her services. They seemed to value the listening ear more than the medical care, which always was for very trivial problems. Kely chafed frantically one day while she opened up the office for nothing more than a simple hematoma on his finger that he got slamming it in a door. Underneath it all Shona believed their impatience could be put down to rank, and hoped that if fabulous wealth ever befell her she would try not to become that spoiled.

Still there was the mystery of the flowers. They kept coming, a fresh vase of them every day. The whole-house computer's security system was supposed to set off an alarm if anyone entered, but the first morning Shona held open office hours there was a huge vase of yellow chrysanthemums on the dining table. She hinted to her visitors that she would like to thank the donor, but no one admitted to the gift. Puzzled and a little taken aback, Shona set the computer to detect intruders, but the next morning there were bouquets of alstromeria and Dutch irises in the examination room and on the table she liked to sit beside in the garden. The flowers were taken away every night and replaced every morning. Shona never managed to see who or what changed the flowers, and Saffie went crazy every morning.

As for visiting the houses, Shona had carte blanche. She and her family could have eaten every meal every day at one neighbor's or another. Behind their own walls her hosts were open and friendly, their archness and coldness set aside. She wallowed splendidly in soap operas with Laren and Finoa, talked fine fabrics with Baraba, and had cook-offs with Dwan. None of them ever invited another person or couple at the same time. It was as though they were reluctant to share her company.

Chirwl had invitations galore to visit homes. All the families asked him almost daily to come by. Keeping in mind her sense of uneasiness from the first Friday party, Shona always accompanied him on these outings. She cited Alien Relations rules, and most of his hosts accepted Shona's presence without question, but Finoa seemed impatient to have the ottle to herself. The most privacy she'd been able to obtain was when Shona allowed Finoa to take him on a grand tour of their home in the third week of her tenure. Before they had left Setve's house Shona had instructed Chirwl to stay in his pouch and not to get out of it for any reason when she was out of sight. Finoa's obsession with getting Chirwl alone made her very uncomfortable.

"A pleasant occupation afternoon," Chirwl chittered, as they rode back to the surgery, as Shona had come to call their adopted home, in the handsome dark-green cart.

"So, what's the rest of the house like?" Shona asked.

"Rooms in profuse mass, like divided cells." When Shona looked alarmed, Chirwl tittered. "Mitosis!"

"Oh, you mean there's a lot of them," Shona translated, with a laugh. "I thought you meant they were secure rooms for keeping prisoners."

"There are prisoners," Chirwl said seriously. "Many small animals, as in your lab, but unhappy. And strange smells I breathe, like incense musk. I think my friend Saffie would growl at them."

"If Finoa and Robret are doing genetic research, she

will have animals," Shona said. "It's an ugly truth. What did she talk about?"

"Many subjects. I am not bored with her."

"Well, I'm not bored with her, either. She wants you to come back again soon. I think we may wait until next week," Shona said, shifting the pouch on her lap. "Your social schedule is cutting into my work schedule."

"I could go by myself," Chirwl offered. "The house would drive the cart for me. But I do not think I want to. The scents raise for me discomfort."

"Now, that is very well put," Shona said.

Three

"Mama!" Alex called. "Mama! Guess what?"

"What, sweetheart?" Shona asked. The house computer directed his shout to her office intercom speaker. "Wait, here I come." It wasn't too difficult to follow the sound of ringing footsteps on the hard parquet floor. The five-year-old came barreling down the long gallery toward her and jumped into her arms. Shona staggered backward. "You're getting so big!"

"Mama, Tumi has a tiger! His name is Jamir. We had fun. He's not soft at all, and he makes a noise like a purr. Tumi says it's a growl, though."

"Really?" Shona asked, amused. "Did you have fun with Tumi?" On another, more populous world, Finoa's eight-year-old Tumi would be unlikely to play with a child so much younger, but Shona guessed that children here had little choice.

"Yeah! It was great! Tigers eat more than five kilos of meat a day, and sleep more than sixteen hours. Except he didn't sleep when we watched him. He watched us back. It made me feel scared, the way his eyes are, but he let us pet him anyway. I wish we could have a tiger, too."

"I see," Shona said, sensing an unsubtle suggestion for a future birthday gift. "Well, why don't you ask where his parents got it, and I'll see if I can send away for one. What kind of power cell does he run on?"

Alex wriggled away from her with a disdainful look on his face. "Mama! He's not a toy. He's *real*."

"Is he in a cage?"

"No! He's in the garden."

"Oh, honey, then how could he be real? There probably aren't five hundred tigers left in the universe. He wouldn't stay in a garden. They need miles and miles of space to roam, and they eat lots of meat. There isn't that much live-able land on this world, and this is the only inhabitable continent. It's got to be an automaton of some kind."

"No, he's real. Tumi says he's magic," Alex insisted. "He keeps them from getting sick. It works, too. He never gets sick."

Shona nodded. Finoa was using a little psychology on her son. She had used similar psychological tools with her own children. Jill had a fuzzy bunny toy named Escarole that could eat nightmares. Alex had declared that he was too tough for nightmares, and they had better not try and invade *his* dreams. He preferred his animals big and tough. Naturally he'd like a bigger, better fuzzy toy.

"Can I look up tigers on your console?" Alex pleaded. "Why are they striped when lions are plain?"

Alex in search of information could spout out questions faster than he could breathe. Shona tried to answer the first couple, then settled him down in front of her console to search the data out for himself. Once she had saved her data in her retina-scan-protected file cache, she logged him onto the console as a user and left him to it.

Little needed to be done, since the roboservers took care of cleaning Setve's clinic. In her module, adjacent to the medical center, Shona washed out the rabbit and mice cages and put down fresh bedding for them. Moonglow and Marigold wriggled their noses as they sniffed the carrot tops and beet greens Shona had plucked for them in the garden. Their purpose was to test food for safe consumption by humans, but they were enthusiastic eaters to begin with. The mice had chewed through the last fiber-core roll she'd saved for them from the plasheet printers. She found a chunk of soft pine in the woodpile and gave it to them with a smug feeling of doing something good for the environment.

"Have fun, guys. It's organic!" She left them sniffing it closely with twitching noses and whiskers.

Alex still sat at the console board in the office, his tongue out as he concentrated.

"Mama, can I send Papa a message?" he asked.

"Of course, sweetheart." She entered the address header for the *Sibyl*, and showed him how to find the icon when he wanted it. Hethyr had given her the frequency for the communications satellite that served Jardindor. The message would reach Gershom in a few weeks.

"Hi, Papa!" Alex said, waving at the video pickup embedded in the screen. "I'm fine and Jill is fine. We have a pool so I can swim every day. Oh, wait, you saw it," he added, wrinkling his nose. "Why don't we have a pool big enough? When there's no gravity we can swim in the air."

"Honey," began Shona. Alex off on a tangent could fill whole disks. Alex grinned.

"Oh, yeah. Today I went to play with Tumi. He lives next door, except next door is far away. He has a real tiger. I petted him. He's called Jamir. Tumi said I can feed him next time I come."

After some prompting from his mother, Alex delivered more news of the family, and finished with, "We're having fun but I miss you. Bye."

"I know it's silly," Shona said, at the next Friday house party she attended, in the walnut-paneled sitting room of Laren and Bock's gigantic thatched-roof, black-and-white house, "but Alex is a very truthful child. He keeps insisting that Tumi has a tiger in the garden. It isn't like him." Everyone seemed to be looking at her with an expression she couldn't read. Shyly, she looked down at her punch cup. A child's tale was too trivial to mention, she supposed.

"I achieved the Cow-Face Position this morning," Baraba said, perhaps too brightly.

"Very good!" Angeta cheered. "Did it hurt?"

The carmine-haired woman shook her head. "No. Well, not the second time. You have to stretch *religiously*. It helped that I assumed the Stork Pose for a while before, controlling my breathing, and meditating on a mantra. I chose 'su.' "

"A nice, calm sound," Finoa agreed, turning to Shona. "We've been enjoying our visits with Chirwl. Do you find that having him with you stimulates or relaxes you?"

Shona thought about it for a moment. "More stimulating, I think. He does like to talk, and he challenges me constantly with his observations about why I do the things I do."

"Do you think of him more as a pet or a companion?"

"Not a pet! He's much more intelligent than any animal. Ottle intelligence is equal to or higher than humanity's. As a nontechnological race they are closer to basic survival than we are. They question and discuss everything, breaking every subject down to its component parts. They look at things in ways I never would. I think you could compare them to the ancient Greeks of Earth. If we taught them physics, and convinced them of the need for it, they'd probably be able to design interstellar transport that would knock your eyes out. One of the things I envy about Chirwl most, though, is that he can communicate with my cat and dog. I don't know if he translates their speech, or if he's just better at reading body language than I am."

"Having pets is considered good for one, though, isn't it?"

"Absolutely! Stroking an animal lowers your blood pressure. If you have to exercise a dog it means you need to go out. And having to care for another living being keeps you involved in life. I think it's very beneficial."

Finoa paused, then sat forward, her eyes fixed on Shona's. "What about animal therapy?"

Shona frowned. She noticed how intently the others were listening, including people in groups adjacent to their little circle. "What do you mean? I've read research in which children with autism were allowed to interact with dolphins. Some of the studies impressed me greatly. A reasonable fraction of the children were able to achieve natural function, and others showed improvement, but no one has ever been able to determine how that improvement came about. Beyond that, I've heard of few other instances where animal therapy was efficacious. I've never prescribed it myself."

Finoa settled back, her lips pressed together. "I see."

All the others sat back as well. Shona felt she'd touched a nerve. She had gone over Setve's records, but couldn't recall seeing a notation for an autistic child. Maybe that information had been expunged before her arrival. Was Setve off-planet in search of a dolphin?

"Are the mountains inside the terraformed territory yet?" Shona asked, appealing plaintively to her neighbors. "I've never been on one, in atmosphere, that is."

Bock gave a sour look to Finoa and came handsomely to her rescue. "What's your fancy, darling? Laren and I have some very fine foothills, and we can give you a fabulous deal on an alp or two, though the monodnocks are out of stock."

Shona giggled. "Anything. Setve's property seems to be mostly forest. I haven't reached the end of it yet."

"Well, come over some early morning, and prepare to sweat. I love climbing. I'll fit you out with equipment and show you. Oh! Am I boring you?" he asked, as Shona stifled an involuntary yawn.

"No," Shona said, but she got to her feet. "I'm afraid we didn't get much sleep. It's taking a while for the children to adapt to the big house. I tried to get Jill to sleep in her own bed last night."

"Not a success?" Dwan asked, sympathetically.

"Not a total failure," Shona said. "But I want to start out tonight before she's overtired. Good night. Bock, Laren, thank you for a lovely evening."

Laren was on his feet. "It's always a pleasure to see you."

"Oh, can't you leave the ottle?" Baraba said, from the ring of seats surrounding Chirwl's "throne." "We're having such a wonderful discussion of plant hybridization."

"I'm so sorry," Shona said, gathering up the ottle in his backpack pouch. "Good night to you all."

The Taylors withdrew with as much dignity as haste allowed. Laren accompanied her to the door and saw the cart rumble off into the twilight. He stalked back to the window seat. Finoa turned a blank face in his direction.

"I am very disappointed in our new doctor," she said.

"Did you expect she would understand right away?" Laren asked. "You were much too hard on her."

"What if she doesn't understand at all? What if she never comes around to our way of thinking? If she never can accept it at all?"

"She could quit and leave in a huff."

"And take the ottle with her," Baraba said forlornly. The whole room knew she had spoken out of turn. Finoa glared her back into submission.

"And taking our privacy with her," Robret pointed out. "That's what's important. Our way is the wise way. The best way!"

"Do you think she suspects anything?" Agneta asked.

"Certainly not," Finoa said. "How could she?"

"She's a good person," Dwan said, coming to her friend's defense. "And she's very wise, too. I think she would understand how we believe if we just tell her the right way."

"We may not have the leisure to do things our way. She's not stupid. The boy has already seen—" Kely shut his mouth immediately when he realized he was criticizing Finoa's own son.

"Tumi has always been strong willed." Finoa's tone was final. She was admitting the fault, but there was to be no further discussion on that point.

"No one wants to argue with you or Robret, but why?" Laren said with sudden bitterness. "Only six of us can be the chosen, but you're stringing us all along. You want Shona to change her mind, you convince her."

Finoa withdrew from him, seeming shocked and saddened. "I am sure that you must be wrong. I am only the guardian. I'm trying to do what is best for us all. I assure you that the chosen will be the best of us all."

"Engage her," Robret recommended. "Win her over. Find out what she thinks and what she knows. Then we can go on living our lives the way we like them."

FOUR

"It is a beautiful day," Lani offered shyly. She was sitting in Zolly's room on a low, yellow silk pouffe beside the other girl's personal communications console as Zolly scrolled down the screen. "We could go outside."

"What's so interesting?" Zolly said, without looking away. "It's just nature. It's there all the time."

"Not for me," Lani said. "We don't see blue skies."

"You live in space all the time?" the dark-skinned girl asked, her attention drawn momentarily away from the screen. Lani nodded. "Very rad."

"Unless I go away to school next year." The doubt she felt must have shown on her face. The indicator went "ping!" on the personal snack-maker beside the chairs. Lani opened the retro-styled chrome cabinet and took the iced lime drink from inside.

"You don't want to leave your family?" Zolly asked, leaning over to program a peach parfait for herself. Her thick ponytail of tightly plaited, curly black hair dropped over her shoulder. The beads at the end of each braid rattled. Lani's long, straight, black hair had been similarly dressed. She'd enjoyed playing hairdresser with her new friend. "I know what you mean. I don't know what it will be like when I go. Except for moving here, which I don't remember because I was too young, and taking Melody to school, we haven't been off the planet. Well, Mommy has. She has to go to annual meetings on Alpha. I would like to go with her sometime, and shop in *stores*. Have you done that?"

"Oh, yes. Every time we stop. On space stations and once on a colony, but they had only one mall."

"Tell me," Zolly said, leaning forward, her large eyes aglow. "Is it wonderful? You getting to handle all kinds of merchandise, not having to guess what it is like ahead of buying it?"

"We see lots of merchandise at depots and factories," Lani explained. "My father is a trader."

Zolly patted her on the knee. "Oh, that's right! So your ship is like a traveling store! Oh, that would be heaven. I wish I could see it."

"When he comes back I know he will let you. But it isn't glamorous, like stores. Everything is in impact crates, not hanging up."

Zolly laughed with delight. "But that would be like opening presents! What fun. I can't wait until he comes back. But I want to go to *stores*. I think that would be bliss. To try on clothes in front of the mirror, instead of using a computer model of yourself. To have clerks bring me hundreds of pairs of shoes. To try on all the jewelry at once."

Lani thought that last scenario was unlikely, given that sales personnel were notoriously security-conscious around teenage shoppers, no matter how wealthy. "The part I like best is the aerosol booth in the cosmetic stores. You put your chin on a rest. They program which kinds of makeup you want to try, and the machine sprays on microthin layers."

"And you don't get any in your eyes?" Zolly asked. Lani shook her head. "That is even more rad. Why microthin?"

"It wears off in a few minutes. No remover necessary. Then you can try on some more."

"Fabulous! I'd be there all day. We should do it, you and me," the other girl said, grabbing Lani's hand. "Next year, when we're both away at school. Meet at a big shopping station over the holidays, and just go into every store over and over again."

Lani just smiled.

"We know about you, you see," Zolly continued. "We heard you were very rich. Why do your parents have to trade and doctor, if you have all the money in the galaxy?"

The terms didn't seem mutually exclusive to Lani. To an uncomprehending Zolly she explained, "They like to work. My mama likes to help people." Her friend shook her head.

"She's a nice lady. And a good doctor. Except I overheard Shelia complaining that she made her use nonorganic eyedrops on Darrlel. I thought she would split something, she was so mad."

"If Mama said he needed them, then he did," Lani said firmly.

Zolly shook her head. "I dunno. If she had used goldenseal and eyebright, it should have taken down the inflammation. Might have been slower than chemicals but it's healthier for you."

"But it wouldn't stop the infection. I had pinkeye once. Jill caught it from another baby on Alpha. It spread fast. We all got it."

"All right, isolation and goldenseal." Zolly crossed her arms and raised her chin defiantly. She couldn't seem to let herself be in the wrong. Lani didn't say anything, but she did not let her eyes drop from the other girl's strong gaze. After a moment Zolly laughed. "You don't say much, but you're thinking hard at me, aren't you? I wouldn't let anyone talk down my mommy, either. Come on up here." She moved her hips over and patted the empty expanse of bench seat beside her. "I know! Let's play Top Tag."

"What's that?" Lani asked curiously. "Do we run around?"

"No, we sit right here. It's shopping!" Zolly said, cheerfully. "It's your money. You can spend what you like, right?"

"Yes," Lani said warily.

"Then you don't have to ask anyone's permission to play. If you want to. It's fun."

"All right," Lani agreed, hopping up. "How?"

"Look here," Zolly said, widening the twist on the rectangular color screen until both of them could see it well. "Pick out something to buy. Then, I'll choose something. Then you take a turn, and so on. When we are all finished, we'll add up the score to see who wins."

It sounded like an odd idea, but Zolly was so excited that Lani started to feel excited, too.

"All right."

"Good!" She put her hands on the controls and started scrolling around. "What shall we look at first? Fashion? Jewelry? Art?"

Catalog downloads were generally free if one allowed the business to send them on a regular basis. Because space travel often meant that a catalog might pursue a shopper over several beacons and change of direction, the sales could be outdated by the time it was downloaded. Zolly's catalogs were being updated continually, with all products guaranteed to be in stock. These advertising supplements were much more interesting than the usual flyers, packed with all the animations and tri-dee demonstration clips that the businesses could afford, designed to lure a good customer into spending as much money as possible. Lani found herself captivated by the mini-movies and songs in each of the advertisements. One, a heartfelt love ballad sung by a smooth tenor to a perfume in a pink glass flask, so entranced her that she played it over and over.

"We're *shopping*. Come back to that later," Zolly said impatiently, hitting the Escape command. Lani was jolted away from the enwrapping warmth of the male voice. "Pick something so I can have a turn! What about that?"

She pointed at an advertisement for the personal snackmakers. "You like mine. I bet you'd enjoy having one of your own. It freezes ice cream, or whips mousse, makes savory cheese crisps—anything you like. There's two models. One uses nutri, and the other uses real ingredients, like milk, sugar, and eggs. Mine uses real ingredients, of course," Zolly said proudly, taking a big sip of her peach shake. "Healthy. But they taste better, too. What do you think? The boxes are only half a meter square, so shipping doesn't cost a fortune. Why not? All the kids have them."

Lani tilted her head, studying the image. "I like it . . ."

"Well?"

"All right," Lani said, hitting Accept. The unit only cost a couple hundred credits. This wasn't so bad. She shifted the keypad over to Zolly, who leaned over the controls with the concentration of an attack pilot.

"I know there is a new music site here somewhere. There've been coming attractions for this new headset. It promises you feel like you're at a concert, and it can expand to up to six listeners. That's more than enough. Counting you there are only four girls our age, and no one else understands our music, don't you agree?"

Lani thought about it for a moment. "That's true."

"Ah, here it is!" Zolly exclaimed, triumphantly.

Both girls sighed in ecstasy at the object on the screen. On a background of velvety blue scattered with twinkling stars, a gold visor had been joined by a wide band to three curved panels about the size of an outstretched palm. The two on the sides fitted over the ears, and the one in the center curved up over the back of the skull like a modernistic tiara. The whole unit sparkled with glitter embedded in the amalgam. As it rotated the girls heard tantalizing bars of music purportedly coming out of the sixteen concealed speakers. In the animation the visor popped apart into its component pieces so the girls could see how it went together.

"I love it," Zolly said. "Only three thousand credits. It's mine." She hit the key to accept the purchase. "Do you want one, too?"

Lani leaned close to the screen. Arneguy Resources was the manufacturer. If she wanted one, Gershom could go directly to Fatima Arneguy, daughter of the president, who was the vice president of order fulfillment. She would sell the Taylors a unit for less than half of the stated price. She started to say something about that, but Zolly had already whisked the browser back to the index.

"Your turn! Oops, that's cooking equipment. I don't cook," Zolly said proudly. "That's for machines."

"I like to cook," Lani said. "Mama is teaching me recipes her family brought to Alpha from Earth. And Dwan knows a lot, too."

"I know, but why do they bother?" Zolly said, bored. "The robots are more careful than humans in keeping the nutrients intact. That's what they're here for, to free us up for more important tasks."

"Like shopping?" Lani asked, with a twinkle in her eye.

"Absolutely!" Zolly said, giving her a hug. "Oh, you're not going to buy that boring thing, are you?" She pointed at the screen, where Lani had halted the browser on a small countertop machine for making sauce.

"No," Lani said. "My father can get it much cheaper. But it's nice."

Zolly took over the controls and brought them back to the fashion index. "How about one of these?" she asked, pointing at a black coat with fuchsia trim at collar and cuffs. "It's cuddly as anything."

Lani considered it too extreme for her tastes. "I like this one better," she said, pointing at a long duster in a deep green with gold trim down the front facings.

"Get it!" Zolly ordered.

Lani's fingers hovered over the Accept key. "I shouldn't."

"Why not? It will look smashing on you."

"My father knows the distributor. He can get it for me at a fraction of this price."

"Well, then," Zolly said, impatiently, "find something he cannot get. How about this?" She indicated a complicated necklace of illuminated stars set in enamel. "Pick your birth sign, or your favorite constellation."

Lani's eyes lit up. "I like the Seven Sisters you can see from Sol system." A flick of the hand, and the purchase was made. Zolly took over and began to look for herself.

"If we're having concerts, I must have something new to wear. I think Partridge has a new line available this month. Yes," she breathed, sitting back as graphics exploded out of the tri-dee tank toward them.

Exquisitely handsome young men and women paraded up and down a miniature catwalk, twisting and turning so the viewers could see every angle of the clothing they had on. Deep colors like aquamarine and amethyst were lit warmly by concealed lights or accented with dazzling crystals.

"Partridge is different because the models are allowed to smile," Zolly said. "They have it trademarked now, you know. Do they have that beige suit in my size? They do!" She started to reach for the key. Lani caught her hand.

"Don't," she advised. Zolly looked surprised.

"Why not? I like it. It will fit me."

Lani gestured at the screen. "You don't want to pay these prices," she explained. "I have a suit just like it in deep red. My father will get it for you from Partridge for 20 percent of what is being asked here. This site charges full retail. That's too much."

Zolly finally fixed her with an exasperated look. "Lani. You just don't understand. The idea is not to spend the least, it's to spend the most!"

Lani blinked. "It is?"

"Of course! What is money for, if not to keep score in the grand game of life—a quote of my father's. If I didn't blow three thousand credits a day my parents would think I was sick. The others all do it. It's *fun*. We don't have a lot

of fun around here. Stop thinking like a tradesperson."
Lani started to protest, and Zolly raised her voice over her
objections. "Think *rich*. You are rich. Come on. What's the
most expensive thing you ever bought?"

"Oh," said Lani, comprehending at last. "Well, I once
bought a bank."

Zolly laughed. "A bank? I have a hundred banks. China,
metal, papier-mâche, wood, even one made out of plat-
inum my grandmother gave me when I was born."

"Not that kind of a bank. A mercantile bank. A business."

The other's dark brown eyes grew wide. "*Rad*. So, what
is the too-coolest thing about owning a bank?"

Lani shrugged. "Well, you don't have to decide between the electric blanket and the toaster. They send you
both."

"What does *that* mean?" Zolly laughed.

"I don't know," Lani said frankly. "It's a joke the president told me when I met him."

"I never bought a business," Zolly said, with interest.
"Let's see what's for sale. Maybe I will buy a nice shop on
a space station. It will give us something to visit when we
go on our great escapade. Perhaps a branch of a jewelery
store. Or silks. I love silk. I think my mother will go spare
when I tell her." Zolly giggled.

"Isn't that bad?" Lani asked, worriedly.

"She's used to it," the other girl said offhandedly, hitting the Search key. "Look, right there: franchises for
sale."

"Is there anything you can't find?"

"You can buy *anything*, if you know where to shop, and
if you're willing to pay whatever it costs."

"Even a tiger?" Lani asked, flippantly.

Zolly narrowed her big black eyes into slits. "What put
that into your head?" she asked.

"My little brother. He has been talking about nothing
else since he visited Tumi."

"Oh!" Zolly said, nodding. "So you are interested.

That's good. I thought you and your mom weren't part of us, but I guess you are. That's a relief. My mother will want to know."

Lani didn't really understand what her friend was talking about, but Shona had said often that she wanted the family to fit in as long as they were on Jardindor. She nodded.

"Right!" Zolly exclaimed happily. "Now, let's really spend some money!"

FiVe

"I have," Laren said defensively, "a cough."

The spare man sat with his arms folded on the examining table in the office. He turned glares at Shona, his partner, the diagonostic machinery, and Saffie, who was curled up underneath it. At the Carmodys' specific request Chirwl had been banished to the outer office. Shona wondered what was wrong. Laren's hair was ruffled into a crest like a fighting bird. Beside him sat Bock, larger, milder, watchful, with his big hands clasped. Shona pulled up her chair until she was sitting beside them, her head lower than theirs, allowing Laren the position of superiority. He needed the confidence. He was having a very hard time speaking. She could tell he didn't want to be there, but obviously Bock had forced him to come.

"I have noticed your cough," Shona admitted.

"So has everyone else, it seems," Laren said, with a sour glance at his partner. Bock gave him a placid look.

"Everyone gets sick once in a while," Shona said.

"Not me. Not here. It's not allowed. Oh, spacewrecks, *why* can't I just say what I mean?" Laren appealed to her.

Smoothly, she took the initiative. She leaned forward and took his wrist, casually counting his pulse.

"You can talk to me in confidence. That's what I am here for. I'm your doctor. I will not judge you. You have complete privacy here. What other symptoms have you noticed? There are other symptoms?"

Laren made a face. "Damn it, yes, there are. I don't see how anyone's missed those, either."

"I'm new here," Shona said cheerfully. "I haven't seen anything myself. What is worrying you?"

After one more resentful glance toward Bock Laren threw up his hands. "I'm tired all the time. I've tried fighting the fatigue with herbs, homeopathy, yoga, deep breathing, you name it, but nothing works for long. I can get up from a good night's sleep and be tired by midmorning. I can't focus on my work. The buyers in my decorating salons and antique stores are becoming very impatient with me because I'm late on the current season's line. My attention to detail sometimes goes right out of the atmosphere. I've been making bad decisions. And my muscles ache. Not just the muscles. The joints, too. Especially around my elbows and knees. I'm not arthritic," he added, with a sideways wary glance at her. "I drink enough cider vinegar and honey to pickle an orchard. I'm losing weight. Food doesn't go right all the time. Simple things I used to love to eat disagree with me. The other day I ate an avocado and I nearly stopped breathing. There was a pain here." He indicated the right side of the bottom of his rib cage. He shifted uncomfortably and Bock shifted closer to put an arm around his shoulders. Laren looked plaintive. "I feel as if I'm getting old."

"And you're only fifty-three," Shona said, after checking his record on the computer. "You don't look even that age, apart from being somewhat too thin. *Leucocephalus?*" she read off the screen. "That's 'whitehead' in old Latin. Was Setve treating you for acne?"

"No, and I wish he was here now," Laren said, then paused, ashamed. "No offense."

"None taken," Shona replied. "I'm sure you would be more comfortable with your own doctor."

Saffie heard Laren's plaintive voice and came over to put her head on his knee with a gentle whine of concern. Laren gave her a smile but didn't pet her.

"Thank you, but I don't need what you have to offer right now."

Shona had no idea what that meant. Probably part of the local custom that she still struggled with. She pinched up a fold of skin on the back of his hand and was alarmed at how long it took to settle out.

"I know." Laren smiled ruefully before she could speak. "I'm very dehydrated. Water races through me. I hardly dare drink in company. Never alcohol anymore, and I do like a good glass of wine. That brings on a pain in my belly, too."

"What medications are you taking?" Shona asked.

"If you mean commercial medicines," Laren said stiffly, "nothing."

"I mean your personal regimen," Shona corrected herself hastily. "What vitamins and herbs do you take? Teas?"

"I don't see what bearing that has," Laren said, looking more mulish than ever.

"If you're taking anything that might mask more troubling symptoms, it would help if I knew about it," Shona said reasonably. "For example, if you're boosting your immune system with echinacea . . . ?"

"Yes," Laren admitted at last. "I take echinacea."

"And what else?"

"I'll message you a full list, if it has anything to do with how I'm feeling!"

Shona regretted again Setve's apparent willingness to let his patients overmedicate themselves. "Laren, you've been very open in talking about your health in public. All I'm asking for are specific supplements and, if you can tell me, what quantities."

"That's true," Laren admitted, with rueful humor. "I'll make up a list and send it. I'm sorry to be so offensive."

She rose briskly and put her stethoscope buds in her ears. "Well, we'll give you a full checkup and see if there's anything to be concerned about."

The scope's small screen confirmed what her ears told her. His pulse was threadier than she liked. She ran a blood sample through Setve's impressive computer. It spat out its reading, but continued chuckling along. Shona gave it a troubled glance.

She scanned the small plasheet, then reread it carefully. Bad news was always difficult. She paused for a moment, finding phrasing that wouldn't send the reluctant patient fleeing, but would give him the information he needed to cope.

"I see an elevated white count," she said. "And a high level of antibodies. That suggests an infection, but I'll have to get a blood culture to identify whether it's bacterial or viral. I already see EPV. Epstein-Barr syndrome could account for some of the symptoms you describe, especially the exhaustion, but it wouldn't cause the high level of leukocytes. It suggests that there might be a different causative organism. What worries me more is that your liver is showing signs of distress."

"I told you, I've stopped drinking," Laren protested.

"The liver doesn't just filter fats and alcohol, though I found it telling that you're having trouble with fatty foods like avocados. It deals with toxins of other kinds: dietary, environmental, anything that gets into the body by any means. It's your second line of defense. Could you have eaten some contaminated fruit? Pesticides can break down your immune system. It's meant to work that way on insects."

The men shook their heads. "Not a chance," Bock said. "All imported food has been irradiated and passed by the Interstellar Foods Commission. All of the food grown here is organically raised. No pesticides, no herbicides. We are very careful."

"Bacteria from the soil or hydroponics, then?"

"We wash everything in an organic bacteriocidal solution."

Shona frowned. "Then that suggests something in your

home environment. Are you being exposed to anything unusual in your daily life?"

Both men exchanged alarmed looks. "No," Bock said at
last.

"Maybe it's something you're not aware of in your
home's system," Shona said. "Environmental medicine is
my specialty. I would be happy to come in and do an analysis of your home's filtration systems." The men looked
horrified. "At least I could rule out anything in the house
itself as the vector for your condition."

"No," Laren said. "Absolutely not."

Shona knew how the Jardindorians prized their privacy,
but she pushed a little harder. "Laren, if it's something
your living system has in common with others it's possible
that more people than you are being affected but are
asymptomatic as yet."

"You'd have to go everywhere in the house, see everything?" Laren asked.

"Yes," Shona said. "Otherwise I might miss what's affecting you, and that would do you no service."

"I'm sorry," Laren said, white around the lips. "We cannot just allow you to go marching all over our home. Not
a chance! Black holes, if it was even thought that we were
spreading a disease around the colony . . . !"

"That's not what I meant," Shona began. "We need to
talk about the correct therapy for you, and I need more information—" But Laren wasn't listening. He sprang up
from the examining table and went straight out the rear
door. Bock shot her a look of apology and set out after his
mate. Shona hurried to catch him.

"Are you feeling ill, too?" she asked in a low voice.

"We're not here to talk about me," he said. "Just Laren.
I've got to go." And he did. Shona let the door close between them and sat down to think.

Saffie came over to lay her head on Shona's knee and
turned big, sympathetic brown eyes up to her. Shona
scratched the dog between the ears.

"I can't administer medical care to him if he doesn't

want it," she mused aloud. "But his condition is bad. It could turn very serious very quickly. I know how important privacy is here, but is it worth their lives?" She couldn't solve the mystery without more information, and they weren't willing to give it to her. Not yet.

She stared out the big window at the mountains peeking over the pine forest. Jardindorians, for all their luxurious lifestyle, lived close to a potent source of toxic chemicals. Laren and Bock's home was closer than most to the force field. It was possible that an undetected, temporary or permanent leak was allowing polyphenols and other dangerous materials out into the terraformed environment. She would have to start examining her other patients for the same immune-response symptoms, and see if anyone else was willing to let her look for pathogens and poisons in their homes.

Not for the first time she wondered how Jardindor had been released for settlement. It should have been fully terraformed or fitted with protective domes before habitation was permitted. A second mystery. But in the meantime she had offended one of her patients, the first one she'd seen who really needed her help. She was going to have to figure out how to break down the barriers, for his own sake.

A "ping" sounded as the blood analysis finished. Shona pulled the plasheet out of the tray and read down the traces of pathogens, minerals, bacteria, and viruses. As she had feared, Laren had been exposed to biphenyls and polyphenyls, but suspected that those only exacerbated his condition, which was a bacterial infection that had been going on for a long time. As to which one, she would just have to wait for the details when the culturing was completed. Until then, the best thing to do was to get him on a broad-spectrum antibiotic, and start looking for a root cause. His life could depend on it.

"And of the man who will not answer his console?" Chirwl asked Shona as they sat in the cart on the way to Dwan's mansion.

"He'll have to get in touch with me at some point. In any case, we will see him at the Friday party. I think Agneta is hosting this week. She's a wonderful cook. Mm! I dread the time when it's our turn. My food is mud pies compared with the cooking on this world."

"Then the impression should be of not of this world," Chirwl said reasonably.

"What should I do?" Shona asked, with a laugh. "Serve them nutri?"

As Shona pulled into the circular, gravel-covered driveway in front of Dwan's mansion, she heard a cheerful shout. She turned to see Alex and the other children waving at her from the side garden.

"Stop here, James," she said aloud. Obediently the green cart came to a halt. She and Saffie jumped out to meet the children, who were racing toward her, trampling Dwan's lavender in the process. Highly excited and fragrantly scented, Alex and Jill leaped into their mother's arms.

"Mama, Mama! I learned about acids and alkalis today!" Alex shouted. Dwan, smiling and waving, threshed slowly toward the road, gathering handfuls of flowers from the fallen stalks. Shona, her arms full of children, could only grin back. "Dougie and I went to see Jamir. His urine is very acid. Is that because it smells bad?"

"No, honey, it smells bad because it's very acid," Shona explained, giving them one more big hug before setting them down. "I guess the pretending goes on," she said to Dwan as her friend reached the carriage. "Alex has really formed an attachment to Tumi's toy. It must be a very realistic one."

Alex gave her the look he reserved for when his parents were being very stupid. "He's not pretend, Mama. He is real. So is Dougie's monkey. Well, he's Dougie's mama's monkey."

"Alex, you shouldn't say things that aren't true, especially in front of the lady," Shona said. Dwan broke eye contact, picking up her son and burying her face in his hair. "I'm sorry. It's not like him to make up stories about people."

"No!" Alex insisted. "Chirwl knows. He's seen him."

"What?" Shona asked bemusedly, looking at her friend for an explanation. "Chirwl?"

"Secrets are not mine," the ottle said, twitching his whiskers. He regarded Shona with sympathy. "Much is not told that is still smelled."

"I do have a monkey," Dwan said in a very small voice, still not meeting Shona's eyes. "A real monkey. His name is Kajiro. He's very smart and gentle. I've taught him to pick berries and flowers. I think he enjoys it." She stopped, sensing having said too much.

"Flowers!" Shona said, enlightenment dawning suddenly. "*That's* how those bouquets have been getting into my house. The security program is looking for someone *walking* in. No wonder Saffie's going crazy smelling his scent on the vases. She's never met a monkey before. How does he do it, cling to the roboserver arms in the ceiling?"

"Yes," Dwan said. "He learned that when he first came here, before we taught him how to live in a house. He hasn't destroyed anything, has he?"

"No, indeed, he must be very careful. I've wanted to tell whoever it was how much I've enjoyed the flowers. It's so nice of you." Shona grinned, thinking of a monkey swinging from room to room with her friend's secret offering of flowers clutched in one of his prehensile feet.

"It's nothing," Dwan said, shyly. "I just wanted to welcome you. Then you've been so nice I . . . I just kept it up."

"Well, it's been one of the things I look forward to in the morning. I'm glad to know how it was done. It's been puzzling me a lot. Can I meet Kajiro? Does he live in the pool house?"

"No," Dwan said, leaning low after looking around nervously. "He lives in the house. He's got his own room. You've never seen that part of the house. You . . ." She glanced around again. "Come on, but hurry."

DWAN led the group through the great room, but instead of turning left in the blue-carpeted corridor behind it toward the children's bedrooms and play area, she turned right. They hadn't gone more than a few meters before Saffie raised her nose from the floor and let out a bay. Shona looked at her in alarm, but the dog's tail was wagging. She was about to solve a mystery that had been troubling her for the last several weeks.

The Taylors were devoted to nature programs beamed from Earth, though those tended to concentrate with depressing regularity on animals that no longer existed either in the wild or in captivity. Shona knew there were several kinds of monkey. She tried to guess before Dwan opened the door at the end of the hall what Kajiro would look like.

To her delight and surprise, the inhabitant of the huge, airy room was a small, intense creature about two-thirds of Chirwl's size with a lion's mane of white around his wrinkled pink face. The room contained several small platforms on high poles with thick, ropelike vines festooned between them. The little monkey flung himself off his perch and handed himself rapidly down, dropping the last meter to land on his mistress's shoulder. Chittering, he clung to Dwan's hair and studied Shona.

"Oh, he's adorable," Shona said. Chirwl, in his pouch on Shona's back, stuck his head up to see. Kajiro, startled by the ottle's sudden appearance, screamed. Saffie barked, and the monkey stopped screaming to scold her. Chirwl berated both of them for bad manners.

"What is he?" Shona asked, laughing, over the din. "Hush, Saffie!"

"He's a Japanese snow monkey," Dwan explained, detaching its paws from her hair. "He's normally better behaved than this."

"Well, I am very pleased to meet you, Kajiro," Shona said, addressing the round brown eyes directly. The monkey chattered shrilly and offered her a tiny black hand. Shona laughed with delight and took it. Its texture was interesting, similar to Chirwl's hand-paws in that it was hard and knobby, but his fingernails were very like a human's. "Thank you for your kind delivery service. You've made my mornings very happy."

"You are another person, but my friend Saffie worries him," Chirwl said. Dwan looked at the ottle with a hungry expression, and Shona realized how lonely she was. Kajiro would be a kind of company, but he couldn't converse intelligently the way the ottle could. Chirwl wasn't a pet.

"What a nice surprise," Shona said. "He must be fun to have around."

"Fun?" Dwan asked. "I suppose. He's a responsibility. It's all worthwhile, though." Dwan fell silent again.

"See, Mama," Alex said. "I told you he was real."

"You're right, sweetheart. I apologize. But if Kajiro is real," Shona asked Dwan, hope dawning as the point from which she had been distracted earlier came back to her, "then what about Jamir?"

"Yeah!" Alex said. "Let's go and see Jamir!"

"Is *he* real?" Shona pressed Dwan.

The taller woman backed away, looking as frightened as her monkey. "I . . . I don't like to discuss it any more. I can't really say . . ."

"Then who *can* say?" Shona asked, in her gentlest voice. "Should we go and see Finoa? I will ask her myself. I'll tell her I found out about Kajiro by accident."

"No!" Dwan exclaimed. "I mean, no. You'd have to get Governor Hethyr's permission. She's in charge," Dwan added weakly.

"Then let's go see her," Shona said, holding out a hand to her. Very slowly and with the greatest reluctance, the Jardindorian woman lifted Kajiro off her shoulder and set him on the nearest post.

"All right," she said.

SiX

HETHYR paced from one side of her sumptuously furnished office to the other. Shona sat in a chair in front of the desk, Saffie at her feet. Dwan, looking as rueful as a dog that had been whipped, occupied a curved antique couch a couple of meters behind. She refused to meet anyone's eyes. Hethyr had heard Shona's opening queries over the comm-unit, and blew up in fury the moment she had walked in.

"Your job here is not to snoop into the private lives of the citizens. You are to provide medical care. Nothing more!"

Shona watched her with astonishment. "I was only curious, as anybody might be. My son, who does not usually lie or tell wild stories, came home from his new friends' homes full of enthusiasm about seeing exotic animals. Naturally I wanted to find out what was behind it."

Hethyr rounded on her, sticking a finger nearly into Shona's eye. "You came to spy on us, didn't you?"

Saffie growled at the threatening tone. Shona rose, taking her dog's collar in her hand. "Governor," she said coldly, wrapping the leash around her wrist, "let me re-mind you that *you* contacted *me* and offered me a job. I had never heard of Jardindor until I got your message. If you are unsatisfied with my discretion or behavior I tender my resignation. I'll contact my husband and have him pick us up at the earliest possible convenience. I ask only that you pay my wages up to this point and allow us some suitable accomodations until our departure. We'll prepare to move out of Dr. Setve's house at once. I'm sure you'll want to make it ready for your next contract physician."

"Wages!" Hethyr exploded. "I should prosecute you for invasion of privacy!"

"Now, please, let's all calm ourselves," said a new voice. Finoa, in a pantsuit of flowing silver-gray, entered the room, stepping swiftly between Shona and Hethyr, whose face was now a fine shade of purple. "There's no need to be unreasonable."

Shona felt her eyebrows climb her forehead. Finoa draped an arm over the governor's stiff shoulders and drew her back, giving the doctor a gracious smile.

"I regret we weren't here when you arrived, Dr. Shona. Hethyr is tense, as she might well be. We'd been preparing to take you into our confidence over this small matter, but we were going at our own pace, and you stumbled upon part of our secret a little before we were ready. Forgive Hethyr her outburst."

Hethyr gaped at Finoa. Whatever she'd expected her to say, Shona could tell that this was not it. She had no time to think for herself, as Robret leaned forward to take her hand and led her back to her chair.

"What are you doing?" Hethyr hissed. Finoa turned so that her superior height blocked her actions from Shona and put a finger on Hethyr's lips.

"Shh! What were you doing? You don't want her going off-planet, not now. Not yet. Calm yourself, Hethyr. You know what's at stake. You should be more diplomatic."

"Diplomatic! She knows!"

Finoa smiled, her mouth twisted into an expression of

scorn. "She doesn't know what she knows. We will make
certain that her knowledge is steered correctly so that we
get what we want from her. Don't charge in and ruin this
for us, Hethyr."

"You have no authority over me! You're not governor
of this colony."

"And I hope I never am. But what I am is more important to it at this moment." Finoa held up a warning finger,
with her sternest face. "Don't say another word. Let Robret."

Hethyr seemed about to protest, but Finoa turned away
from her, refusing to acknowledge the woman's authority
or temper. Robret had already begun to bring his charm to
bear on the little doctor.

Robret knelt down beside Shona's chair, balancing his
elbows on the arm so that she felt his presence but did not
perceive herself to be trapped by it. Finoa admired her husband's instincts. Shona was off-guard; that was good. Perhaps Hethyr had not done so much damage after all.

"I'M sorry that Hethyr got all set off like that," Robret
said to Shona. His voice was deep and very soothing. "Are
you upset?"

Shona became aware that she might look no better to
the newcomers than the angry governor, and made an ef-
fort to bring her breathing under control. "Yes, I am. I feel
vulnerable here. I'm dependent on you for my employment
and my living arrangements. I thought the terms of my
tenure had been spelled out completely in the agreement I
signed. Nothing in that document said that there was a security concern. I displayed a little normal curiosity—
human nature—which was kindly indulged by a friend
whom I believed had the right to do so. When I sought further information I was threatened with termination, and I
still do not know what I am accused of doing wrong."

"She didn't mean to overreact. We were going to tell

you, but we were hoping to gauge how you would react before we did."

Shona frowned. "Tell me what?"

"Shona, what do you know about Animal Magnetism?" he asked, gazing warmly into her eyes.

The big bear of a man was staring at her with warm, honey-colored eyes. Shona glanced away from his intense gaze to Hethyr, whose face was a stony mask, and Dwan, who looked frightened. Shona swallowed. She felt as though she was on trial or facing a difficult exam.

"I believe that some people have a kind of charm that draws others to them. It's more basic than charisma—I've met a couple of men whom I thought had animal magnetism. They were, well, sexy. Though one of them wasn't handsome he still attracted women by the drove."

Robret smiled, and she realized he had some of that raw charm himself. "That's not exactly what I mean, though it's related. In this case the attractiveness would be more of a result than a cause. You see, when you handle or interact with certain animals, that contact bestows on you certain qualities." Shona opened her mouth, but he pressed a little closer, stilling her protest. "Please, hear me out. As I'm sure you know from history, let alone your medical studies, our ancestors believed in totem animals."

"Yes, that's true," Shona said thoughtfully. "Tribes would adopt a beast that embodied characteristics they wanted to have, like lions for courage, owls for wisdom, gazelles for speed, and so on. It was a superstition."

"They did exactly what you say, adopting a creature they admired to gain its attributes," Robret said, nodding. "But what if I told you it was not a superstition? What if I told you that interaction with those animals does impart those characteristics?"

"I've never heard of any scientific basis for that," Shona said evenly. "What I do know is that millions of animals over the centuries were killed because humans thought ingesting or wearing parts of them made them stronger or more virile. It's an appalling part of our history." She looked at Hethyr. "I hope you're not telling me that you are reviving vile traditions like that. It's against all decency."

"Not at all," Robret said, recapturing her attention. "We're not so barbaric to kill these animals. Mere contact bestows those qualities on us."

Shona gaped at him. "You can't expect me as a woman of science to believe such a thing."

"Hear me out, please, Shona. Science has ignored a great many things over the ages, things that have been proved in the long run to have validity. Why, don't you recall when chiropractic medicine was considered charlatanism?"

"Well, yes," Shona began.

"And you did say yourself that you know of successful research involving dolphins?"

"Yes, but—"

"And I have read a good deal about the benefits of pet ownership, especially for the elderly or isolated. You said yourself that you felt better taking care of your furry friends, including this gentleman here," he said, indicating Chirwl, who was listening with outspread whiskers.

"That's true," Shona said.

"Well, your friend there has a dolphin," Robret said smoothly.

Shona raised an eyebrow. "She has a monkey."

"*And* a dolphin."

Slowly, she turned to look at Dwan, who was redder than ever. "You have a pet dolphin?"

"A therapeutic dolphin," Dwan said. "Three-eet is my friend. It's part of our family wellness routine. He lives in the pool house. That's why I've never taken you there. It's . . . private. You understand."

"Forgive me," Shona said, thinking of the studies. "Wait, I didn't see any reference—" She stopped short, almost surprised into discussing her patients' records in front of others. Robret seemed to pick her meaning directly out of her mind.

"That's because there is no history of any of the conditions normally associated with dolphin therapy. This is something new and special. We here are fortunate enough to be able to experience Animal Magnetism, to experiment with it, because of our situation."

"And what situation is that?" Shona asked.

"Why, that we can," Robret said, simply.

Because they could afford to do so, Shona understood.

"We take very good care of our charges, I promise you. Would you like to see them? I can't speak for the others, but we would be glad to let you see our special friends. It would be an honor. I hope to convince you that what we are doing here is true and remarkable. Would you like that?"

"Yes, I would," Shona said at once. Whether or not they were practicing a very novel form of quackery, the concept of seeing a number of rare animals in the flesh piqued her interest.

Whether or not Jardindor *was* the seat of a very novel form of quackery, Shona did not care, not at that moment. She was too busy holding her breath and staring. Before her eyes was one of the wonders of the universe, a beast that she thought was nearly extinct, except in government-maintained nature preserves. The male tiger, 230 kilos of orange, black, and white-striped muscle, paced slowly back and forth on the grass. His golden eyes were fixed upon her even when he turned to pace back the other way. His expression was one of idle interest. He didn't seem threatened by the presence of half a dozen humans and one ottle. Saffie had been left behind at the governor's mansion, for her own protection, Robret had explained. All of the children had remained at Dwan's home. Her husband had been pried away from his keyboard to keep an eye on them.

Shona marveled at the size of the tiger's paws, as big across as her own head. Wickedly sharp, curved claw tips showed between the huge pads as each foot lifted and was set down. Dappled by shadows thrown from the high bushes surrounding the sheltered enclosure, the stripes on his back, legs, and flicking tail formed an everchanging pattern that hypnotized Shona as she watched him. He was beautiful, the most beautiful thing she had ever seen. She let out her breath with a sigh of pleasure.

"He is called Jamir," Finoa said, "but I believe you know that already. My son was . . . indiscreet. He is very trusting, as most children are. As are young of most species. Tumi should not have let your children back here, but once he had we ought to have spoken openly with you about what they saw. I apologize for allowing you to misjudge your son, but as you may guess, some secrets are important."

"Yes, indeed," Shona said, absentmindedly, not wishing to take her eyes off the tiger. "He is . . . bigger than I imagined tigers would be."

"Over two and a half meters from nose to tailtip," Robret said proudly.

"I've heard they remain wild throughout their lives, but the boys can pet him?" Shona eyed the creature warily. He was *huge*. Muscles bunched and unbunched under the silky hide, ready to spring. At that range she couldn't outrun him, but the couple at her side weren't at all worried.

"He's quite docile," Finoa assured her.

"What do you feed him?" Shona asked. "He must eat kilos of meat every day. You don't have herds of livestock."

"Certainly not!"

"There are mass refrigeration units built into every home, full of frozen fodder," Dwan said. "You have one, too. I can show you later." She quailed as Finoa rotated magnificently to glare at her. Shona didn't understand why. The tall woman turned back to Shona and smiled.

"Would you like to stroke him?" Shona nodded. Robret led her forward. "He won't harm you. He's used to humans." The big man laid a hand on Jamir's neck. The tiger stopped pacing and sat down, hind legs first. The striped tail flicked in a curve around his back feet, and he sank heavily to the ground. Shona fancied she could hear a thump as he settled. "Go on, scratch his ears. He likes it."

Shona touched the round ears lightly with two fingers. They flicked. Encouraged by Robret, she scratched harder around the ear cup and down the middle of the forehead, her fingers disappearing in the thick pelt. The fur was coarser than she had expected, like coconut matting, and it had a pleasant though strong musky scent. The liquid-gold eyes squinted halfway shut, and a low-pitched purring sound came from his chest.

"Why, he's like a big cat," she said. Encouraged, she began to fondle the big head in the same way she scratched Harry's. The tiger tilted his head toward her. She used both hands. The rough fur scraped her skin but the sound he made was so appealing that she kept going. "How beautiful!" She glanced around at the part of the garden they were in. It was rectangular and ran a few dozen meters down its long axis in the direction of the distant mountains. Shona realized it paralleled her own garden next door. A hedge with a fence separated the tiger's space from the family's kitchen-garden and scented knot garden that flanked the sprawling house. "Does he live in this small enclosure? I thought tigers were jumpers. How do you keep him from wandering away?"

Finoa cleared her throat. She hesitated a moment before she replied. "He stays close. He doesn't like to be far from his companion."

Shona's eyebrows went up. "Do you have a female tiger, too?" That would be riches beyond compare. She looked around for Jamir's mate.

"No." Finoa's mouth curved in a tiny smile at her eagerness. "No, his companion is not of the same species." She pointed at the thick brush. "You can see her if you look closely."

Shona followed the direction of her hostess's hand and peered at the undergrowth. It did feel as though something was watching her, but she couldn't see. Suddenly she became aware of a shape, a shadow looming against the trees. What could be that big? "What is she?"

A gray tendril of flesh as thick as her arm curled out of the brush. A snake! Automatically, Shona recoiled. But no giant python or boa constrictor dropped out of the trees to slither toward them. Instead, a gray head the size of a medicine ball adorned with twin sabers of pale cream color followed the curling appendage, followed by sail-shaped ears, tree-trunk legs and a body covered with saggy, leathery skin. Small brown eyes in wrinkled sockets regarded her with intelligent humor.

"I don't believe it," Shona gasped. "She's . . . an *elephant?*"

"Yes," Finoa said. "Her name is Lady Elaine."

Shona started toward the big animal almost in a trance. Raised on colony and dome worlds she had never had the experience Earthborn children had of visiting wildlife parks and zoos to see the rare creatures that had once roamed their planet's plains and jungles. All she knew of them she had seen in tri-videos, in books, or painted on the side of a set of ancient wooden blocks that she'd played with as a child. Elephants were at the same time beasts of burden and treasure troves of resources. Their ancestor the woolly mammoth had been hunted for its pelt, meat, and ivory tusks, a material that took fine carving better than almost any substance in existence. The ivory was the reason for its peril, as poachers destroyed viable populations in search of an ever-shrinking supply of the desirable big tusks. Lady Elaine's were intact, gleaming white. Shona wondered how she'd ever missed seeing them against the darkness of the undergrowth.

A snarl brought her up short, as Jamir leaped up from the spot where he had been reclining and interposed himself between the doctor and Lady Elaine. He bared impressive white fangs, and the pupils of his gold eyes glowed green. The growl seemed almost to come from beneath Shona's feet. She froze. Fear tingled in her belly.

"Robret, what is he doing?" she asked.

"Jamir!" Robret shouted. "She's a friend!"

The tiger blinked. He did not move, but his stance relaxed very slightly, the muscles in his back going from coiled to merely taut. In the meantime the elephant had stretched her trunk over the head of the tiger and dropped it onto Shona's hand. It, too, felt coarser than she had expected. The moist tip sniffed its way up her arm, into her hair, across her face and down her chest. It withdrew, pausing in the air like a woman with her finger raised to consider a thought. Jamir growled again. Robret strode to her side and pushed the tiger away. It turned and stalked to stand with its flank against the elephant's huge leg. His fierce expression dared anyone to come close to them.

"I'm sorry, I should have warned you," Robret said, putting his arm around Shona's shoulders. She found she was trembling and leaned against the big man to steady herself. "Jamir doesn't like anyone touching or challenging Lady Elaine. He's appointed himself her protector."

"It's unusual to have two such different species so close to one another, isn't it?" Shona asked, once she'd gotten her breath back. She shrugged off his arm and planted her feet firmly on the grass, determined not to be frightened. None of the others were.

"He's taking care of her in her condition," Finoa said, from behind them. "Lady Elaine is pregnant."

Shona spun, unable to believe her ears. "She is? How long?" Finoa stared at her. Shona ducked her head, abashed. "I'm sorry to pry. It's just that I'm amazed to see a live elephant—"

"Being touched by one, in fact," Chirwl said, speaking for the first time. "The proboscis takes in more sensation than a smaller nose."

"Yes," Shona agreed, "then to hear there's a baby elephant on the way . . . this is so wonderful. I can hardly take it all in."

"She's in her seventh week."

"Oh," Shona said, a little crestfallen. "They carry for

about two years, don't they? I'd just hoped to see the new baby delivered." Finoa smiled her superior smile. Shona forgave it. The woman had plenty of reason to be proud. She turned to look at the elephant and tiger again. She was seeing Terran wildlife for the first time in her life. She wanted to pinch herself. "Oh, I can see even more why you would be cautious about having anyone knowing about her. A live elephant is valuable, but a mother and baby would be beyond price."

Nobody spoke. Shona understood she'd overstepped the bounds of local propriety again.

"Trees make a small cage for such big creatures," Chirwl observed.

"That's true! I'd heard elephants wander for miles in search of food," Shona said. "And they're hard on the local vegetation." The picture in her mind was a two-dee video from the twentieth century of a large herd stripping the branches from trees to eat and use as fans. Little had been left behind of the forest, making the elephants very unpopular with their human neighbors. This enclosure was pristine, except for a few piles of waste. "Both of them seem very tame."

"The answer is quite simple, and one that I am surprised that you, as a woman of science, as you call yourself, would not have deduced," Finoa said with some asperity. "We sedate her, of course. We cannot afford to have her wandering off into the no-man's-land. She is too valuable, and she could get hurt trying to force her way past the terraformers. Jamir, too, has to be under constant sedation. Otherwise he would be too wild to handle, and that would defeat the purpose of our research here."

Shona felt as though she'd been slapped. "I see," she said stiffly. "Forgive the question. It was sophomoric. Aren't you concerned that the sedative might affect the fetus?"

"No. Sopophedrase has been used on animals for over a hundred years," Finoa assured her. "Under far less benevolent circumstances, such as those wretched little traveling circuses and zoos with cages. I have the documentation on the chemical. I will message it to you. You may find the abstract interesting."

"Thank you," Shona said, keeping her replies formal. The warmth she'd felt toward the animals had frozen solid under the icy regard of her hostess. She hardly wanted to look at Dwan, whose expression pleaded for understanding. They needed to talk later where they couldn't be overheard. "I'm not as familiar with veterinary sedatives as I am with human equivalents. I treat my own animals under direction from a veterinarian I correspond with on Earth, and I have no experience with wild animals. Thank you for introducing me to your . . . charges. You have given me a great deal to think about. I had better go back now and see my children. I owe Alex an apology."

Robret took her hand and looked deeply into her eyes. "We look forward to telling you more about Animal Magnetism. Do you have any more questions?"

"Just one," Shona said. "What kind of bird do Laren and Bock have?"

seven

"**And** Jamir is strong enough to kill a whole deer by himself," Alex said, through a mouthful of chicken and dumplings. Alex had forgiven her instantly for disbelieving him, not just because she'd been too stupid and adult to believe him though he loved her anyway, but because it gave him a fresh audience for all the things he'd been thinking for weeks about animals. "You're lucky. Tumi won't let me see Lady Elaine. He says his mother gets too mad if he bothers her. She hides in the trees when we're out there. But I like Three-eet. He whistles when you give him fish. I keep asking if I can swim with him, too, but Dougie says it's a family thing. Sometimes Dwan says I'm getting to be just like one of the family, but she always says no about Three-eet. When are *we* going to get a dolphin?"

"We're not, honey," Shona said, cutting up a dumpling with her spoon for Jill. "We're only on this planet for another few months. Dolphins need plenty of clean seawater. We have no room for a proper-sized lake on board the *Sibyl*."

"We could use one of the cargo pods," Alex suggested, with a winning smile. "We don't need all three of them. Oh, wait. Your lab goes in one," he said accusingly. Shona laughed. "Besides, Three-eet lives in a pool, not a lake. He wouldn't need much room. You could put him in my cabin, and I can sleep in a bunk with Eblich. He's small, too."

"No, darling."

"How about a monkey? I'm sure Papa will say yes."

"I have enthusiasm for Three-eet," Chirwl said. "My theory is such an animal has language discernible by study. I wish to learn how he communicates with other intelligent. I believe I can learning dolphin the same way ottles learned human. If Dwan let me."

"She could hardly say no, under the circumstances," Shona said, "but I think she's as curious as the rest of us. If you succeed you'll be spitting in the face of generations of scientists before you who've tried to figure out what they're saying."

"Would not spitting be rude?"

"No, it's a way scientists communicate," Shona said. "Go for it! You can take the cart whenever you want, but bring Saffie with you."

Lani smiled but kept her eyes on her plate.

"Did you know about all these animals?" Shona asked her. "Did Zolly show you her family's menagerie?"

Lani shook her head. "No. I think only the children speak among themselves."

"Too young to understand discretion," Shona said, nodding. "The teenagers know how to keep secrets. Well, it's understandable that they'd be reluctant to tell us, since we're transients. The population here is too small to defend such treasures. What they do have on their side is distance. Jardindor is simply too far off the spaceways for anyone to drop in on the chance that a rumor of fabulous beasts worth a thousand kings' ransom is true."

"I am close enough," Lani said shyly.

"Would you like to see them?"

"Oh, yes!"

"I'll ask Finoa when it's convenient for you to stop by." Shona grinned. "She couldn't expect me to keep the secret from you, since the little ones have known all along. It's exciting. I feel just like Alex. I can't stop thinking about them. Wait until I tell Gershom."

"I already did!" Alex protested.

Shona reached across the vast table to pat his hand. "You're right, darling, you did. But I'll tell him I saw them, too. It was a huge surprise. Dwan was so apologetic when she admitted she had been hiding Three-eet from me."

"Introductions would be awkward," Chirwl admitted. "The functions suggested by Finoa and Robret does not come to mind on animal charge viewing. With machines for every other, why there are not more for those?"

Shona grew grave. "I agree with you. The Jardindorians are mistaken if they honestly believe that animals are a remedy for ailments, whether real or imagined. Tigers can't make you stronger. Elephants can't improve your memory. Lizards can't . . . cure your acne, or whatever it is they are claiming. They're just indulging themselves. I've got a bone to pick with Dr. Setve."

"Are you sure it is he who has trembling ethics?" Chirwl asked.

"You mean shaky ethics. I believe so. He's in charge of their medical care. He must condone it. I intend to stay long enough to talk to him in person about this *fraud* he is perpetrating. None of these people are sick."

"What about the man who was angry?" Chirwl asked.

Lani looked a question. Shona nodded acknowledgment. "Laren Carmody came to see me. In fact, I believe that his problem is caused by interaction with his . . . totem creature. I think I may hear from him before very long." She sighed. "I just keep thinking about that tiger. I don't know much about the big cats, but if Harry was pacing and glaring like that I would know he was unhappy."

At the sound of his name the Abyssinian cat looked up from his bowl near the wall and came over in hope of a taste of chicken.

"Perhaps Jamir needs someone who can understand him, as Harry has our listen," suggested Chirwl.

"That," said Shona, picking a morsel of food out of her plate for the cat, "is not a bad notion."

ChirWL could be right. These animals might need an advocate. The situation required more study. Tigers were virtually extinct. What if the choices for Jamir were either to live in a captive setting or to die when the next opportunist found him? What if the only answer for the survival of Lady Elaine's offspring was not to let her tear up her environment but to keep her in a small area and provide fodder and constant medical supervision? She let Alex babble on during dinner, not really hearing him, but putting in all the right maternal noises when he stopped and looked at her. She was grateful to Lani, who asked Alex questions and smiled at his comments, giving Shona a chance to think.

When the meal was over Shona had no idea what she'd eaten. She sent the children up to play in one of the bedrooms.

"What about the dishes?" Alex asked, eyeing the table. It was his turn. Shona could tell he was hoping for a reprieve.

"Just this once," Shona said, "we will let the service robots clear away the dishes. But just this once."

"Super!" Alex crowed. He tagged Jill and ran out of the dining room. The toddler protested and scrambled away after her brother.

"Whew!" said Shona, watching them go. "Servers, clear and clean." The robot hands swung down from the ceiling and began to convey the plates one at a time firebrigade style toward the kitchen.

"Mama, may I borrow the cart?" Lani pleaded. "Zolly has asked the other girls over for tonight."

Shona brightened. At least there was one positive facet of this posting: Lani had a peer group for the first time, and she was enjoying it. "Of course, darling. Are you all staying overnight?"

The girl looked hopeful. "May I?"

"Absolutely. If you enjoy it you can host your own slumber party next."

Lani's dark eyes glowed. "I've never had a party."

Shona felt a pang of conscience. She put her arms around the girl, now a few centimeters taller than she was. "Your father and I have kept you all to ourselves long enough, sweetheart. It's time we learned to share you. When you come home tomorrow we'll make some plans. We'll do whatever you want."

Knocked completely silent by the awe-inspiring notion of being a hostess, Lani ran to her room to pack a bag. Shona got on her communications console to check with Hanya. A party was indeed going on, the big woman assured Shona.

"I expect it will go on all night, of course," Hanya said, with a grin. In the background, Shona heard the strains of the latest teen music playing. The other girls had already arrived.

"Is that Dr. Shona?" Zolly crowded in behind her mother. "Tell Lani to hurry over. The others are already here! What kind of pizza does she like?"

James was summoned from the outbuilding. Her face glowing, Lani climbed into the seat. Her spine bolt upright with excitement, she was whisked away, a princess going to the ball in her mouseless pumpkin carriage. Shona grinned as she walked out to sit in the garden.

Days were growing longer. The sun was still a good distance above the horizon. From the comfortable embrace of the sling lounger Shona watched pinkish clouds ambling slowly across the sky. What a fantastic sensation to realize that she might be the only person in the universe seeing that sight at that moment. Lani, on her way to her first real party, was too excited to be paying attention to anything, the other children were inside, and no one else on Jardindor seemed to take advantage of the fantastic gift they had outside their doors at any time of the day or night.

"They all ought to try living in space for a while," Shona said aloud. "That'll teach them to appreciate atmospheric phenomena when they see them."

"I remark with happy upon their presence," Chirwl's voice said from almost underneath her elbow. Shona shot up out of the sling onto her feet.

"Blue Star, Chirwl, you startled me out of ten years' growth!"

The ottle crawled up onto the frame of the chair and rested his front legs on the swaying glider seat. "How to detect and enumerate so clearly the age lost?" he asked.

"Oh, never mind, it's just an expression," Shona said, sitting down in the chair again. Her thoughts had been broken by the ottle's unexpected appearance. She laughed.

"What for is the humor?" Chirwl asked.

Shona threw out an arm to indicate the endless gardens. "I was just thinking. I came out here to be alone to think. You turned up just now, and I felt as though the garden had just become crowded. There are hundreds, no, thousands of empty acres out there, and I just pulled in my elbows because you're here."

"Is it proximity that makes the crowd?"

Shona shook her head. "It couldn't be. On the ship we're almost tripping over one another, and no one is worried about it. Even living on Mars I had very little private space. Here I could run naked for miles and not one other warm-blooded creature would see me. It's a wonderful strangeness. It makes me feel as though I'm someone else."

"Do you feel someone-elseness when you are another somewhere-else than this?"

"Yes," Shona said, after a moment. "At first I experienced fear at sleeping in those big rooms by myself. I got so used to defining my personal space by a kind of echolocation, by my relationship to you and the children and the walls of the ship. When those had all been moved away I didn't know where my own boundaries were. I am not sure I know all of them yet. I think it's simply adaptation."

"Self-normalcy is called for."

"Don't I know it," Shona sighed. "At least we're all sleeping in separate bedrooms again."

The ottle wiggled his whiskers at her. "For why then the contemplation of emptiness?"

"You know the human tendency to fill up any available space?" Shona said, with a wry grin. "I just discovered I'd filled up this whole huge yard with me."

"You must remember who you are when you are not here."

"Now, that is very clear thinking," Shona said, rising to her feet. Night had fallen. The greenery had turned into an irregular dark carpet at their feet. "I'd better see what kind of trouble the little ones have gotten into in all their space. Then I'm going to send to Gershom. I always feel better after I've talked to him. Do you have any message for him?"

"No, with thanks," Chirwl said, huddling into a comfortable position on the seat of the cast-iron chair. "I already feel normalcy."

WHEN she touched the console icon for personal mail the first item that sprang up was a personal message from Bock.

"Please accept our apologies for walking out on you the other day," the dark-skinned man said, with a rueful smile. "I would like to make amends for our abruptness. I'd promised you a walk on the mountains. How about Saturday?"

"Oh, yes!" Shona sent an enthusiastic thank-you, then checked for off-planet messages. She had plenty of mail from friends and relatives, issues of medical journals and correspondence from her peers in environmental medicine, and half a dozen messages from Susan. She scanned the list twice, feeling her heart sink: there was no word from Gershom. Though he sent every day it was likely that the path taken by the *Sibyl* to fulfill all the orders Governor Hethyr had given him might cause a delay of a day or two in between sendings. For a moment Shona felt bereft. No matter. She hit the keys for a new message and smiled at the video pickup.

"Hello, love," she said. "Well, I've had quite a day. This won't come as new news to you, since I know Alex has been telling you all about Jamir for weeks. I feel silly. He was telling the truth. Jamir isn't a robot. He is a real animal." Shona paused to grin, feeling the awe and delight well up inside her, and knew her husband would share them, however vicariously the sensation had to be at many light-years' distance. "A *tiger*, Gershom. You can't believe how beautiful he is. And almost more amazing, they have got an elephant. A live elephant! Finoa's said I can come and observe them occasionally. It'll be a treat. I plan to ask her if you can see them, too. But they're not the only surprise: everyone seems to have an exotic or three in their backyards. Dwan's got a dolphin and a monkey, and the governor herself has a *wolf*. You know how I love animals. This is heaven for me. But you will not believe why they've been imported here. Let me tell you . . ."

Shona related as much as she could of what Robret had told her about Animal Magnetism, and described meeting Kajiro, Three-eet, and Argent. "This may turn out to be the best posting we've ever had. All this, and they're paying me, too!" She smiled. "I can picture you sitting and listening to me babble on about all this. You're a darling. Oh! I have another big piece of news: Lani was invited to a sleepover. She was so excited. We are really going to have to insist she go to an academy next term. She needs more socialization than she gets living in a fishbowl with all of us. I'm downloading brochures, but if you come across any interesting schools while you're visiting suppliers, please send me some data. I'd better go and make sure the kids are still in bed. I love you." She touched her fingers to her lips and brought them to the video pickup in the center of the screen. "I miss you." She felt the loneliness in her heart when she reached out to touch the Send button.

EiGHt

WOrd spread quickly throughout the colony that Shona was now in on the secret, so it was safe to talk to her about their practice of Animal Magnetism, or more specifically, the problems that arose from it. The Jardindorians were embarrassed when their healing animals inflicted damage on them and sought to conceal the ill effects in all but the most pressing of cases.

"I think there ought to be a chaperone present," Ewan said, early Friday morning. He had called before breakfast to make certain she had no other appointments scheduled, and asked that she leave the rear office door open so he could enter unobserved. The tall dark-haired man wore loose, blue cotton pajamas, and he was standing a trifle oddly. Shona's invitation to him to sit down had been refused brusquely, followed by hasty apologies. He'd also handed Saffie away from offering her usual enthusiastic good morning and retreated to a safe point behind the examination table. "Of the same gender. I mean, mine."

Shona raised her eyebrows. "A chaperone? The only males in the house are my five-year-old son and my cat.

Oops, sorry, Alex is at lessons with Dougie Sands. Why do you feel you need someone present at this examination? Do you think I'm going to make a pass at you? Is Baraba worried about that?"

"Er, no . . ."

"Are you worried that I'll feel you're making a pass at me?"

"No!" Just the way his hands automatically sprang toward his crotch told Shona that sex was the last thing on his mind at the moment. "What about the ottle? Is he here? He could, couldn't he? I'd just feel better telling another male . . ."

"Ah," Shona said. "Well, Chirwl's not really a male as we think of it. Ottles have three genders . . . but the mechanism works very much the same way. I can get him, but are you sure you want him? He has a rather interesting take on human sexuality." As he hesitated, she added, "And I'm not certain he'll understand what he's supposed to keep confidential. I think it would be better if we left this between you and me."

"Oh." Ewan's shoulders drooped. "I . . . I guess it will be all right."

Shona patted the examination table. "So let's see what the trouble is."

"I don't want anyone else knowing about this," Ewan said, as he undid the drawstring of his pants.

"Of course not," Shona said. She pulled on a pair of gloves and waited. Down came the cotton trousers, and Ewan's secret was out.

"How did you get gouges like that . . . *there?*" Shona asked, unwinding a bloodstained cloth from the man's penis. The muscular, tanned thighs were unhurt, but four parallel cuts as if from a knife blade were incised on the skin.

Ewan muttered something.

"What was that?"

"It was Pepe," Ewan repeated, too loudly.

"Who's Pepe?" Shona asked, dabbing antiseptic in the

wounds. They had stopped bleeding, but they looked nasty. Better to use liquid sutures on them than simple butterfly dressings, she thought, reaching behind her for the squeeze bottle. When Ewan didn't answer she looked up at his face. It was scarlet.

"Our parrot," Ewan said, staring straight ahead at the wall. "Are you sure that door's locked?"

"Yes, of course. But why would you let a parrot . . . ?" Shona tried to find a way to express her question, but ended up silently gesturing.

"It's a ritual for vitality," Ewan burst out.

"It's what?" Shona demanded.

"Well, you know," Ewan said, "parrots can live up to one hundred years. And they can keep on reproducing almost all their lives. Especially the males, so . . . it's a ritual. I know it works. I feel stronger every time I do it. Pepe just got . . . upset this time."

"Mm-hmm," Shona said encouragingly, not knowing where she was getting the strength not to burst into hysterical laughter right in her patient's face. "Well, I wouldn't recommend using this ritual again. Parrots have very strong claws, as I don't have to tell you. He could do *more* damage next time." She nodded meaningfully down at the wounded member, now neatly wrapped in a white gauze tube. Ewan looked nervous.

"He won't," Ewan said. "I'll increase his sedatives. Setve said I could give him more if I had to."

Shona was alarmed. "You really shouldn't do that. Too much medication could shorten his life."

"Well, what does that matter?" Ewan asked, sharply. "He's just a parrot. I'm the one who matters here."

Shona flushed. "This was a completely avoidable injury. Using your penis for a parrot perch is preposterous. Punishing him for behaving normally is cruel."

"How normal is it for him to squeeze me like that! I thought it was going to come off!"

"You're not a tree branch. It's natural for him to hang on tightly. Couldn't you . . . couldn't you find another way to tap into his talents? I'm sure some other kind of contact would give you the same results." Which was to say, nothing, but Shona didn't want to say it out loud.

But Ewan wasn't taking any advice from the temporary help. His face wore a shuttered expression. "Thank you, doctor. I appreciate your service, but you don't know anything about modern medicine." With dignity, he pulled up his pants and stalked out of the office.

The door slid shut behind him. Shona could indulge in a good laugh then, and she did.

"It's too bad he's not the one with psittacosis," Shona said to Saffie, who tilted her head curiously when her mistress stopped making raucous noises and squatted down to scratch her floppy black ears. "Then I'd have a good excuse for taking poor Pepe away from him! Blue Star, a parrot perch!"

EWAN stood awkwardly at the edge of the pool while the ottle and the dolphin studied one another. The big room was warmer than Chirwl was accustomed to, but he knew from study of encyclopedia entries that many dolphins lived in warm climates on Earth. The human-settled part of Jardindor was an artificial climate in itself, but its mean temperature in this latitude did not reach the comfort level of the aquatic mammal. He was pleased to be lying on the tiles that surrounded the pool. They felt cool under his furry belly and helped to abate the heat.

The chamber had very plain walls, painted pale blue with a small amount of green mixed in, and was furnished with only two metal chairs, a table with a glass top, and a small refrigeration unit. Unless the dolphin was of a contemplative and meditative nature it probably craved new sights to engage its mind. He was eager to learn what it was thinking.

A fascinating face the dolphin had. If one allowed for the hydrodynamic design of its head he could see how it related to other Terran mammals. The large eyes brimmed with curiosity.

"Should I just leave you all alone?" Dwan asked, gazing at her nonhuman guests.

"Not to run," Chirwl assured her. "Why is he called Three-eet?"

The cheeks of the woman flushed red. Chirwl had observed this reaction in her. It occurred in her much more often than in Shona, but as frequently as Lani. It was a similar response to the ottle move of burying one's head under one's front foot to display shyness and discomfort.

"It's as close as we can get to the noise he makes most often. A hiss and a sharp whistle, then another sharp whistle."

"It is likely then not his name. He will not be exclaiming his identity. He is here, and he is aware of you, and knows your awareness of him."

Dwan's color became more pronounced yet. "If it means something rude I hope you'll tell me."

"I will," Chirwl promised her. "But it is likely a noise of alarm, a challenge, or a query."

"Would any of you like something to eat?" Dwan asked, backing toward the door.

"Perhaps. Sss-sharing food often helps make friendships."

Dwan departed. Chirwl continued to study the dolphin until he heard her return. Though Chirwl knew the humans here relied upon their mechanicals to do most of their carrying, she herself brought a tray. With care she set it down on the floor beside him. She pointed at a large bowl almost the size of a pail filled with large chunks of translucent red flesh.

"This is what Thr—I mean, *he* eats. It's raw tuna. I know he likes it. He seems more eager to get this kind of fish than most of the others. We try to give him a varied diet. Here are some biscuits for Saffie." The dog perked up her ears. Dwan reddened again, but this time with pride as she pointed at the two other dishes on the tray. "This is my favorite summer salad: chicken and mixed lettuce with lots of fruits and nuts. But no dressing. And Shona said you like Crunchynut bars." The blue plate was piled high with the cellulose-wrapped candy bars. Chirwl's whiskers twitched with pleased anticipation.

"She is patient though I take of her supply without thinking sometimes," he said, blinking up at her gratefully. "They are not well-budgeted for among us. You are thoughtful. I look forward to enjoying."

Dwan stood up hastily. "I'll just leave you alone. Tell the house computer if you need anything."

The door closed behind her. Chirwl turned back to the dolphin, whose intelligent black eyes were fixed on the bowl of fish.

"You would like some of this?" he asked, pointing a sharp claw-finger. The dolphin seemed to lean closer. "You understand much Standard. I have read of the Rosetta Stone. Standard shall teach us each the other's tongue. Yes?" He picked up a chunk of tuna. "Tuna. What do you call it?" The dolphin looked at him curiously. Chirwl gestured. "If you wish this, what do you say tell?" He put as much of an interrogative tone into his question as possible. Humans would have trained Three-eet to listen for such a rise in the voice. "Tuna. You shall ask for the next piece yourself."

He threw the fish to Three-eet, who gulped it and dove underneath the water. Chirwl knew that its skin was delicate, needing constant moisture. A second later the animal surfaced, spraying droplets of salt water everywhere. Saffie, getting a sprinkle on her nose, jumped up and away, but Chirwl stayed steady. He lived half the time in the water. What was a drop or two?

"Do you wish more?" he asked, gesturing at the plates in turn. "Or would like this?" He pointed, and named them more slowly. "Salad. Tuna. Chocolate. Biscuits. Tuna?"

"Threet!" the dolphin whistled. Chirwl offered the piece of fish, which vanished down the toothy gullet as quickly as had the first. He was pleased.

"I have now a sound, but whether it means 'that' or 'tuna' I do not know yet. But we shall work our way to understanding. Again. Tuna? Biscuits?"

"Bark!" Saffie stood beside him, her long, black tail waving. Her big jaws were open to show her long, pink tongue in her happy, hopeful expression.

"We are not studying the language of dogs today," Chirwl chided her. "But you are right to say I did not offer to you as I should. Biscuit?"

The dog nosed forward, taking the bone-shaped cake. She retreated to a dry spot a few meters from the pool and settled down to gnaw and crunch her way through the treat. Chirwl glanced back to see the dolphin watching the dog curiously. "Would you like to try a biscuit?" he asked. His paw hovered over the dish.

"Threet!"

"Good," Chirwl exclaimed happily. "We make progress." He threw a dog biscuit to the dolphin. It submerged, but surfaced, rising almost out of the water on its tail. The biscuit shot out of its mouth and went flying. It hit the wall and shattered. Three-eet leaped up and dove into the water headfirst. Saffie got up to investigate the broken pieces. Chirwl considered the dolphin, whose nose came poking up close to him. "You did not like that. Shall we try again?" He put his paw over the dish of biscuits. "Yes?"

"Ek-ek-ek-ek!"

"A protest of no," Chirwl said, triumphantly. "Ah! I learn a new word and you try a new comestible. You do not like it, but that is progress, too. Soon we shall have more to say to one another. We have time. Tuna?"

"Threet!"

NiNE

"Dr. Shona, how lovely to see you!" Baraba greeted Shona and her family at the door of their fieldstone mansion that evening. She glanced at the children who barreled past her over the threshold and gave a smile to Lani and to Chirwl, who rode in his pouch on Shona's back, as usual. "I know this is earlier than usual for our little get-together, but as I told you on the console, it's a special occasion. I hope you've had a pleasant day?"

"Very nice, thank you," Shona said. "Oh, look, Alex, there's Dougie. I like Melny's braids, Baraba. They're so becoming."

"Thank you!" the hostess beamed. She was proud of her young daughter, and today was the girl's birthday. Shona had spent the rest of the day going through Dr. Setve's patient files. Baraba seemed to have brought Melny in whenever the girl had even the most minor sniffles. Shona also knew, from digging after an obscure reference that led to more secret files, that besides the parrot that had injured Ewan, somewhere in the enormous house was a hot room containing a Galapagos tortoise named Earthstone, who was over ninety years old and three hundred kilos in weight.

Now that she knew what the others were hiding from her, it was easy to figure out what the mysterious references were in the health profiles. Not that Setve would have needed a lot of reminding. He cared for the animals as well as the humans. In the secret files were images and statistics about each animal involved in the Animal Magnetism program. Shona now knew that the cluster of pink and yellow feathers that Wenya Paci wore in her hair had been shed by a rare rose cockatiel named Pinky she had gotten three years ago to increase her acuity of vision. The "thorn" mark on Kely's thumb turned out to have been a bite from his devenomed cobra. Scrapes on Rajid's side had been a near-miss bite by their captive reef shark. Dwan's scratches that she had previously blamed on their own cat were Kajiro's work.

The other thing that had come to light was Setve's compensation. Shona felt she was being well paid for her six-month contract, but it was a pittance compared with Setve's income. For his services he received thirty thousand credits per family per month. That multiplied out to well over six million credits with no deductions for services or planetary association fees. Shona knew about PAFs; on Jardindor they went toward such expenses as terraforming and power-plant maintenance. Everyone deferred to Setve, he owned part of a planet that could only appreciate in value as it became more Earthlike, and he worked only as often as one of his hundred patients came to see him, which was not often. He was, to coin an animal-oriented phrase, in the catbird seat.

Part of the hefty compensation had to be for confidentiality. Shona got her children settled in the playroom that adjoined the vaulted great room and emerged just in time to bump into Ewan.

"Oh!" she exclaimed. "Hello there! How are you feeling?"

Ewan backpedaled hastily. "Very well, very well." He

glanced up over her shoulder, then shot away across the room to grab a tray of glasses off the platform of the autoserver. He stayed as far away from her as he could. When she caught his eye he glanced down shamefacedly toward his crotch. Shona had to suppress a giggle. She could understand why he didn't want to talk to her: she might let something slip about his morning appointment.

"Pretty wood," Lani said, looking around the big room.

Shona smiled. "It is beautiful, isn't it?"

To complement the whitewashed, rough stone walls, most of the furniture had been hewn out of thick slabs of natural wood joined with round wooden pegs. The surface of the wood was smooth to the touch but not even. Shona enjoyed the texture as she ran a hand over a tabletop. It had a vitality that nothing on a spaceship could equal. Though she and Gershom had never wanted to be groundbound, she felt a pang of envy. To have the opportunity to indulge herself in such comfortable, old-fashioned surroundings was something she had not appreciated before.

Hanya arrived, Zolly towing her toward the entertainment area. With a look for permission at her mother, Lani shot off to join her and Clea, who was already scrolling through the music lists for songs she wanted to hear. Shona smiled and joined Hanya.

"Lani's been able to talk of nothing but your wonderful party," she said.

"Did she say anything?" Hanya said, heartily. "That girl hardly uttered a word the whole evening. She is a lovely guest. We would be happy to have her visit any time. Any time. No call needed."

"Lani is going to have a party, too," Shona said, settling down in tapestry-covered cushions on a settee that looked like it had come out of one of the Gothic churches she saw in ancient two-dee videos. She put Chirwl's pouch down beside her. The ottle wiggled hastily out of it and scuttled toward the Sands family, who were just arriving. "I haven't hosted in so long, not since I got married. If you have some advice, I'd appreciate it."

Hanya laughed, her musical voice ringing off the exposed rafters. "Dear Shona, it's so easy! Just make sure there is plenty of food, and cover your ears! Amir and I fled out to the aviary to get some sleep. I thought we could get some peace out there, but in the middle of the night they decided to go out to the enclosure to visit Peggy, so the shrieking came out to us." Shona nodded. Peggy was the pigmy hippopotamus in Dr. Setve's files. "They were awake all night long, and awake before noon to eat an enormous brunch. You would not think four little girls could eat the way the way a hippopotamus does and stay so trim."

Shona made a few mental notes as she accepted a hot drink from Ewan. He carefully kept from meeting her eyes and moved away as soon as he could. Mona had joined the teen clique next to the entertainment center. Zolly pulled her close and whispered in her ear. All four girls burst into shrill giggles. Shona glanced around. If Mona had arrived, Laren and Bock were present. She was determined to take Laren aside and make him commit to an appointment.

"The whistling fascinates," Chirwl was saying in his shrill voice, as Shona sipped her tea. "I believe we make progress. Because it, too, uses high-frequency tones my own language may approximate at a remove." Shona glanced over. As usual, the ottle was surrounded by an eager crowd. At the center of it were Dwan and her husband.

"I am amazed," "Captain Code" was saying. "Hmm! I'd love it if we could work out what all Three-eet's shrieks and cackling was about. I know dolphins are as intelligent or more intelligent than humans, but we just haven't had a reliable means of translating. I just hope what he's saying doesn't turn out to be 'So long and thanks for all the fish.'"

Chirwl's whiskers tilted forward. "He has not the means to depart. Why would he say such a phrase?"

"Old joke," Sands said. "Saffie's been very good, hasn't she? We can't let Lark in with Three-eet. She's too hyper."

"Saffie's a very mellow dog," Shona assured him, leaning an arm over the back of her chair. "If it's a problem, she can wait outside the pool house while Chirwl's communing. Do you really think you are beginning to understand what he's saying?"

"It needs to try," Chirwl said. Everyone started speculating on the possibility of learning dolphin language. Dwan's cheeks were flushed with excitement.

"If you are successful with Three-eet," Finoa said, "you must see if you can learn to speak with Lady Elaine. Elephants are just as intelligent as dolphins."

"Not proved," Captain Code said tersely.

"Nonsense, Ev," Finoa retorted, her thin face flushing. "It's been proven that elephants have a complex matriarchal civilization. How would that be possible without a coherent language?" She turned to Shona. "Chirwl is welcome to try. Of course, you must come with him if you wish. Please call first, but come any time."

"Really?"

"Of course. Your daughter, too, if she wishes." Shona stood transfixed, starry-eyed with joy at obtaining blanket permission to see the elephant and tiger any time she liked. But Finoa's friendly gestures were strictly confined to people she wished to please. Her face hardened as she turned back to Captain Code. "Ev, you're a fool. I have disks full of data, studies that analyze elephant behavior dating from as far back as the middle of the Terran eighteenth century—"

"Hush, everyone, hush!" Baraba said, coming forward into the center of the room with her hands raised. "We are not *alone*."

At once the Sandses and Malones halted their argument and fell silent. Dwan grabbed Shona's arm, putting a finger to her lips. Shona stopped talking in the middle of a sentence, and looked curiously at her friend. Dwan gestured with a hand toward their hostess.

Baraba beamed at her guests. "As you know, today is Melny's tenth birthday. She's halfway to adulthood, as she keeps telling us." The audience gave appreciative chuckles. "So we have a lot of special surprises for her."

Shona leaned over to whisper in Dwan's ear. "Should I have brought her a present?"

Dwan shook her head. She leaned over to whisper back, her eyes dancing with glee. "There's not a thing that girl doesn't have."

"Want to introduce to you a marvelous performer. I'm sure you all know him already. Please welcome— Leonidas!" Baraba stood back, clapping, as a man strode in, beaming. Shona didn't believe her eyes for a moment, then frantically joined in the applause. Andreas Leonidas was a legend on every planet and space station across the human-settled galaxy. He did impressions, told stories, but what he did best was sing. Shona had several of his recordings on her console, both audio and tri-dee.

Leonidas beamed at them, displaying impressive square, white teeth in a handsome, tan face whose full red lips should have made him look feminine, but there was no doubt of his maleness. With his famous mane of black hair waving just above his broad shoulders, he looked like a king lion walking upright. He must have been nearly fifty, but he looked a vital and sexy thirty. He caught Shona staring and winked one bright blue eye at her. He lifted a microphone in one hand, and a beam of light leaped down from the rafters to surround him in a halo.

"Hello, friends," he called. Speakers hidden in the walls picked up his warm baritone voice so it seemed to be coming from all around them instead of just from the man himself.

"Hello," Shona heard herself reply, along with all the others.

"I can't tell you what an honor it is to be here on Jardindor, land of the fountain of youth." He held up a hand to still the protest that rose to the lips of his audience. "Now, that's what they say. I don't know if it's true, but I've never seen such a crowd of beautiful people. Especially this young lady." He stepped to the edge of the cir-

cle to take Melny's hand. The girl blushed a deeper red
than her hair. He spoke, focusing his intense gaze on her.
"Hello, Melny. I understand it's your birthday today."
Melny nodded, dropping her eyes. "Well, that's wonderful.
Come out with me and we'll let your friends celebrate your
one and only tenth birthday!" He drew the little girl out
into the circle of light. "Everyone, let's sing 'Happy Birthday' to this beautiful young lady. All together now!" He
raised his microphone hand, and a fanfare came from the
concealed speakers. Leonidas dropped his hand, and the
group began to sing. Melny blushed deeper, but with a
smile of pleasure.

As the last note died on the air, Leonidas bent to give
the girl a kiss on the cheek and delivered her to her beaming parents. He took a step back into the spotlight. Music
rose around him, and he began to sing.

Now and then he'd allow his invisible accompaniment
to die down to an undertone while he did impressions, told
jokes, related anecdotes from his career, and told bits of
current gossip. In spite of themselves, the Jardindorians
began to loosen up. By the time he announced an inter-
mission everyone that Shona could see was smiling.

TEN

With a flick of the performer's wrist, the lights came up again, breaking the spell. Shona glanced at the chronometer on the wall and discovered to her astonishment that over two hours had passed. The group, released from thrall, moved around, exercising limbs. Roboserver limbs reached down from the ceiling to offer drinks and canapes from trays. Shona grabbed for a fruit drink, suddenly aware how thirsty she was.

Lani appeared next to her, her dark eyes glowing. She looked at Leonidas, now surrounded by a crowd as he circulated with a well-deserved drink.

"He's so *good*," Lani said, admiringly.

"Oh, yes," Mona said. "Finoa campaigned to stop any live shows, but Melny said her mother wasn't going to listen. She says Finoa doesn't rule the world. A girl only turns ten once, you know. I had acrobats for *my* tenth birthday. How about you, Lani?"

Lani glanced at her mother, wondering how she could compete with her friends and their opulent lifestyle. Shona didn't bat an eye.

"We were traveling at the time," she said. "Lani had her tenth birthday among the stars. We were en route between Karela and Mars, in fact."

"Oh, lucky you," Zolly said fervently. "I wish we would travel."

"Well, hello!" the rich voice interrupted them. Leonidas bore down upon the knot of women. One by one he kissed the girls' hands. "I hope you like my show so far."

"Oh, yes!" Lani exclaimed, as he came to her. The singer stopped, his blue eyes intent upon her.

"What an exotic beauty we have here," he said, patting her hand. "I saw you during the show. You listen to music with your entire body. You probably have musical talent of your own." He paused, pursing his red lips. "I feel as though I've seen you before. I couldn't forget such a lovely face, with such hair, such eyes. Are you a model? Have you been on tri-dee?"

"No, not exactly," Lani managed to stammer out. Shona was proud of her. Not all that long ago Lani might have run from the room if a stranger talked to her, especially one offering such outrageous compliments, but she did retreat half a pace.

"Of course you have seen her," Zolly said, throwing her arm around her shy friend's shoulders and shoving her forward. "She is Leilani Taylor. Her mama is Dr. Shona Taylor." Zolly presented the two of them as though she had invented them.

Leonidas took Shona's hand and bent over it. She felt his warm lips brush her skin and her whole body quivered. "So, you're famous, too," he said. "I am delighted to meet you. I saw your tri-dee program. Not with you in it, of course, but I recognize you from the news items before. It was all true, wasn't it, all of the events in the show?"

Shona opened her mouth to give him a facetious reply, when she noticed Dina hovering almost at her shoulder, openly listening to their conversation. She edged to one side to make room for the taller woman, but Dina didn't step into the gap. Instead, she glanced away. Leonidas had noticed her, too.

"Oh, come," he said, gently putting a hand around her arm. She looked alarmed. "You're a big fan of mine, I can tell. Wait! Let's immortalize the moment." He snapped his fingers, and a hovercamera, which Shona had noticed roving around the room, zoomed in. He draped his arm over Dina's shoulders and beamed at the lens. Dina gave a weak smile. "There!" the singer boomed, picking up her hand and plastering a smacking kiss on the back. "If you will give me your address I will transmit a copy to you. I am so delighted to meet you. Thank you for listening to my performance."

Dina, the sickly smile still on her face, retreated into the crowd. Leonidas watched her go, a grin tilting up one side of his mouth.

"She was watching you, not me," he said. "That's not very neighborly, is it?"

"Oh, I don't live here," Shona said. "I'm here on contract for six months."

"Ah! Like me. Although I'm only here for six hours."

Shona blinked. "You came all this way for a six-hour show?"

"Yes-indeedy-do," he said, with a winning twinkle in his bright eyes. "Very strict time limits, too. But as a gig it was hard to refuse. My agent, Vanessa, quoted them a ridiculous sum. They met our price *and surpassed it.*" A lift of his winglike eyebrows showed how rare an incident that was. "First-class accomodations all the way from Earth, although on a small independent freighter the last leg of the journey, plus per diems and a very handsome fee. I didn't mind the break away from daily performances. The captain of the freighter gave me an empty cargo pod to rehearse in."

Shona was amazed. "An empty cargo pod? They were running partly empty, all this way?"

"Mmm-hmm. That's right, your husband's a shipper, too, isn't he? I remember that from the tri-video."

"Independent merchant," Shona corrected him. "What's the name of your captain? We might know him."

"Dave Potter? A few cents shorter than me? Mustache? His wife's a sweet thing with blue eyes. Amey? And about five crew. The ship is the *Delos*."

Shona smiled. "I know them well. If I don't get down to the spaceport in time, please give them my regards."

Leonidas looked around. "He might be coming down here. He had a shipment to deliver in person, and very mysterious about it he was, too."

Shona started to ask him what was in it, but she noticed Hethyr drawing close on her other side. Leonidas was right. They were keeping her under close observation.

"I'd heard that Laren Carmody lived here," the singer said. "I love his furniture designs. My flat on Mars is all furnished with his Silver Nebula line. Costly, but marvelous."

Shona looked around. "He's not here," she said. "I was looking for him earlier." Mona, like the other teenagers standing with Lani, was listening to every word she and the star exchanged, but even when Shona met her eyes she didn't say anything. That worried Shona. She raised an eyebrow. The girl shook her head hastily. The message was as clear as a beacon: don't say anything.

"Oh, Leonidas!" Baraba sang out, bearing down upon her quarry like a hawk swooping. She fastened herself onto his arm. "Melny would love to have her image taken with you. Please come right over here." She gestured toward the end of the room where the girl stood framed by piles of gift-wrapped packages. Leonidas was clearly to be portrayed as one of those presents. Shona felt a wave of dismay. Her neighbors—her employers—did seem to consider him a purchase.

"Just one more moment, dear lady," the singer said, detaching her hand and kissing it. He turned back to Shona. "Would you mind posing for a picture? It would be a coup for me to tell people that I met you."

"Oh, yes!" Shona exclaimed. "But the honor is all mine.

I . . . my family . . . I mean, we've all been huge fans of yours for years." She felt her cheeks burn.

"Now, that's genuine," Leonidas said gently, the huge façade put aside for one moment. "Thank you. I'm so happy I have been able to bring pleasure to you and your family. I love what I do, but it's nice when someone else appreciates it, too." He dragged Lani in with one big enveloping arm and Shona on the other side. "Goodness, you're a little bit of a thing," he said, giving her a warm hug. They posed for the floating camera eye. The brilliant light flashed. Leonidas kissed her hand again and bowed. "Bless you, Dr. Taylor, and may you keep safe. You were born under a chancy star. Now, dear Baraba, I'm at your service."

As soon as he was gone, taking his aegis with him, Shona took the slender girl aside. "Mona, where *are* your parents?"

FINOA watched the crowd around Leonidas. She tried to believe that the attraction was largely lost upon her. He was a successful animal, no more, adapted to please a large crowd in exchange for emotional and financial rewards. He was no different than, say, a brightly plumed male bird attempting to win a mate by putting on the most elaborate show of which he was capable. To her relief his time on Jardindor was strictly limited. Baraba would pay for bringing him here at all, against her instructions.

This was not the first time the Joneses had rebelled. Finoa could usually talk one of them around, but if both of them were threatening to strike out against her very practical suggestions she would make certain they regretted it. The Carmodys had been fomenting unrest among the families. That could not be allowed to bloom into a full-out rebellion. The nascent culture—and Finoa's very favorable rank within it—was so fragile that more than one stress placed upon it could cause it to fragment into two groups: one led by Finoa, and one not led by Finoa. That must not be allowed to happen. Not with the first of their goals just in reach.

It was bad enough that people had begun to feel it was all right not to attend the Friday events. She thought she had made it clear they were mandatory, if one wanted to keep one's name on the list of candidates. Mona's excuse that Laren and Bock had had an argument was not good enough to keep them from attending. The room was big enough, stars knew, to keep them nearly a degree of longitude apart. She had a great temptation to send over to their house and demand their presence. Let them have their private fight in public. A little embarrassment would be good for them.

She beckoned to Hethyr, who had had her audience with the distinguished guest and was now settled in the most comfortable of the overstuffed chairs. Hethyr sprang up and shouldered her way through the crowd toward her. Dina, noting that her mate was on the move, glanced in the direction she was heading and made her way toward Finoa. The scientist was pleased. At least her influence hadn't diminished in other quarters.

"She made the arrangements personally while she was off-world three months ago," Hethyr said, not waiting for Finoa to ask. "She knew I wouldn't approve it, but it would look too strange if I denied landing permission to the ship once it was here."

"We could have claimed quarantine," Finoa said peevishly.

Hethyr blew over her bottom lip. "And backed it up with what? They'd just have gotten on the horn to Dr. Shona, who wouldn't know what we were talking about. Then she'd come and ask me what was going on. She's not afraid to ask questions."

"Isn't that the sign of a good doctor?" Dina asked, defensively.

"She's an *employee,* and should do what she's told. Besides, she spent a lot of time with that off-worlder. What did she say to him? Did he ask any questions?"

"She's a fan," Dina said. "She didn't say a single thing she shouldn't have."

"I'd better ask her myself," Finoa said, craning her neck to look around. The singer was at the buffet, letting the four teenage girls feed him tidbits like a little bird. There was the doctor's daughter, but where was the doctor?

Finoa collared Ewan, who was making the rounds with homemade fruit brandy.

"Have you seen Dr. Shona?"

"She left just a moment ago," Ewan said. He offered tiny glasses to each of the women. Finoa accepted one with a queenly nod. Ewan had a talent for distillery; no doubt it was connected to his prowess as a chemist. "Said she forgot something at home. I called her cart. I hope she hasn't gone to try and find a present for Melny. I told her it wasn't necessary. She's going to miss the presentation."

Hethyr looked at her wrist chronometer. "Isn't it time Leonidas went away?"

Ewan frowned. "Our contract with him is for six hours: orientation time, a five-hour show, and transits in between. It isn't up yet."

"It is up," Finoa said firmly. "I don't care for your family sneaking around behind my back, Ewan, but now that I know what you're up to I intend to put a lid on it."

Ewan looked stricken, his healthy tan fading to a sickly gray. "You can't cut Melny's party short, Finoa. A girl only turns ten once! Let Leonidas finish his show. Melny's been looking forward to this for months. Think how Tumi would feel."

Finoa made a face. Tumi *would* be upset if she deprived him of a long-promised treat. "Oh, all right, but hurry. The off-worlders have to be out of the way before the presentation."

"They will be," Ewan assured her.

ELEVEN

"**HUPPY** up, James," Shona said.

The dark-green cart increased its rate from its customary amble until Shona could actually feel the breeze brushing her cheeks. The faint chemical odor of the atmosphere became more evident at that speed. She sneezed. The cart slowed to a halt. Shona groaned.

"That was *not* an order to stop," she said. "Get going." The cart started rolling again.

It had taken a little time and all her experience being the mother of a teenager herself to persuade Mona to talk. Her parents had ordered her not to say anything, especially not to Finoa or the governor. Her story was that they were fighting and didn't care to appear in public while they were having a spat. Shona wondered how many people would believe the excuse. She didn't. In her experience, if she and Gershom were having an altercation the last thing they wanted to do was stay in a cabin alone with one another. Company was the best remedy for a fit of bad temper. Shona took the girl into the children's room, where the happy shouts of the little ones made certain no one could overhear them.

It didn't really take long to worm the truth out of Mona. She was worried, almost frightened.

"Papa's turned yellow," she said, clutching Shona's arm. Her big hazel eyes were fixed on Shona. "Papa told me it's just a passing thing, from something he ate, but his eyes are yellow, too. It's *creepy.*"

"What else?" Shona asked. "Is he active? Is he sticking to his normal schedule?"

"No way. He's been lying on the couch listening to meditation music. Not even Akeera—" The girl clapped her hand over her mouth.

"I already know about Akeera," Shona said. "Go on."

The symptoms Mona described were the same that Shona had observed when Laren had come to her office, but they sounded worse. Laren was deteriorating. She hoped that she could pull him out of it. She made Mona promise not to say where she'd gone.

Saffie started barking immediately when she heard the rear door open. She came racing into the office, sounding furious. Shona almost laughed as Saffie saw her mistress and backpedaled, her feet sliding on the slick floor until she slid into a heap.

"Yes, it's me, sweetheart," she said, falling to her knees beside the big dog and ruffling her ears with both hands as Saffie scrambled to her feet. "You're such a good watchdog. I wish I could explain the house security system to you. Did you eat your dinner?" Saffie panted for joy. Harry, asleep on the examination table, rose, spine first, into a croquet-hoop, then jumped down to get his share of attention. "Hello, you," she said, fluffing up his fur. "Did I get any calls?" The cat slitted his eyes and purred.

"No? Good. I need to pay a house call. I just came back for some instruments and supplies. I think Lani may have to walk you. I'd better leave her a message." Shona threw all the equipment she could think of into a padded case,

then sat down at the communications console and put in
Lani's code.

"Honey, please listen to this in private." She waited,
giving the future Lani a chance to stop the recording or
chase out anyone who was in the room with her. "I'm
going to the Carmodys. No one else needs to know that, I
don't have to tell you. I don't know when I'll be back.
Make sure Chirwl gets home all right. Put the little ones to
bed. Thank you, sweetheart. I don't know what I'd do
without you. Love." She hit the Send key and turned to
Saffie. "I might need you, Saffie. Having you process a
vaccine is faster than waiting for the machine to analyze
and synthesize one. How about a ride?"

At the sound of the magic word, "ride," Saffie began to
pant happily, bounding all over the room, to the annoyance
of the cat, who immediately retreated to the top of the console with a peevish comment.

"Don't you worry," Shona told Harry. "I think I'll be
needing your talents later on."

Feeling like a spy about to go on a covert mission,
Shona shouldered her bag, patted the cat, and slipped out
the rear door. Saffie trotted at her side, tongue hanging out
in joyful anticipation of a trip in the cart. Shona was less
confident about what she'd find at the other end. Behind
her, the console began to signal an incoming message.

"HE looks terrible," Bock said.

"Stop it," Laren ordered, waving a hand feebly. "You
cannot discuss me as if I'm not here."

Shona, standing at the side of the bed, had to agree with
Bock. Laren, always slim, had dropped more weight than
anyone of his size ought to. His ribs showed. His skin was
a shocking shade of yellow. The portable diagnostic computer, taken from her own module, showed a decline in
liver function even more drastic than before.

"You should have called me," she said.

"And have everyone know you made a house call for

me?" Laren said. "Not a chance. No one can know—" He started coughing.

"Don't be ridiculous," Bock said, taking his mate's hand tenderly between both of his own. "Everyone will know something is wrong. You can't just drop into seclusion. Not here."

"I thought everyone here was very keen on personal privacy," Shona said, without looking up from the readings. "That's what Dwan said. And Hethyr."

"Some things are private and personal," Laren spat, "but everyone must know the reason you are one minute late to a Friday night gathering. They're mandatory. Did you know that?"

"Oh, come on," Shona said, looking up with a grin. Neither of the men were smiling. "Why?"

"Finoa. She has to keep tabs on us. We're all subject to her whim."

"Why?" Shona asked, tsk-tsking to herself over the bilirubin levels, which were astronomical. "You're all important in your own rights."

"You mean rich," Laren said, peevishly, but his tone softened at the shocked expression on her face. "Look at that, Bock. She's caught Dorianism. You've started thinking like one of us, darling. Back in the real world we all talk about money and possessions. It's normal. You don't push it into the face of someone you like, but it comes up, and no one's freaked out about it. Here, though, the normal, nice, capitalistic way of things is all upset. We're reduced to banal conversation, when we're dying to gossip about one another. You know, in the beginning Animal Magnetism was a good thing." He coughed, and tears filled his eyes. "I'm so damned weak! I hate this. And you're not going to tell me it's because of Akeera." He set his jaw to challenge Shona.

"I'm not here to lie to you," Shona said, looking him squarely in the eye. Bock clutched his mate's hand, his brow wrinkled with concern. "It is serious. You must have suspected something, or you would have come back after

I'd left you a message. It's not what you think, though. I've never seen a case of it in my lifetime. It was the symptoms that puzzled me at first: exhaustion, coughing, fever, chills, the beginnings of pneumonia, skin sensitivity, aversion to light, and complications of the liver. But once the blood culture came back there was no doubt at all. It was common on Earth up to the late twentieth century."

"Is it bad?"

"Yes," Shona said, gently. "The antibodies in your bloodstream show it's definitely a greatly advanced case of *candida psittaci.*"

"I beg your pardon?" Laren asked, aghast.

"You have psittacosis," Shona said. "Ornithosis. Chicken fever. It's a minor ailment spread from the droppings of infected birds. Have you ever heard of zoonosis? It's a disease that different species can catch from one another. That's how I knew you had some kind of fowl here."

The two men glanced at one another a little uncomfortably.

Shona gave a rueful smile. "I think you know I'll never really be one of you, but I wish everyone had decided to trust me earlier. It would have been easier on you, to start with."

"Well!" Laren said. "Now that we've all apologized, what happens? Is *sitiky* fatal? Do I update my will?"

"I hope not," Shona said sincerely. "Psittacosis is highly treatable, but you have let it go untreated a very long time. All it would have taken in the beginning was simple antibiotics, so we'll start there. Both you and Akeera."

Bock frowned. "I don't like that, introducing unnatural substances into either of them."

"You have to, or both of them could suffer a relapse. Have you had any symptoms yourself?"

"No."

"All right," Laren said, waving a fretful hand. "Let's get going. If you think I like this color yellow you're insane. It's démodé. Come on, Dr. Shona. Do your worst."

Shona pulled Laren's sleeve up, applied a palm-sized

dome-shaped device over a prominent vein in his arm and pulled the strap snug. "The rapid-infuser will give you a large initial dose of antibiotics, and follow it at the appropriate intervals over the next five days with the remainder of the medicine. You don't have to think about it at all. You can even bathe with it in place. Once we've got the infection under control we can concentrate on your liver. I'll have to monitor you daily, but I'll be discreet."

"I believe you," Laren said, patting the bump that showed through the sleeve. "It's working? I don't feel a thing."

"Good," Shona said, with a smile. "You're not meant to. It's the same gadget I use on my children. Jill hates direct-app innoculations, and she spits out oral meds."

Laren grinned back. "That's me, a big baby. Now what?"

"Now," Shona said. "I need to see my other patient."

"All right," Bock said, rising. "Come out to the aviary. It's this way."

"No." Laren arrested her with a pleading look. "Stay with me. Bock, will you go?"

"Of course."

As soon as the large man was out of earshot Laren beckoned her close. "He worries too much. Can you make him stop worrying?"

Shona moved to sit on the edge of the sofa and took his hand. "It would be a disservice to both of you to lie to him. How do you really feel?"

Laren dropped back against the intricately patterned tapestry cushions. The yellow of his face contrasted unflatteringly with the rich colors. "Bad. It hurts or burns all the time in here." He indicated his belly. Shona picked up the hem of his shirt and palpated the liver through the skin. "Ow!"

She gave a quick glance over her shoulder. "How long have we got?"

"A few minutes."

Shona reached into the bag for the portable imaging device and ran it over the exposed flesh. What she saw dismayed her, and she wasn't quick enough to wipe the expression off her face.

"Bad," Laren said. "Don't tell him. Help me if you can, but don't tell him. He'll blame himself."

"It's not his fault. I've got to do some more tests. Tomorrow, whenever is convenient for you."

She put the device away and stood up to return to her own chair, but Laren took her hand. "Stay with me," he asked plaintively. "It's nice to have company, and you look as though you belong here. You have such a fresh, natural look about you."

"Thanks, I think," Shona said, embarrassed.

While they waited she had time to admire the sleek, comfortable furnishings. The men favored natural materials and fabrics, like most of their neighbors, but here and there a wedge or streak of a rich color peeked out, reminding her of planetary sunsets and glimpses of lush gardens.

"Did you design this room?" she asked.

"Yes, I did, you clever child. Do you know my work?" Laren asked, peering at her humorously. "I wouldn't have thought a spacebound family would be interested in my creations. They tend to take up a lot of room."

"I like them," Shona said. "I wish you'd been able to come to Baraba's this evening. Do you know who Leonidas is?"

"Of course. Who doesn't? He's a genius."

"Baraba brought him all the way here for Melny's birthday. He says his entire apartment on Mars is filled with your furnishings. He loves you. He wanted to tell you so. I'm sorry you missed one another."

"Ah." Laren leaned his head back on the broad arm of the tweed-covered couch. "I can die happy. A legend loves me."

"I don't want you to die at all," Shona said. "We're going to have to tell Bock how serious your condition is."

"When you're not even sure what it is? Not a chance. He will worry. You don't know how he worries." A scuffling sound arose in the hallway behind them. "Here they come."

Shona knew she would remember the moment for the rest of her life. She turned slowly, wanting the surprise to dawn slowly and last. Bock gave her a smile that was almost shy as he held out his arm. On his hand was a thick leather gauntlet that reached over his elbow, and on the gauntlet perched a mighty bird with dark brown feathers, a huge hook of a yellow beak, and a shining head of white feathers. *Leucocephalus.*

"This is Akeera."

The great bald eagle, standing over sixty centimeters high, cocked its head and fixed a large, sharp eye on Shona. She rose, and the eagle's intent gaze followed her.

"Can I touch him?"

"Move slowly," Bock advised her.

Her feet shuffled over the thick carpet as if she were sleepwalking, unable to break contact with the eagle's eye. He looked as though he was nearly her size. As she got close and started to raise her hand Akeera baited, shuffling his big talons uncomfortably. He opened wings big enough to envelop her and Bock together, opened his mighty beak, and spoke.

"*Peep!*"

Shona stopped, startled. "What was that?"

"That's how he talks," Laren said, looking perturbed.

"That's all? That little, tiny baby cheep? I thought eagles screamed."

"Only when they're defending their nests. Otherwise, they sound like chicks."

Shona started laughing. The ridiculous contrast between the magnificent creature, legend and symbol of nations and worlds, and the silly little thing it called a voice struck her as so funny she had to go and sit down. "I'm sorry," she said, wiping tears from her eyes with the side of her hand. "I don't mean to insult Akeera, but . . . *peep!*"

Laren grinned suddenly, and she realized his annoyance

was put on. "I think it's rather endearing, really. It makes him vulnerable and approachable. Mona loves it."

Bock stroked the big bird's neck and head until Akeera settled his wings about him with a sound like a rattle. He strode off his master's arm onto an ornate bronze contraption that Shona had noticed but thought was a fancy coatrack or an abstract sculpture. It was a perch, a custom-made eagle perch designed by a master craftsman.

Shona took out another infuser, the smallest one in her pharmacopaeia, and filled it with the antibiotic. "How much does he weigh?" she asked Bock.

"About four kilos," he said. Shona adjusted the device so it would dispense the correct amount and approached the eagle very slowly. Bock helped her to strap it onto Akeera's leg, just above the yellow, scaly foot and below the white-feathered knickerbocker. With Bock guiding her, she reached high to find just the right place at the back of his neck among the crisp, silky feathers where he liked to be scratched. Akeera watched her with that intense, round eye, until she backed away and sat down.

"He's wonderful," Shona said. "And so calm. I thought he'd be more wary of strangers."

"Isn't chemistry miraculous?" Laren asked, with a grimace. "He's on his own meds, dear. We can't have him flying all over the place, or we'd never see him again. Jardindor's a big planet."

"Oh," Shona said, hoping she had managed to keep the sadness out of her voice. That big, beautiful bird was drugged, just like all the other animals.

"I wish we could," Bock said. "It'd be marvelous to see him soaring."

That must have reminded him how ill his mate was. His gaze bent to Laren, who was in no mood to be mourned over just yet.

"Stop it," he said. "Dr. Shona will think we're always this gothic."

"You can't be," Shona said, her eyes twinkling. "Then you would have gotten a vulture." The men laughed.

"So . . . what health virtues do you distill from having an eagle?"

"Keen vision, of course," Bock said, ticking them off on his thick fingers. "My family's got a history of eye problems. Endurance. Strength. If Akeera really tried, he could squeeze my arm off with his talons."

"Just what I need when I'm dealing with suppliers," Laren added.

"I see," Shona said, inwardly fretting for these people. She liked and respected them, but their gullibility shocked her. She looked at Laren with sympathy. She hoped that his willingness to believe in miracles would not cost him his life.

"At last," Finoa breathed, as the canned music died away and Leonidas bowed his way out of the room. Finoa twisted away from Robret to go make sure he was really going. She followed them into the foyer, where a stocky man with light brown hair and a mustache was waiting.

"Captain Potter?" she asked, before Baraba could introduce them.

"Right," the man said. He jerked his head toward the outside. "Your other delivery's here. Ready to take you back, Mr. Leonidas."

The singer's eyebrows had gone up at the mention of the delivery, and he looked as though he was hoping to be allowed to stay to see it, but there was no welcome on the faces in the circle around him except young Melny, who was still staring up at him with adoration. The man had nothing if not poise under difficult circumstances. He chucked the little girl under the chin with a cocked finger, and turned to Potter.

"Well, folks, it's been an experience. Captain, after you."

They mounted the waiting cart, which drove out of the circle of light at Baraba's front door. A few seconds later, another cart drove into the light. A big crate was in the cargo area at the back. A man with a long, rectangular face and a strong jaw wearing olive-green coveralls and a cap climbed down from the seat and came up the stairs.

"Have you got it? Hurry up and bring it in," Baraba said, excitedly. Then she recognized the man, and her whole body stiffened. "Setve."

"All in good time, Baraba," he said, taking the crew cap off his sandy red-brown hair. "Well, Finoa. How's my replacement working out?"

"Well enough," Finoa said frankly, because that's what Setve would expect of her. "She's a good doctor, but a lot nosier than I thought she would be."

"Well, you know what to do," Setve said. "Get rid of her. We can't afford to have our work undermined." He turned to Ewan and slapped him heartily on the back. "Ready to meet the new addition?"

TWELVE

"I wish I hadn't agreed to do both of these at once," Shona grumbled, running her hands through her short hair. She and Lani sat over the console with overlapping lists on a split screen. "Why can't we have cheese pastries for the buffet and your snack bar, honey? They're delicious. We can just have the 'bots make a big batch and split them."

"No one has the same things at two parties, Mama," Lani explained patiently.

"Is that right, Hanya?" Shona asked. The Kadasis were sitting in on the session via comm-unit at their house.

Hanya's rich voice came rolling from the speakers. "Oh, usually, usually. We are very spoiled, you know. If you serve the same food twice it shows you are stuck in a rut."

"Oh, that won't do," Shona chuckled.

Lani let out a giggle. So did Zolly's disembodied voice.

"What did you think of the platypus?" Zolly asked.

"Strange," Lani said, playing with other selections. Shona watched her carefully. Four teenage girls could eat a lot of food, but not as much as Lani was programming.

She suspected they were going to have a lot of leftovers. "Cute."

Zolly chuckled. "It was adorable. I wanted to pick it up out of the water, but it moved too fast! Also, Ewan said it would bite. With what?"

"It's got vestigial teeth in its beak," Shona said absently, filling in "tenderloin tips, rare, with blue cheese sauce" on her side of the list. If this was the only elegant party she ever hosted, she was going to do it in style. "But in any case it's not used to being handled. It won't trust humans."

"Have you seen it yet?" Hanya asked her.

"No," Shona said. "I'm grass green with envy. Too bad I had to go home."

"What did you forget?" Zolly asked. "Mona said you went home for something."

Shona had forgotten all about her fib. "Oh! Well, you know, I really just wanted to be alone for a few minutes. I've been in love with Andreas Leonidas since I was little. It was so exciting to meet him. The time got away from me. Thank you again for bringing the others home, Lani."

"Finoa was furious that he came," Zolly said, with smug satisfaction in her voice. "I thought he was lovely. Mmm, that voice! And those eyes. I adore sapphire eyes. But there's a rumor that you didn't go home, Dr. Shona. You didn't answer the console."

"That's enough," Hanya commanded, cutting her daughter off. "Gossiping like that. At least have the decency not to do it in front of us stuffy old grownups."

"But I just want to know," Zolly protested. "Like all this week, Mona's been saying you've been coming over to their house. She won't say why."

"I wish Mona hadn't blabbed," Shona said, with a sigh. "Everyone must be talking about it, aren't they? I guess I will have to tell you so there won't be any more rumors. Laren is teaching me to play mah jongg. He doesn't want anyone to know until I'm very good at it so we can sweep the tournament he's planning next month."

"Really?" Zolly asked, fascinated. "You have never played before?"

"I used to, but not since medical school. Since then I've been too busy," Shona said blithely, making a note about nondrippy finger foods for the children. "I'm enjoying playing the game with them. Laren especially. He's very good."

"He's a demon," Hanya declared. "I think he can read the faces right through the tiles. I have a white jade set left to me by my great-grandfather, who had holdings in old China."

"You *can* read through those," Zolly laughed. "They are lovely to touch, Dr. Shona. You must come and play with us, too. We won't tell anyone."

Shona smiled, glad to have dragged a red herring across the subject of her visits to Laren. The antibiotics wiped out his psittacosis, but removing that infection threw into stark relief the distress Laren's liver was suffering. Using laparoscopic 'bots, Shona had removed a still healthy section of the diseased organ and stem cells from Laren's own dwindling supply of body fat. The two elements had been placed in incubation for the last several days. The technique was an old one that had recently seen a renaissance. Before, cloned or lab-grown organs aged too quickly or had a high percentage of deformities that would render them useless or even toxic to the patient. Shona had read up on the process in Setve's medical journals. She had never tried the new system before, but Laren couldn't wait for a donor, and he was unwilling to sacrifice a genetically enhanced donor animal. Fortunately, the process had worked. Stimulated and exposed to a few healthy cells from the liver, the stem cells had begun to develop. A seed organ, about the same size as the end of Shona's little finger, was nearly ready to reimplant. If only Laren didn't take a sudden bad turn in the meantime.

He put off all visitors but Shona. The sudden isolation aroused his neighbors' curiosity, but since they set so much store by privacy none of them came over unannounced.

Shona knew that now the rumor about mah jongg would make the rounds, scratching the gossip itch. That would serve for a while. She hoped it would be long enough. Even if she accelerated the growth of the new liver the Carmodys would still miss a few more Friday evening parties. Laren, for all his bravado, really feared incurring Finoa's wrath. Shona wished he would discuss the matter with her, but blithely or irritably he would change the subject whenever she broached it.

The other benefit of visiting daily was that she got to spend as much time as she liked with Akeera. The eagle fascinated her. He regarded her gravely from one intelligent yellow eye. He often sat upon his ornate perch in the great room while she treated Laren. His wings had not been clipped, as she feared. He could fly, soaring effortlessly to the high exposed beams underneath the peaked cathedral ceiling. Shona never tired of watching him stretch out his great wings, his movements majestic and langorous. The drugs Bock had to give him daily were desecration, she felt. He ought to be clearminded and free.

"Beautiful," she murmured.

"What?" Hanya said, snapping Shona out of her reverie.

"Oh, this is going to be a beautiful party," Shona said, coming to herself all at once. "Lani and I would love to come and play games with you, but next week, when I'm finished being frazzled."

Hanya laughed. "It won't be so bad." A beeping sounded. "Oh, that's my message from my contact on Alpha. It is something I must reply to instantly. I must disconnect. See you Friday!"

"Thanks for all your help," Shona said, closing the contact. The menu for both parties was finished. Looking to Lani for approval, she saved the file and sent it to the house computer. "Now all we have to do is enjoy our own entertaining."

Lani looked excited and nervous. "I want to send to Papa," she said. "I want to tell him about my party."

"All right," Shona said, rising. She dropped a kiss on the girl's shining hair. "Close down when you're finished."

"POOL small," Three-eet complained, bumping the tiled sides again and again. "Small small small. Before endless water. Long journey. Dark, small. Now, light, small, lonely." The last was a sorrowful cry that echoed off the walls of the pool house.

"Not lonely before?" Chirwl asked, combining twists and flips with the cry and the negation sound that he had learned from the dolphin. For the first few days of his investigation he had remained on the side of the pool, but his observations had led him to understand that the dolphin's language involved body movements as well as sounds, which came from the blowhole on his back. Three-eet had seemed suspicious when he'd slipped into the water to swim with him, but when Chirwl mimicked everything he did, including an attempt at a tail-walk, he'd tossed his head and let out a raucous sound like human laughter. Thereafter Chirwl's attempts to compile a pidgin language from the dolphin had gone much faster, using Standard as a bridge to comprehension.

"Negative. Another before. Two in dark. In light far away. Phweep far from me."

Chirwl came up for air, his round, flat body bobbing easily on the surface. The pointed face emerged only a short distance away. He whistled so his shrill voice echoed, too. "You could hear the other?"

Three-eet—his own name for himself was a similar-enough sound that Chirwl continued to think of him by the name the Sandses had given him—affirmed it. "Hi-how-you sound. Wall-hole"—he nosed toward the garden door—"open. Hi-how-you, hi-how-you." As he repeated it, Chirwl was aware of the supersonic overtones of his cry. He could understand how the sound could carry a considerable way under water, but a surprising distance in the air, as well. Since Three-eet knew what to listen for he would have heard even a faint cry at that frequency. "Then fear-distress. Predator come! Alarm!"

Three-eet threw himself high into the air and came down on his belly with a splash that resounded throughout the room.

"Predator? There is no predator on this planet," Chirwl said.

"There is! There is! There is!" Three-eet shrieked, tossing his head.

"What is it?" Dwan Sands's voice came from a far distance, and Chirwl heard the sounds of her footfalls approaching. The slender woman burst through the door. Chirwl paddled close to the edge of the pool. Three-eet flicked a tail to join him, now calm. "What's wrong? I heard a huge boom!"

"It is all right," Chirwl said, lying on the surface of the water. "Three-eet tells me his expression for emergency. It is not fact, but demonstration."

"Oh," Dwan said, the worry on her face changing to open interest. "Are you really talking to him now?"

"It is pidgin between us, but it progresses," Chirwl said, crawling out on the tiles and shaking water out of his sable-brown fur. Dwan threw up a hand to ward off the spray.

"Ek-ek-ek!" Three-eet shouted suddenly. "No no no! Not D'wan."

"I not say," Chirwl replied, in a staccato chirrup that calmed the dolphin down at once. Asking why Three-eet did not want him to tell the human about the subject of their conversation would have to wait until she left. There were plenty of other things he wanted to know. "I am curious: why choose this configuration of confinement? It is small for an animal who ranges."

"Well, Setve said this is all the space Three-eet would need," Dwan said, wrinkling her brow. "The water's kept at an optimum temperature, and it's filtered all the time. It should be very comfortable."

"He is cramped," Chirwl explained.

"Oh!" Dwan exclaimed, her hand flying to her mouth. "I'm sorry. We didn't know . . . I mean, we can't understand him."

Chirwl tilted his head to one side to regard her. "You cause him to reside with you, but you do not consider how he abides in his previous living conditions?"

The woman's skin reddened, a sign of embarrassment. "We took Setve's recommendations. We thought it would be enough. Is he . . . is he unhappy?"

"What does she say?" Three-eet asked. Chirwl slid back into the water on his belly to act out his reply.

"She asks mood. Unhappy? Discontent? Frightened? Happy?"

"Content," Three-eet replied, flipping onto his back and waving his fins. "More space happy. Fish plentiful good. Content."

"He is content," Chirwl translated. "But would like more room. Much more room," he added, as the dolphin began to bump the sides of his tank again.

Dwan started toward the door at once. "I'll see what I can do."

"HE said there was another dolphin somewhere in the colony?" Shona asked, as she cut out shortbread rounds with a cookie cutter on the vast countertop. All around them the robot arms were at work peeling vegetables, grinding up tomatoes for juice and sauce, crumbling cheese, rolling pastry. "And a predator got it? EarthGov would like to hear about that. Someone falsified a report, or Jardindor would never have been permitted to begin terraforming. Hmm." Shona paused to eat a scrap of dough. "That would explain the traces of chemical waste from outside the barrier that Harry keeps sniffing out in the park.

"I do not think it was native," Chirwl said. He was lying flat on the counter, watching her hands. His paw shot out and caught a sweet crumble that she had missed, and popped it into his mouth. His whiskers twitched while he chewed. "A most enigmatic final cry from Phweep was 'stripes.' Nothing in tri-vid taken beyond the barrier shows the terrain a striped creature must have evolved into for camouflage. Nothing of size capable of alarming a grown dolphin."

Shona's eyebrows went up. "Jamir?"

"Phweep would not know name given to the tiger by humans, but it is my guess as well," Chirwl said. "Phweep—"

"Please stop saying her name," Shona said, clapping her hands over her ears. "Three-eet's real name is a sharp enough sound. My ears can't take too much of it."

"That is the chief barrier between humans and dolphin comprehension," Chirwl said. "The height of frequency of language sounds. My voice he has no trouble with." He reached for another hunk of dough.

Shona slapped his paw away. "Don't eat raw dough. Here." She opened the cooling cabinet to which the robot bakers transferred the pans after the timer went off and slid thick, buttermilk-colored rounds off the tray. "Try these. Watch it; they're hot."

Chirwl took the cookies gingerly in his sharp little claws and climbed down to lie on the cool slab of marble set into the low table used for making bread and pastry by hand. "As for where the second dolphin lived, I believe it was here."

"Oh!" Shona said, shutting the cooling cabinet with more force than she had intended. "The pool! That's why Saffie can smell blood out there. It never occurred to me, but Dr. Setve must have had an animal or two of his own. Jamir *killed* Phweep."

"Dolphins have some defense," Chirwl said, "but they can run only to the end of their confinement. And the predator could swim."

"Oh, poor Three-eet. He's probably been wondering if he's next."

"I would think so," Chirwl said thoughtfully, breaking

the hot shortbread into small bits to cool more quickly. "But not possible, is it? Jamir walks in trance now, so as not to prowl away. Three-eet is not clouded, but where could he go?"

Shona frowned, pressing the last wedge of dough into a disk with her palms. "That's true. I wonder how long it's been since they started using sedatives. I bet it dates from that time. I just can't get anyone to tell me anything about it. Even Laren talks with deep awe about his interaction with Akeera as if it was something holy. It's like . . . a religion, and I think Finoa is the head of it."

"But how is this like the mystic explanation of the world to them?" Chirwl asked.

"They don't question anything. I wish they did." She looked around for the house computer's pickup, though she didn't need to. "Cencom, put the cookies in with the other desserts."

FOr once the huge great room with its peach walls and high, white ceiling did not seem to be too big. That Friday morning hidden doors, the existence of which Shona had never suspected, opened in the wall beside the fireplace, revealing dozens of chairs and occasional tables, screens, and statuary stacked to the roof. The roboservers went to work arranging them around the room.

The clatter of heavy thumps was what had brought Shona running. She and the children watched with fascination as the long mechanical arms dropped down from hidden recesses in the fancy plastered ceiling to hand the chairs out bucket-brigade style until the big chamber had been made cosy. Statues and folding screens allowed small groups of chairs the illusion of privacy, but none were out of easy hailing distance from the ones nearby. Along the wall adjacent to the fireplace big trestle tables were erected and draped with white cloths. Shining platters were laid carefully at either end, flanking a wealth of beautiful crystal bowls. One of those would be filled later with pesto she had made with her own two hands with a marble mortar and pestle, using basil she had picked herself in the garden. It had been a matter of pride to complete the task, but now she knew how much work it was to make pesto for a hundred and how long it was taking to get the garlic smell out of her system. But it was good pesto. She let the computer make several containers more, now in the deep freeze, that she intended to load aboard the *Sibyl* once Gershom came to pick her up.

"Shouldn't we get dressed?" Lani asked, watching the mechanical arms with huge black eyes.

"Oh, yes," Shona said. "If you'll help me get the little ones cleaned up first. Cencom? Where are Alex and Jill?"

"Alex . . . is in the pool room. Jill . . . is in the great room."

Shona looked around. The toddler was not in sight. "Oh, well. I guess that Jill won't be able to wear her *very pretty new dress* that Governor Hethyr was so generous to send over. And she looks so nice in yellow!"

One of the white-clothed tables giggled. Shona tiptoed over and picked up the edge of the cloth. The child huddled amid the wooden legs, her hazel eyes full of mischief. "There you are! Let's go have a bath, all right?" Jill held up her arms to be picked up. Shona lifted her and planted a big kiss on her cheek. "Oh, lovey, you smell like Saffie."

"I will get Alex," Lani promised, gliding toward the door.

"Are you wearing that peach silk dress?" Shona asked. The girl hesitated and looked back, one hand on the lintel. "Oh, come on, sweetie. You will look so beautiful. You should look your best. You're a hostess tonight, remember?"

Lani glanced shyly at the floor. "All right." She slipped out the door. Shona surveyed her party room one more time, gave a sigh of satisfaction, and went upstairs to get ready.

Thirteen

"**HOW** lovely you look, Agneta," Shona said, showing the older woman into the great room where a couple dozen people were already mingling. "That blue lamé goes so well with your eyes. What will you have to drink?"

"I'm on a juice fast today," Agneta said, with regret, looking over the array of wines the roboservers were pouring. "It does wonders for my digestion. Do you have any fresh juice?"

"We have any kind you would like," Shona said. "A raspberry-banana smoothie, perhaps? No fat, but very good."

Agneta smiled with relief. "That sounds delicious, Dr. Shona. Kely! I wanted to talk to you. My maple leaves are curling at the end."

Shona gave the order to the house computer and escorted Clea past the staircase where the other children were playing pirates with Alex and Jill to join Zolly and Lani. Shelia and Dina arrived together, chattering. Hethyr and Jesper came behind them, talking more quietly. Hethyr's teenaged birth-son, Lewis, was listening intently. Shona grinned. He was sixteen, beginning to be considered an adult but trying valiantly not to let it seem as though he cared. Dina's birth-daughter, Jonquil, was skipping with Darrlel. She had on a gray string necklace that looked as though it had been braided out of Argent's fur. The child adored her family's wolf. If, as everyone seemed to believe, wolves could enhance strong family feeling and the stamina to run long distances, it was doing the job with Hethyr's family. Saffie greeted the child at the door, and took a good sniff of her necklace. Shona shooed them both off to the staircase, where they joined the game in progress.

Mona arrived alone, but no one remarked on her parents' absence. The rumor about the spat was now widely accepted. Finoa still seemed to be displeased at Laren's and Bock's absence, but she wore a smug smile as she entered the grand room that suggested she owned the world and everything in it. She accepted the offer of wine and held out her hand, ready for the roboserver to deposit the glass. She barely seemed to taste it. Shona was surprised at her absent expression. The wine was a rare vintage. She'd seen it listed on manifests of luxury goods that Gershom had delivered. It sold for six hundred credits a bottle. A sample she'd tried before the guests had arrived had been so delicious and heady that she was ready to grant the vintners the privilege of charging such an outrageous sum.

"Good evening, Dr. Shona," Robret said, dropping his heavy hands on Shona's shoulders from behind. "May I have some of that fantastic wine my wife is ignoring?"

Shona jumped with surprise and glanced at the front door. Robret laughed. "Habit," the big man said apologetically. "I came in through the clinic door before I thought about it. We're all so used to sneaking in here that we're not used to coming in by the front."

"Of course you may have some wine," Shona said, as her pulse returned to normal. "Cencom!"

Half a dozen guests arrived at the open door at that moment. Shona flitted off to greet them.

"Done?" Finoa asked.

"Done," Robret replied, holding out his hand for the glass that descended from the ceiling.

SHONA, carrying a tray of tiny hors d'oeuvres from group to group, was delighted at how well her party was going. A last turn around in front of the mirror upstairs had reassured that she looked like a hostess. Hethyr and Dina had most generously sent over an ochre silk dress with a draped front and an uneven petal hem that complimented her figure and complexion. The bronzy-gold helped to pick out the golden lights in her hazel eyes and her brown hair, done up in a silky chignon. The bone-colored shoes were her biggest concern. She hadn't worn high-heeled slippers for a long time, since the *Sibyl* hadn't paid a call into a port with a really fancy restaurant, but they felt good. The centimeters they added to her very modest height helped her confidence.

Lani, excited about her own party that would begin when the big gathering broke up, was holding court in a circle of plushy armchairs near the confectionary table. She had on the peach silk dress and looked like a million credits. The other girls admired the gown loudly when they had arrived, and settled down to talk about their favorite music and other topics. Shona could occasionally hear a giggle break out, and glanced over with a smile. Once Lani caught her eye and smiled back, her dark face radiant with joy. Shona offered the platter to Amir, Hanya's husband. He took a selection on a small, priceless china plate and gave Shona a wink.

She smiled. Noticing that the caviar toasts were gone from the arrangement, Shona lifted the platter up over her head. Automatically, mechanical arms reached out of the ceiling to retrieve it, and placed another, full one in her hands.

"I'm getting spoiled," she admitted to Dwan, whom she

noticed watching her. "When I started planning this, I was going to cook everything myself."

"Oh, you can't," Dwan said, picking a cheese straw off the fresh tray and nibbling it. "Food for a hundred? We're next week, and I'm getting exhausted just thinking about it, but the house will do it all." She bit into the canape. "These are delicious."

"Don't thank me," Shona said. "The computer made them."

"You chose them, didn't you?" Dwan asked. "You chose it, and you arranged it, and everything's beautiful. You look lovely, and so does Lani."

Shona gave her a one-armed hug. "Thank you for the confidence booster. You look wonderful, too. I wish Gershom could have been here."

Chirwl trotted into the room and lolloped up to a high, mushroom-shaped cushion that Shona had set up for him near the desserts. His admirers gathered around him, offering him profiteroles and caramel meringues from the goodies on display. Chirwl accepted them all, chattering about science and philosophy in between munches. He could never resist sweets. To Shona's relief these human-made delicacies hadn't seemed to affect his metabolism or his teeth.

"Dr. Shona!" Finoa called. She and Robret had found a seat by the fireplace. "Come and sit with us."

"Just a moment," Shona said. She handed the tray of hors d'ouvres to the roboservers and made a quick run down the hallway toward the back of the house. The weather had warmed up gradually over the past couple of weeks, and Setve's glorious display of jasmine trees were blooming. She wanted their delicate scent to waft through the house.

She entered the code to unlock the door to the pool room and the door leading outside from there. Just to make sure that no one's records or any dangerous medications were in reach, she went to try the lock on the office. Both doors were secure. Satisfied, she trotted back to her party.

"There you are! Come join us." Finoa patted the empty half of the loveseat she was sitting on. She shivered. "Do you feel a draft in here?"

Shona nodded toward the back. "I just opened the doors to get some air circulation. It's so nice outside."

Finoa gave her an odd look, and Shona remembered how little advantage they took of their remote paradise. "I see. You may want to shut them. People might feel uncomfortable. Unsafe."

"But why? There's no one else on this planet, is there?" Shona asked.

"Laren and Bock, naughty men," Finoa said. At the sound of her parents' names, Mona glanced up, then hastily turned her head away. Finoa didn't seem to have noticed. "I know you won't break a confidence, but how long do they plan to stay away? We miss them. Are they ill?"

"They're fine," Shona said, mentally crossing her fingers and hoping she sounded casual. Laren had shown Shona his mail program, displaying dozens of calls from Finoa and her husband that he had refused to answer or reply to. "Hmm. I don't see Baraba and Ewan yet."

"I'm sure they'll be along," Finoa said, with a kind of grim satisfaction. "Tell me, Dr. Shona, Chirwl was explaining to me that there are three genders on his planet. How different is his DNA than ours?"

"It's similar enough that it makes me begin to believe the seeding theory of the universe," Shona said. "They can eat our food, and our plants can take advantage of their soil, for example. The three genders are really two plus a null. The genes that transmit gender information come from the two parents who donate sperm and egg to the third, who acts as the host mother. Where both gender genes agree, it becomes either an egg donor or a sperm donor. Where they're heterogenous, they cancel one another out, and the offspring becomes a host mother."

"Fascinating," Finoa said, nodding. "So Poxt biology

divides the female's function between two beings. Not a breeding pair: a breeding trio."

"Correct," Shona said. "Chirwl could have told you all this."

"I'm afraid I offended him," Finoa said, looking a little ashamed. "I asked if I could examine him."

"I'm afraid you walked into a quagmire there," Shona said. "Ottles are very private about reproductive matters. It's not unlike Jardindor, now that I think about it. They live in cluster colonies, and they communicate a lot, but reproduction is no one's business but their own."

They watched Chirwl for a few moments, chatting with his admirers. Finoa leaned toward Shona. "Don't you worry that he'll make himself sick with all those cakes and cookies?"

"Chirwl has a capacity for goodies that surpasses even my son's," Shona admitted with a grin. "I trust Chirwl to stop eating if he starts feeling as though he's getting a tummy ache. I have traditional ottle stomach remedies on hand in case he overindulges. It's not often. He can take care of himself."

"So I have observed. I would like to see more ottles living among humans. We could gain so much from interaction."

"So would I," Shona said. "But that will be their choice. They're still trying to make up their minds about us."

"I hope both of you—all of you—will come and visit Jamir and Lady Elaine again," Robret said, holding up his glass for a refill.

Shona smiled, catching her breath at the memory. "I have to thank you for the invitation. Lani was so excited. She *talked* about getting to pet Jamir, and you don't know how rare an event that is."

"Speaking of Chirwl," Finoa said, persuasively, "it would be such a pleasure to have him come, too. You may accompany him, if you wish, but he'd be perfectly safe with us, I promise you."

"Well, I don't know," Shona said. She didn't want to offend the imperious woman. She offered a tentative smile. "Let me think about it."

Finoa's brows drew down. Robret's deep laugh boomed out. "Finoa's not used to hearing refusals! You are a refreshing addition to the community, Shona," he said. "I'll be sorry when you go. Setve isn't nearly so much fun."

"Thank you," Shona said, rising. She didn't want her relief to show. It was growing harder to say no to Finoa. There was nothing she could put her finger on, but Chirwl's feelings and her own kept telling her that unsupervised visits would be a bad idea. "I'd better circulate some more." But she glanced around. The party seemed to be progressing very well without her help. The roboservers were passing drinks and food. Fairly soon, she could signal to the house computer to bring out the larger plates and serve the main courses. She was looking forward to finding out what Dwan and Amir thought of the beef tenderloin dish. It was a favorite of hers that she'd first tasted in a restaurant on Mars when she and Gershom were dating. She circulated through the group, accepting compliments on the food and wine, and making small talk. This was easy! Why had she been so worried? Shona forced herself to take a deep breath and let it out slowly. That was better.

A faint, high-pitched hum was the computer's signal to Shona that another guest was coming up the front walk. Shona glanced through the voile draperies. Baraba, at last! Shona started toward the open front door. She was concerned for the other woman. Her hair was askew, and her grim-set face was pale.

Shona hurried to greet her, but the woman pushed her aside. "Where is she?" Baraba shrieked. She stormed down the hall into the great room with Shona on her heels. She pointed at Finoa, her hand shaking with fury.

"Where is it?" she screamed. "Where did you take it?"

Finoa had risen to her feet, with Robret a looming presence behind her. "Dear Baraba," she said, in a calm, patient voice that reeked of saccharine, "I've warned you before not to challenge me. Now you're paying the price, and a hefty one it is, too, isn't it? How much for the habitat, plus whatever you paid, with shipping on top of that . . . ? Normally I'd just *remind* you what you'd stand to lose, but I decided not to wait for the future. You were just a little too bold in your arrangements, and that could have been bad for all of us."

"Who died and left you God?" Baraba shrieked. "Give back that platypus! We paid for it. It's ours! You can't just march in and take it!"

"As far as you are concerned," Finoa said, evenly, "I *am* God. Now, go home. Perhaps, one day, if you show proper contrition—yes, contrition—you can have it back." Baraba stared at her, her mouth agape. "Go!"

To Shona's amazement, and probably Baraba's, too, the carmine-haired woman closed her mouth, spun on her heel, and stalked out.

The room, which had fallen silent when the newcomer had burst in, suddenly broke out into a nervous prattle of sound.

"Good Lord, look at the time," Ev Sands said, springing out of his chair. "Dwan, it's nearly the girls' bedtime."

"Oh!" Dwan, giving Shona a guilty glance, rose to her feet.

"We have to get back and feed Argent," Dina said. "What a lovely night, Shona. Thank you." She grabbed Hethyr's arm. The governor gave a hard look at Finoa, but allowed herself to be led out of the door. Most of the others blurted out excuses, and slunk or frankly ran out the door. Shona tried to stop them, but none of them wanted to stay in the room, as though punishment might descend upon them if they remained. Abandoning full plates and glasses, with no regard for their fine garments or awkward shoes, the guests fled. None of them could look at Shona.

Soon no one was left except Finoa, Robret, Hanya, Chirwl, and Lani's friends. The four girls, all clasping one another, stayed in a wide-eyed huddle near the fireplace. Her face devoid of emotion, Finoa stayed in the same erect posture she had been in, like a rock around which rapids broke. Suddenly, she turned, smiled, and offered a hand to Shona.

"What a lovely party," she said, clasping Shona's nerveless fingers warmly. "I look forward to the next time you have us all over. Come and visit us sometime. Come along, Robret."

"Of course, my dear." The big man followed his wife into the hall.

The sound of the door slamming broke the spell.

"What did that mean?" Shona broke out. She stood forlornly in the midst of the ruins. Her voice echoed off the ceiling as metal hands reached down and began to pick up the discarded plates. "What just happened?"

"That's it?" Laren demanded, regarding the two-centimeter chunk of bright red tissue with a chary eye. He was lying on a priceless marble table in the Carmodys' great room. The table had been scrubbed with antiseptic. Most of him was hidden beneath sterile drapes. His curly, graying hair was concealed under a surgical cap like hers, and she had tucked his hands inside sterile mitts in case he moved them too near the incision site. "I thought you were going to grow me a new liver."

"No," Shona said, putting the sterile dish back onto her instrument tray, which stood on a gilded, glass-topped occasional table that was probably worth as much as the *Sibyl*. Bock hovered a few feet away, worrying about his mate but unwilling to watch the operation up close. The removal of the donor tissue had been too upsetting to him. "You are. You're the perfectionist. I expect this to be the most beautiful liver in all of humanity. In the entire mammal kingdom. Now, lie still." She brought the broad circle of the numbing probe into contact with the skin. The vibrations it emitted made the pain receptors go dormant within its circumference. This way there was no chance of anaesthetic causing complications during or after the operation. If he started to show distress she could increase the amplitude. Pulling on the goggles that displayed what the fiberoptic camera 'bot was seeing, Shona reopened the first laparoscopic incision, and began.

"Not very impressive," he said sleepily.

As long as he didn't move, Laren could remain awake. Shona had given him a mild sedative to help him deal with the mental trauma of undergoing major surgery.

"Just think of it as though I'm planting a liver seed," Shona said, humorously.

"I'm an awful gardener," Laren said. "Interior design's my strong suit."

"This *is* interior design," she said, and Laren chuckled.

The Nentnor process created an entire single organ from body stem cells, by tweaking a gene here and there, link by link if necessary, to get rid of a trend of impairment. Unlike previous methods of regrowing organs it worked every time, though it was nervewracking to look into the tank and see an entire upper intestine developing there like a deformed garden hose. The liver, which regenerated rapidly in the body, could be removed from the tank when it was as small as a pencil eraser, just under a centimeter across, and implanted by its minuscule ducts and blood vessels. This was larger, but it would save Laren's system some strain.

"So I hear your party was the bomb, to scare up an ancient expression," he said, managing to show malicious humor even though he was keeping his breaths shallow.

"Bomb is right," Shona said, monitoring her robots as they slid easily through the peritoneum and into the body cavity. The original liver looked worse than before. She had been planning to use heat-excision to destroy it as soon as the new organ had reached a viable size, but now that he was open she was going to remove as much of the old one as she could. At any time it could go toxic and cease to function altogether. She'd found plentiful traces of the chemical she now was certain had caused the organ to become diseased. There was no shortage of it behind the terraforming force field, only a few miles away from where she now stood. If Governor Hethyr cooperated, she was going to test everyone for sulfur dioxide poisoning. "You should have seen Baraba's face."

"And I never got to see the platypus," Laren said, puffing out his lower lip in a pout.

"Neither did I. Finoa refuses to tell anyone where it is. Will she ship it off-planet?" An awful thought occurred to Shona. She paused, calling the 'bots to a halt. "She won't kill it, will she?"

"Finoa? Black holes and constellations, child, no! The high priestess of animal preservation? She might have killed Baraba, but she didn't. I suppose the little beast will become part of her own menagerie, and none of us will ever get to see it."

The flip way Laren referred to Finoa emboldened Shona to ask. "Laren? Is she a priestess? Is Animal Magnetism a religion? I've been afraid to ask because I think I'm going to offend someone, and I never intend to."

Laren let out a bark that ended in a short groan as his belly contracted. Shona increased the numbing and he relaxed.

"You sweet young thing, you," he said, his breathing shallow because the numbing ring was affecting his diaphragm. "I could eat you up. Of course not! We're just health fanatics—and look at me."

"You're going to be fine," Shona said, mental fingers crossed.

"Now, that," Laren said, settling back and closing his eyes, "is something I plan to use religion to hope for."

Shona worked in silence. She could feel Bock's eyes on her from across the room. An occasional questioning peep from Akeera was the only sound, apart from her monitors. She was relieved to see pulse rate and blood pressure remaining normal. Laren was in no distress. The miniature robots connected blood vessels and capillaries to the tiny liver. In case there was infection, Saffie was incubating a sample of Laren's blood. The resulting vaccine, drawn at the site of injection, should help Laren through recovery.

•

"Where's the family?" Laren asked, drowsily.

"Lani's at home. The girls are still there. I'm very grateful to Hanya. After everyone ran away she stepped in and insisted that even though one event was ruined there was no need to spoil everyone's fun. They all insisted on helping me clean up, though the house took care of the mess. They're such nice girls. The children are with Dwan's, having lessons as usual. She called this morning to apologize for running away, but she's afraid of Finoa."

"As are we all," Laren said. "Don't hold it against Dwan."

"I don't," Shona said. "Heavens know there are people I'm afraid of, too. Saffie and Chirwl are there, too. Chirwl says he's making real progress with Three-eet."

"Wonderful," Laren drawled, relaxed. His eyes kept drifting shut. Shona smiled and carried on with the operation.

One by one, the tiny robots dragged cauterized blood vessels to the infant organ many hundreds of times their size. The image on Shona's monitor bloomed as the 'bots employed their cautery attachment. A faint movement within the translucent, dark-pink capillaries showed that blood was beginning to flow. Shona counted veins and arteries, then recalled her team of robots. With a sigh, she took off the goggles.

"Done," she said.

Laren met her eyes. "Thank you for that. And thank Finoa."

Surprised, Shona wondered momentarily if Laren had misled her about their devotion to Animal Magnetism. "Why Finoa?"

Laren grinned, as if he guessed her thoughts. "It's her technology you used. You said you were employing the Nentnor method of stem cell differentiation to grow me a new liver. She perfected it. Instead of a hundred misses for every successful attempt to reproduce organs, it works nearly every time. Yes?"

Shona frowned. "Yes, that's right." Her eyebrows went

up as enlightenment dawned. "That's right! I've been talking to her about the system, but I never connected her to her own breakthrough. Blue Stars!" She gave a sheepish grin. "I wish I could tell her how well it worked. But I won't."

Bock snorted with laughter, the first sound he'd made in hours. "She knows. Finoa misses nothing."

"Let's get you back to bed and settled. You need to sleep." Shona swabbed her hands with a cleansing wipe and put them under the sterilizing light before folding away the surgical drapes and checking Laren's dressing.

"That's all I want to do," he said sleepily, as they transferred him gently to his own bed and pulled a light coverlet over him. "Talk, talk, talk, that's all you do, sweetheart. It'll be the death of you."

Shona smiled gently as Bock guided her out of the bedroom and closed the door.

fourteen

"**HUCH!** Huck! Huck!"

"Oh, no!" Shona exclaimed, standing up from helping Jill on with clean, pink denim overalls in the little girl's room. The toddler giggled.

"Harry make a messy."

"Yes," Shona sighed. "Harry making a messy." The whole-house computer, sensing the voice of a designated family member, had broadcast the sound Harry was making to speakers all over the house. No doubt about it: wherever he was, he was throwing up. She hoped it was nothing more serious than a hairball.

"Computer! Where is Harry?" she demanded.

The mild female voice responded from the hidden speakers in the walls. "Harry . . . is in the office."

With a groan she finished closing the fastenings on Jill's outfit and carried the little girl downstairs. As soon as they were on the ground floor Jill wriggled loose from her mother's arms and went running toward the front of the house to the great room, the children's designated play area unless Shona was entertaining, which she had not done since the disastrous party of the week before. The memory of everyone running away haunted her dreams like scenes from a horror video. Shona turned toward the rear of the house, wondering how much of a disaster the cat had left her. When his stomach was upset he tended to bury things in invisible "sand," sometimes sensitive lab equipment, sometimes her clothes, but only, she reflected with mock despair, items belonging to people he liked. He liked Shona very much.

When she got to the lab the situation wasn't as bad as she had feared. The usual data crystals and plasheets had been knocked to the floor. The roboserver arms were already at work cleaning up the floor. Most of the . . . matter . . . was bright green, and therefore likely organic in nature. Harry had retreated to the top of the communications console, tucked up into a bundle of distrust and self-pity.

Shona gathered the long-legged cat into her arms and scratched the top of his head.

"Serves you right for trying to eat the entire garden single-handedly," she told him. "Do you realize you are consuming a fortune in herbs every single day? Gershom would go spare if you did that on the ship."

The cat purred. Naturally he didn't care at all. Shona carried him around the office, observing how efficiently the house system had noted where things had last been, and restored them to those locations as soon as the surfaces were cleaned. The arms, after delivering a final squeeze of citrus oil to freshen the air, folded themselves back up against the ceiling. It wasn't until that moment Shona noticed the light blinking on her console.

"Probably messages from the girls for Lani," Shona said, sitting down in front of the console with the cat on her lap. But to her delight, the code that showed on the screen was hers. "Gershom!" she said, with pleasure. She noted that the amount of memory the message contained was considerable. The last few days' calls had been so short. She missed him.

Her husband's narrow face appeared on the screen. His long, black hair was floating around his head like seaweed, which probably meant the ship was in zero- or low-gee. Shona frowned. The vertical line between his dark brows meant he was worried.

"Hello, love," he said. "I hope you and the children are doing well. You must be very busy in your silk-lined office. It's been a while since I heard from you or the kids. Is there anything wrong?"

"What?" Shona demanded, unsettling the cat, who protested. "I send every day."

"You'll be happy to know that we're busy." While Gershom's voice continued, telling her about the current deal he was making for silk-cotton carpets from a dealer on a space station, Shona ran through the list of messages in her Transmitted file. There was the list, dating from the day the *Sibyl* had departed. Shona hadn't even been able to wait a day before sending Gershom a love-note. Thereafter she'd recorded at least once a day, sometimes more than that. Every one of the messages was tagged with the code showing the comm-unit had made its connection with the local comsat. But that was all. Only a message reaching Gershom would show the string of linked satellites it would have had to connect with to reach him. And since his were reaching her, there had to be a fault in the transmission end.

"Our delivery is as close to your side of the galaxy as we can get. We're going to try and stretch our fuel to come visit you. From what the crew has said about unwelcome visitors you may have to see me at the hotel on the landing strip. It's isolated, but it's comfortable." He leaned forward seductively. "If you can get Lani to watch Alex and Jill for a while. A *long* while."

Despite the warmth that she got from knowing how much he missed and wanted her, Shona was worried. She needed to talk to Governor Hethyr at once. A colony's comsat was its lifeline to the rest of civilization. If it had gone faulty there was no way they could communicate with anyone else until a ship came into orbit. They might end up waiting until Gershom or another delivery ship arrived for rescue.

"HELLO, Dr. Shona," Hethyr said, glancing up from the plasheet report she was studying. "You sounded very upset on the comm-unit. Please sit down." She waved a short-fingered but competent hand at the chairs ranged around her desk.

Shona dropped into an antique wooden chair without observing its beauty or quality. "I think there's a problem with the communications satellites. Have you had any difficulty sending messages?"

"Why, no," Hethyr said, calmly. "My mail is going out just fine. Why?"

"I've just received word from my husband that he hasn't received any of our messages in more than two weeks. Over twenty messages, missing!"

"Oh, they're not missing, Dr. Shona," Hethyr said, putting down the sheets. She folded her hands and leaned over them. "They didn't go through."

"Do I need a code to link into the system?" Shona asked. "Is there something else I need to do so my messages go out?"

"You have a code. What you have not done," the governor said, her eyebrows drawing down over her brows, "is maintain patient confidentiality, as we requested you do when you arrived here."

"I beg your pardon?" Shona asked blankly.

"I've been stopping your outgoing transmissions. All of the messages we stopped made some reference to our practices, to our animals. You are revealing doctor-patient information, which is not within your rights to do."

"But these are to my husband," Shona explained. "I haven't told anyone else what I've seen. I've sent plenty of other messages. But it would be difficult to conceal the animals' existence; my children have seen them, and they send to their father."

"Yes." Hethyr nodded. "I stopped those, too. See here, Dr. Shona, if I had had my way, we would have waited a little longer to talk to you about Animal Magnetism until we were sure you understood. I believed you when you said you embraced natural healing, but I am beginning to doubt my previous impression."

"But I do!" Shona protested. "Except in cases where it cannot be avoided, I've used natural remedies and treatments. Anyone who is willing to admit that they have come to see me will tell you that. That doesn't give you the right to cut me off from communicating with my husband."

"It's what you are communicating that is the concern. We accept that it is unavoidable that you and your children will tell him about our lifestyle, but we must prevent you from transmitting that information on open beacon. What you tell him in person is up to you, but I cannot and will not jeopardize Jardindor. We're vulnerable to theft or attack. No one is close enough to protect us, and we do not have armaments. We are already vulnerable in that you know what we do not wish the rest of the galaxy to know, that we are acting as stewards to some of the most precious and most endangered creatures ever to live. You must understand that, having unusual animals in your own household. Elephants are so very rare, you know."

Angry as she was, Shona couldn't deny that Hethyr had a point. "Yes," she said. "I know they're virtually extinct. It's a marvel that you have one here, and one more to come. The problem will be with convincing Alex. He's so excited that he's looked up every elephant joke in every database he can find."

Hethyr gave her a wintry smile. "I'm a mother, too. Thankfully, a certain amount of what children say can be put off to imagination. It's what you, as an adult, let slip."

"I am aware of the position that I could put you into,

and I am watching my tongue. I've heard about Finoa's research," she added.

Hethyr frowned. "I see," she said.

"I am sorry," Shona said, with a sigh. "Another secret?"

Hethyr screwed up her face. "I suppose it was unavoidable. I'm an administrator. We keep security all the time. I've never been able to prevent scientists from talking to one another. I don't know whether it's a good thing or a bad one, but it makes my job harder."

"I'll do what I can," Shona promised. "I will keep mention limited to personal contact when I see my husband. I know he'd be thrilled beyond words to meet these animals. He will be able to, won't he? You can rely on his discretion. I will assure you that we won't even inform our crew."

"He will need to sign a confidentiality agreement," Hethyr said.

"But he is not employed here."

"If you wish him to see our charges, he will sign it. We can even forbid him from touching down."

"He must touch down," Shona said. "He has to pick up my module. And what about all the goods your people ordered?"

"Orders," Hethyr said, with the air of someone who holds all the cards, "can be cancelled."

Shona thought with dismay of the thousands of credits' worth of computer educators and luxury goods that Gershom would have to take back with him. Their credit history was shaky enough that they had to put a deposit on luxury goods that they took on consignment. "I am very sorry. I won't put any more information into my messages, and I will go over the children's outgoing mail, too, but I do insist that you let me send them. They are private, after all."

Hethyr paused, then tightened her lips. "You will be given appropriate access to the satellite, but I have one more matter to raise. I don't customarily tell people what they can and can't say in private communications, but I must say I was shocked at the insulting and offhanded characterizations you made of your patients and their beliefs. I am giving you the benefit of the doubt that you merely meant to be amusing. I am keeping that information to myself. I won't even tell Dina, so you can maintain some pretense of respect for your patients. They may continue to like you, even respect you, remaining unaware of what you really think of them." Shona opened her mouth and shut it several times, but Hethyr had her there. She probably had been scathing on the subject of pseudoscience and the gullible nature of the Jardindorians, never knowing it would be heard by someone other than her own husband, who knew how much emphasis to put on her comments.

"I apologize," Shona said, in a subdued voice.

Hethyr waved the apologies away. "Just watch what you say. I'll be keeping my eye on you from now on."

BY the time Shona drove away in her cart, she was furious. Part of her anger was at herself, for ignoring one of her mother's cardinal rules of behavior: never commit to disk anything that you wouldn't like to see on the evening news. She knew that transmissions could be and were routinely cracked by government security. She should have kept her observations to herself until she and Gershom were in private. It was trying that there was no one nearby with whom she could talk out her frustrations with her life and her job. It was unfair to load the burden on Lani, who was coping with the troubles of being a teenager and a stranger. Chirwl, coming from a very different culture, would try but not really understand the nuances.

Suddenly, what had looked like a cushy assignment with gorgeous accomodations, gourmet food, and an easy workload turned out to be a pretty cage. She'd been too free with her feelings and opinions. She must now wait out the full six months before she could relax and be herself once again. Hethyr had given her a warning—a merciful one, in retrospect—and Shona meant to take it to heart. She would give Hethyr no more reason to be disappointed with her. It was true: she'd been laughing at their pursuits. Was Animal Magnetism really so bad, if it hurt no one?

But it *was* silly, and it *was* hurting someone: the animals themselves. Chirwl had been telling her about his conversations with Three-eet. The dolphin was cramped in his pool. He didn't like the smell of the chemicals the Sandses used to sanitize it, and the fish was always thawed, never fresh. In spite of their protestations that they loved their totem animals, their owners kept them drugged, in straitened surroundings, or both.

And Hethyr was wrong: others did know of Jardindor's treasures. Plenty of people were in on the secret. Those who sold the animals to Jardindor might not know their eventual destination, but the animals didn't get to the planet on their own. The crews of the cargo ships had to have a general idea what they were carrying, if only to assure themselves that their load was neither dangerous nor illicit. What was to stop them from talking?

Money, Shona realized, as the cart turned off the wooded lane into the semicircular driveway in front of the grand house. They were being paid well for their silence.

That brought another thought to Shona's mind, one that worried her. Money could also pay for their complicity. Shona knew there were plenty of independent merchants out there who would look the other way. She knew Dwan believed that Three-eet and Kajiro had come to her legitimately—but what if they hadn't? Jardindor was so remote that if a stolen object was brought here it was likely that no one would ever know, and no one would ever tell—no one but a stranger. She had to be careful not to arouse suspicion, but she wanted proof.

She strode into the house, heading for her lab. It was time she asked Gershom to look into the matter, but it would take special care.

"Mama!" Jill cried as Shona passed the door of the

great room. The toddler ran out to meet her. Chirwl and Saffie loped along behind.

"Oh, honey!" Shona exclaimed, sweeping the little girl up into her arms. She was dismayed to have forgotten about her. "Chirwl, thank you for watching Jill. I've got to take care of something. Can you play with her for just another few minutes?"

"Certain," Chirwl said, stretching out a hand-paw to Jill.

"No!" the toddler declared, wrapping her arms around her mother's neck in a stranglehold. "Mama!"

Shona looked down at her daughter's head, buried in her neck. "What did she do?" she asked Chirwl.

"The house has already cleaned itself up," the ottle said, switching his whiskers from side to side.

"Meaning you won't tell me," Shona said. "All right. Come along. I have a use for a penitent little girl."

"Sweetheart," Shona said, looking intently into the communications console's pickup. "I miss you. I'm sorry you haven't gotten my other messages. You know what the beacons can be like. They get overloaded, or an ion storm catches them. We've been fine. I've been out hiking in the meadow every morning with Dwan and Lark. The fresh air is *marvelous*. I don't think we'll ever get Saffie used to the treadmill again. I'm not sure you can ever get me used to it again.

"But we're out of touch here. We get all the tri-dee programs, but the news is weeks out of date by the time we get it. I want you to tell me everything that's *hot*. It'll make things more interesting." She swept up Jill, who was playing on the floor with Chirwl and Saffie. "And now a word from your younger daughter. Say hi to Papa, honey."

"Papa!" Jill exclaimed, looking around for him.

"Papa's not here. Send me lots of news, sweetheart," Shona told the pickup. "Got to go. Love."

She closed the file and hit Send. Gershom was no fool.

He'd understand what she meant by *hot*. In the meantime she intended to dig deeper into Setve's files, to see if there was any evidence in them to back up her suspicions.

In the meanwhile, her mailbox was filling up again. Having delivered her ultimatum, Hethyr had allowed Shona's messages to be delivered.

"Hey, twin," Susan MacRoy's cheerful face appeared on the console screen. "Hello to the outside edge of everything! Miss you! You haven't sent me a message in an age. What's been going on?"

Shona felt a deep pang of loneliness. She wished Susan was there beside her so she could unburden herself of her discomfort and discuss what to do. The temptation to raise a public stink over the locals' treatment of their animals arose in Shona's heart. Here was the very person who could get the matter the most attention. The urge grew greater as Susan continued. "I've got editors asking why I was researching Jardindor for you. Is it as wonderful as everyone thinks it is? Buzz around the starlanes is that it's an El Dorado, streets paved with gold, fantastic creatures."

Shona gave a rueful chuckle. "More than you know."

"As much as told me that if I could provide anything in the way of exclusive facts I could have forty-five minutes on every tri-dee band from here to the Horsehead Nebula. You could get a goodly fee out of them for providing info. Tempting, eh? What do you say? Send lots of video. No one's ever seen the place. The construction company responsible for the terraforming is tighter with data than an airlock. I couldn't even get confirmation that they were doing the job, except that I got a friend in the communications industry to print out for me the beacon string from some of their messages back to the home office. How about it, sweetie? A big exposé like that would give me a boost. My series on designer body parts tanked in a shockingly major way. It shouldn't have, except I didn't know the head of Galactic News Network had had her butt reworked by the most scummy medical firm with a reputation for shoddy culturing." Susan gave a humorous grimace. "Wouldn't you like to know you'd fallen for a scam artist, even after the fact? So I'm persona non grata. Give me a break."

Shona shook her head with regret. Even if she wanted to, her outgoing communications were being monitored and edited by Hethyr. She had to be guarded in what she said and didn't say. Fortunately, she and Susan had been friends long enough to have code words that Hethyr couldn't possibly know about, no matter how good her spies were. She pasted a smile on her face and hit Reply.

"Hi, twin. Too bad about the body-engineering documentary. I thought you did a great job. I wish I could help out. My contract forbids me to say much about Jardindor, except that it's interesting." "Interesting" originally meant that there was something Susan's mother and father or Shona's aunt and uncle didn't want them to talk about, and that they should meet at the earliest possible opportunity. "But I'm out of here again in five more months, give or take two weeks. If you can swing some free time, Gershom and I will meet you anywhere you say and have a real vacation together. You know all the hot spots. Pick someplace that's family friendly"—another, newer code word meaning a location where the Taylors might not be known. Their notoriety of the last several years meant that they were occasionally recognized by sensation-hounds. "The kids are doing well, and Chirwl's got quite a fan club here, which is wonderful. It gives him an audience, and he's not talking *my* ear off all the time. We're eating well. I am learning some new recipes that you will love but are too expensive to make anywhere but here. Can you imagine? I can go outside my door in the morning and gather basil by the *kilo*. There's a garden robot gathering me a kilo of *saffron*. I feel richer than kings. More later. Love you."

She sealed the message and sent it off, hoping all that would get past Governor Hethyr's censor program.

FIFTEEN

"**There,**" Bock said, pointing. "That's the perimeter."

Shona gasped and puffed as she scrambled her way up the narrow crevice to the peak. They had been climbing Mount Akeera since before dawn. Her feet, in new but carefully broken-in hiking boots, were sweaty and sore. She suspected the burning sensation on each heel was a blister. Her hands were torn and bruised from grabbing rocks and branches to help herself along. The hiking staff Bock had insisted she carry was more of a nuisance than a help. After the first two hours of leaning on it and having it shoot out from under her, she had tied it across her back, where it banged into her every step of the way since.

Overhead, the sun beat down on them. According to the local calendar summer had begun only three days before, but to Shona it felt like the hottest day of the year. She crawled up the last few steps and clambered unsteadily to her feet on the small shelf of stone beside Bock. The big man had a few beads of moisture on his dark brow, but otherwise showed no signs of great exertion. He wasn't even

breathing heavily. Shona resented him for just a moment,
then the grandeur of the scene struck her.

They stood on the crest of a high escarpment. Looking
straight down into the narrow rift gave Shona a spiraling
feeling deep in her stomach. She had looked out into infinity from every portal on their starship, but though the
distance was a fraction by comparison it felt different because she could feel gravity's pull. She looked outward instead.

From here the ships in the spaceport looked like a display of miniatures that could be fixed onto a charm
bracelet. The sun lit a curved stripe down the side of each
ship.

Around the spaceport the park stretched outward, like
an elaborate green flower surrounding its sepal. It was
bounded by a thin line, the main road. From it branched
out the arteries that led to each estate. From up here they
didn't seem so far apart, though it was several miles in between the two most distant. Yet the settled section was
dwarfed by the countryside surrounding it. The evergreen
forests were positively primeval in depth and breadth,
miles and miles of trees uninterrupted by civilization. If
Jardindor kept its population small, as everyone vowed
was their intention, that forest would remain pristine forever. Shona applauded their resolve. It did her good to
think that in spite of the ever increasing numbers of humans in the galaxy, taking up more and more land, something like this existed. It was eerily quiet. Only the faint
sound of machinery reached her under the susurration of
the wind. She'd seen vids of Earth. In the audio portion she
always heard birdsong, the busy chirrup of insects, animals
lowing, vehicles humming. If not for the wind it would be
almost as if she were looking at a magificent painting.
Over the far meadows, fingers of light reached down
through the clouds to light up green and gold vegetation.
The surrounding hills, painted in plum and blue shadow,
huddled together like sheep in a fold. All the animal life on
this planet, except for a horse or two, was kept indoors.

"It's hard to believe this has only been here fifteen years," Shona said. "It feels eternal. What a wonderful view! I wish Gershom could see it."

"We negotiated hard to make sure we got the highest point of land in our share," Bock said, with satisfaction. "Ewan and Kely both fought us for it, but after we conceded a major watercourse and a protected slope that is perfect for growing wine grapes, they backed off. If you haven't seen the plat map, it's a jigsaw puzzle bounded by the sea."

In the distance Shona caught silver glints off the surface of the river running down to the ocean. Yelena and Rajid lived nearest to the sea, but so far inland that one couldn't sniff salt water at all from their home. Instead, a brisk wind brought her the tangy aroma of the evergreens. With delight she inhaled their fresh scent. A sour, metallic tang came in with the resiny aroma and caught at the back of her throat. She started coughing. Bock turned to pat her on the back.

"I'm all right," Shona gasped. "Just inhaled something bad."

Bock smiled back, but with worry on his broad face. "The smells hit you sometimes. We can never forget how long there is to go before Jardindor is truly Earthlike. It seems as though we're making progress, then you take a look at all that's left. And sometimes, like this, you just smell it."

"The force field system isn't perfect," Shona pointed out. "They can keep most of the unaltered section isolated up to about five or ten thousand meters, but planetary winds can still scoop up pollutants and dump them on this side of the barrier." She sniffed. "It ought to be more limited than this, though, if what Ewan told me about the generators is accurate."

"Could interruptions in the field let out this much material?" Bock asked, a little uneasily. "Could they be harmful?"

"They certainly could. I have had my cat working on

identifying all the compounds escaping into the atmosphere from the other side of the force field," Shona said. "He doesn't like to work, so it takes a long time. He can smell almost undetectable levels of some chemicals, but it doesn't take a particularly special nose to detect the chlorides and sulfates. They're pretty bad. I've smelled some of them myself, in the heart of the terraformed district. I believe exposure to high levels was partly responsible for Laren's liver failure, coming on top of the psittacosis, which was pretty well advanced by the time I treated it. He was lucky to survive."

"I know," Bock said, bowing his head. "You've saved his life.

"It's my job," Shona said, modestly. "He should have let Dr. Setve treat him."

"He wouldn't. He's too stubborn."

"In spite of what you and I can smell up here, the concentration of chemicals I found in his system were too high for diluted exposure. Did he go out beyond the barrier?"

"Oh, often," Bock said. "He likes to see things that belong to him. Many of our neighbors do the same."

"Wearing protective suits, I suppose?"

Bock looked sheepish. "Not always. You can just about breathe over there, for a while."

"That would explain why I keep coming across noxious odors. You shouldn't be doing that! Unless you're wearing a full environment suit you could be exposing yourself to toxic levels. And you're contaminating your new habitat. You've got clean power, clean air, clean water. You shouldn't be polluting it."

"I know," Bock said, guiltily. "I don't go myself. I warned him it wasn't safe, but Laren can't wait. The terraformers are halfway done reconfiguring a valley he can't wait to get his hands on, though it won't be ready for another two or three years. We want to build a cottage on the south-facing slope."

With one hand shading her eyes, Shona looked where he pointed, at a high, vertical shield of gray.

"He likes to walk around and look at the site. Just there. Thanks to you, he ought to survive to build it, now."

"Just about," Shona said. "If he doesn't make any more unprotected visits over there."

She scanned the landscape. The line of demarcation between the altered and unaltered segment of the planet was easily to spot. On her side, the land was green and alive. On the other lay a knobbly expanse of lifeless brown and gray. Though she couldn't see the force field generators, she could see the sparkle where dust rising from the busy terraformers struck and exploded into its component ions before reaching the lush greenery. The focused beams of the force field destroyed particulate matter between ground level and three to four thousand meters. She could just see the terraformers themselves. Huge, brown boxes on treads, they inched their way almost imperceptibly along the border, moving in an ever-increasing outward spiral. The greatest part of their bulk descended below the surface: the rototiller-like tines that reached deep down into the planet's crust. Toxic compounds and heavy metals were extracted and stored in tanks in the bodies of the terraformers. The land left behind was rendered safe for human habitation. It was a drearily slow process.

"Laren's always in a hurry. I like to say, 'Another year, another yard,'" Bock said with a twinkle in his deep-set brown eyes. "The truth falls somewhere in between. We all gain some acreage every year. There are five hundred sixty machines on the line beyond the barrier, and more every year. Six arrived three weeks ago in the freighter that brought Leonidas. We're always buying more."

"You're joking!" Shona exclaimed. "There are only about three hundred machines working on Mars, a full-scale government project!"

Bock made an offhand gesture. "Oh, you know, there's so much a government has to concentrate its resources on. But *we* can focus. We really mean to have this done as soon as possible." He stared off into the distance. "Some day, I hope we'll be able to let Akeera fly free, and not be afraid that he'll run into the force field, or be poisoned by the air."

Shona looked at him seriously. "You know it won't ever happen. Akeera will never be able to soar above these mountains. Even if you gained another thousand square miles per year it will take longer than his lifetime, and probably yours, too. It's not fair to him."

Bock stared out over the dark gray land, his eyes sad. "I think I've always known it was a fantasy, but it was our fantasy, to see eagles soaring over these mountains. That's why we adopted Akeera, for the qualities he gives us. We wanted to be able to see into forever. He does help us," he said, forestalling Shona's interruption with a raised finger, "but not like that. I don't notice my eyesight being any keener than it was a year ago, but I like caring for him. He gives me something to fuss over, something unpredictable and wild. He's so intelligent and magnificent. In a way, too, he reminds me of Laren. They've got the same profile." He laughed heartily. His voice echoed off surrounding peaks. "I can see Akeera in my mind out there, free, with his wings tilting on the wind."

"He's beautiful," Shona said. She turned to look at the remote peaks still behind the brown haze. "I'm just thinking of his well-being. I'm glad he gives you comfort."

Bock hefted his pack off his back and started to unpack their picnic lunch. Shona sat down beside him and spread out the checkered picnic cloth and pinned it down at the corners with handy rocks. She helped Bock open an impressive array of vacuum jars and bowls. As always on Jardindor, every dish was a gourmet treat. Succulent fresh fruit, caviar on toast triangles, tiny quail's eggs with a brilliant saffron coulis, and an array of other dainties. She tasted a fingerful of duck pate à l'orange and savored the rich aroma with just a hint of citrus. "I suspected Laren's condition could deteriorate very rapidly. I was sorry to be right."

"And what you've done for us since then, not saying a word or so much as hinting he's ill, even though you're a . . . a . . ." Bock bent his head over the bottle of wine he was opening.

"A stranger?" Shona finished his sentence for him, with a twinkle in her eye. "You let me know what was important to you. If it would keep my patient in a positive frame of mind to have everyone think he's just being contrary, I'm happy to go along with the charade! I've enjoyed having you two to myself. I haven't played mah jongg in years. I'm looking forward to the tournament."

"I'm sorry we made you miss the rest of Leonidas's show," Bock said, simply.

"You should have heard him," Shona said. "Bock, Mona told me that Finoa didn't want Leonidas to come here that Friday evening. What has she got against live performers? You had a whole chorus here to greet me."

"It wasn't allowed to leave the spaceport," Bock explained. He scooped servings from each bowl onto a handsome china plate and handed it to her with a cloth napkin. "The facility there is very comfortable, with spas in every room and a fully stocked bar, but they had to go as soon as their performance was over. I hope you enjoyed it."

Shona answered in between bites of her lunch. "Very much. In fact, I was dumbfounded. But I got the impression from others that you used to have acts here all the time."

"We did."

"What changed?"

Bock put down his caviar toast. "Security. It started about the time Lady Elaine was delivered."

"Oh," Shona said. She thought about it. "Finoa must have been going crazy that evening."

"Well, she would have been angry. Finoa isn't afraid of much."

They both sat and gazed out at the vista, enjoying the textures and the muted colors of the land below. They were literally alone in the wide world. Both of them wore pocket comm-units in case an emergency arose at home, though unless someone sent a personal flyer for them it would be hours before they could get back. Bock seemed to feel comfortable, enjoying his picnic on his mountaintop, enough that Shona hoped she could bring up the subject that had been troubling her more and more.

"Why did you—all of you—turn to Animal Magnetism? It sounds to me, and forgive me if I'm wrong, that you don't believe in it yourself. Whose idea was it?"

Bock gave a little sigh. "We are all health nuts. Even me. It started with the dogs. You admitted that having them around is good. It keeps the free radicals of the blood down . . ." He stopped as she opened her mouth to protest. "All right. I'm a programmer, not a doctor. Anyhow, you know what it's like here. Nobody can stand to do anything ordinary. Our dogs couldn't be just any species. They had to be rare and expensive. We had a Martian spaniel. Murphy was a wonderful dog. He liked it up here, too. When he died, Laren was crushed. So was Mona. So was I." Bock fell silent, his upper lip caught between his teeth.

Shona nodded. It was a terrible thing to lose a pet. She didn't want to point out that Martian spaniels weren't particularly special except in their rarity. She'd met a few. They were small, silky, deep golden yellow in color, and very expensive. The breed harked back to an English spaniel female who had mated with a cocker spaniel before leaving Earth. After three weeks in their new home, she gave birth to six puppies, the first dogs born on Mars. The family had been bred to members of both parents' species, and their descendents to one another. The golden coat ran true, as did the sunny disposition, making them appealing pets as well as show dogs.

"We didn't want another dog after that. But people started complaining of ailments that we didn't have where we came from. Agneta contracted some pre-arthritic condition. The capuchin they bought was supposed to help cure it."

"Did it work?"

Bock smiled. "I think the yoga she began to practice helped more, but psychologically? Who knows? Then the

Pacis got their cockatiel. For light sensitivity. They used to live on a station. A tropical bird would have no problem with sunlight. The Sandses got a dolphin."

"So did Setve. But Jamir killed it."

Bock raised an eyebrow. "You figured that out? Yes. That tiger used to range all over the place. We were terrified. Everyone was having a problem with their health pets trying to get out, so Finoa started distributing sopophedrase. Ewan got a tortoise that was supposed to help with the bellyaches the Joneses were having."

"If the tortoise had salmonella it would have made the stomach distress worse," Shona said. "If not that, there are plenty of zoonoses besides psittacosis that can spread to humans. Who proposed bringing in other animals?"

"Robret, I think. No, Dr. Setve. Or perhaps he just approved them."

"Really?" Shona asked. "I would have thought he'd have protested. Caring for wild animals, even ones born in captivity, is not like keeping cats or dogs or small birds. Frankly, they need better hygiene than they've been getting, to protect them as well as you. I've been trying to educate the others, very gently, and warn them that these animals aren't as tame as traditional pets."

"You're not telling me anything I haven't found out. See this?" He pointed to a scar on the side of his face as broad as one of his big fingers. "Akeera gave me that in the first week. I was pretty mad. I was going to send him back, but Laren asked me not to. I would have preferred a chimpanzee, but they're too heavily restricted. Now I wouldn't trade Akeera for anything else."

"You should send him back to Earth," Shona blurted out.

Bock looked away, gazing at his unfinished kingdom to come. "The Terran wildlife preserves are being seriously encroached upon."

"But eagles are protected. And the atmosphere is what he grew up breathing. He wouldn't have to be drugged all the time."

The big man shook his head. "I couldn't do it."

"Animal Magnetism isn't good for them or you. It's much too simplistic a notion. Back in history before we understood science I could have believed in the magic of totem animals, but here and now? No."

Book shook his head. "Setve said, since some animals are clearly bad for you, such as when you're allergic to them, it's possible that some animals are good for you. You know what it's like. You want to believe in something so much."

"Allergies are a physiological chemical reaction."

Bock's hand tightened on his wineglass. "We'd better go down." He gulped the rest of the wine, then rolled the goblet in his napkin. Shona realized she'd gone too far into Bock's personal "no-go" area. In spite of his protests he wanted to believe in some of the tenets of Animal Magnetism. She wished she hadn't been so dogmatic. Silently, she helped clean up the remains of the picnic lunch.

The Jardindorians really were good environmentalists. Bock made certain that they left no trash behind, picking up the stray bits of foil from the bottle seal and putting them into his pack. Once the mountaintop was tidied, Shona reapplied her sun protection, put her hat back on, and shrugged into her pack. Without meeting her eyes, Bock signed for her to lead the way down. She did so reluctantly. There were many tricky passages on the slope. On the way up he had shown her a few paths that looked stable and attractive that led to precipices or crumbly screes. Hardly any visual clues existed to mark the best path, since no native creatures used it, and only three people, now four, had ever walked it since time began.

Where it had been bright and sunny at the top, Shona now found herself having to walk in shadow. Thankfully, the sky remained clear. The promised rain must not be due until later. She hiked down, her mind weighing as heavy as the backpack.

She came to the first fork. Both seemed to curve away down, but there was that scuffed bit of earth on the right where she had kicked a pebble. Not wanting to ask Bock for help so soon, she took that turning. It proved to be the correct one, bringing her within a few paces to an easy but very narrow slope. Gingerly, she picked her way along it. One incautious glance under her elbow let her see the sheer face of the rock supporting her. If she toppled, it would be fifty feet down with no way to catch herself. She sensed Bock's massive presence above her and tried not to let it make her feel nervous.

The air on this sheltered west side smelled sweeter than at the peak. She took deep breaths to keep her pace slow and steady, but also because she enjoyed it. How lucky these people were, she thought. They dreamed a big dream, and they were achieving it. She let out a little sigh. Behind her, Bock's rumbly exhalations changed to a staccato rhythm. He'd heard her, and was chuckling to himself.

With an easier heart, Shona walked down the mountain.

Even though the afternoon was slipping away rapidly, Shona had to halt on a wide curve that stood out like an elbow from the mountainside. She glanced up at Bock, who regarded her with open puzzlement.

"It does your soul good to see such a beautiful vista," she explained. He nodded. Shona took the opportunity to shift her pack on her shoulders. The advice to hikers she found in her health journals suggested a minimum of a half-liter of water for every hour. That was all very well, but water was heavy. She reached around for the flap covering the extendable mouth tube, and had a quick drink. She turned to Bock.

"You should drink some, too . . ." Shona's voice trailed away. The big man wore a haunted look. He was advancing toward her, palms out. "No!" she screamed.

SIXTEEN

Tʜʀᴇᴇ-ᴇᴇᴛ splashed Chirwl with a mighty flip of his tail.

"Pay attention!" the gesture said. Chirwl chittered with laughter. From being wary of communicating with another species, the dolphin had become eager to say all that had been on his mind these long years in captivity. He'd been lonely.

He turned to face Three-eet, surging as far out of the water as he could to say, "I am paying attention to you."

"You have met the striped one?"

"Yes," Chirwl told him. "In safe circumstances. He moves in a dream."

"They feed him bad fish?"

"No," Chirwl said, correcting his actions. Their pidgin language had developed rapidly, but there were still plenty of gaps between intention and understanding. "I do not mean he is sick. Or, yes, it is a kind of sickness, caused by humans."

"These"—Three-eet swung his body wide to indicate the occupants of the house—"do not make me sick, except by neglect, not to let me out of here!" He bumped angrily into the walls, as he did frequently.

"They mean well," Chirwl tried to assure him. "They profess parental-love."

"Are you a captive, too?"

"No. I go where I wish. My human obeys me." It was a poor expression of the host/guest relationship he and Shona enjoyed, but the subtleties would have to wait.

"Order her to free me!" Three-eet said, desperately. "I wish to go back to first waters."

"She would like to," Chirwl said thoughtfully, beaching himself in the shallows of the pool. Three-eet threw himself onto the smooth tile beside him.

"Please," Three-eet entreated, making a wistful noise like that of a juvenile. Then he rose up on his tail and shrieked. "Alarm! Alarm!"

"Ah, here you are," Finoa said. "Are you ready to come with me?"

Chirwl looked up at her in surprise. Three-eet, seeing a stranger emerge suddenly into the room, had thrown himself back into the depths of his pool.

"Greetings," he said. "Shona is not here."

"I know that," the tall woman said, hunkering down. She stood so close to him that her expensive soft boots were lapped by the water. "She didn't tell you to expect me, Chirwl? I invited you both to my home today. She said she was going mountain climbing, but said you could come over by yourself. With your escort, of course," she added, with a courteous hand toward Saffie. The big black dog came over to sniff, then lick, her hand.

"I did not know of this," Chirwl said. "Shona said I may visit? She has said not before."

"Well, she changed her mind," Finoa said, assuming a smile. If Bock had done as he was ordered, Shona would be lying dead in a mountain crevice, and the matter of permission was moot. A regrettable accident. Captain Taylor would have to be summoned to retrieve her body and the rest of his family, including the ottle, who would most

likely return to Poxt. But by then she would have her biological sample.

But how much body language did the ottle understand?
Could he tell she wasn't telling the truth? She tried to be
relaxed, not an easy task when the dolphin behind him was
leaping out of the water over and over and landing with a
belly flop that soaked them both. Finoa blinked, letting the
water run off her face without making a comment. The dolphin was highly excited. Dwan was evidently not giving it
enough tranquilizer. The Sandses had argued to her that it
was not necessary to sedate an animal that was confined to
a tank, but here was visual proof they were wrong. Dwan
stood trembling behind her, but Finoa would have to put
off their reprimand. A more important matter lay here.

"Do come," she added in her friendliest voice. The ottle
leaned closer at the sound. Finoa added more persuasion to
her tone. "I've had the roboservers making your favorite
foods for tea. I've even imported a supply of Crunchynut
bars."

The ottle's whiskers sprang forward. "Ah, my first favorite!" he exclaimed, in his high voice. "That is most
thoughtful kind of you. If Shona has said I may come, then
I shall. Saffie also visits?"

"Yes, indeed. She would be as welcome as yourself."
Victory, Finoa thought, concentrating on not gloating.
"Come, then. Our cart is out front. Yours can follow us
home."

Finoa had to exercise patience as the two vehicles put-
tered slowly along the paved avenue. She must not keep
staring back over her shoulder. After the first two such
glimpses the ottle began giving her very odd looks indeed.

Dwan had nearly caused trouble, muttering that Shona
had given her no idea that Chirwl would be taken out of
her care that day. Silly creature. She knew what Finoa was
about. She stood to benefit by it, so why was she protest-
ing? Why was Dwan being loyal to Shona? She was an off-
worlder, after all, with no place in the future of Jardindor.
Finoa stiffened her back, making certain her face was not

visible to the occupants of the second car. Shona had no place in the future at all, in fact.

"AS you can see, my work is going quite well," Finoa said, gesturing at the monitors lining the automated section of the lab. "I think I'm really making some progress in refining my regenesis technique. It has for many years been the standard with regrowth of skin tissue, especially in cases of excision or extreme damage by fire or chemicals."

Chirwl, in his pouch on Robret's back, kept his claws from touching his bearer. He did not like the big man's gait. It was not smooth, like Shona's. Even Robret's breathing was too jarring, as though he was nervous. But why? If they wanted him to visit alone, without his friend Shona, they must be pleased that he was here at last. Yet they seemed uncomfortable. He did not like the labs. Since he had seen them on his first visit, he wondered why it was necessary to show him around again.

Saffie whined as they passed the cages of guinea pigs and rabbits. She would have chased them if they were free, but she had sympathy for their captivity. So did Chirwl.

"If tissue is easily made, why require living animals?" Chirwl asked.

Finoa's mouth drew together like the top of a string bag, disapproval and concealment of her thoughts in the same expression. "They're not for experimentation. They are the results of my work. An ancient philosopher, Havelock Ellis, said that 'the byproduct is sometimes more valuable than the product.' In this case, I believe it may be priceless."

"You breed these rabbits?"

"I . . . do."

"How are they unusual?" Chirwl asked.

"They are not unusual in any way. That is what is important about them," Finoa said. Several infant rabbits, all black with white noses, occupied one glass-walled container. She opened its lid and took one of the babies out. It huddled quivering in her hand, its oblong ears flattened against its tiny scalp. "These are three weeks old, looking forward to the normal lifespan that any rabbit might have. They are free from disease and genetic abnormality."

"At the cost of any harm to the mother?"

"This is their mother," Finoa said, proudly. She pointed to a huge cabinet with a clear, boxlike compartment on top. Inside, under a cup-sized dome, was a mass of white fibrous tissue. Deep within it, four small, pink bodies, each the size of Chirwl's nose, was visible. "This is the last batch remaining ex utero. And this is their father. The DNA and stem cells to grow them come from him." She showed him a black rabbit all by himself in a larger cage nearby. The rabbit, unaware of its scientific significance, chewed alfalfa with a great twitching of his white nose. Finoa returned to the cabinet structure. "If you look closely you can see the placental mass alongside the embryo. They remain here until they are large enough to be implanted in utero. It is my intention to develop my process further, at which time I will not require a living host mother, but that is in the far future. At present it functions, which is an important step forward."

Chirwl peered at the machine.

"Shona uses a device like this in the borrowed laboratory."

"Yes, a much smaller one," Finoa said. "Not as advanced, of course. This is my prototype. . . . You say she used it? What for?"

Chirwl twitched his whiskers. Shona told him that no one was to know what went on in the clinic. "I cannot say with precision," he said. He didn't like to tell untruths. Equivocation was better than an outright lie. "I am a philosopher, not a scientist."

"True," Finoa said, tapping her lip. "Pity I can't ask her."

"No," Chirwl said. "That would be improper."

"Oh, of course not!" Finoa exclaimed. "What am I

thinking? We are all accustomed to our privacy. I was merely curious."

Chirwl felt his own curiosity perking up. He would have liked to climb down and explore the lab on his own, but each move to free himself was countered by Robret, who held tight to the pouch. "What are those, then?" he asked, pointing a claw.

Another row of glass cases stood at a distance from the working area, behind tables and workscreens. Chirwl noticed something odd about the movement of the animals inside the nearest cage. Robret did not walk toward it. Chirwl tried to climb down, but Robret shrugged and Chirwl dropped down inside his pouch. *Such rudeness,* he thought. But he was an invited guest. He clambered up, eluding Robret's grasp.

"I wish to see," Chirwl insisted.

"Oh, you don't have to look at everything," Finoa insisted, a little alarmed. "You do not have to be so polite."

"It is not mere polite. I wish to see." He began to climb out of the pouch. Finoa threw up her hands.

"No! Very well. Robret, will you?"

Chirwl settled back, satisfied. With the greatest of reluctance, Robret took him to the outer row of cages. The ottle peered at the inhabitants.

There were baby rabbits here, too, but they were larger than the first group, and not perfect at all. One little fellow had only two limbs. One's eyelids were screwed tightly shut all the time. Chirwl wondered whether it had eyes behind them. A pair had truncated ears. The delicate pink interiors were displayed abnormally. Whenever a sound reached them they reacted with greater fear than the other rabbits. Chirwl turned to Finoa, his whiskers spread with curiosity.

"You hide these away."

The scientist seemed at a loss for words. "I . . . it pains me to see them," Finoa said. "They are the result of earlier trials from the same master cells. I care for them, too! They receive the same food and attention as the others."

"They do not ought to exist," Chirwl said severely. "What about the owner of the cells? You usurp his right to create."

"I own that rabbit, therefore I own his cells," Finoa said, her mouth drawing tight around her words.

"Each owns his own cells," Chirwl said, "for where else is identity?"

"In the things one creates!"

"One creates one's own parts. That is biology."

"What about parents, then?" Finoa argued.

"Not the same. The change from the parent-to-parent joining makes a new different," Chirwl said. "That unique is a new being, therefore not one or the other. This is another from the one."

"Well, that is what I do," the scientist argued. "From several I can create one, or many, better than any that came before. Are these then not mine?"

"No. Once they exist they to themselves belong."

Finoa tossed her hair, a sign she was most annoyed. "You would argue, then, against that which created your friend, here." She gestured toward Saffie. "And what your mistress does with the animals in her own studies."

"I do argue this," Chirwl said, firmly. "Where one has not created anything else, one has one's own self. If there were more made from the same against the will of the first, then the original loses meaning."

"*Gains* it," Finoa said, passionately. "It makes the original more important."

Chirwl's whiskers spread out, baring the sharp teeth at the sides of his mouth. "But if the offspring is identical to the first, then there is no first. Do you not have the tale in your history of the dopplegänger? Fear of loss of uniqueness causes insecurity? There is good reason for that feeling. To lose originality stultifies natural striving."

"But if the subject is not self-aware—"

Chirwl cut her off. "Then it is to the self-aware to protect those unable to protect themselves. For the self-aware it is to pursue natural behaviors. This is responsibility."

Finoa pursed her lips, an expression of resigned amusement. "I see, then, that there is no point in asking if you would assist me in my research. I had hoped you might contribute some cells for an experiment." She held up a clean culture dish. "It was in my mind to ask you. I would be honored if you would let me examine your cell structure."

"I most definitely say not," Chirwl said, flinging himself as far away from her as he could get within his pouch. He was horrified at the thought that marched through his head of a thousand misshapen Chirwls, to be examined or exploited who knew how. He braced himself to fight his way out of the pouch, and out of the house if necessary. Saffie would come to the rescue if he was threatened, but would she understand the threat? Robret sensed his struggles and reached around. Chirwl eluded his hands, but could not escape. He took a deep breath to call for the dog, who was watching him curiously from the corner of the room.

Finoa bowed her head, but she put the dish down. "I regret if I've offended you. That was not my intention. I am passionate about my work. I often forget that others do not share my interests, or my philosophy. I will not ask again."

Chirwl saw the surrender in her pose and allowed himself to calm down. "Let us not quarrel about differents. I would be glad to discuss your philosophy, most pleasantly. Theories I do not mind. May we forget the before?"

The woman's long face brightened. "I would be glad to start over, Chirwl. Oh! It's halfway through teatime. Would you enjoy sitting down for a cup of tea and a bite to eat? We've kept you in here a long time without sustenance. I apologize."

Chirwl was mollified. "Very I accept. I would enjoy tea."

FiNOa'S sense of hospitality seemed to have been restored after the brief but frightening argument. She chatted entertainingly about gardening and cookery to Chirwl, who bounced along in his pouch on Robret's back through the winding corridors of the huge house. As they passed under the arch into the great room, Finoa sped up to precede them, her hands in the pockets of her white laboratory coat.

"I hope you will find what we have prepared to your liking," she said. Chirwl peered around Robret's head to see.

A small table had been set up in the very center of the great room, a tiny island of hospitality in an otherwise ocean-sized void. Two chairs and the mushroom-shaped pouffe that Chirwl was becoming accustomed to seeing in every house to accommodate him had been pulled up to it. On the table's white cloth was a shining silver tea service, a three-tiered epergne, bowls, and a vase of flowers.

"Handsome beauty," Chirwl chittered, as Robret set the pouch down on the table-height padded platform. He crawled out and settled himself comfortably on his belly. "I wish to express belated thanks for gracious acceptance and welcome from many weeks."

"It is a pleasure to have you here," Finoa said, sincerely. Robret pushed her chair in, and she busied herself removing silver domes from the plates. "Please, have some cream cakes."

Chirwl brightened as the platter was pushed to within easy reach of his paws. How very friendly this was. Shona's concerns about Finoa were surely exaggerated. The tall woman, after disgusting him so thoroughly, was once again the model hostess. Robret, for all that he seemed sinister during his tour, was his expansive self once again, smiling, his large body sprawling almost bonelessly in the little chair. His hooded, dark eyes were watchful.

"Now, I think you'll find this tea very special," Finoa said, as she tipped the fat china pot over Chirwl's cup.

seventeen

The drop was behind her. Shona tried to sidle away. Bock came after her, panting, his face set and sweating. "What's the matter with you? Bock! Don't hurt me! I've done nothing to you. Please! If you kill me, Laren will die!" The heavy pack threw her off balance and she stumbled. Pebbles shifted under her feet, dropping away into infinity. Her heel slipped, protruding out over the edge. In panic, she jerked it back from the abyss, but overbalanced on the other foot. It skidded. Her arms windmilled, desperately seeking balance. She found herself slipping over the cliff, stepping out into nothing. The sun blinded her. Her heart pounded, choking her. She was going to die.

Then a hard band surrounded her wrist. She squinted up into the sun. A dark shadow blocked her sight of the mountain. Bock had grabbed her hand. She mewed with pain as he hauled her up then backed away from the edge, his arms wrapped around her, enfolding her small frame against his big chest. He staggered backward until a rock turned under his ankle, and he sat down heavily with Shona in his lap. Dust flew up in a cloud where they landed.

"I can't do it," he said, tightly, then threw his head back and shouted, "I can't do it, damn you!" His voice echoed in the silence. He put a big hand on her head, and Shona cringed under its weight. His words came out in a rush. "I'm so sorry. They say kill you and make it look like an accident, but I can't. I'm a programmer, not a murderer. You aren't a cipher. It's all very easy for them to say go do it, but they're not here."

"What does that mean?" Shona asked, still numb. "Who wants me dead?"

"You don't even know what you're doing here, do you?" Bock pleaded. He was covered with dust. "You don't know. It is not fair. You saved his life. I love him."

Shona flung herself away from him. She crawled into the low overhang and sat huddled up, with her knees underneath her chin. Bock sat where he had dropped down, his back to her, his head hanging.

"I came to practice medicine," Shona cried. "That's what you hired me for. I'm just a substitute until Setve gets back. Not to do you any harm."

Bock rolled his hands into fists. "But *he* didn't see . . . what was wrong with Laren. Why didn't he? Akeera has been sick for ages, and Setve didn't do anything. Akeera was making Laren sick. It wasn't his fault. We love that damned eagle. Setve was going to let them both die. You saved both of them. Except for Mona, they're the people I love more than anyone in the universe."

"Then why?" Shona pleaded, the pounding of her heart making her voice rough. "Why are you trying to kill me?"

Tears ran down Bock's dusty face. "Because you will tell people. You keep breaking rules. You tried to tell your husband, on open transmission. You think the encryption's unbreakable, but it isn't. Anyone who really wanted to could do it. No, that's not true. I could do it. That's what I do. I program so-called indecipherable keys, but there is always a way in."

Shona gawked at him. "Everyone is upset because I

tried to tell Gershom about the animals?" Bock shook his head.

"That's part of it. No, that's not the whole truth at all. Do you even know what Finoa does?"

"Yes. She's a brilliant geneticist. After Laren reminded me she'd worked on the Nentnor process, I found some of her abstracts on line. She's cutting-edge. Her biotechnology saves millions of lives a year."

"More than that," Bock said. The way he spoke made Shona curious. In spite of her fear, she peered at him curiously.

"Is the Nentnor process connected with the research she's doing now?"

Bock looked grave. "Of course. I'm surprised a smart girl like you didn't put it together."

"Isn't she working on a new wrinkle to improve tissue growth in burn victims? I thought she was investigating embryology."

Bock dropped his eyes. "She is. Didn't it ever occur to you that Lady Elaine has been here years, yet she's been carrying only a matter of weeks?"

"Of course! There's no male elephant here." Shona's eyes went wide. The scientist in her made the connection, and a whole continentful of lights went on. Human cloning had been banned for decades, but animal cloning was not illegal—though the in vitro process required eggs and host mothers to implant them into. Those clones often suffered from genetic abnormalities, most of them didn't take, and the clones had aged as though they were born at the age of their cell donor, meaning a kitten cloned from a twelve-year-old original had a very short life span. Finoa had revolutionized the process and taken the cruelty out of it. Tweaking a single stem cell into an entire embryo, where one could plan every last gene, and could make certain of its viability long before implantation, was brilliant. Organs produced by the Nentnor process enjoyed full, healthy existence. So if Finoa had made the jump into creating whole embryos they would almost certainly be perfect and healthy. Shona was excited at the notion. "So that's why Laren called her the high priestess of animal preservation? That's what you're all doing here. How marvelous! You're reestablishing dying species using her stem cell process."

"That sounds so unselfish," Bock said, uneasily. "No, some of us are here to collect our own private zoos. Finoa's a fanatic. You are stepping on a lot of toes, and they want you to stop it."

"But my contract is for six months. I was bound to find all this out. Why wasn't I simply told there would be secrets and offered a confidentiality agreement in advance?"

Bock grimaced and glanced away. "You know how the people here think. They probably thought you'd never notice."

"Not notice an elephant?" Shona shrugged. "Well, I almost didn't. But Jamir's been sniffing around my garden. Saffie scented him on the first day. Anyway, why hire me if the eventual outcome was to murder me?"

Bock studied her face. "You know what Finoa's doing, and even now you don't understand. You have a shipful of rare species. That's why we wouldn't hire just any doctor. It's your menagerie. It's the ottle. And all your other little treasures: a purebred cat—a real Abyssinian. A vaccine dog. Genetically hybrid mice. Lop-eared rabbits. We brought you here because of them. You didn't even realize that might be an attraction. You're the custodian of a gene pool that is the envy of anyone on this planet, wealth or no wealth. And Finoa has evolved the means to take advantage of that."

Shona was mortified. "She wants Chirwl for experiments?"

"No!" Bock exclaimed. When Shona cringed he lowered his voice. "She wants to breed from him. Everyone was wild for the idea. Their own ottle. An alien of our own. We'd be the envy of every other collector in the galaxy— if they knew. It would be satisfying that itch each of us has. That's why they asked you to come here." He reached out and put a hand on her knee. She was in such a state of shock she didn't recoil. "You're so naïve. You've got a treasure trove of rare animals, and we knew they'd all come with you. We each have one or two rare beasts, but we each have room for a zoo of our own, and we will have them, over time, if Finoa's research is successful." He gave a sad little shrug. "One day, they'd be able to run free, in jungles and forests where no one would ever molest them."

"That won't be for at least a hundred years," Shona insisted. "Bock, my specialty is environmental medicine. Based on the sheer volume of toxins and naturally occuring compounds on the unreconstructed part of this planet I can foresee pathologies that could affect all of you in time, but those animals have less immunity to foreign pathogens than you have, and they don't understand what is happening to them. Some of you are already showing symptoms. I've treated a number of cases caused by the environment—that over there." She stabbed a hand down toward the barrier where the terraformers chugged patiently along. "It's not fair to any of these precious creatures to be trapped here, multiplied into an infinity of miserable existence. It's wrong to keep them drugged all the time. That, too, will eventually do them cumulative harm, no matter how benign the sedative is. And trapping them in little yards and inside aviaries is cruel. You know that. They should be returned to their native habitats."

"I know, I know," Bock said, mournfully. "I know it would be better for Akeera. I know it. But he's part of the family. How do I know he'd be all right if he went back to Earth? You know how bad the pollution has been. He might get captured and put in a cage again, by someone who won't love him like we do."

"What about that huge protected wilderness in the Rocky Mountains?" Shona asked. "It's almost a third of North America now."

"Yes, with agricultural and industrial areas crowding it on both sides."

"He could soar the skies, fish in the lakes." Shona

stared into Bock's eyes, which were beginning to well up. "He would be free."

Tears spilled over and ran down Bock's cheeks. He was the quiet one of the couple. Shona knew from weeks of watching him and Laren closely that though Bock was not openly demonstrative, his feelings ran very deep. Where Laren chattered and gossiped and vented, Bock sat and watched, only acting after thoughtful consideration. She knew he had been thinking about this for some time. He knew he ought to set the eagle free, but was reluctant because Laren didn't want it to happen. She went and knelt with her arm thrown as far as it could go around his massive shoulders. Bock picked up her free hand and cupped it in his big palms. His dark, chocolate-brown eyes met hers.

"You need to leave Jardindor," he said, sincerely, urgently. "You have to go as soon as you can. When you do, will you take Akeera with you? Get him back to Earth?"

"I will," Shona promised. She looked away, out over the wilderness, almost dreamily, as the afternoon painted every peak bright gold. It seemed to be unspoiled, but until the terraforming was finished it would always be tainted by the poisons on the other side of the barrier. The exotic captive pets would never live to roam free. "I'd like to take all of them with me."

"Oh, no," Bock rumbled in alarm. "They will kill you."

He did not mean the animals. Shona realized she'd spoken without thinking. "Don't tell anyone I said that," she pleaded. "Don't tell anyone that . . ." The words "that you made an attempt on my life" died before she could even get them out of her mouth. She gestured at the cliff with a feeble hand. "Otherwise, how can I go on living here? I can't just leave. I have no transport. I need to wait for Gershom. And what about the children? I have more than three months left on my contract. I don't want them terrified the entire time that something is going to happen to them. Please, Bock!"

"I won't say a word," Bock promised. "I'll tell Finoa no

opportunity ever came up to . . . do what she asked. Remember I owe you, for Laren's life. *We* owe you. But she may ask someone else. You have to watch yourself. You're in danger. Don't make yourself vulnerable. Don't tell people you're going mountain climbing. Don't go swimming without several witnesses."

Shona gave a bitter laugh. "I'll have to stay in for the next hundred days, just like the rest of you. Do you know what a treat it's been to be able to roam around in atmosphere? To look at it through a window will almost be a punishment. But I'll do it," she added resolutely. "The children won't like it, but their safety is more important than their happiness."

Bock shook his head. "Hiding in that house is not as safe as you think. Remember, your computer can be programmed from outside. Finoa and Setve were close. They had the codes to one another's houses. You may have changed the locking mechanism, but you have the same source code."

Shona's hand flew to her mouth as a memory struck her. "The night of my party Robret came in the back door. I know I had left it locked. So that's how he did it! You know how the house computers work. Will you help me?"

Bock looked relieved. "Yes, of course. But don't tell anyone what you know. You have to act normally. You don't know what I was supposed to do. You just had a nice day out mountain climbing. I'll take the pressure for not doing it, but it won't be the last try, if you don't act more cooperative, Shona." He looked deeply into her eyes. "Don't trust anyone. You shouldn't even trust me. Just . . . stop saying the things you do. No one around here is used to hearing the word *no*. They like to give things, but only when it's their own idea. They'll never accept the idea of 'give back.' Except for Akeera, the other animals are here to stay. Face that, and concentrate on getting yourself away from here alive."

Shona privately vowed to try and urge more conversions to reasonableness, though she agreed with Bock that it would be difficult. "I'll be more cooperative. I'll pretend I'm going along with everything, if only to get my family safely off this planet."

"That's good enough," Bock said. "I'm on your side. Laren, too. Just remember that if things get sticky."

"I'll remember," Shona said. "Thank you."

The journey down the mountain took half the time as going up had, but it felt twice as long.

Eighteen

"**Where** is he?" The doctor's voice issued a strident demand.

Finoa turned in horror. Standing in the doorway, with her hands on her hips, dusty and sunburned, was the last person she had expected to see on this planet, or on any other. Alive! Shona Taylor was alive! Hastily she dropped the sample dish into her smock pocket, hoping that Shona had not seen it. The big black dog lying down in the corner of the laboratory let out a pleased whine and trotted over to the newcomer. "Dr. Shona! What a . . . pleasant surprise."

Shona knew exactly what kind of a surprise it was to see her. Poor Dwan trailed behind her like an unhappy shadow. Shona owed her another apology for the strips she'd torn out of Dwan's hide when she'd arrived at the Sandses' home after the grueling downhill trek and found two of her charges missing, but that would have to wait. She was storming the temple, trying to rescue the unwitting sacrifice. Finoa did indeed look like some kind of arcane high priestess, garbed from neck to heels in white samite in the midst of her gleamingly chaste white-and-silver laboratory. By contrast, Shona must resemble an angry dust bunny who'd clawed her way out from underneath a primeval sofa to haunt her.

"Where," Shona repeated, slowly and dangerously, ready to tear the place apart if she didn't get an answer, "is Chirwl?"

Finoa stepped hastily aside to show a sprawled mass of brown-black, a blot on the whiteness. "He's here," she said.

With an exclamation, Shona rushed to the ottle. He was lying on his back on a waist-high mobile surgical table, all his limbs splayed helplessly around his flat, round body. His slack jaw, faintly open to show his tongue and teeth, was tilted toward the ceiling. Shona lifted his head. It rolled in her hands. Just the faintest fluttering of eyelids reassured her he was alive. She peeled one back to have a look at the eye. His translucent nictating membrane was tightly shut. Behind it, the pupil was wide open. It responded sluggishly to light. She bent to listen to his breathing. Ottles, a species that spent a lot of time in the water, had a very efficient respiration system, which meant they used oxygen more efficiently than Terran-born creatures. In the noise of the lab it was hard to hear the light breath sounds. She marched over to Finoa and grabbed the stethoscope off her neck. With that she could monitor respiration and heart rate. They sounded normal. She glared at the high priestess, who was weaving her aristocratic fingers together.

"What happened to him?"

"We were having tea," Finoa said, defensively. "He was eating rather a lot of sweets. Suddenly, he . . . toppled over."

"What? What did you give him to eat?" Shona demanded. "I want to see it."

"You shall. There was nothing unusual. Salmon sandwiches, caviar on toast, crème fraîche on cucumber rounds. Cream puffs. Passion fruit tarts. And Crunchynut bars." Here Finoa wrung her hands. "He ate so many of them. I wondered whether he might make himself sick."

"Could they have become contaminated?" Shona asked, applying the tympanum of the device to Chirwl's chest again. "In storage or transit?"

Finoa looked horrified at the accusation. "Certainly not!"

"Well, he's eaten Crunchynut bars every month since he came to live with me. *And* he's been eating the food on this planet for months now, and has never had a reaction before. Certainly not like this. I want to know what was different this time."

"He chose the quantities he wished to eat. Are you accusing me of poisoning him?"

Shona glared at her. "I hardly bear a lot of good will for you at this moment. You virtually kidnapped him from Dwan's house, when I'd given him specific instructions not to go anywhere without my knowledge. You knew that. Since I'd be away all day you knew I wouldn't find out about this until I got back. I'd come home to a fait accompli."

"Chirwl came willingly," Finoa said, aware that she was on shaky ground. "I didn't force him. You can't call it kidnapping."

"You lied to him," Shona said furiously. "You told him I'd given you permission, when you know perfectly well I had not. You kept him here against my wishes. You ignored the door signal. I knocked. I pounded. I pushed the button for fifteen minutes. You ignored my console calls. I had to signal Alexander to call Tumi to open the door for me. How dare you trick Chirwl? And now he's ill. He had better recover without any ill effects, or I am going to raise a black hole over this household that will suck it out of existence."

"He will!" Finoa exclaimed. She thrust out a trembling hand. "Look, he's moving."

The ottle's eyes rolled, then his limbs curled instinctively against his body in a defensive posture. The thick hide and layer of fat on his back served to protect him from his species' ancient predators, though it was not very useful against unscrupulous scientists. Shona cuddled him against her chest. It was a risk. If he was disoriented, he might lash out and bite or slash as he woke.

"Chirwl, it's me," she said, cuddling his face into her neck like a mother nestling an ottle pup. Alien Relations didn't like its hosts interrrupting the aliens' personal space, but Shona had read studies that it helped them feel safe. He fought her as he struggled his way back to consciousness. She ducked as a fistful of sharp claws narrowly missed her cheek.

"Unsafe!" the ottle squealed, then chittered in his own language. "Pained! I am in the dark! An obstruction!"

"That's my head," Shona said, apologetically, tilting it back. Chirwl lifted his face and blinked as his eyes focused. His body relaxed. She set him back on the table, but kept a hand on his foreleg.

"My friend Sss-shona, you are returned," the ottle said. His head swiveled around. His dark, puzzled gaze returned to Shona's. "This is not where I was. I was here before there."

"You . . . became unconscious in my entertainment room," Finoa said. "During tea? Do you recall?"

"I . . . remember," Chirwl said. He put a paw on his belly. "Too much full." He yawned. "I wish to sleep again." His eyes started to drift closed, and he snuggled against Shona's chest.

"We're going home now," Shona said briskly.

ROBReL appeared, holding out Chirwl's pouch, and vanished into the depths of the house once more to return carrying a box of food Finoa assured her was a representative sample of the delicacies she had served for tea, including a few of the suspect Crunchynut bars. Shona accepted it without another word. She nudged the somnolent Chirwl into the pouch, which she then shrugged onto her back, re-

fusing Robret's proffered assistance. She and Dwan, who
had not spoken the entire time, marched out of the house
and climbed with dignity into Dwan's cart. She sat on the
seat, bolt upright, staring straight ahead.

With an uneasy sideways look at her, Dwan gave the
order to move. The vehicle rolled. Saffie, who had climbed
patiently into the rear seat, sprang at her friend Chirwl and
sniffed him all over, thrusting her big nose into and underneath the pouch, half-shoving Shona off the seat.

"Stop it, Saffie," Shona said, shoving back. The dog
dropped down, surprised at her mistress's harsh tone, but
she quieted without making a fuss. Shona stiffened her
spine, refusing to show weakness or fear as long as that
woman could possibly see her out of a window.

The moment that they were among the trees on the lane
and safely out of sight of the mansion, Shona felt the resolve drain from her. She let herself slump. It had been a
tiring day. An attempt on her life, in between grueling treks
up and down a mountain, only to be followed by the discovery that her precious alien charge had been abducted
was as much as anybody could take. She choked on a
breath, and in a moment found herself sobbing helplessly.
Dwan let the cart come to a halt and put her arm around her
friend.

"I'm sorry," Dwan said. "It's my fault. She said it was
all right with you. I thought you'd changed your mind. I
know I let Finoa push me around. I wish I had your
courage."

"It's not that," Shona said, and opened her mouth to
pour out her story of what had happened to her on the
mountainside. Then she realized that as much as she liked
Dwan and as much fun as they had had together, she did
not know if the Jardindorian woman was part of the con-
spiracy to steal her animals. She could not trust her with
the whole truth. "I'm very tired, and I was so frightened
when you said he was missing. Taking care of him is a
grave responsibility. Ottles are the only intelligent alien
species that we've made contact with. Alien Relations

would throw me out an airlock if something happened to
him. And he's my friend. I worry about him. To see him
like that, sick and unconscious, as though he was on a dis-
secting slab . . ." She tried to finish her sentence, but her
lips refused to make coherent words. She just let herself
cry as Dwan patted her shoulder.

"I am well and together with you now," Chirwl assured
her in a drowsy voice, sticking his whiskery face over her
shoulder. His vibrissae tickled her ear. "Do not weep for
what did not happen." Shona shook her head.

"Let me take you home," Dwan said, comfortingly, giving the command to the cart. "Lani has the little ones in
their rooms, and she's ordered dinner. For once you should
just take it easy and go to bed early."

"Maybe I'll do that," Shona murmured. Whether Dwan
had ulterior motives or not, it was nice to have someone
making friendly noises to her. Finoa was a menace. She
wished fervently that Gershom was not light-years away.
Shona wiped her eyes with her dusty sleeve and sat quietly
as Dwan drove her back to the doctor's mansion.

LANI met her at the door and put her arms around her.

"I didn't know he was gone," she said. "I was visiting
Zolly."

"It's not your fault, sweetheart," Shona said, hugging
the girl back. "Just Finoa trying to get her way. I'm . . . annoyed, but it's over. I'm just so very tired."

Lani's large eyes were sympathetic. "I have fed the little ones. Would you like dinner alone?"

Dwan gave them both an awkward pat on the shoulder
and tiptoed out the door, shutting it behind her. Shona
sighed and set Chirwl's pouch over the back of a chair in
the foyer. The ottle crawled out over the top and sat on the
cushion grooming himself. Saffie settled heavily against
Shona's ankle and put her chin on her paws. Shona undid
her belt and strung it through a chair rail. Every muscle
seemed too weak to move. Her back and legs hurt, and the

throb in her head was an ominous warning that if she put anything in her stomach it would immediately come back. She smiled reassuringly at the worried girl.

"I think I'll just find something simple in the kitchen and take it to the lab with me. I need to send a message to Gershom. It's been a very long day." Lani peered at her questioningly, but didn't ask again. Her actions were always more eloquent than her tongue. Shona chuckled ruefully. "I'll be all right, darling. You are a treasure. Thank you for taking the burden off me."

"Of course, Mama," Lani said, looking pleased.

"I would weigh less if possible," Chirwl said, absently. Still slightly wobbly, he lay on the cushion worrying at the fur on his arm with his teeth.

"You're not the burden, either," Shona said, ruffling his sleek head. "You're a joy, too. What's the matter there?"

"A scratch seems to be here," Chirwl said, holding his arm up to her. "Perhaps a cup broke under my fall. I have no remember of it."

Shona got down on her knees to look at the extended foreleg. The wound on the upper part of the limb looked deepish, but no blood stained the flattened and wet fur. "That's not a scratch. That's a cut. A very clean cut. Come to the lab. I want to take a look at it."

Under the microscope the wound proved to be a very neat incision that cut through all the dermal layers and through the muscular tissue. A minute hole had been drilled into the bone.

"I don't know what she was doing," Shona said, frowning at the scan, "but it looks like I walked in just in time. She didn't have a chance to accomplish whatever it was, nor to seal the cut so you wouldn't feel it when you woke up."

"She may have so informed me," Chirwl said, his eyes tight shut as Shona probed the incision, then ran a regrowth stimulator over the freshly cleaned site. He claimed the cautery light hurt his eyes even with safety goggles on.

"Finally she revealed to me the cause of her work. She grows babies from cells."

"I know," Shona said. The tiny wound sealed itself, and she cleaned her hands. "Bock told me. Her work could mean new hope for thousands of endangered species."

"It is trouble," Chirwl said, twitching his whiskers imperiously. "If she has stolen from me, I must have back. Tomorrow you shall ask her. The destiny of one's cells is up to oneself."

"I know, I know," Shona said, wearily, sitting down on the rolling stool beside the table. "We've had this discussion before. I know your feelings. I can't do it tomorrow. There's . . . a reason I don't want to challenge her just now. Please."

The ottle gave her an odd look. "Something more that you wish to speak of happened?"

Shona paused, thinking of Finoa and the cold purpose with which the scientist had acted, in her pursuit of the Taylor menagerie and instructions for the removal of its caretaker. She was overwhelmed, but she owed Chirwl the truth.

"You are right to concern yourself," the ottle agreed, once she had explained her experiences of the day. "A fearsome situation. Do you trust he will not attempt again?"

"Yes. You should have seen how upset he was," Shona said, remembering.

"I will continue on my guard," the ottle said. "This is even more a reason to see if there was anything taken from me."

"We will," Shona said. "I promise. But not now." Her spine sagged. "I'm so tired."

Chirwl looked at her wisely. "You have used yourself up." He glanced through the sheer curtains at the darkened garden. "The false sun will show soon. Sleep will heal the body." He put his paw on her hand. "We are friends. What you need I will give when it is right."

"Thank you," she said. "I'd just like to be alone now."

The ottle scuttled out of the room. Shona punched the

stud to close and lock the door. If the children needed her
they could ring the signal on the outside or call her on her
console, but privacy, real privacy, was what she needed at
that moment.

ThE pounding wouldn't stop. Bock sat on the couch in the
great room with his hands clenched between his knees.
He'd been in the same pose for hours, it seemed. He felt
unable to get up and do anything. He knew it was late.
Akeera stood on his perch with his white head hunkered
down between his wide black shoulders, deeply asleep.
Mona was only visible in silhouette against the blue-white
light that came from her comm-unit in the corner. Laren,
lying with his head on a down-stuffed pillow and his feet
on Bock's thigh, drew back one leg and prodded him in the
side with one sock-clad toe.

"She is not going to go away," Laren said. "You're
going to have to answer it."

Bock raised his eyes to study his beloved's narrow in-
verted triangle of a face. It gleamed a pale ivory in the light
of the dimmed globe lamp hanging in the air above the
couch. His face had been so yellow for the last few weeks.
That it wasn't pink yet showed his tentative hold on health,
a hold that Bock had nearly jeopardized with his actions
that day.

"Go on," Laren insisted. "Get it over with. Then you
can clean up. You're all dusty."

"I've been a fool," Bock said.

"We've all been fools. Go."

Dumbly, Bock rose. He touched the controls set into the
priceless mahogany paneling. The door slid silently shut.
Bock continued to meet Laren's intelligent, sardonic, and
sympathetic gaze until the polished wood cut off his view
of the great room. Then he went to answer the door.

He pulled the front door open with such force that the
woman on the other side nearly fell in out of the night. The
high color in Finoa's cheeks showed she was in a temper.

"How dare you keep me standing out here so long!" she said. "Your front garden is open to the road. Anyone might have seen me. Me! Spotlighted by your coach lights, banging on the door like a tax collector."

"I apologize," Bock said, slowly. "Won't you please come in?"

At the sound of contrition in his voice, she abruptly recovered her aplomb. Head up, Finoa marched past him down the wide hall toward the great room. Stopped by the seamless wooden wall, she spun on her heel. "Open it."

"You wanted to see me," Bock said.

"I want to see both of you. I've been sending you messages for hours."

"Laren and Mona are not accepting visitors this late." It sounded unnecessarily blunt, but he refused to apologize or explain.

Finoa glared at him, but he knew she couldn't force her way through solid wood, nor batter through the slug-and-laser-proof shielding concealed within the cladding, nor could she figure out the encoding that would open this or any other locked door in his house. She knew it, too. His family was safe. "Very well," she said. "We'll talk in here."

Bock gestured to a wrought-iron chaise upholstered in bottle green velvet, one of Laren's favorite pieces. "Won't you please sit down? May I get you something to drink?"

Finoa, of a height with him, met his eyes with a gaze so sharp it felt as though she was boring into his brain. "Don't you try to hide behind empty pleasantries, Bock Carmody. Why didn't you follow my orders?"

He tightened his lips. "There was no opportunity."

"No opportunity?" she echoed, disbelievingly. "You were out with her all day long. No one was within miles of you. Not one soul on this planet could have seen it."

"I had no chance!" he said, raising his voice. Laren would hear him.

"Ridiculous," Finoa sneered. "You have no spine, is what you mean. One push! That's all it would have taken. Then, no more inconvenient questions, no more nosing into our way of life. I had the shock of the century, seeing her parade into my lab, when I thought she was safely dead."

The heavy syllable shoved at Bock's already battered conscience. "You think it is so easy to kill, then you do it. I won't. Neither will Laren."

"You won't." Finoa fixed him with an eye as sharp as Akeera's. She stepped up until they were almost nose to nose. Bock kept his face impassive. "You know what this means?" she snarled. "I won't give you another chance. It's the end of your share in the dream. Any of you."

"I know," Bock said, refusing to let her see how shaken he was. "Even . . . all that is not worth the life of a friend."

Finoa studied him as she backed away. "Very well. You've made your choice. I'll show myself out."

Bock watched her disappear into the night, heard the crunch of the gravel as the wheels of her cart rolled down the drive. As soon as he was certain she was gone, he locked and sealed the door.

The other two looked at him when he returned to the great room. Laren didn't need words to understand what had happened. He glanced a question. Bock nodded. Making a little face, Laren wriggled down into his light silk coverlet and indicated to the house computer to restart the symphony he'd been listening to through the speakers concealed in the body of the couch. Bock met Mona's large, worried eyes and came over to her.

"May I use that for a moment, little butterfly?"

Silently, she nodded and made room for him on the bench seat. She'd only been looking at catalogs, so there was no communique to save or close. From his capacious memory he entered Shona's personal comm-unit code, adding a private encryption command that would cause Hethyr's snoop program to miss this entry.

"I've burned our bridges," he said. "We're allies now, for better or worse. I will try and help keep you alive until your husband returns. Remember your promise." With a firm gesture, he sent the message.

Nineteen

ONCE the impact- and radiation-proof shell of her personal lab module was closed around her she allowed herself to collapse like the contents of an egg, boneless and helpless. How foolish she had been, believing that everywhere she went she could count on good will! She sprang for the communications console and turned it on.

As soon as the message program indicated it was recording, she blurted out, "Gershom, we have to get away from here. They brought me here to steal the animals, and now they're trying to kill me. I don't know who I can trust anymore. I'm afraid for the children. . . ."

Suddenly, she smacked her palms down on the console. No! She couldn't send a communique like that. Everything she transmitted was read by Governor Hethyr. Whether or not Hethyr agreed with Finoa's methods, she believed in Animal Magnetism. Like the others, she was involved in the plot to amass her own private zoo. She must have known why someone had insisted they hire Shona Taylor and not some other, less encumbered *locum tenens* to replace their vacationing physician. To tell Gershom was to tell Hethyr, and to tell Hethyr was almost certainly to inform Finoa that her plot was known. Shona clicked the key to erase the message. She was not thinking clearly. Resolutely, she pushed herself away from the console and stood up.

A thought stopped her at the door. She didn't want to go back into the house just yet. She was so tired. It felt good to be protected, enfolded in familiar surroundings. Now that she had used Bock's special codes on the house computer to seal the doors, Chirwl and the children were relatively safe in the house.

She activated the audio pickup on the shell of the module so she could hear if the children called for her. Later, when she was rested and could think more clearly, she could examine the house computer's programming and figure out where Finoa's "back door" was situated. Finoa wanted the animals' DNA, and in spite of Shona's impulse to see her as an ogre she would almost certainly not hurt them, or the children. But Shona was another matter. Her knowledge made her vulnerable. The capsule was secure, and the children could reach her in it if they needed her. Should she sleep in there?

Who could sleep? Shona thought, flinging herself into a frenzy of pacing up and back. But each step reminded her of how tired she was, and how long it had been since she had rested or eaten.

She eyed the tray of cheese and fruit she had brought into the lab module. Those strawberries were such an unbelievable shade of red, brighter than rubies, more lustrous than silk, dotted with the tiny jewels of their seeds. She reached out to take one, knowing that it would be damp from rinsing in pure water, slightly scratchy in texture, fragrant with a perfume that lifted the senses. But could she trust even the food? All the wealth of Jardindor was suspect now. She had just come to understand the price she was expected to pay for borrowing it.

This lab module, though, was hers. She knew every cranny, every scrape on the white enamel interior, every

sticky hinge. She was safe here. A faint rustling from
Moonbeam and Marigold attracted her attention. The soft-
eared brown rabbits lolloped over to the edge of their little
habitat and stared at her meaningfully. Their dishes were
empty. She could at least attend to that. They twitched their
noses at her when she lifted the lid to put in fresh food and
check the filtered water dispenser attached to the side wall.
She tickled the soft fur on the back of the rabbits' necks.
They ignored her, more intent on the bowls of kibble and
lettuce.

She glanced toward her own plate of food, still not willing to touch it. There was always nutri: safe, boring, available, tastes-of-nothing nutri. Those ruby-colored
strawberries and peridot-skinned apple slices took on the
air of blessed ambrosia in comparison.

Shona threw back her head and groaned at her own ignorance. What was she thinking? She was standing in the
middle of a facility intended for biological research. If the
food was poisoned, she could easily find that out.

She took samples from each item on the platter and ran
them through analysis. Everything came up untainted by
either poison or biological hazard. Feeling a trifle foolish,
she ate her meal. She willed herself to relax. She must
relax, or she would upset the children. They must not know
what had happened to her. They would worry, and they
might talk.

How horrible that ignorance should be their only shield.
For the sake of her children and the animals in her trust she
had to go on pretending that nothing had happened. It had
been very hard to maintain the correct air of righteous in-
dignance when rescuing Chirwl. She had to come up with
a plan to protect herself and her family.

She glanced at the communications console. Its screen
stared blankly back at her. It was pointless to ignore it. No
one could jump out at her from its insides. There ought to
be some word from Gershom, and maybe she could think
of what to do. She sat down and switched the box on again.

In her planetary mail she had several messages from

Laren, Dwan, and her other "friends," none of which she wanted to answer or even hear just then. The little icon appeared in the corner of the screen, indicating that the console was connecting to the beacon in stationary orbit above the planet. Her mailbox began to fill up.

The usual wealth of advertisements went straight into the Delete zone. At that moment she could not think of a single thing that she wanted to buy, short of a tesseract teleporter to get her back to the *Sibyl,* and those hadn't been invented yet. A bloc of messages from Gershom appeared in the queue, along with half a dozen missives from her professional bulletin board, a review of her last paper, a message bearing the return address of Alien Relations, and one sending from her aunt and uncle on Mars. Shona immediately punched up Gershom's messages. The tension holding her body taut melted away when she saw his face.

"Hello, darling." Gershom smiled at her. Shona smiled back. "Well, the current champion of the galaxy in the Ganzara World online role-play game is Eblich . . ."

The first six messages were short transmissions full of chatty news and little messages of love that made Shona tingle inside. By the context he still hadn't received her sendings yet. Gershom had recorded a half-dozen messages that had likely been gathered into a bundle for transmission. The *Sibyl* had accepted a handful of reasonably lucrative short runs to refill the coffers, but he was on the trail of additional luxury goods that he hoped would interest the folks on Jardindor. Shona replied to that one guardedly, hinting that he shouldn't overload himself on speculation. He'd be better off collecting freight charges for actual orders than carrying the cost of goods. She hated to dash his hopes of good sales to the Jardindorians, but it was better that he be forewarned than unable to dispose of a big shipment of luxury goods. Then she came to the last message in the queue.

"Hello, love," he said. "Glad to hear from you at last. I got a lot of messages all at once, but they seemed a little

broken up. Transmission must have been interrupted by a
sunspot or something. We've been busy. I accepted a quick
run from Unity to Peshawar Station and back with a load
of Colors soda. We didn't break . . . too many containers.
It took a steam cleaning to get it all out of the cracks." A
rueful smile. Shona could imagine the sickly sweet smell
of spilled soda wafting out of the cargo hold. *Ugh.* "The
money's decent but not generous, same as any standard
run. The kids look like they've grown, and it's only been
two months! I miss you every night. Tell Chirwl we ran
into another ottle, an ovadonor. Hir name's Brandwr, says
they know each other. I like his host. Orvald's a traveling
musician, but he looks like a stevedore: big and burly, with
a mustache you could lose a muffin in. I took the two of
them from one station to another, and they worked their
way. Nice folks. I'm attaching some of his music for you
to listen to. I'll send more later, but we're going to jump,
and I'll lose this beacon. Tell Lani and Alex and Jill *Daddy*
says hello."

Shona let the program freeze on his image, reluctant to
let it go. She checked the monitor: this message contained
many times the memory of the first six. She clicked on the
icon at the top right of the image. A menu came up; Gershom must have recorded a file of his new friend Orvald's
playlist. But what about the information she'd asked him
for?

She tapped the first choice. As Gershom had said, Orvald was a big man, but his thick hands were extraordinar-
ily deft on the strings of his ancient wooden guitar. The
ottle, an older Poxtian with a few white hairs in amongst
the sable, rested with its head and forepaws on his knee,
listening with the alert black gaze Shona knew so well.
Mellow music came out of the speakers. She listened for a
while, then selected the next song, watching the screen
carefully. The gentle sounds soothed her, but she was impatient. Where was the hot list?

She scrolled up and back through the entire message
again. No text. Then she brought up a digital image of the

message. Not all of that hefty file was music wave forms. Something was attached to the first part, Gershom's message. But how to access it?

"Tell them Daddy says hello."

That must be the password. "Hello," Shona told the screen. "Hello." She tried it in several different tones of voice, including matching Gershom's cadence. Then she recorded his own voice saying the word and played it back. Nothing. What was she missing?

. . . *Daddy* says hello."

Shona grinned. That was it. The children usually called him Papa. "Got you, darling. Daddy."

Immediately Gershom's face shimmered and vanished. Beneath lay the familiar form of the hot list. Shona's fears were pushed aside in favor of intellectual curiosity. This either contained or did not contain the answer to the question she'd asked herself a couple of weeks ago, and it might help her to understand what had happened to her that day.

Every spacer knew this document intimately. In the upper left corner was the date of issuance. She was required to enter on the line beneath it her name and the date she received it. As soon as she keyed it in and waited for the video pickup to record her image, the file accepted and locked the data. Now, short of corrupting her own console memory, she could not alter that entry. Once she had registered, the file came to life.

The icon in the corner indicated over a million and a half entries. Shona elected first to scroll through the file without choosing search criteria. It was fascinating what a bizarre range of things had been lost throughout the galaxy, everything from clothing to buildings. Because the "hot list" usually dealt with high-value merchandise, rotatable tri-dee images of each item in and out of its shipping container was the first notation. She could also browse by owner's name and/or location, or along a searchable text. Entering the word "animals," Shona was rewarded with a veritable zoo.

From aardvarks to zebra mussels, it seemed that every animal in the bestiary had been separated from its owner at one time or another. A few of the entries were marked "probably expired," based upon the date of theft or disappearance, added to the likely lifespan of the animal involved. One listing moved Shona deeply: the image of a bowl of goldfish. The accompanying explanation was offered by a small, toffee-haired, brown-eyed girl who appealed for the return of her pets. Patricia was an apartment-dweller on Mars, she explained, and the fish were the only animals she was allowed. Could she please have them back?

A man, whom Shona guessed to be her father because of his near resemblance to Patricia, appeared next to say that he would pay a reward and *reasonable* expenses for the return of his daughter's property. The details followed in print.

Such offers constituted legal contracts. If a shipper wrote to claim the reward, barring bankruptcy or other legitimate obstacles, the owner was obligated to pay. Even if no reward was forthcoming, shippers were morally and legally obligated to return cargo that they found to be stolen. Shona became overwhelmed by the thousands of extracts and further reduced her search by entering the word "elephant."

The familiar gray shape appeared on the screen. It seemed there was only one elephant missing at present. "Please return Lady Elaine to me," pleaded the owner, a slim, dark, mustachioed man named Dan Patel. Lady Elaine! Shona let out an exclamation. "She's a priceless part of Earth's heritage. If you find her and can't get her back to me, please take good care of her. She's a great old girl. She's not cheap to feed, so between her care up to the point when she went missing and my search ever since, my finances are not good, but I'll give you whatever I've got left if you'll can find a way to bring her back to me. I know it's not much of a reward, but you'll be preserving an irre-

placeable part of our planet's history. Thank you." Patel's
contact information followed.

Even the same name. Shona shook her head at Finoa's
nerve. The woman had stolen an elephant and didn't attempt to conceal it even by changing her name. At once
Shona bookmarked the entry, then put in "tiger."

More sparkles as the system searched. Again, only one
extract popped up. On the screen, a slim man with a
hatchet profile ran his hand nervously through close-
cropped salt-and-pepper hair. "I'm Steve Lopata. If you lo-
cate a male tiger—yes, a tiger—240 kilos, five years old,
get in touch with me. He vanished, crate and all, off a
short-hop surface transport going from Winter Park,
Florida, to the spaceport in Cape Canaveral. I . . . I hardly
know where to start. Look, he eats only meat. He can survive for a while on nutri if you supplement him with vitamin B-12 and taurine. He's meant to be part of a breeding
program on Proxima 4, where we've got most of a pastoral
continent wide open and waiting. Please. There are only
one thousand tigers left in existence in the *galaxy*. I'm begging you: if you are offered tiger parts or a pelt, pay *anything* if you can obtain the animal himself alive. I will
make sure you are reimbursed. If you could just see him:
he's a fascinating, beautiful, majestic animal who deserves
to survive. Please help me. I'm traveling a lot between
Earth and Proxima. I'm still looking on my own, but if you
find him, please contact me." He started to say something
else, then changed his mind. "Here's the last picture of
him. Thank you."

Shona's heart went out to Lopata. She peered at the
low-resolution image of a striped shape prowling restlessly
under a hot, tropical sun. The video had been cut from a
larger scene in which the tiger was not the center of focus,
but she was certain that Lopata's tiger could be none other
than Finoa's Jamir. The scan of the animal's genome followed. If she could get a hold of some of Jamir's DNA she
could make sure, but how many lost tigers could there be?

She marked the location in the list. Two list searches,

and so far, two hits. Jardindor's wonderful Animal Magnetism cult looked as though it was a haven for stolen goods. One by one she searched for matches to the exotic animals that lived with—she could no longer say were owned by—her neighbors. Nearly every one turned out to be snatched from private individuals, or, more worryingly, from national or planetary trusts. Even, and here Shona felt a big ball of ice in her belly, a bald eagle had gone missing from the North American continental preserve on Earth, its discarded tracer band discovered in a Golden, Colorado, recycling plant. Akeera. Poor Bock. Poor Laren. Or *should* she be pitying them? Shona drummed her fingertips on the console top.

To do them justice, her neighbors didn't strike her as thieves. They weren't afraid to pay for what they wanted. They were proud of their ability to pay. Jardindorians bought anything they desired, raising their offers until the seller could no longer resist. Therefore, they would believe that they had purchased these animals legitimately. Therefore, and Shona was stretching a point, though not far, none of them knew they were illicitly obtained. Therefore, logically, some outside agency was arranging the thefts and making the purchases without their knowledge. The only person who seemed to come and go from Jardindor with any frequency was Dr. Setve. Therefore, logically, Setve must be the "fence." He and Finoa were close, so Shona had to assume that most likely the biogeneticist knew what the traveling doctor was doing. She must. No wonder Finoa wanted to get rid of Shona. Not only was she garrulous and observant, but she was the wife of a space merchant who knew the ropes and who would no doubt have questions as to how such a great quantity of these very precious and restricted life-forms came into the hands of a small and notably wealthy population that was so far away from the common spaceways that nobody could drop in to make a casual inquiry.

Shona pushed back from the console to think. It certainly didn't comfort her to have her suspicions confirmed.

At the time she'd asked Gershom for the list it had seemed a remote and absurd possibility that the Jardindorians wanted to keep the animals secret for anything other than privacy reasons. Now that she knew the animals were here illegally she was morally bound to get them off planet, all of them, and return them to their owners. It was her duty, both as a merchant with a license to lose, and as a humane individual who loved animals. But first she had to think about getting herself away. She could help none of these creatures if she was dead.

Still, now she had an ally. Bock was dedicated to his family, and he felt indebted to Shona for saving his partner's life. He had already made her promise that she would see to Akeera's return to Earth. If she told him the truth perhaps he would help her get all of the animals away.

The scheme would take a great deal to arrange. It might be impossible, if her movements were constricted from fear of assassination. Bock had not revealed the reason why he and the others were obedient to Finoa, but the tie was strong, and the next attempted killer wouldn't have Bock's reasons to spare her. But was Shona's death really necessary to Finoa's project?

No, Shona thought, as she browsed through the hot list, marking down yet another missing animal, not as long as she led the scientist on to believe that she would have access to her pets' gene pool. That was what she really wanted, after all. Shona would have to appear conciliatory and eager to make friends again, perhaps letting it be known that if the other woman apologized she would be more open to having Chirwl visit her alone again. Maybe Shona should offer to let her meet the rabbits and mice. Anything to buy more time.

It would take time to contact each owner and inform them their animals had been found, then figure out how to transport each animal safely. She needed to let Gershom know he was going to have a much bigger party to pick up than the one he'd left on Jardindor. Oh, if only he would hurry up and return! With three months to go in her con-

tract, almost anything could happen. She had to work out
how much room she would need aboard the *Sibyl* for each
creature, and how much fodder. She started to make a side
list of the information she needed on her console, then
hastily erased it before it could auto-record. If Hethyr
could break the encoding on her outgoing messages, she
might be able to remote-read her files. The hot list was all
right: it was auto-encoded to the console it was on. She
glanced around for traditional writing materials. Jill liked
to use her styli to write on the walls. Later. Her head was
throbbing.

It was after three o'clock in the morning when she resolutely recorded another message to Gershom. "Hi, honey.
It's been *very exciting* around here. I'm training for a mah
jongg tournament in a couple of weeks. I know that sounds
tame, but you have no idea how much controversy a little
game can stir up! I wish you could *be here* to cheer me on.
The kids would love to see you." Shona babbled along for
a little while, then took a deep breath. Now the awkward
part. "It sounds like you're being very successful hunting
down everything on Hethyr's list. It must be like a scav-
enger hunt, running all over. I envy you visiting Chun Op-
penheimer & Co. I love their silks. Isn't DirectLearn's
main depot on that station on the other side of Sol? And
then you have to look at personal comm-units, but new
things are coming out all the time, and you *know* how people change their minds. Why, I bet they're wondering if
there isn't a fancier model to buy. You should make sure
that the current models can be returned for credit. It isn't
their fault if trends change.

"You know how I miss you. Six months is too long to
go without seeing you. If you could hop back here *soon*,
you'd make me *very happy*. Miss you, darling. Love."

There, that sounded innocent enough. She sent it off,
hoping Gershom would read between the lines. She didn't
dare attach a concealed message, not having so convenient
a cover as recordings of a traveling musician and his guest
ottle. This sending must be in the clear, so it would not be

stopped on the way out of the system. She didn't want him to drop everything to come. She was afraid, but she was beginning to get her confidence back. She could cope, for a while. He must not fail customers who were counting on him. The Taylor family was going to have enough of a sticky financial situation if Shona defaulted on her contract. But if she was able to get off the planet alive with those poor animals the Jardindorians were unlikely to want anything from them except their hides.

TWENTY

The bartender squinted at the four men who sauntered in the door of Cargamil Station's Last Chance Saloon and Pizzeria. They walked with the slight unsteadiness of men who'd been in low-gee for a long time. The tall, youngish one with the long black hair seemed to be the leader. Yes. The others hung back slightly while the slender guy ordered pitchers of beer, fried vegetable chips, and a couple of extra-large pizzas with everything.

"How far you going?" Scot Melbourne asked, keying the entry into the kitchen computer. He pulled the beers himself. The autobar could do it perfectly, but spacers liked seeing something done by humans when they came into port.

"Marsport," the tall man said, with a smile. "About two weeks' transit to go. We're looking for short hauls between here and there. We've got room." The burly one behind him picked up the tray of pitchers and balanced it neatly on one hand.

"We're off the *Sibyl*," said the short, skinny guy. He

presented a credit chit for payment. "Any messages left for us?"

Melbourne was surprised they'd ordered their food first before asking for mail. Folks usually couldn't wait to hear from home. Leaving and picking up messages at the local bar was common practice among the smaller space merchants. He reached into his pocket for his personal screen. Should the station's system be hacked, or should the bar computer be compromised in some way, he didn't want to be the one responsible for messages being lost or garbled. The screen was clipped to a retractable tether that ran around Melbourne's ample waist, and the unit was password-locked. The only way anyone was going to get at the private data for his guests was over his dead body, and he knew every dirty in-fighting trick ever hatched. He scrolled through the list of waiting mail.

"*Sibyl, Sibyl* . . . Is one of you Eblich?"

"That's me," the skinny guy said. "Is it from my wife?"

"Here," Melbourne said, handing him the screen so he could read the message.

"Anything bad?" Gershom asked, leaning over Eblich's shoulder to read.

"No problem. My niece is coming back through this station on her way to a survey job," the navigator said, scanning the print, "in about twenty days. She's got her new baby with her. We'll be long gone. Damn. I was looking forward to seeing the little guy. I'll leave a note saying sorry we missed them. Thanks," he told the bartender.

"D'you want to download the message from your niece?"

"No. Not necessary. Thanks." He handed back the unit. Melbourne pocketed his screen and went over to refill a drink for a guy signaling him at the end of the bar.

"*Sibyl,* huh?" asked a man sitting nearby as Kai carried the drinks to a vacant table.

"That's right," Gershom said, offering a hand. "Gershom Taylor, captain of the *Sibyl.*"

"Marcus Rosen. *Blue Danube.*" He was typical of the

long-haul spacer breed, rangy, his naturally tawny skin bleached from limited exposure to sunlight under atmosphere. His black hair, long like Gershom's, was shot through with silver, suggesting his age to be fifty or thereabout. His prominent nose gave an otherwise undistinguished face some character. He squinted at Gershom. "I think we met once, back along about five years, maybe a little longer. Didn't you make a stop on Karela after the plague?"

"That's right. My wife's a doctor."

"Hey-yyy, that's why I remember. She's the famous one, right?"

Gershom made a face. "We prefer to call her 'well-known.'"

Rosen grinned and glanced about. "Is she here with you? Gone shopping?"

"No." Gershom took a gulp of beer, noticing that a bunch of the other spacers were listening in. "She's working. Got an assignment on Jardindor." No harm in people knowing that.

"Really?" Rosen asked, impressed, as Gershom guessed they might be. "Jardindor! I hear they've got more money than the government."

"Jardindor?" said another traveler, sitting down at the *Sibyl*'s table. "I hope she's doing okay. When was the last time you heard from her?"

Gershom glanced warily at the other, a heavyset woman with rough hands, bulky arms, and dark blue hair. "Why do you say that?"

"Weird things happen to people who go work on Jardindor. My name's Kim Fletcher, skipper of the *Patmos*." She extended a hand to Gershom and Rosen. "We dropped off a geology specialist about three years ago. I knew the man well. I'd worked with his company a bunch of times. Most careful man in the galaxy. Knew everything there was to know about petrography and tectonics. Killed in a *landslide*. Now, I ask you."

"You think there's something going on there?" Ivo asked, peering anxiously at the woman.

Gershom frowned. "My wife's not involved in earth-moving or anything hazardous like that. She's a physician. She's there on a temporary contract, a consultant."

"So was my mate," Fletcher said. "He was the best that there is, lived through six dozen missions just like that. He can hear tectonic plates shifting—or he could. Dammit."

"Things happen, Kimmy," put in another spacer, from two tables away. She grimaced.

"That's not the only thing I've ever heard about Jardindor, Angus," Fletcher said gruffly. "After Barak died I started asking questions. Over the last couple of years there's been a lot of 'accidents.' A lot of temporary workers who go there never seem to make it off again. Oh, their families get their wages—most of 'em. But there's something going on there." She drank up her beer and departed.

"Good traveling to you," Gershom said. A man raised his glass to Fletcher in a toast, then went back to the conversation he was having with a female dressed in a clingy dress that fastened in the front with magnetic clasps. A couple of newcomers hailed Rosen and slid onto the stools at his table to talk. Gershom didn't like Fletcher's story of the careful engineer's accident. Shona's last few sendings to him had worried him. He caught his crew watching him carefully.

"The nearest booth's just around the corner," Kai said quietly.

Gershom nodded and slipped out of his seat.

The credit-reader in the communications booth chuckled for a while over Gershom's wrist-chit, but it finally consented to link him into the system. Dozens of messages for his ship queued up. He forwarded most of them to the console in the *Sibyl*.

Five messages from Shona were at the tail end of the queue.

"Hello, darling," the first one began.

He'd known her now too many years not to be able to tell when she was unhappy. A tiny line etched itself between her straight brows, and the sides of her mouth looked pinched even when she smiled. The gaiety when she talked about the upcoming game tournament sounded forced, and there was real worry in her eyes when she spoke about the children.

"And Chirwl . . . is having a ball. He's the real social butterfly of the family. I think they'd forgive the rest of us just hopping up and leaving the planet if he would stay. He has so many invitations . . ." The way she'd hesitated told him she had meant to say something else and stopped. Why? He halted the transmission. She must have discovered that her communications were being tapped. Again, why? All he could guess was that it had something to do with the hot list. Strange that she'd asked for it after all these weeks. Had some of that fabulous artwork been illicit? Was that the great secret of Jardindor, that all those wealthy captains of industry and intergalactic artists were smugglers? That would be ironic. If she'd discovered some kind of irregularity it would make things awkward for her.

"Lani has formed fast friendships with Mona and Zolly. It's so nice that she can be with girls her age. I hope she stays in touch with them after we go . . ." Shona gave what was meant to be a carefree laugh, but it was strained. Gershom found he was tightening his hands into fists. Something had her worried to death.

"And you know how people change their minds. Why, I bet they're wondering if there isn't a fancier model to buy. You should make sure that the current models can be returned for credit. It isn't their fault if trends change."

That tore it. Gershom pounded a hand on the console top. She was warning him that there was trouble, and she couldn't talk about it on an open channel. But he couldn't find an underlying message.

"Miss you, darling. Love." That sounded sincere. She

was nervous. No, she was frightened, but not code-red kind of worried yet. He replayed the message to make sure he'd heard it all correctly.

He stared at the frozen image of her face. He should go back and get her. She didn't say directly that she wanted him to come. She had coped with dangerous situations before. Wasn't she a tri-dee heroine in the eyes of his fellow indies? He was proud of her for her courage and resourcefulness, but if she was afraid to tell him what was going on she clearly didn't feel as though she was in control of the situation.

What could he do? It would take the *Sibyl* nearly a month to get back to the remote edge of the galaxy where Jardindor lay. He had contracts to fulfill, even if he followed her very broad hint and jettisoned the remainder of Governor Hethyr's orders. He still had to go the rest of the way to Mars. Their livelihood, if not their reputation, depended upon his reliably completing assignments. Yet, she was all alone out there. He clutched at the console, as if by force of mind he could reach out and feel Shona's hands on the keys. Then, an idea struck him. She was not alone. Resolutely, he signed off and loped hastily back to the bar.

"HOW bad is it?" Ivo asked later, as they left the bar.

"Pretty bad," Gershom said. A couple squeezed past them, more intent on each other than the four strangers in the hollow metal corridor. Gershom waited until they were out of earshot before continuing. "She's frightened. She's found something out, but she didn't tell me. She must be afraid of surveillance."

He played the message again.

"Hop?" Eblich said. "Did she say hop?"

"She did," Gershom said, palming the crash doors that led to the dock where their ship was being fueled. "Not as bad as a 'skip' or a 'jump,' but bad enough." His crew regarded him sympathetically. They loved Shona. She was one of them. Each of them thought of her as a sister or a daughter.

"What can you do?" Eblich asked at last.

"I've done it, back in the bar. Please heaven she's still all right when help reaches her."

TWENTY-ONE

Friday afternoon, Shona, in her best green dress, stood in the Sandses' great room holding a tray of hors d'oeuvres while Dwan flitted around, tweaking a tablecloth here, straightening a flower there.

"It looks fine," she said, as her friend whisked past her, not hearing a word. Dwan was too nervous to pay attention. Lani, clad in simple red silk and similarly burdened with a salver of party snacks, shot an inquiring look toward her mother. Chirwl, already on the mushroom-shaped seat that everyone now had in their homes for his comfort, twitched his whiskers in their hostess's direction. Shona nodded agreement. She put her tray down on the nearest end table and went to take Dwan's hands. She angled her head around until Dwan had to meet her eyes.

"It's almost six o'clock. Why don't you just let the house computer take over the finishing touches? You'll be exhausted by the time everyone is here."

Dwan plumped into a chair. "Oh, you're right. I'm making too much of this. I do it every few months. Why am I so nervous? It's just the usual Friday night house party. What could go wrong?"

"Exactly," Shona said lightly. "Spoiled food. Malicious gossip. Roboservers dropping chafing dishes in people's laps. Children breaking up the furnishings. Just like every week. Nothing to worry about."

"But I do," Dwan said, making a long face. Shona was ashamed for having teased her. "I want everyone to like it. Everyone does judge everyone else."

"My mother said my grandfather had an expression: 'Shame the devil,'" said Shona. "Put on a mask. Don't let anyone know their comments bother you."

Dwan laughed. "I'll try. Uh-oh, look, here comes Agneta. Computer! Straighten up the room, please. Ev! Guests!" The robot arms reached down and began delicately to turn vases and pick invisible bits of fluff from the carpet. Shona took the tray from Lani and put it into a waiting pair of metal claws. Dwan hustled to the door.

"Good afternoon, Agneta. How nice to see you," Shona heard her say at the door. "Finoa, you look lovely in dark green. Come in, please."

"Fake confidence," Shona said to herself. She smiled at Lani's puzzled expression, and straightened her back.

"AND so, I will be going back to Earth to reorganize the central office," Hanya said, settling the folds of fuchsia silk around her ample knees. "What a nuisance. I was not planning to go until after . . . for a few more months."

"It's a shame you couldn't trust your manager," Robret said politely. "Face time is very important, though."

"Yes, it is," Hanya agreed. "Nothing equals personal contact. That is why I must go, even though it will take months that I would make better use of right here."

Ev Sands offered around a brandy bottle and a fistful of delicate balloon glasses. Shona brought her attention back from a smiling refusal in time to hear her name mentioned.

"Face time is very important," Finoa repeated. "Don't you agree, Dr. Shona?"

Shona froze. It was the first time the other woman had spoken to her since her arrival. Finoa had ignored her elaborately, seeming to be surprised to see Shona there. She also made a tremendous show of greeting Chirwl from across the room, then sitting down as far from him as she could get without surrendering the center of attention. Shona knew she was up to something, and she'd been on guard until that moment.

"I do," she said, evenly. "For example, I've never found it helpful to conduct examinations by console."

"Is that what you've been doing with Laren and Bock?" Finoa asked, in a very innocent voice. "Correct me if I'm wrong, friends. It seems that the only one of our number to visit the Carmodys in all these weeks is Dr. Shona! Whatever is going on over there? Have we all acquired chronic halitosis?"

Shona reddened. Bock had told her about Finoa's repeated attempts to see Laren. "I certainly can't say from here," she said, with more asperity than she intended. "Besides, I don't discuss my patients' conditions in public. Perhaps you'd like to make an appointment, and we'll settle this matter in private?" Finoa's long, pale face hardened at the sally, which had elicited a snicker from several of the listeners.

"What I want to know, with no offense intended, is why are *you* so favored when their longtime neighbors are being neglected? Why, I can't even get a call returned."

"Are you feeling neglected, Finoa?" a sardonic voice asked from the door. "My goodness, that won't do!" Laren stood framed in the entryway. Shona almost melted with relief. The lean man spread out his hands theatrically, and sailed into the room. He swooped down on Finoa and gave her a hearty, smacking kiss on the cheek.

"How are you, dear?" he asked. "Hot as an oven, isn't it? I decided to dress for comfort, if not for fashion. What do you think?"

Finoa eyed Laren up and down. He had on a shirt made of a very sheer dark-green gauze that didn't leave a centimeter of his torso above the waist unrevealed. Shona held her breath while Finoa eyed Laren up and down. Shona had healed the incisions from removing the remaining shreds of his diseased liver during his very last treatment only two days before. There was a chance some of the new pink skin might show. Whether the moiré weave of the shirt concealed it or Laren had covered it with surgical cosmetics, she could see nothing. His slim middle showed fine muscular development, not at all what would be typical for someone who'd been gravely ill and on his back for several weeks. Shona had overseen his practice of isometric exercises and yoga, and Bock had made certain he didn't overdo. Finoa shifted her glare to the doctor, who met it with a bland expression. Whatever Finoa suspected, she would never know the truth. The new organ was about half adult size already, and Laren barely needed the follow-up visits Shona was going to make anyhow. As long as he was careful what he ate and drank, he would do fine. Finoa returned her gaze to Laren, and held out her hand to him. Bock moved up protectively behind his shoulder.

"It's good to see you, dear," Finoa said, sounding sincere. "Ev is circulating some excellent brandy. Why don't you have some?"

No alcohol! Shona thought, letting out an inadvertent exclamation. Finoa caught her in her bright gaze and narrowed her eyes. So. She had *some* idea. Shona wondered how.

"No, thank you," Laren said, as Ev hovered nearby with the delicate glasses. "I'm on a juice fast today. Could I impose on you, Dwan, my silent sweetheart? Anything, so long as it's plant-based in origin and not later than last Tuesday. Carrot juice? Wheat grass?"

"Er . . . tomato?" Dwan asked, hustling to the pitchers on the bar.

"Delicious!" Laren said, throwing himself in a chair beside Finoa. Bock settled more quietly onto an overstuffed ottoman an arm's length away. "So, darlings, how have you all been?"

"It was a good party," Shona assured Dwan, as she gathered her children together. The dark-green cart awaited them on the steps. Behind them, Laren seemed reluctant to leave. He had held court all evening, blithely ignoring hints from his neighbors who pushed subtly for the details of the fight that had kept him and Bock from being seen together in public all those weeks. "Really. You are such a good hostess."

The taller woman blushed. "It's hard," she said in a low voice, helping Shona get Chirwl's pack onto Saffie's back. Hefting him herself would ruin Shona's best dress, and the ottle enjoyed the alternate means of transport.

"Why don't you and Ev come over for dinner tomorrow?" Shona asked. "By then you'll be feeling better."

Dawn looked greatful. "I accept with pleasure," she said formally. "Thank you."

"Don't mention it," Shona said.

"Dr. Shona," Finoa called. She was collecting her silk shawl from Ev. She held up a hand as Shona turned. Shona waited as the tall woman glided down the steps to her. "Dr. Shona, I wanted to have a word with you in private."

They had not spoken again all evening. Shona had not found a convenient opening, and did not want to risk another contretemps in public. Her original intention to be placatory seemed to have flown out the window. But Finoa did not look angry.

"I wanted to talk to you, too," Shona began, gathering the words of regret she'd prepared for this moment. Finoa held up a hand.

"You've been ignoring my calls, and I can't say I blame you," the taller woman said. "You won't believe it, but all I want to do is apologize. You're right, I was high-handed. I'm used to getting my way." She made a self-deprecating face. "I prefer it, I admit. It was wrong of me to persuade Chirwl to visit. I knew your rule. Forgive a scientist's mindless zeal. But in the end it didn't matter," she said ruefully. "After all that he refused to assist me in my work, so all my enthusiasm was for nothing. Then he was injured in an accident in my home. Please accept my heartfelt apologies. It was never my intention to cause him harm."

Privately, Shona doubted it. In light of the unmistakably deliberate wound on Chirwl's foreleg she wondered how much Finoa expected her to believe. But for three more months of peace, she was willing to extend the polite fiction.

"I was wrong, too," Shona said, allowing Finoa to grasp her fingers in a seemingly companionable grip. "Alien Relations reminds me so often of how careful I need to be of him that perhaps I overreact."

Finoa beamed. "Then we're friends again. I'm so glad. I was hoping so. Robret?"

Her massive husband appeared soundlessly at Shona's side, making her jump. He held out an armload of packages. Finoa selected the largest and lightest.

"This one's for you, Shona. It's a climbing rose from my own garden. It has the sweetest scent I've ever smelled." She pulled away the paper to show three thorny green stems laden with shiny green leaves and pink blossoms a few centimeters across. The roses' delicious perfume wafted around them like a sumptuous cloud.

"Oh, we couldn't accept . . ." she began.

"Please," Finoa said, forestalling her protest with a raised hand. "Oh, there I go again. Please accept it. It would give me great pleasure if I knew you would enjoy it."

Shona relented. After all, the gift of one plant was a small thing to Finoa. "Thank you," she said. "It smells wonderful."

"And this is for Alex," Finoa said. She knelt beside Shona's son with another package, this one wrapped in purple tissue sprinkled with sparkling stars. He regarded her with suspicion. "Tumi thought you'd like it. He hopes you'll be able to come back and visit very soon."

Alex glanced at his mother. She nodded. With one eye on Finoa, he tore open the paper. "Yow!" he exclaimed, holding up a gleaming, smooth-surfaced, silver robot about 30 centimeters high. "It's Nano-Man!" He immediately knelt on the ground and started playing with it. Shona cleared her throat. "Oh. Um. Thank you, ma'am."

Finoa trilled out a liquid laugh. "You're welcome." To Shona's embarrassment, she had gifts for each of them. Lani got a pair of glittering earrings that Shona judged to be worth a month of her pay. Jill clasped a handsewn velvet dolly. There was even a bag of biscuits for Saffie. "And this, dear Chirwl, I offer in apology for my poor hospitality. I hope we will be able to visit again soon."

"It is not necessary to provide gifts," Chirwl protested. His whiskers stood out in surprise as he unwrapped a fine box of smooth, dark wood that had fine tracery carved inside a circle on its lid. "It is for storing of notes and reading matter. This is home done or similar."

"That's right," Finoa said, pleased. "I'm so glad you recognize the style. I've been in touch with the human settlement on Poxt. They said these are ottle symbols representing wisdom and education. I hope you don't mind that it's of artificial manufacture, not from your planet. It would have taken too long to wait for a shipment from Poxt. My roboservers made it from wood grown on our property. I was careful to make sure the design was like those your people use."

"I am pleased by the thought," Chirwl said, rubbing the surface with his hand-paws. "My offense is forgotten. It is kind to go to so much trouble. I am impressed by this box."

"You are kind to forgive me enough to accept it," the tall woman said, with an inclination of her head. "Well. Good night to you all." She gestured to Robret. He followed his wife to their cart where Tumi sat fidgeting.

"Thank you," Shona called after her. She took another deep sniff of the rose before she stowed it in the back.

Climbing into the driver's seat, she gave her command. "Home, James!" The cart lurched into motion.

"That was very nice of Finoa," Lani said, as soon as they reached the road.

"You mistrust her sudden generosity, too?" Shona said. Lani paused for a moment, then nodded.

"It is not simply guilt?" Chirwl asked, wriggling up between them.

"I'm not sure if it is guilt," Shona said thoughtfully. She still had not discussed Finoa's attempt to get Bock to kill her. In light of the fact that Finoa was still unaware her plan had failed, it might seem like ordinary etiquette. "It may just be the proper response in this culture, honey, showering someone with gifts when you've offended her. They certainly are generous on other occasions. I am probably being remiss in not having presents to reciprocate." She shook her head. "Participating in this insane comedy of manners is beginning to make me second-guess my own intentions. I wish we could get back out into the spaceways where people are more direct with one another."

The red-and-white house loomed up over the treetops. Jill let out a pleased little crow.

"Home!" she said.

Shona felt her heart lift when she saw the house, then beat back the feeling. Dr. Setve's house was *not* home. She stiffened her back. Home was the *Sibyl*, and she couldn't wait to get back to it.

Alex had an odd expression on his face when he climbed down from the cart with his new toy clutched in his fist.

"Well, what's wrong?" Shona asked, lightly. "That's a very handsome gift you have there. You should send a special note and thank Ms. Finoa. That robot is just like Tumi's."

"It is Tumi's," Alex said, holding it up for her to look at. "It's got a chip on its foot from when we dropped it down the stairs."

"That's very odd," Shona said to Lani, as they bundled

the little ones off to their rooms for evening baths a while later. "Why would Finoa give Alex her son's toy?"

The girl frowned. "Maybe she thinks Tumi's outgrown it, and she's passing it along?"

"Human children change rapidly," Chirwl pointed out, from his pouch on the wall. He scribbled something on a wood chip, then carefully placed it in the new box Finoa had given him. The house roboservers had mounted a shelf for it on the wall beside him so he could reach it easily. "Finding new applications for targeted operations does not always work. It is best to pass along to another user. That is a key component of my argument against the complexities of technology. The mind can make more use of simple objects, which change with maturing."

"That makes sense," Shona said. "Even if that's the case, Alex has no business being upset about it. I certainly wouldn't look a gift robot in the gears, not even as a hand-me-down. Those things cost a fortune."

"If that's why," Lani said, her eyes full of doubt, echoing Shona's own feelings.

EVERYONE was too strange on this planet, Shona thought. Quashing her own doubts she got the children settled in bed. Jill wanted a special story about her new doll, which taxed Shona's tired brain, but Chirwl came to the rescue with a few insights on what a rag doll would think about humans with bones. Both children cuddled around the silky ottle, rapt and giggling. Alex was interested in all the gory details of rag doll anatomy, but thankfully, Jill didn't understand the more technical facts Chirwl included about tendons and sinews, focusing on the social aspects of being the only flexible person in a universe of stiff-legged beings. Gratefully Shona left Chirwl to his talespinning.

"You should rest now, Mama," Lani said, as Shona saw her to her room. Harry, asleep in the middle of Lani's vast and sumptuous peach bed, rose and stretched langorously.

He trotted over to rub against her legs. Shona bent down to raise the cat to her shoulder. He exhaled a deep, fishy purr in her ear.

"In a little while, sweetheart," Shona said, leaning over to kiss the girl on the cheek. The gift earrings glittered against the girl's dark hair and skin like stars in a twilit sky. "Those look very pretty on you. I'm going to send a message to Gershom, then I will go to sleep, I promise you." With Harry kneading at her shoulder, Shona backed quietly out of the room and closed the door.

Shona carried the cat in one arm to the front hall. She'd put Finoa's rose in the conservatory until she could figure out what to do with it. Bending at the knees so as not to disturb the cat on her shoulder, she dipped down neatly and picked up the pot. Harry's head went up at the scent of the flower. At once, he tried to climb over her back toward the pot.

"Stop that," Shona scolded him, lifting his claws out of her tunic. "You are not going to eat this flower. It was a present. I don't want you coughing it up all over the hallway."

Harry squalled a protest all the way down the corridor, but fell silent as Shona stepped through the doorway into the darkened conservatory.

Shona didn't bother to put on the lights, instead navigating in the cool blue-white of the moonlight lancing in through the cut panes of the glass roof. Shona put one hand on the exterior door, then changed her mind. Better break the habit of walking out at night. As much as she enjoyed her starlit strolls, who knew what could be hiding out there, waiting for her? The water in the big pool rippled gently in response to the vibration of her footsteps on the floor. It reminded her that a dolphin had been killed in that very room by a wandering tiger—a hot tiger.

She put the rose on a table by the rear door. It would catch the morning sunlight. By then she would have decided where to place it permanently. In the meantime, she wanted to muse about Finoa's change of heart. Harry, his quarry now out of reach, elected to snuggle in her arms and knead at the inside of her elbow. She took him with her into the lab.

Three short messages from Gershom were hardly enough to make up for the fact that he wasn't there. Each time she entered a reply she had to stop herself from begging Gershom to come and get her off planet. How could she say that she kept a hyposyringe of a powerful anaesthetic by her always, in case she was assaulted again? That there was a supply of food and water on hand in the module, in case she and her family needed to retreat to it? She wondered if he'd read her concern from her previous message.

An unfamiliar address in the queue of waiting messages made her frown as she tried to recognize it. When she opened it, the face of David Potter, with his sandy hair and whiskery mustache, appeared. He grinned at her.

"Hey, Shona," he said. "Sorry to miss you when we were on Jardindor. I didn't know you were there until I ran into Gershom on Unity Station. He and Amey and I had a really *hot* time together. He's gone way in toward Europa for those silk carpets he wants your folks to look at. Hope we run into you some time. Amey sends her love to the kids. I hope you're going to send me some pictures. I haven't seen Alex since he was a baby. Take care."

The image froze on the screen. Shona's tired brain tried to make sense of his message. Why was he contacting her now? The Potters had been here months before. They'd known she was on Jardindor; Leonidas would have told them. There was something important in the message, then, something Gershom must want her to know. What was the key? She listened to it again. That was it: the way Dave had emphasized the word "hot." This was another Trojan horse message, with the keyword to conceal the really important part.

"Hot," she said aloud.

Suddenly the screen broke into a cloud of sparkles, indicating the same kind of tight encoding that Gershom had used. David's face was there again, but with a different expression.

"Hope you get this okay," he said, leaning close to the pickup. "Gershom is worried about you. He's heard a lot of things about the people you're staying with, and after the stuff he told me, you ought to get out of there as soon as you can. He is too far away to help, but Pop and Mom Meader are on their way back to Jardindor with another load of terraformers. We all know them from way back. They're the grandparents of all us indie spacers. They'll pull you off-planet. From my mark, they're about three, three and a half weeks away from you. I hope this reaches you in time. They won't have a chance to give you much notice. Keep looking out for code words in messages. None of us will blow this open for you. We indies stick together. You keep yourself safe. If you need to Trojan-horse another message to Gershom, send it through me or the Meaders. Good luck." A soft voice, the speaker not visible on screen, murmured something. "Amey says good luck, too."

Shona smiled. She no longer felt quite so alone. Bless the Potters and the Meaders. Three weeks! Having a deadline served to focus her mind on her tasks.

She exited from encrypted mode, hit the reply stud, and put on her brightest face.

"Hi, Dave and Amey! It's so nice to hear from you! I wish we'd been able to see each other. Your kids are getting so big. Has it been that long? Anyhow, here are some updated pictures of my brood. Lani is getting so beautiful I'm thinking of making her wear a biohazard suit when we get back to civilization. Hope we can get together soon. I'll be finished with my contract in another twelve weeks. My best to you both."

There, that ought to allay Hethyr's suspicions. The governor would know about the approaching trade ship, but now she wouldn't make any connection between it and

Shona. She brought up her stored pictures of the children. She knew she shouldn't draw attention to the riches of Jardindor, but that image of Lani in the peach boudoir, an exotic fairy princess caught at her toilette, was her favorite. She hoped Hethyr would assimilate that and not stop the message on that account, as long as Shona showed no animals but her own. She selected five more of the children in various places around the big house.

Now, to build her own Trojan horse.

In encryption mode she opened a new message, choosing the address from the hot list. She smiled her most businesslike smile at the pickup.

"Mr. Lopata, my name is Shona Taylor. I believe I've located your tiger . . ."

HEr eyes burning with fatigue, Shona leaned back from the video pickup to massage a crick in her back. The time on the chronometer in the corner of her console screen blinked an accusing number at her. Three o'clock! Harry had long ago abandoned her lap for a cooler bed in the sink. She'd been so motivated she had hardly noticed the passage of time.

The moment the first note was time-sealed she was committed. She had to get the animals off planet. Now, all she had to do was figure out how.

She didn't have to worry about Finoa. Such a short time frame would hardly give her a chance at Shona.

★UPPEr torso of adult female A observed entering juvenile C's quarters, upper manipulatory limb powering down light-emitting module. Darkness, 85 percent. Scanning . . . Juvenile C exhibits resting behavior. Respiration . . . regular and rapid: twenty-two breaths per minute. Pulse, seventy beats per minute. Muscle tone, slack.★

The small silver robot's eyes gleamed with a blue light. It turned its head as its internal controller continued to

monitor the house through surrounding walls.
*Scanning . . . Juvenile D exhibits resting behavior. Adult
female A in Juvenile D's chamber, exiting. . . . Adult female B exhibits resting behavior. Alien life-form E exhibits movement. Waiting . . . waiting . . . alien life-form
exhibits resting behavior.* It turned its head again. *Adult
female A . . . out of range . . . adjudged no hazard.*

Fluidly, it rose to its feet and picked a careful path
through the small obstacles littering the thick carpet. Adult
female A had not secured the door. A silent pulse from the
robot informed the house computer to open the portal fifteen centimeters, wait until it had passed through, then
close the portal.

The robot stepped down the center of the corridor, monitoring the major life-forms. Adult female A was perceiv-
able only faintly, indicating thick shielding in between her
and the robot's sensors. A receiver located in the little automaton's torso began to listen for the pulse of components
it required for its assignment. The first was in the next
chamber on the right. Adult female B lay within. That door
was secured. Two pulses were needed to inform the computer what the robot required.

The chamber offered no obstacles to negotiate until it
reached the dressing table, its upper surface twenty centimeters too high for the robot to reach. At the robot's command, a mechanical arm dropped down from the ceiling
and lightly scooped up the small automaton, bringing it
close to the table.

The robot needed no other illumination to see the object
of its search: a pair of earrings. With swift motions, it
clipped the lowest dangling solids from the bottom of each
one. Those crystals contained temporary instructions and
would be destroyed after a single use. The server arms
lowered the robot to the floor and silently shut the door behind it as it continued its quest.

Warning, nonhumanoid A approaches.

Saffie raised her head as the little robot went by, sniffed,
smelled no human or animal scent, identified the intruder

as a machine. Plenty of things in this house moved by themselves. But this one carried faint traces of Alex's and Lani's scents. Neither of them was with it. Should it be out wandering by itself? With a questing noise, Saffie rose to her feet and sniffed along behind the striding robot.

It was behaving like an animal. Saffie wondered if she could make friends with it, and if it would play with her. Or if it was more like her mistress. Would it provide her with a share in a midnight snack?

It stepped mechanically down the corridor all the way to the end. Saffie kept half a pace behind it, smelling its track. It must be more like a human, for the door opened for it, admitting it and Saffie into the conservatory. As Saffie sniffed around for fresh scents, the robot made straight for the small potted rose. A roboserve arm assisted it to the top of the table, where the robot dug in the dirt until it came up with a cubic datacrystal.

Saffie was so intent upon her investigations that she didn't notice the robot as it left the room. The door slipped shut between them. Saffie recovered and galloped after it, to be met with the solid surface of the door. She pawed at it, then sat down and barked loudly for her new friend to come back. It must have forgotten about her, for it didn't return.

It took Saffie's canine brain only a moment to realize that she was locked up in a room she was not supposed to be in alone. Feeling guilty, she slunk to the wall behind the pool with her tail between her legs and her ears flat against her head. She was a bad dog.

No midnight snack.

The robot, having located all components for its objective, sent a pulse to the house computer asking for the location of its central processor. On quiet feet, in the dark hall, it marched onward, its programming set in place.

"SaFFie was in the corridor when I went to bed," Lani said, kneeling with her arms around the big black dog.

"Well, that's a relief," Shona said. "I thought I must have locked her out here when I came in to drop off the rose. I just don't know how she got in here."

"I heard nothing," said Chirwl, "but I was engaged deeply in study, then slumber."

"I didn't do it, Mama," Alex said, very solemnly.

"I believe you, sweetie. And Jill can't work the locks, so it's a mystery." The dirt in the flowerpot had been disturbed. She glared sternly at Saffie. The dog ought to know better than to dig in houseplants. If she'd done such a thing on the *Sibyl,* Gershom would have given her a good scolding. The dog looked up at her with sad brown eyes. As it was, Saffie had had enough punishment, spending the night locked up in the conservatory. By the time they'd found her that morning she had been so desperate to go out that she had urinated in the drainage grate beside the pool. If she hadn't been in a restricted part of the house, the doors would have opened when she scratched, allowing her outside to do her business. The roboservers were hard at work deodorizing and sanitizing the system.

Saffie felt betrayed. Alex held her new friend in his arm. Not only did the silver being not acknowledge her, it did not attempt to make her feel better about her disgrace. Saffie appealed again to Shona, who reached down and scratched the side of her jaw.

"Oh, what's the use. Come on, girl," Shona said. "Let's all have some breakfast."

Saffie sighed. That was the way a friend should act.

TWENTY-TWO

Laren discarded a tile from his hand. Three of Circles! Shona, to his left at the priceless octagonal table in the gaming room, stabbed at it with her forefinger, then quickly discarded the White Dragon she'd been holding on to.

"You can't take that from me unless you're completing a pung or a kong," Laren chided Shona. She looked guilty. "Aha! I thought so. You've only got a chow. You know that means you can only take from your left unless you're going mah jongg, and I would bet my last yard of silk you're not ready to do that yet. Computer! Reset the tiles one move."

The virtual reality display shimmered slightly, dumping the useless blank tile back into Shona's holdings. She sighed.

"I knew I shouldn't have, but I couldn't help reaching for it," Shona said plaintively.

Laren gave her a summing look then exchanged glances with Bock. "You've blossomed from a decent player to a nearly great player under my excellent tutelage. These little mistakes tell me that your mind is not on your game. Something has you preoccupied and rather excited. Is it anything you can tell us? We are at your service. Give. Dish. Disseminate."

Shona hesitated. Lani, filling the fourth chair at the table, looked from one adult to another, then pushed back her chair and headed for the door.

"No, don't go, honey," Shona called to her. "You're right," she said to the men. She'd held on to the secret so long it was hard letting it go at last. Her tongue didn't want to move, but when she thought about the fact there was so little time left until her deadline words started tumbling out.

"We're leaving Jardindor," she blurted out.

"Good," Laren exclaimed. "And bad. We'll miss you very much, but under the circumstances it's probably the safest thing for you all. When will you be going?"

"What circumstances?" Lani interrupted, looking from one adult to another.

"Lani—"

Bock held up a huge hand for silence. Shona clamped her mouth shut and waited while he rose from his chair and examined the room. He felt along the server arms and peered into hatches and under component covers. He returned to the table and gave her a brief nod. By now Lani looked very worried. "You can tell her," Bock said.

"Honey," Shona began, taking Lani's hand, "while I was mountain climbing a couple of weeks ago, I nearly had a little accident."

"Don't try to spare me," Bock said, humbly. He bowed his head. "I almost pushed your mother off a cliff." Lani gasped, her eyes huge. "Finoa blackmailed me into it. But don't worry; she's lost her hold on me. On us," he said. Laren gave a grim nod of agreement. "We've decided."

"Everything's been all right," Shona said, clasping Lani's hand in both of hers. "I promise you."

"That's why you won't let us go visiting," Lani whispered.

Shona felt heartsick at the way her daughter's face paled. "Yes. I didn't tell you why before because I didn't want to worry you. I don't believe you're in any danger. Just me."

"But that is bad," Lani cried. "Mama!" Shona went to put her arms around Lani. The girl buried her face in Shona's hair. She patted Lani on the back, murmuring soothingly to her.

"I take it you're planning to escape on the cargo ship that's on the way," Laren said, and smiled at Shona's astonishment. "Now you look as surprised as your daughter. Everyone knows it's coming. We all look forward to arriving ships the way nineteenth-century Terran-Americans must have looked forward to Wells Fargo stagecoaches. Everyone is expecting at least one package besides the five terraformers we commissioned. Until the tachyon mail system can deliver solids, we're still dependent upon traders. Fine. We will treat your secret as our own. You can count on our help. Do you plan to slip away, or do you need our interference so you can be waiting at the pad when it touches down?"

Shona glanced at Bock. "I need more help from you than that. I . . . have to take . . . a lot of . . . cargo with me when I go."

Laren's eyebrows went up. "Cargo? I know we've been giving you a lot of gifts, but surely it will all fit inside your shiny white module."

Shona hesitated. This was going to be *very* awkward. "It's not gifts. The Galactic Government circulates a hot list of stolen and missing merchandise," she began. "To keep our licenses all indie merchants are required to try to return objects we find to their original owners. They're very strict about their interpretation of the rules, and I have to tell you that our livelihood depends on following them."

Laren's left eyebrow went up. "I hope you're not going to say that some of the terraformers are stolen. We bought them directly from the manufacturer. A benefit of having a business of one's own," he said blithely to Lani, who was not nearly over her fright. "They're tax-deductible."

"No," Shona said, slowly. "Not the terraformers."

"The art? The construction materials? You can't disassemble our homes and take them away. Isn't possession nine-tenths of the law? Lewis's flitter? Most of us would like to see that go. That young man is a menace to navigation on these country roads."

"Let her tell it," Bock said. His tone was mild, but Laren treated it as a command. He looked apologetic, turning his long face into a humorous tragedy mask.

"You know what I'm like. I'll keep guessing until I get it. Tell me."

"One moment," Bock said. "Computer!"

"Ready," the disembodied voice of the house computer said.

"Somo-nambu-confabulation."

There was a pause. All the roboserver arms halted, and the computer-generated mah jongg set faded away. "Ready."

Bock sat back with his arms folded. "You can speak freely. The computer will not now quick-record your words, waiting for a command. It's a little buffer that can be read by the right programmer."

Shona looked at him. "How did you do that with just a few words?"

"Every house on the planet has emergency backdoor codes. I've just suspended all computer activity in this room, for a few minutes. Tell him."

"It's none of the inanimate objects here," Shona said. Laren's eyes narrowed. "I'm very sorry to have to tell you, but it's the animals. Most of your animals were obtained illegally. Now that I know about them, I am required to try and get them back to their owners or guardians. I know that it's a lot to ask, but I want to enlist your help in getting them off-planet. After that, Gershom will help me take them all home."

"No," Laren said firmly, understanding at last. "Under

no circumstances. My eagle stays here. He's mine. Tell them you couldn't do it."

"But he's stolen," Shona explained. Laren had put on the same sulky face as Alex did when she told him he couldn't have something. She pressed on. "He belongs on a Terran wildlife preserve. The forestry service employees were frantic when he disappeared. They found his ID band in a trash-reclamation site. They thought he'd died in there. They searched the whole facility, then decided he must have been shipped off-planet."

"How do you know it's my eagle?" Laren asked, the light of challenge in his eyes. "There could be other bald eagles that have gone missing. Who knows? Someone might have hit another one with a flitter or a transport, or found it dead and didn't want to take the blame."

Shona could tell he was floundering for an answer.

"When available, there's a DNA profile attached to each entry. I compared the one on the hot list to the tail feather you gave Alex for his collection. I'm sorry, but there's no mistake."

Laren lifted his sharp chin in defiance, rendering his resemblance to the eagle that much more marked. "I don't believe you. Akeera is mine." But he looked at the solemn faces around him, especially the sad-eyed visage of Bock. He paused. "Is it true?"

"Yes, it is." Shona stood up. "Come and see for yourself. All of the proof you need is in my lab."

LAREN stared at the console screen, flipping from the DNA sample back to the excerpt from the Terran Fish and Wildlife Service. His face had been locked into a stone mask as Shona had led them to her module, but confronted with indisputable proof his expression had changed to that of a man stricken. "I don't believe it. All this time, while I've been thanking fate and time for bringing me a symbol, a totem, a wild spirit, a pure expression of all those virtues I admire, he turns out to be nothing more than stolen prop-

erty. I'm devastated—I can hardly tell you how I feel."
Bock put his hand on his partner's shoulder. "I'm all
right," Laren said, his voice tight. "All the others are like
this, too?"

"Not all, but most," Shona said, calling up the bookmarked list. Laren scrolled through the items grimly.

"Hethyr and Dina have dodged disaster," he observed.
"Argent must be just what Setve said she was: an orphaned
cub who couldn't be returned to the wild. But she's a
chaste exception to this shocking list. Earthstone is illicit,
and that couldn't have been an easy heist. Dwan's Three-
eet is here. And poor Zolly! She and the girls really like
playing with Peggy Potamus, though now that she's close
to three hundred kilos she's rather a dangerous swimming
companion in that great mudhole of hers. But you have to
take them all away," Laren said, with a flicking gesture. "It
is the right thing. It will not be easy. We'll have to come up
with a plan to spirit them off at the right moment when no
one is looking."

"Why?" Lani asked. "Why not just ask everyone to let
us take the animals back?"

The men stared at her blankly, then Laren laughed and
squeezed Lani's fingers affectionately. "Because they'll
say no, dear child. Just as I did. They'll hold fast to what
they think is theirs. You'll *have* to do it by subterfuge. And
what makes me sad is that if you succeed, they'll all start
over again, no doubt paying a ruinous premium to our supplier for a certificate of ownership."

Shona nodded. "Your supplier. It's Setve, isn't it?"

"Yes, it's our rambling physician," Laren burst out bit-
terly. "He charges us a mint for our medicine animals,
doesn't he, Bock? We had no choice but to pay whatever
he asked, since our own efforts to obtain eagles and tigers
and wolves on our own was as unsuccessful as if we were
trying to find unicorns. That's why we all don't have a
menagerie apiece now. Akeera cost us as much as one of
those terraformers out there. We were so happy to get what
we wanted we just never asked enough questions, and let

him take whatever extortionate profit he wanted. He must make enough to retire every time one of us sends him on safari. To be honest, this is why we wholeheartedly support Finoa's technology. Making a new animal from cells is cheaper than having Setve import them one by one."

"Probably," Shona said, thoughtfully, "his profits are not as great as you may think. Beside the difficulty of getting and transporting restricted animals, he must have been paying heavy bribes."

"Well, it must stop. Once you're gone, we'll do what we can to prevent this interplanetary smuggling ring from starting again, even if it means we'll never get what *we* want. That was Finoa's great threat, you know. This will tie the final ribbon around it. I'm ashamed that I was even an inadvertent part of the scheme. . . . What are you staring at, Bock?"

"You're going to help," his partner said simply. "I never thought you would be able to let Akeera go."

For the first time tears formed in the sardonic eyes. "It won't be easy. I . . ." He took Shona's hand. "Dear doctor, when you come for him, please, just make certain I'm not there. I won't be able to stand seeing him go away."

Shona nodded. "I will take very good care of him, I promise you."

Laren bowed his head, silent for a long time. Soon, he raised his head, then blinked hard. "All right. Let's make plans. We have to be very quiet about this, or sll-ccchh!" He made a throat-cutting gesture with one finger. "Who knows beside you?"

"Lani and Chirwl," Shona said. "She heard it for the first time when I told you, just a few minutes ago. Chirwl has made such good progress communicating with Three-eet that he might be able to help ease the trauma when we have to move him. I'm not telling the little ones until I have to."

"Can we be overheard in here?" Laren asked.

Bock looked at Shona. "Has Finoa ever been in here?"

"No. It's voice-sealed except to my family."

"Then we can't be. You'll need code words to every-one's homes. I have those. But how will you get the animals away?"

A shuffling sound made them all freeze. Laren's eyes flew wide open. "What was that?"

For a moment Shona feared that Finoa had managed to insinuate a spy into her house after all. But Bock leaped forward, and with a sweep of his meaty arm, came up with the hidden intruder.

"Alex!" Shona exclaimed.

"I wasn't listening," the little boy protested, cringing in the big man's grasp. "Well, I didn't start out to listen. I came to clean out the rabbit hutch. Then I heard what you were saying." He turned huge, frightened eyes to Shona. "Is someone really going to kill us?"

Shona gathered him up in her arms. "No, honey. Mr. Laren is exaggerating, isn't he?"

"That's right," Laren said, leaning confidentially close to Alex. "But there will be trouble unless you can really keep a secret. Can you?"

Alex's big hazel eyes scanned those of the adults around him and went very solemn. "Yes, sir," he said.

"Maybe you can help," Bock said, picking the boy up and putting him on his knee. He tapped Alex's small shoulder with a big forefinger. "Did your mother just tell me that you kept Akeera's tail feather in a collection? What kind of collection?"

ALEX tiptoed into the lab with a huge storage container in his arms. He put it gently down on the floor and unsealed the plastic lid "Here's one of Jamir's whiskers and some fur from when we combed him. And a painting Kajiro did with Dougie's fingerpaints. Some of his hair's stuck in the paint, but it's okay except for that. This is everything except Marvella's egg. That's in a case over my bed so it doesn't get squished."

"You show a lot of forethought," Bock said. He looked

into the container at the neatly arranged rows of scales, talons, feathers, clumps of hair, and bits of shell. "I don't want to mix everything up. And this is incontrovertible proof?"

"Absolutely," Shona said. "I'd already compared the DNA of each specimen to the excerpts. It's what made me decide to reply to the owners. I'll give you an uncoded copy of the list for comparison. That should convince anyone who is willing to listen."

"Alex, may we keep this?" Laren asked him, seriously, man-to-man. "We will need it later."

Alex's lips puffed out in a pout. "But I wanted to have souvenirs of everybody!"

"Honey," Shona said, "I promise you, you'll get all the souvenirs you want."

Alex thought about it for a moment. "All right."

"That's all we'll need," Laren said. "Now, close the door, and we'll talk about what you need."

"HEY, Shona!" the fair-haired woman said cheerily, beaming out from the screen. "No word from you in ages. Are they keeping you that busy? I thought you'd be going stir-crazy by now, shut away from the rest of the universe on a backwater, however elegant. Miss you and the kids. I got a short word from Gershom when he was close to Biloxi Station, where I was when I sent him a joke I found in a database. Hey, I thought your assignment was very hush but everyone seems to know where you are. Word gets around about famous people like you. Are you sure you don't want to help a struggling journalist out with an exclusive? Since you asked, here's a scan of my latest mini-doc. I think I was brilliant, but the ratings were so-so. Love you!"

Finoa frowned. She turned the monitor on the governor's desk back toward Hethyr. "That was the final message she received last night? Were there replies?"

The stocky woman matched her frown. "Yes. I audited

all of the outgoing transmissions myself. As I told you before, I saw no evidence that she's exporting information about your research or anything else we wanted kept confidential. I'm telling you, Finoa, I think you're wrong about her. Ever since my last conference with her she's been good."

"Let me see her replies," Finoa said.

"I will not," Hethyr said, indignantly. "As appointed head of government it's my responsibility to check suspect communications, but I am not authorized to allow a nonofficial to see those transmissions. Every person on this world has the expectation of reasonable privacy, including temporary employees."

Finoa laughed, a harsh sound. "What? Sudden scruples? You have allowed me to hear her messages before, plenty of times. In fact, if I wanted to report you to the Ethics in Government Committee I would have sufficient evidence to have you removed from your office. You were only appointed because none of the rest of us wanted the post."

"I'm a good administrator!" Hethyr thundered.

"Mama?" Jonquil's voice came faintly from outside the office. Hethyr immediately lowered her own.

"That's enough. I don't want my family disrupted," she hissed.

Finoa sat back, at her ease. The situation was at last back under her control. "The easiest way to be rid of me is to let me look at the messages, Hethyr," she said persuasively. "Was there nothing you had trouble understanding? I'd be happy to offer you my help. After all, Shona is a scientist, like me. Your expertise is in land management and legal counsel. If there was any medical jargon that slipped past you, it might be a clue."

Hethyr pressed her hands together until her knuckles turned white. Finoa waited. Implicit behind her demands was the same threat she'd used on Bock, though Hethyr never really needed that much persuasion to bend. As now.

"Very well," the governor gritted out, punching a code

into the console. "She did use some odd wording in one message. You can see that one. But not the others!"

Finoa smiled pleasantly. "Very well. As I said, I only offer my assistance."

Hethyr grumbled to herself as she swung the console to face her visitor.

"Hi, Susan," the recording from Dr. Shona began. "No, sorry, twin, I really can't help you write an expose. It's very *interesting* here, I have to tell you. Everyone is very nice. I miss being out in space. Contrariwise, I could live a long, healthy life here. This is *not* a backwater. The kids are doing well. I'm looking forward to watching your vid. I hope it's something they can enjoy. If they hear Auntie Susan sent something they can't see they'll be so disappointed. I'm counting the days until Gershom comes for us. He's short-hopping right now. I'm suffering from acute separation anxiety and hormone-related serotonin and dopamine depletion. Hey, miss you, too. Send again soon. Send to him, too. He'd love to hear from you. The two of you can work out where we'll meet when my contract is finally up. Make it somewhere with real food. I'm getting so spoiled I'll never be able to look at nutri again. Love you."

"Does that mean anything?" Hethyr asked. "Those last few phrases before the closing? Is it code?"

Code. Finoa drummed on her lower lip with the first two fingers of her right hand. Dr. Shona was just making a joke in medical-speak about missing sexual relations with her husband. However, that curious phrasing earlier in the message was unusual. It did sound familiar to her, but from where? It wasn't a common phrase in use on Jardindor. She and Shona had never met off-world, nor did they have much in common here.

Except for one interest: tri-dee vids, and specifically *Poor Mother McGrew*.

"Season thirty-two," she murmured. Yes. Any really devoted fan of the series would remember it.

That had been the story arc in which Ekarrin, a ten-year-old genius, was being held prisoner by a remnant enemy force that landed on the planet. Before his kidnaping he had annoyed his fellow orphans by inventing a trick of speech. Every sentence he started with "contrarywise," a phrase gleaned from the old Terran story *Alice in Wonderland,* meant the opposite of what it said. The subterfuge came in handy for putting forth a coded message to his rescuers. Ekarrin had been forced to make a recording to tell Mother McGrew to surrender or suffer a terrible attack, but "contrarywise, they have deadly weapons" informed the little band of orphans and medics they had nothing to fear. Dr. Shona was telling her friend that "contrarywise," she was perfectly safe and healthy. In other words, she did not feel safe. Finoa's eyes narrowed. Bock must have lied to her. He had tried to follow instructions. Most likely he had broken down and confessed to Shona. That was why she had been so adamant about keeping her family isolated lately. She was afraid. Good. But here she was telling a journalist of her fears. *That* was bad.

Hethyr could not help but notice the evil look in her eye. "What does it mean?" she asked. "Is she violating our agreement?" she demanded. "If she is I'll fire her and have her transported off-planet on the next garbage scow!"

Finoa waved a dismissive hand, paying little attention to Hethyr. "No, it's not that. There's nothing you should take action on at all."

"Then what does it mean?" Hethyr asked.

"Nothing special," Finoa said, standing up. "It's just a quote from *Poor Mother McGrew.* Doesn't it amaze you that so much of our shared language comes from the entertainment industry?"

With that, she left Hethyr to sort out her bruised ethics. She had a couple of backs to flay.

The console tone sounded. Shona had gone through the motions of having breakfast with the children, though she wasn't able to eat much. She got up to answer the call.

"Shona?" It was Dwan. The younger woman looked

worried. "Kajiro came back with his bouquet. I wondered if you were sick, or if I've done something wrong. I'd hoped you had forgiven me."

Shona had forgotten about the monkey's morning visits. "It's not your fault at all," she said, guiltily. "I've . . . changed the security codes a little."

"I understand," Dwan said. "I . . . I won't send any more until you say."

"Thank you for being understanding," Shona said. She felt as if she'd betrayed her friend with that thoughtless gesture. As if Dwan didn't have enough to contend with having Finoa for a neighbor. "Are you coming to dinner next week?"

Dwan was surprised. "I didn't know if you'd want us after I let you down."

"Not at all," Shona said, feeling guilty and apprehensive at the same time. "We'd love to have you."

TWENTY-THREE

TEN days to go. She'd made it through the next Friday party, though several times when Finoa had addressed her she had had the urge to get up and run away. Thanks to Laren's quick eye and quicker tongue coming to her rescue, Shona had been able to resist the urge to clap her children into body armor and flee into the hills. Every day seemed eternally long. Every time a message came from outside from Gershom or her friends Shona wished they could all climb on a reply beam and ride away.

Yelena was Shona's final patient of the day. The week before Shona had examined a small lump Yelena had found in her breast. It proved to be a small tumor, easily removed and treated with modern medicine. The follow-up visit was uneventful, except that Yelena had brought along a substantial bribe of citrine-and-gold jewelry to keep Shona from telling anyone about the growth, or that she had had to undergo a nonorganic form of treatment. Shona understood her mortification that in spite of her healthy lifestyle she had contracted cancer, but had managed to send her away without the tumor but with the necklace and earrings.

Shona felt guilty enough that she was about to betray her hosts, however righteous her cause. Over the last several days she had sat down with all the presents the Jardindorians had given her. The ones that she felt had been given out of genuine friendliness she planned to take with her. Anything that seemed to have been extorted by her patients' fear of exposure she was labeling for her neighbors to find there in Setve's house once she was gone. She did not want any bribes on her conscience.

Presents that had been given to the children or Chirwl were a more difficult matter. She didn't feel she could compel her family to give them back, even though in many cases their value far exceeded the presents Shona had received. Once Alex had gotten over the dismay at being given his friend's discarded toy, he'd become very attached to Nano-Man. Unless Gershom could negotiate a hefty discount they would be unlikely to afford a toy robot that cost as much as a new ring seal for the *Sibyl*. Then, there were all the clothes. Lani was careful with her garments, but anything the little ones wore couldn't be returned in good condition. Shona would have to consider them consumables, and lump them in with gifts of food, liquor, and candy. Lani would have to make her own decisions.

At that moment the girl was in her room, studying. She'd had an invitation to see Zolly, but admitted that after what she had heard from her mother and the Carmodys she was afraid to go. Shona regretted having told her, but she was going to need the girl's help for their elaborate plan, and she owed Lani a chance to do her own packing.

Shona sighed and looked out the conservatory door, which stood ajar. It was too beautiful a day to keep the house closed up. A gentle breeze brought in the scent of roses and clover. Saffie lay on her belly on the tile floor with her head toward the sunlight. Shona smiled at the dog. Saffie was really going to miss the garden. So was she. Not that she had been able to enjoy it much lately. With Finoa right next door she couldn't wander casually. The garden paths tempted her, but out of the haven of the house Shona had no protection. She had to appreciate the irony: after pushing her patients to get out and enjoy their tame wilderness, she was unable to emulate them.

"Mama," Jill said, coming into the glass-walled room dragging a doll. "What are you doing?"

"Sorting," Shona replied, hoping the answer would satisfy the ever-curious toddler.

"Pretty," the little girl said, reaching for a necklace in the "keep" pile. Dwan had given Shona the string of blue-green pearls, malachite, and gold and silver beads after the dinner party Finoa had ruined. That was a genuine gift, out of the kindness of her sympathetic heart. Dwan could have been a true friend. It was a shame that what she was about to do would certainly make Dwan hate her. Shona fingered the colorful strand ruefully, then fastened it around Jill's neck.

"There," she said. "It looks pretty on you, sweetheart."

Jill crowed with delight. She patted it with her little hands as she turned around, scanning the walls.

"There's a mirror in the hall near the door," Shona said, guessing what she was looking for. "Computer."

"Ready," the disembodied voice said.

"Make certain front door is locked. Go on, honey," she told Jill. The little girl sprang up and started toward the hall, then turned abruptly, as though she had just remembered what she had come in for.

"Mama, I'm hungry."

Shona glanced out at the shadows cast by the sun, guessing that it was about 1500 hours. "You know, so am I. It's about time for a snack. Let me finish what I'm doing, and I'll get something for us to share. All right? In the meanwhile, why don't you go see how pretty you are?"

Jill beamed. "Okay!" She dashed away. Shona could hear her footfalls thud on the heavy carpet.

"The door closes!" Chirwl's voice came in protest over the audio system. "I was smelling the air."

"Oh, Chirwl, I'm sorry. I didn't want Jill going out the front door. We're going to the kitchen for a snack. Join us?"

"I am already coming to meet you," Chirwl chirruped pleasantly.

"HOt fudge sundaes," Jill announced, as soon as they reached the kitchen. "Computer! I want a sundae." She turned to Shona with her lower lip stuck out. She had reached the age-three imperiousness and didn't like to have her orders ignored. "It's not listening to me. I want ice cream. Please?"

"Computer!" Shona called, sitting down at the central island. "Hot fudge sundaes. For Jill, one three hundred–milliliter scoop of strawberry ice cream, thirty milliliters chocolate fudge, thirty degrees celsius, one-third liter whipped cream—nuts, honey?"

"Yes!" Jill said, plumping herself down on the floor with her hands clasped in delight. Saffie sat beside her, panting happily. She sensed that her people were in a good mood, and that boded well for dogs. "Lots. And cherries. Six."

"Thirty grams chopped unsalted pecans, and six maraschino cherries. And sprinkles," she added, noting her daughter's shining eyes.

Jill jumped up. "Red and blue." Shona grinned. It was so nice to be able to indulge her children in such a treat. Real ice cream, all the way from Earth. Another one of her borrowed treasures.

"Red and blue what?" Alex said, coming in with Nano-Man under his arm.

"Sprinkles," said his mother. "We're having a hot fudge sundae snack, but only small ones. The Sandses are coming for dinner again."

"Okay! I want a pineapple split with vanilla ice cream and mango sherbet and lots of fudge. And sprinkles."

"Ugh," Shona said, making a face, but she gave the order. "Lani?"

"Yes, Mama?" the soft voice came through the house audio system, as the computer found the girl and opened up communications to her location. Music and Zolly's cheerful voice over the console could be heard in the background.

"Ice cream?"

"Yes, please! I will call you back, Zolly . . ."

Chirwl waddled in and clambered up the face of the nearest cabinet to the countertop, then leaped across to the island. He rolled onto his back and clasped his hand-paws on his chest. "This is most pleasant," he said, watching the robot arms splitting a pineapple with a knife and placing two succulent filets into a long dish. "Delicious aroma. I shall share the remainder."

Another trio of mechanical hands waited patiently behind the first two with containers of ice cream and a scoop. Deftly, they measured out the correct amount of each flavor and placed it in between the pineapple halves. Fudge and whipped cream were poured liberally over the whole creation, and cherries were placed at the peaks of each fluffy whitecap.

"Just like in the picture," Alex said, pleased, as the hands delivered the sundae to him. "Hey, computer, may I have a spoon, please?" The hands swung down, began to move along their ceiling track toward the utensil storage.

"Lazy," Shona said, countermanding the order. "Get it yourself, please, and bring enough for all of us. Napkins, too."

Alex grumbled a little, getting down from his stool and rustling through the drawer with loud clatterings. "I don't want my whipped cream to melt down."

Lani glided into the room and perched on the stool next to Shona. She glanced with interest at the tin roof sundae Shona was eating, so Shona ordered her the same thing.

Chirwl propped his fountain creation, full of fruit and chopped candy bars, on his belly and ate it with a modified baby spoon. He rocked back and forth with delight.

"Excellent flavors in combination," he said. "This is a most useful sort of technology."

"And it's centuries old," Shona said. "Ice cream long predates electricity."

"Most appealing," Chirwl said, licking his whiskers. "Nonmechanical and delicious."

"I love it," Jill said, brandishing her spoon. "I like Jardindor. I wish we could stay here forever."

Alex turned and gave his mother a very adult glance full of meaning. Shona realized Jill was the only one who didn't know their situation. With any luck, she wouldn't have a clue until ten days from then when the Meaders touched down and helped them pack up . . . everything.

Beep-beep. Beep-beep. Shona glanced up at the sound. "Someone's calling. Computer! Answer, please."

She waited. "Hello?" She heard a brief buzz, then nothing. "Hello?"

"Whoever it was hung up," Alex said, his mouth full of fudge sauce.

"I guess they didn't want anything," Shona said. With a shrug she went back to her sundae.

THE computer recognized the control code in the databurst. *Override program,* its internal system was informed. *Safety protocols—off. Loading datacrystal subprogram—active.*

ALEX let out a loud burp as he pushed his bowl away.

"Manners," Jill said, wiping her mouth with the back of her hand.

"Sorry," Alex told Shona, pointedly ignoring his sister.

"That was delicious," Lani said softly.

"Most flavorful," Chirwl agreed. "All empty spaces within me have been happily filled."

"Mine, too. I think dinner's going to be late tonight," Shona laughed, as the roboserver arms picked up all the dirty dishes and squeegeed the surface of the island clean. She looked around at the circle of smudgy faces. "Maybe I ought to let them wash you, too."

The arms reached down again. Shona watched them idly, admiring the intelligent design. A lens was placed at the juncture of each pair of tonglike pincers so the roboservers could "see" what they were doing. One dropped down toward her hand. She moved it aside. It moved with her, then clamped onto her wrist.

"Hey!" she exclaimed. "Let go! Computer, error! Have roboserver arm release my hand."

"Ready," the computer voice said. Another server dropped down next to the first one. Shona snatched her free hand out of its way. Instead, it clamped around her thigh. Shona found herself yanked into the air. She writhed, trying to get free.

"Mama!" Alex howled, jumping down from his chair. He pulled Jill away from the table. She screamed. More hands descended from the ceiling. Lani leaped up and ran for the door. It didn't open. She pounded on it, first with open hands, then fists. Hands descended on her shoulders, lifting her right off her feet. Chirwl sprang at the roboservers that grabbed at the children, trying to pry the fingers apart. An arm shot out of a wall and picked Chirwl off the mechanical assembly. The pincers closed on his neck. He squeaked once as his air was cut off.

The servers holding Shona shifted. She thought she could break out of their hold, but more came in, closing on her wrists and ankles. She was flipped over so she was hanging stomach down in the air. All four units pulled in opposite directions, making her spine crack. She gasped with pain. The house was going crazy! What had gone wrong?

"Mama!" Jill shrieked. She was hoisted up toward the

ceiling and whisked along the track toward the disposal unit.

"Jill!" Shona screamed. She lost all fear for herself, struggling to get one hand or one foot free. Her left hand tore loose, the skin ripped by a sharp metal edge. Blood seeped out of a jagged cut. Immediately another roboserver swooped in and recaptured her wounded wrist. As if to punish her, the clamp twisted the arm ninety degrees. Shona nearly fainted from the pain.

Chirwl's limp body followed Jill's, held tightly by the silver band around his neck. It took six hands to hold Alex, but he, too, was being swept toward the disposal. The bin's broad lid opened up, awaiting its first deposit.

"Computer, stop this! We are humans! We are alive! Close the disposal unit! Release all humans and ottles at once!" Lani was carried past her, held by five robot arms, her eyes huge with fear. "Computer! Halt! Cease program! Reboot!" The servers rolled inexorably forward. Jill was nearly dangling over the open disposer now. She was hysterical with terror. Shona fought harder. She had to save her daughter!

There had to be a way to stop the malfunction. Bock had made the house computer stop functioning with just a few words. What was it he'd said?

"Sumi . . . soma . . . somo . . . !" she blurted desperately. It was something like that. Blue Stars, what had he said?

She realized suddenly that the arms had halted their motion. Alex was kicking furiously at his bonds. He'd managed to get one leg free, and was battering the assembly holding his other leg with the toe of his shoe. She'd gotten the first part right, but she couldn't remember the other strange syllables.

"Lani," Shona said. "Honey, what was that code Bock used to block the computer the other day? *Think,* Lani. It was three words." She glanced at the ottle, swinging from the server arm. "Chirwl! Can you hear me?" How she wished he'd been in the room that day. He had a wonderful memory.

"Somo-nambu-something," Lani whispered. "I thought it was funny."

"That's right," Shona coaxed her. "Try and remember, darling. Somo-nambu-congratulation? Conflagration?"

"I think it was flab-something," Lani said.

"Confabulation?" Shona asked.

Suddenly, the arms opened. Shona threw her hands down to break her fall. She landed on her elbows and knees on the hard floor. Lani fell on the table. They both scrambled to their feet to save Jill, but they were too late. With a wild yell, the little girl dropped into the disposer.

"Jill!" Shona threw herself over the edge and stretched both arms down into the bin. Thank the Blue Star, the unit's operation had been suspended along with the room's other functions. Jill lay on a pile of half-digested banana peels and pineapple rind with her eyes wide open. She was too shocked to cry. Shona pulled her out and sat on the floor cradling the child, rocking her. Alex, with bruises on his cheek and knees, crawled over to put his arms around his mother and sister.

Lani sank beside them with Chirwl in her arms. He wasn't moving. All of them needed medical attention. There was only one safe place.

"Come on," Shona said, struggling to her feet. Her wrists and ankles hurt terribly, but nothing seemed to be broken. "Head for my lab. Hurry."

Alex clung to Shona's leg as she listened at the door. "Ready?" she asked him. With a solemn face, he nodded. "If you see Saffie or Harry, grab them. Let's . . . go!"

Shona shouldered the door open and dashed through the dining room. As if they had been waiting for her, roboserver claws reached for her. Jill screamed. Shona ducked her head over the toddler, and shouted out the code words.

"Somo-nambu-confabulation!" The arms stopped moving at once.

"Somo-nambu-confabulaton!" they all yelled together at the robot arms in the hall.

Saffie heard their voices and came galloping up the corridor, pursued by the vacuum unit, which was whipping its hose attachment at the dog's back. Shona shouted again. The vacuum stopped. They ran toward the clinic.

"Harry!" Alex exclaimed. He dove toward the conservatory door.

"Alex, come back!" Shona called.

"Somo-what-mama-said!" Alex yelled. He came pelting out of the glass house with the cat in his arms. Harry must have been attacked. His tail was puffed up like a furry balloon. Alex's face bore pink scratches from grabbing the frightened cat.

The arms in the clinic snatched at their clothing until they were stilled by the magic words. Shona shifted Jill to her hip so she could press her palm on the identification plate on the module door. The door slid aside. Everyone piled into the room. Shona hastily palmed the door shut and flattened herself against it. Safe.

"How is Chirwl?" Shona asked Lani. She handed Jill to Lani and laid the ottle on the floor. She put her head down on his chest to listen. With her fingers she pried open his mouth and flattened his tongue to clear his breathing passage. Immediately, his chest expanded, and he gasped. "Chirwl, can you hear me?"

"I live again," Chirwl whistled. He felt his neck with his claw tips. "Hard grip . . . why were the machines angry?"

Shona glanced at Jill, who huddled in Lani's lap with her head pressed into Lani's shoulder, her small body shaking. "It was just a mistake," she said, pointedly. "Honey?" she asked, coaxing Jill to look up. "It's all right. We're safe here. These walls can stop a meteor bombardment. I want to look at your wrists."

Jill shook her head, refusing to lift her face. "But the ceiling tried to eat me!" she wailed.

"Oh, honey, it was an accident," Shona said, wishing she believed it. "The computer had the hiccups. It thought you were a plate. How about that? You might have gotten a bath in the dishwasher."

Jill's lip stopped quivering as the corners of her mouth tilted up at the funny image. "Would I have to go round on the turntable?"

"Yes, you would," Shona said. She picked the toddler up by the middle and swung her in a circle. "Round and round . . ."

Jill let out a shriek of fear. Shona had accidentally clutched the child where the mechanical arms had grabbed her. Immediately she dropped to her knees, cradling Jill. "Oh, honey, I'm so sorry. Oh, darling, I'm bleeding on you." Tears running down her face, she rocked the child.

Alex crawled over and tugged on her arm. "Hey, Mama, I made a joke. What kind of peas perform in circuses?"

Grateful for the distraction, Shona asked, "I don't know, honey. What kind of peas?"

"Calliop-peas! Get it?" He nudged Jill, laughing in her face until she laughed, too. Shona threw her arm around him. Thank heaven for him. Sometimes he was so grown-up.

"I think you need a nap," Shona said, picking Jill up very gently. "Come on, let me take a look at your owies. Then, I'll put fresh bedding on the crash couches."

"Stay with me, Mama," Jill pleaded.

"For a minute," Shona said. "But Saffie will stay with you the whole time. Maybe even Harry, too." At the sound of her name the dog stood up, tail waving. The cat, his back fur still bristly, looked planted for the duration out of reach behind the equipment on the corner lab table. He didn't seem to have been injured, so Shona concentrated on everyone else's cuts and bruises, including her own.

When Jill finally fell asleep, Shona tiptoed out to tend to the others and, at last, herself.

"It would seem that call started it," Chirwl whispered.

"The one where nobody was there," Alex added.

"Someone was," Lani said, with a worried frown.

Heavy pounding on the module shell startled them all.

Shona grabbed all of her family in her arms and put her body between them and the door. Was this another attack? The audio pickup crackled into life.

"It's Bock," a deep voice said. Chirwl scurried away from the group hug and up onto the console. He turned on the external video pickup. The dark-skinned man's face appeared on the screen. "Ev called me. They've been trying to get in. The roboservers are all going berserk. Has there been a malfunction?"

"Oh, yes!" Shona said, about to pour out her terror to him when she noticed Ev's and Dwan's concerned faces behind him. They must be talking on Bock's pocket comm-unit. "Oh, heavens, I forgot all about them coming for dinner."

Bock grimaced, and Shona guessed how she must look: her hair and clothes were messy, and her face bruised. "I'll shut everything down."

DWƎN was apologetic. "I should have called, but you never forget," she said. They were in the kitchen. She was cooking scrambled eggs and bacon from the refrigerator. Shona stood in a corner with the rolling island in front of her as she cut up melons and strawberries for fruit salad so she could keep an eye on the roboserver arms. They all hung limply from the ceiling, following Bock's deactivation of the whole system, but she didn't trust them. "I thought about it for a moment, then I wondered if I was being pushy."

"There was a call," Shona said. "No one was on the other end."

"Well, it wasn't me," Dwan said. "Oh! Unless I activated your number by accident. I'm sorry.

"I don't understand it," Dwan continued, glancing out into the corridor. The big doors were blocked open with heavy pieces of furniture. Ev and Bock were still in the main computer room. "Setve's system was modernized just a short time ago. Nothing like this should have happened. The governors in the program should have prevented the robots from attacking *people*."

Her children sat in a rapt circle around Alex in the exact center of the room as he told them about their mishap. "And it grabbed us, like this!" His hands formed fierce claws that nipped at Dougie's little sister Ginny, making her squeal with mock terror. Shona was grateful for his resilience. He had already sublimated the terror and was enjoying the adventure aspect of the event. Jill was still asleep in the module. Chirwl had elected to stand guard over her. He claimed he hadn't been hurt, only choked unconscious. Shona had examined him and decided he was telling the truth. Ottles were strong and resilient.

It had grown dark by the time the men returned. Bock's face was grim.

"I've never seen anything like this," Ev said, holding out a handful of little components, all blackened and cracked. "Half a dozen datacrystals just corrupted, and two of them practically melted. That's usually caused by a power surge, but we haven't had a big lightning storm in weeks."

"I'd better check the power plant," Bock offered. "It's on my way home."

"Would you like some dinner?" Dwan asked, holding out a plate of food.

"No, thank you," Bock said very formally. "I had better go home. Mona cooked dinner. She would be very disappointed if I didn't do justice to the meal."

The Sandses shook hands with him.

"I'll walk you to the door," Shona said. Dwan rose. "No, everyone go on and eat. I won't be long."

"It was sabotage," Bock said in a low voice, as soon as they were out of earshot of the kitchen. "Those components were planted in the system. I can't tell you how long ago. The attack was triggered by some outside agency."

"The console call," Shona said.

"Yes. It came from Finoa, but you had already guessed that, hadn't you?"

"Yes. But how could she have put anything into the house computer? Ever since Gershom set up the security system no one but me could have entered that room without my permission." Then a memory came back to her. "But Robret came in the back door during my party. I know I locked it."

Bock shook his head. "He and Setve are close. He'd know the override codes for the doors. If he attempted to enter secure areas an alarm would have gone off."

"Well, it wasn't noisy enough to mask an alarm," Shona said. "Then who? And when?"

"Unless they walked in there on their own, I have no idea."

Shona frowned. "Well, I have." She told him about Nano-Man. Bock pressed his lips together.

"Yes. That would do it. Those toys are easy to program. She must be mad. I have never known her to behave so irrationally. If she knew all of what we are up to she would be worse. I've told you to be careful. Now you must be much more careful. Trust no one. Laren and I will do our best to help safeguard you. It is only another ten days."

"Nine and a half," Shona said. A wail interrupted them. "Jill's awake. I'd better get back in there."

"Call me any time," Bock said.

"I will. Oh, I've been so upset I haven't asked: how's Laren?"

Bock smiled for the first time. "Perfect. He sends his love." He kissed her on the cheek, then disappeared out into the night.

TWENTY-FOUR

THERE was no hiding this attack. By the next day the news of the alleged malfunction was all over the colony. Shona received calls from all of her neighbors offering apologies for such a terrible accident. She accepted them with bemusement in her voice. She still had to pretend outwardly that she had no idea what had caused the computer to go awry. Yet she knew the truth, and Finoa knew she knew, and she knew Finoa knew she knew. Shona's greatest advantage was that Finoa could not know of her impending departure. Bock had cautioned her never to speak of it openly on a communications channel, nor to send details in unencrypted messages.

In the afternoon Bock delivered in person a small data-crystal containing override codes for all the houses in the settlement. He helped her work out program sequences that would cause each house to send its transport cart to the nearest point to each animal's location, load it safely, and converge upon Shona's module at approximately the same moment. When that moment would be, however, she had yet to work out.

"Let's see," Shona said to herself, making a note on the list of animals she had made on a piece of stationery. Like everything else on Jardindor it was gorgeous, expensive, and nearly priceless. It was also literally the only paper she could find in the house. Every sheet was translucent as a plasheet, except that it had an enticing crispness not found in plastics. She and Gershom had carried some quality stationery as cargo once, but never owned so much as a page of it, and there she was scribbling over its pristine surface with one of Alex's art pencils. She wished styli worked on paper, and that one could eradicate marks with the touch of an icon, too. The beautiful page was covered with erasures, crossings out and diagrams that reminded her she was a doctor, not an artist.

"Elephant. Pretty much the whole sleeping room, because Jamir is going to be in with Lady Elaine. I wonder if Peggy and Three-eet can safely cohabit once their sopophedrase wears off. Hippopotami are supposed to be pretty aggressive, but I heard dolphins can take care of themselves. But would he be vulnerable when he sleeps?" She paused. Peggy probably couldn't use a seawater pool. That meant two tanks, both of them very cramped. It was a shame she couldn't ask anyone for advice.

She scanned down her list. Oh, but there, she'd forgotten about the platypus. Chirwl had not seen it on his visit to Finoa's house, but it must be there. It, too, lived in water. They were supposed to be very aggressive, too. And was it a saltwater or freshwater beast? Must she arrange for three separate tanks, if Peggy and the platypus needed different water temperatures?

Chirwl was over at the Sandses'. If the family left him alone with the dolphin he was going to try to explain to Three-eet the upcoming transit. Shona wanted to lessen the trauma as much as possible. "Tell him," she'd suggested to Chirwl, "that at the end of the journey he'll be back in his home waters." She hoped.

The logistics of bringing them home amounted to a lot more than just moving the critters. She was going to have to take food for them, lots of it. She'd been planning to strip out Setve's freezer for fish and meat and take all the fruits and vegetables that she could out of the orchard and the garden—thank heaven it was full summer. The rewards wouldn't come until she'd returned each animal. Her wages, which she was certain she would now not be able to collect, could go to pay for the food. If not, she was leaving Setve an IOU, collectible much later, when she had earned the money to pay for the food. She was certain he would be reluctant to sue her in court, knowing that the details of what she was doing would come out. The IOU was protection against a financial judgment, which wouldn't require an open trial.

She also needed things like fresh fodder for the elephant, the zebra, and the other bulk-eaters. Hanya stopped by that morning to express sympathy at the exact moment Shona was having the long grass along one side of the property mowed and gathered up into bales. She'd had to explain hastily that she was concerned about not being able to see the road in that direction, toward Finoa's. Hanya nodded knowingly, and gave Shona a pat on the arm before she went.

Shona knew there was one more item she had to deal with before her new "guests" were on board: sanitation. Since none of these passengers could be counted on to use a disposal, she needed bedding that she could recycle or sift. And there would be a lot of shoveling and scrubbing. But, oh, for how long? She had better assume it was going to be for a month. A "clean room" needed to be maintained to use as an infirmary, though she still had little experience in veterinary medicine, and for the children to stay in until transport aboard the Meaders' ship was accomplished. Thank heavens that most of the animals were small. Even so, it was going to be a tight squeeze.

The real question was, could she pull this off? She would have only one chance. The transport issue was going to be enormous. She had to whisk everything out from under her neighbors' noses and into her module correctly the first time, and she was going to have to do it very quickly. Lani and Alex were ready to lend their help. All they needed was the right diversion. But what? She couldn't simply point in the opposite direction and shout, "Look over there!" She needed hours of time.

She almost laughed. The obvious time to have that diversion, when everybody would be concentrating on something else directly under their noses, was the mah jongg tournament. It was going to be held at the Governor's Mansion. Since Hethyr was not in possession of a stolen animal, Shona did not have to worry about extracting Argent while the entire community watched. Hethyr and Dina were keen mah jongg players.

Ah, but not everyone was playing. Hmm. She needed a second diversion, one that would get undivided attention. Why had the Jardindorians summoned her here? She would let it be thought that she was going to give them what they wanted. Shona scribbled down a few notes, and finished them with a triumphant flourish. There! She had it all in place.

"HEY, there, little Shona." Pop Meader's cheerful face appeared on the screen. Everyone was "little" to him, including Gershom. His lean frame was nearly two and a half meters tall. "We just came out of jump on the edge of the system. Old Bessie's navigation system needs a little bit of an overhaul, so we don't like to come in too close to a star. Best as I can figure it, we're going to make landfall in your neck of the woods on around about Thursday, planetary date, three days from now. Say, this is a pretty system. I haven't been here in a while. Mom and I are looking forward to seeing you, honey.

"If you can spare an old man time for a visit, let us know. I'm *assuming* you have time for Mom," he added with a glint in his eye, as a spare woman with thick, straight white hair pulled back in a knot slid in next to him in front of the pickup. "It's me you have to make special consideration for."

"This old man's always trying to fish for sympathy," Mom Meader said, with a grin. Her smile threw her beautiful cheekbones and jawline into relief. "Don't you pay attention. Gershom said you'd be glad to have company. If not, at least we've kept our word to say hello. We'd have done that anyhow."

Shona didn't wait for the message to finish. They could not land on Thursday, or her plans would be ruined. At once she hit the reply stud.

"Hi, Mom and Pop!" she said. "We're really looking forward to seeing you on Friday. It's been a long time. I'd love to have you stop by. Give me a call when you're close! Wait until you see this place. It's wonderful. Safe journey!"

With trembling hands, she sent off the message. All her plans turned upon him catching the clue she gave him.

FINOA'S precise hands plucked the caul from a newborn rabbit, turned the tiny, squirming creature over to examine it, then placed it against the doe's teat. It snuggled in and began to suckle, a sight that would normally have had Finoa regarding it with maternal pride. Instead, her face was stiff and expressionless.

"It looks perfect," Robret offered. He stood on the other side of the incubator, watching his wife cautiously.

"It is," she said, snapping the syllables off. "We won't have the results of my greater experiment yet. The control organisms are all coming out without flaw." She sounded like a robot. Robret knew that meant she was unbelievably angry.

"It had to be dumb luck," Robret said.

"I don't believe in luck," Finoa said, closing the incubator and looking him square in the eye. "She could only have overridden the computer and stopped the house from carrying out my instructions with the base code, and there is no way she could know it."

"Bock Carmody and Everette Sands both know it," Robret pointed out. "They have been defending her."

"Against me?" Finoa asked, standing as erect as a statue. "That would be foolish. They know what power I hold in my hands."

Robret shook his head. "Hethyr is right. You are starting to sound like a soap-opera character."

"She stands in the way of my legitimate pursuit of scientific progress," Finoa said. "Look at the way she interfered with my work with the ottle. In the wild, doesn't a mother have a right to defend her cubs? She has inconvenienced me, she's put my work in jeopardy, but worst of all, she's embarrassed me. Such a perception undermines my authority."

Robret's eyebrows rose. "Are you ready to try for an ottle embryo?"

"No," Finoa said. "Not until the host mother is ready again. That will only be a few weeks from now. I can wait."

"Is the tissue sample you obtained sufficient?"

Finoa pursed her lips. "I doubt it. He is an alien organism. The similarities between Terran species and Poxtian species may not be enough for the process to produce healthy offspring. I will undoubtedly need more."

"You won't get it," Robret said. "Shona's on guard now. You can hardly get her alone to talk at a Friday party, and the ottle's nowhere to be seen if you go in for an appointment. I've tried two or three times. The last visit Ev Sands was working on her console. I think he was there to watch me."

"Well, we can't do anything until after the cargo ship has come and gone," Finoa said, turning away to wash her hands. "They expect to see her alive. But during the mah jongg game I plan to arrange for a little accident."

Robret understood. "Jamir's been a little testy lately."

"He is on half rations until Saturday." She smiled, a

cold, wintry expression. "Who could have foreseen that he would get out again?"

"The house codes have been changed," Robret said. "I have tried the doors every day while she's taking her children to Ev's for school."

"The dog has to go out," Finoa said, taking a portable ultrasound unit out of a cabinet. "The children play outside. The door will be opened from the inside. It's just an . . . accident waiting to happen."

Robret paused for a moment, then nodded. "I suppose you're right. After all, she's not one of us."

"She has never fit in," Finoa said over her shoulder as she left the lab. "I have to check on Lady Elaine."

TWENTY-FIVE

THE morning of the tournament dawned clear and beautiful. Shona was awake as soon as the sun rose. As much as she could do ahead of time, she had done. Her things were packed, as were Lani's and Alex's. Shona distracted Jill by letting her play in the pool with Chirwl while she collected all the little girl's clothes and treasures, and tucked them into a storage compartment beside her crash couch in the soon-to-be-stuffed laboratory module.

Chirwl trotted into the dining room, his fur still spiky from shaking himself dry.

"Are you ready?" Shona asked him.

"All as much as possible, save for nutrition," the ottle replied calmly, clambering up onto his chair. Shona cringed as the roboservers swung down, but they behaved themselves, serving Chirwl's breakfast without a hitch. "My friend Saffie and I will be safe."

At the sound of her name the dog looked up from her bowl. She looked from Chirwl to Shona. Shona patted her on the head and gave her a sausage from her own plate. She felt a little guilty involving her pet and her friend in her plot, but she could think of no other ruse that would keep the Jardindorians' attention off her, her module, and the arriving space ship.

As soon as they finished eating, Shona took the children out in the garden. Over the hedge she could see Saffie, with Chirwl perched in his pack on her back, trotting away down the road toward the ocean. The smaller house cart rolled almost silently alongside. Saffie kept trying to get up on the cart and ride, but Chirwl coaxed her to stay on the road. Shona heard the dog whine in confusion and disappointment as they disappeared beyond the trees.

"Good luck," she whispered.

HEtHYr and Dina went all out in their efforts to make the mah jongg tournament an occasion. The portico of the opulent Governor's Mansion had been covered by a half-curtain of red silk with a circular pictogram painted on it in black. Each of the guests, when he or she arrived, was forced to bend slightly to pass beneath it. Inside, the entry hall had been draped with priceless tapestries. Every parent instinctively grabbed for his or her small children's hands to keep them from pulling the colored hangings down.

Alex let out a happy cry of recognition. Dougie ran up to greet him, followed by Lark, the greyhound. She had a wide gold collar wrapped around her neck. Dougie was dressed in a little embroidered coat that fastened with silk frogs and a round cap with a button on top.

"You look cool," Alex said enviously.

"We've got outfits for you and Jill, too," Lewis said.

"We have games planned following today's theme," Zolly said, resplendent in aquamarine damask slit up the side to show soft silk trousers. Her thick, curly hair had been pulled back on her head and decorated with a tall, enameled comb. "Come on!"

Alex gave a worried glance to his mother, but she gestured that he should go with the others. It would be a few hours more until she needed to make her move.

The great room was divided by plants and waist-high screens into a grid of nine zones, each tinted by different colored lights.

"Feng shui," Dina said, mysteriously.

Game tables were set in each of the eight outer squares with room for four players each. Plenty of chairs for spectators sat on slightly raised platforms around the outer edge. In the center was a single table with a ribbon hanging around it on low pylons. Shona guessed that was where the championship round would be played. The chamber was filled with people chattering in small groups. The competitors wore silk cords around their right wrists, the color of which indicated their assigned tables. On one side of the great room was a table decorated with jasmine and orchids. Pendant gems, each a different color of the rainbow, set on golden chains were nested in bowls of white rose petals, four on either side of the centerpiece, which consisted of a polished wood carving of a dragon with five toes on each foot—an Imperial dragon. It was holding an ancient box whose lid was open to show a mah jongg set inside. The tiles were yellow with age, had been incised and painted with a hair-fine brush in black, red, blue, green, and gold.

"This set was owned by an ancient emperor of Terran China," Hethyr explained. "It goes to the winner of today's contest. They can't make ivory sets any longer."

"Hah," Ewan said. "Unless Finoa's elephant loses a tooth, huh?"

Finoa glared at him. "That was in very poor taste."

She might have pursued him further, but Ewan retreated behind Bock, who regarded the scientist with a mild look.

A buffet was laid out along the opposite side of the great room, all nonmessy finger foods, like pâté in tiny pastry shells and vegetable coins topped with crème fraîche and caviar. Though it was lunchtime, Shona doubted her stomach would tolerate food. She chose a cup of jasmine tea and went to her seat in the green zone.

"You look pale," Agneta said, sitting down beside her.

"It's the lights," Shona said, with a weak smile. "I'm just nervous. I've never played competitively."

"*Any* time you play mah jongg it's competitive," Agneta assured her.

"Where's Chirwl?" asked Robret, appearing suddenly and silently at her shoulder. Shona gasped, and the hot liquid sloshed in her cup.

"At home," Shona said, when she'd recovered enough to take a sip. "He came up with a new topic to add to his dissertation."

She could tell he was disappointed, but could not bring herself to say, "You'll see Chirwl another time," because if everything worked out, he never would. He was too dangerous an acquaintance.

Hethyr appeared at the doorway. Her stocky form was gloved in a shiny red silk satin jacket and trousers embroidered with phoenixes and dragons. Behind her, Dina stood smiling in white silk, with the same embroideries. Hethyr cleared her throat, and everyone turned to look at her.

"Will everyone take their places, please?" she said. "The game will begin at the stroke of noon."

In truth, Shona thought, as she scooted her chair in.

THE first round would take about two hours. The semifinals, between the winners of all eight tables, would run the same. The two top scorers from those tables would meet in the center. Shona hoped that she'd given Chirwl enough of a head start. Saffie needed to leave at least a three-mile spoor.

"Are you ready?" Laren said, coming to lean over Shona's shoulder. He looked a little pale, but as witty and dry as ever. "I expect to face you in the finals."

He winked as he went to sit down at his table in the pur-

ple zone. Shona relaxed a bit. Her allies were gathering.
She glanced back at him gratefully. He flicked his hand
impatiently, as though to tell her to concentrate on what
she was doing.

Lewis, dressed importantly in dark-blue silk, marched
around the room, depositing polished wooden boxes on the
tables. Ewan, as the player sitting in the East position,
opened the box on the green table. Inside was a mah jongg
set carved of white stone streaked with bright green.

"Gorgeous," Agneta said. "Imperial jade." The characters on each were incised and brightly painted with marvelous skill. All three suits, circle, wan or character, and
bamboo, were depicted using different textures. The season and flower tiles were tiny landscapes. They must have
taken a craftsman a year to create.

"Priceless," Shona breathed. The others shot her a look
of disapproval. "Sorry." She'd broken that cardinal
Jardindorian rule about discussing value. Ewan's left eyebrow stayed up near his hairline while he built the tiles into
four walls, then dealt them out four at a time to the others.
Shona, at North, dropped her eyes to her stake, and busied
herself arranging her hand. Ewan waited until all of them
were ready and looking at him. He tossed a tile into the
now empty center.

"Four wan," he said.

POP Meader leaned over from the helm and peered at the
big blue circle on the tan planet rotating swiftly underneath
his ship's belly.

"Looks like a big eyeball, doesn't it? Hello, Jardindor,
this is the *Elizabeth R.*, coming in with a shipload of goods
and your terraformers," he said into the audio pickup. "Requesting landing instructions for our shuttle."

"Ready," said a computer-generated voice.

"Aw, heck, it's one of those," Pop said to Mom Meader,
who was at the navigation station of the elderly cargo ship.

"Hook into it and let it guide us in. I've got to get on the horn to Shona."

SHONA held her breath. It was the last round. She was in East position, looking at a hand that had been dismaying when it was first dealt, but she had had some amazing luck: three flower tiles had turned up, including her own Plum Blossom, giving her score a good boost and one double. By ruthless discarding she had made three pungs, sets of three identical tiles, one concealed. Only about sixteen tiles remained in the walls. The cool jade tingled under her fingertips. She and Robret were nearly neck and neck, having driven Ewan and Agneta into negative territory. She, Shona thought smugly, could win. Engrossed in the game, she had entirely forgotten her fear. To finish, she needed one more set of three, a pung or a chow, a small straight, plus a pair. She already had a pair of North Winds. They'd be of no value to her as scoring tiles, since she was East, but when she had drawn the second one she decided it was worth keeping. The remaining tiles in her hand were a Four of Circles and two Fives. All she needed to win was another Five or a Six. If she drew a Six, she would win, but with a low total, maybe not enough to best Robret's score so far, but if a Five, she'd have a special hand worth an extra hundred points.

Spectators had scooted their seats forward. They were whispering about the hands they could see and speculating on the others. Finoa's table had already finished its round. The serene expression on her face told Shona that she had been the winner. She pulled a chair off the dais and tucked it right in between Shona and Robret. It made Shona uncomfortable to have her mortal enemy centimeters away. She focused her attention on the tiles.

Agneta was an aggressive player, snatching up her new tile and smacking her discards down into the center. Ewan wore a sly grin that led Shona to believe he knew what she was looking for but was holding it back to spike her hopes.

Robret never lost his cool. He could shoot a look at the rejected tiles and rearrange his hand to accommodate them before Shona had time to blink.

Four remaining. Shona felt the tension between her eyebrows. She had not seen either of her hoped-for numbers. They must still be there. They must! It was her turn. She reached for the second-to-last tile in the wall.

"Excuse me," Dina said. "Dr. Shona, Lani is here to see you."

The other guests made way for the girl, who was pale and worried.

"Mama, didn't you get my message?" she asked, rushing to Shona.

"No, honey," Shona said, checking her shiplink. "I had to turn it off during the game."

"Computer!" Dina announced. "Scroll incoming messages for Dr. Shona."

"Ready," the disembodied voice said. "One message."

"Never mind," Shona said, pushing back her chair to take her daughter's hand. "What was in it, sweetheart? What's wrong?"

"Saffie is missing. She got out."

Now for the performance of a lifetime, Shona thought, pulling Lani close. She lowered her voice, but not so much the people hovering beside her couldn't hear. "How long has she been gone?"

"I don't know," Lani said, truthfully.

"This is bad," Shona said.

"What's the matter?" Dina asked. "Surely she'll just come home."

Shona shook her head. "She's gone into heat. There are too many male dogs in the colony. She mustn't mate. I've got an agreement with the breeder who sold her to me. Her fertility is controlled by contract. If she has puppies they'll all be vaccine dogs. They'd be born here, and I'd be in deep trouble. I would have to pay a hefty fine if I bring them off-planet with me."

She could see everyone looking at one another wondering if the others had gotten the same idea they'd had: to capture Saffie and breed her to their male dogs. Because it would put Shona in a bind, they might be able to negotiate possession of the offspring of a rare and precious species, and the rest of the universe need never know. *Uh-uh,* Shona thought. *You've had the last of your rare species. I'm about to see to that.*

"We'll all help you find her," Robret said immediately. "Which way did she go?"

Shona turned to Lani, who had not seen Chirwl and Saffie leave.

"I don't know. She's always been curious about the ocean."

"Isn't she wearing a transponder chip?" Finoa asked.

"Yes, but it doesn't transmit," Shona said. "Those interfere with our navigation equipment. Hers is only detectable if you run a reader over her. We'll just have to track her somehow."

"Argent's an expert tracker," Dina said. "Do you have anything that belongs to her?"

Lani was ready for that question, too. "Yes. Here is her blanket. I . . . I just held on to it when I left the house." She held out the plaid wool square, almost reduced to a rag by Saffie's nibbling around the edges.

"Is she likely to have taken off across country or on a road?" Robret asked.

"Probably she'd stay on the road," Shona began. "She's a ship dog, not used to wilderness . . ."

That was all her erstwhile neighbors needed to hear. Everyone demanded the house computer bring around their carts. Lewis ran for his flitter.

Shona, with Lani behind her, made her way through the crowd to the children's crèche. She was taking a gamble that no one would return home for their dogs lest Dina and Argent steal a march on them and follow Saffie's track before they could. They'd follow her footprints, which Shona guaranteed they would find.

"What's going on?" Alex asked. Jill swarmed up into

Shona's arms. She was wearing a miniature happi coat and black silk slippers. Alex threw aside a Chinese warrior's helmet but kept on the surcoat of sewn plates.

"Saffie ran away," Shona said. "Everyone is helping us to look for her."

"Oh, no!" Jill cried. "Saffie all right?"

"I'm sure she's fine," Shona assured her. She looked around for the children's toys and outer clothes. Jill's green sunhat was stuffed underneath the drawbridge of a toy castle, but her jacket and Alex's were neatly hung up with the other children's garments. Shona took her time getting them ready. The house was deserted by the time they got to the front door.

"We have to find Saffie," Jill said, nearly in tears.

"We will, darling," Shona said, as she stepped over the threshold. "Swordfish," she said over her shoulder. She didn't hear the humming of the household system, but knew it was working. The message she had had Lani send to the house contained embedded instructions designed by Bock. It would call all the other houses and set off their house systems, then shut down to prevent the communication system talking to any of the other houses for at least twenty-four hours. It would also wipe her digital password out of the computer so Hethyr could no longer read Shona's mail. That measure of privacy she was taking back as soon as she could.

All hundred Jardindorians crowded the crushed-stone circular drive in front of the Governor's Mansion, getting into their carts and arguing with their neighbors to get out of the way. They were all focused on the prize ahead of them, not thinking of their own homes. The race was on. Shona knew they wouldn't miss the intercommunication systems until after Saffie was found. They each hoped to get the black dog home before anyone else. She recalled what Bock had said about rare breeds, the rarer the better, and what was more rare than a pedigreed Bernese Mountain vaccine dog? Lani's wide eyes were on her as she ordered the cart to move.

"Where is Saffie?" Alex asked, knowingly, as soon as the other carts had pulled ahead of them on the road. Shona smiled at him.

"She's out there with Chirwl, who's telling her where to go. I only hope they can get back in time. Are you all packed?"

"Uh-huh. Can I bring Nano-Man? It's not his fault he was a traitor. I can reprogram him."

"Certainly, sweetheart," Shona said. "We can download instructions from the company as soon as we're back on the *Sibyl*."

"Poor Saffie!" Jill kept saying. "She might be hurt."

TWENTY-SIX

AS James rolled into the drive of the doctor's mansion, Shona saw a virtual traffic jam around the back corner that housed her laboratory module. Bock's program had worked exactly as he had said it would. She could see that most of the animals had already arrived. Some of them, like Stripes, the okapi, had been tethered to keep them from jumping off the flatbed carts that had carried them. Others were in cages, leaping from side to side and chittering agitatedly. The rest were fairly placid and easygoing, eating hay or feed. More food was piled up on the rear of the carts or on top of the cages. A heavy metal container with air slits near the top had to be Peggy's conveyance. As yet the pigmy hippo was still calm. Shona heard serene grunts echoing from inside the shelter.

Two very large carts trundled up just as Shona ordered James to a halt. If nothing else had convinced her she was really concocting the Great Animal Escape, this did it. Her heart almost leaped into her throat to see Jamir prowling up and back in his caged enclosure. Behind him, on a vast platform surrounded by endless bales of hay, stood Lady

Elaine, calmly chewing on a mouthful of fodder. Her pregnancy barely made a bulge in her great, wrinkled sides. If Shona hadn't known about her condition, she'd never have detected it. Lady Elaine's trunk curled gracefully around underneath her mouth to tuck in a wisp of grass. She lifted her head, and met Shona's eyes. Shona gulped. This was the moment of success or failure. If anyone came along now, it was all over. Heaven knew what they'd do to her— or her children. A sick feeling grew in the pit of her stomach.

"Circus train!" Jill shrieked happily.

Shona grinned, the tension easing. The procession of arriving animals did look like a parade. She might as well get into the spirit of it, or she was going to exhaust herself with emotional storms before they ever got onto the ship.

Which, when she came to think of it, was her next concern.

"Did Pop Meader get in touch with you?" she asked Lani, as they picked the children off the cart and hurried into the house.

"Yes," Lani said. "They have to deliver the terraformers first, then they are coming here. It won't be long."

"I hope not," Shona said, locking the door behind her. "Toast and jam!" she shouted.

Whirring inside the door frame told her that the locking mechanism was sealing and shutting off input from any system for the next forty-eight hours. She glanced into the rooms as she passed, making certain that nothing she wanted to take with her was still in them. She would not have time to double back again.

"Are you all packed?" she asked Alex and Lani.

"Yes, Mama!" they chorused. Alex took the steps two at a time to the upper level.

"Are we going on a trip?" Jill asked, looking around her in bewilderment and excitement.

"Yes, we are," Shona said, picking her up for a hug. "We're going to see Papa."

"With all the animals? Yay!"

After that, Shona had no worries about Jill kicking up a fuss. She started listing everything she was going to tell Gershom when she saw him. "And we slid into the water, and the dolphin laughed at me, and Kajiro pulled my hair. . . ."

Chirwl wouldn't be back until the last minute. With Jill clinging to her back like a papoose Shona ran upstairs for his pouch and the file box Finoa had given him. Luckily ottles didn't have very much in the way of possessions. On the other hand, she was dismayed at how much she had not packed up. Personal care items were still arrayed around her bathroom. She swept bottles and tubes into a basket. There wasn't room for them all. She glanced at them to see if there was anything she was desperate not to leave behind, and decided there wasn't time to make that decision. Anything she couldn't carry in one trip would stay behind. None of it was irreplaceable. Time was much more precious, and seconds ticked away with frightening rapidity.

She left Chirwl's possessions on the landing while Lani went to help Jill get her clothes and toys together. She had to start overseeing the loading of the animals into the module before Pop Meader arrived with the loader.

Screaming assaulted her ears as she went out the door beside the module. She ran to see what was wrong. The noise was coming from the monkeys. They didn't seem to be in any distress. In fact, they were playing, throwing shells and pieces of fruit at one another through their cage bars. In fact, she was surprised to see how unworried they seemed about the tiger, whose cage was in their midst.

Jamir was anything but calm. He paced back and forth, always keeping his face toward Lady Elaine's conveyance, which stood several yards away from him. Once in a while he sprang toward her, only to crash into the bars and fall back again. After licking his shoulder with a huge, sandpapery tongue, he began his restless circuit again.

She needed to get the small animals settled first. With the help of the robot arms, which extended all too readily into her module, she stacked the cages one on top of another in her sleeping room. She didn't have to leave very much space between the rows. With luck, the cages could be unstacked and given more room once they were on board the *Elizabeth R.* She smiled a little to herself as she thought about how the animals would feel once the sopophedrase was out of their systems, some of them for the first time in their lives. They would know what it was like to be alive. The only one that had ever been really free was Three-eet, though according to Chirwl he knew he was imprisoned far from home. It was a terrible choice: one could be aware and unhappy or drug-impaired and unknowing. She felt sorry for the animals. Someone had to do this for them. She was glad to be the one.

Her mind turned to Three-eet. He'd have to be lifted into the module tank and all. Ideally he would be lifted down into his half of the bathing pool on a stretcher manned by six or eight strong people. She had no choice but to lower the tank into the water and roll it over, and hope he didn't get hurt in the process. She was counting on Chirwl, who would escort him from the Sandses', to explain it to him in the pidgin language they'd developed between them. Three-eet and Kajiro would be the last animals to arrive. In the meanwhile, she had the first passenger for the freshwater side: the duck-billed platypus. The small, dark-furred creature shot out of its aquarium-like travel container like a missile and began diving ceaselessly back and forth, looking very much like Chirwl playing in the water except for its absurd beak. Fascinated, she watched it for a moment, wondering what kind of psychic benefit Ewan and Baraba believed they would have gotten from it.

"I'm ready," Alex said, rushing in. He was breathless. His arms were piled high with toys. Amir's spider monkey reached through the cage bars and grabbed one from him. "Hey!"

"Don't worry about it now, please," Shona begged him. "Find Harry. I want you to strap him into his crash bed."

"Okey," Alex said. He squeezed over to the storage

compartments where the rest of his luggage was stored and stuffed his burden inside. He slammed the lid hard, making Shona jump and the little animals shriek.

"We are ready," Lani said. She arrived at the door of the lab with a pack on her shoulder and a suitcase in one hand and Jill clutching the other hand.

"Zoo!" chortled the little girl. "Let me see!"

Shona looked up, distracted, her hair askew, as she turned away from counting the hundreds of white-wrapped freezer packages, square containers of grain, and baskets of produce.

"Oh, not now, honey! Please, Lani, take her into the conservatory for now, will you?"

"Of course, Mama," Lani said.

The big animals would have to go in last. In the meantime, Shona had the robot arms lift all the floor plates to load in all the frozen meat, fish, grains, and fruit into the cold-store containers. When they were full the module would be close to its maximum weight, but still lighter than any of the terraformers. There should not be any trouble carrying it with the loader.

One by one, Shona escorted the cages and containers into the module. Pepe, Ewan's parrot, screamed defiantly as she set him down on top of the examining table in the lab. Akeera, by contrast, was dignified on his perch. The great bald eagle batted his wings a little, then settled down to watch the activity around him with one sharp yellow eye. Maat, the cobra, lay in a coil at the bottom of a clear plastic terrarium. The snake had a big bulge a few centimeters behind her head, showing that she had had a meal very recently. At least there was one animal Shona didn't have to worry about feeding for the next few days.

She hurried back and forth out of the clinic's rear door, making sure the carts were rolling up in their turn. As each was emptied, she sent it home. Yelena's, the closest to her target, had had to go first, even though that meant shuffling the crate with their dwarf zebra just inside the conservatory until Shona could place it. The little reef shark was in

a kiddie wading pool underneath Shona's worktable. With
luck, the race to the seaside or up the mountain would keep
the neighbors just long enough so that no one saw the
cart's return. Who was next? Oh, no!

Earthstone. The giant Galapagos tortoise might not
have been as large as his fabled ancestors on Earth, but he
was big enough for all practical purposes, or impractical at
that very critical moment. She eyed the humped shell, over
a meter across, and the wise, wrinkled little head that con-
templated her from its base.

"Alex," she called. Her son came racing out of the module. "When you were playing Noah's Ark, did you discuss
how to get a tortoise to move?"

"No problemo!" Alex disappeared through the door.
While Shona waited impatiently with one eye on the horizon, he reemerged with a mango in his hand. He smashed
it on a corner of the step so that the luscious orange flesh
showed through the shaded green-and-yellow rind. Shona
could smell the fruit's perfume rising from the bruise. The
scent certainly got Earthstone's attention. The beady black
eye tracked Alex as he waved the mango under its nose.
"Here, turtle, turtle, turtle."

At last, like an avalanche beginning, the tortoise rose a
few centimeters and began to lumber slowly after Alex
into the module. Shona followed, fascinated.

A mechanical roar made her heart race with fear. She
rushed outside, terrified that some of her neighbors had at
last given up the chase for Saffie and had caught her in the
act.

No, thank heaven. The noise was coming from a cargo
loader. The vast machine, nearly as tall as the trees, boxy,
white enamel sides chipped and scratched from a thousand
deliveries, trundled up the driveway toward the house.
Under a square dome at the top Shona could see two figures waving at her as she emerged from the module: Mom
and Pop Meader. Thrilled with relief, she found herself
jumping up and down like a child. She waved to them as
they drove the huge machine over the lawn and brought it

to a stop beside her. Pop's long figure, clad in a black-and-white shipsuit, swung down from the cab.

"Hey, Shona girl, what's all this? New pets?" His mouth smiled, but his eyebrows were drawn down over serious eyes as he came over to engulf her in a huge hug. Behind him, Mom Meader was stepping lightly down the ladder on the side of the machine.

"They're coming with us, Pop," Shona said, rushing to hold hands with his wife. "Hello, Mom. I am so glad to see both of you!"

The graceful woman bent to give Shona a kiss on the cheek. "Me, too, darling. But you didn't tell me about all this."

"I couldn't," Shona said. "My transmissions were being intercepted. The Jardindorians can't know what I'm doing. I've sent them on a wild-goose chase. We've got to hurry up before they start coming back!"

"Hold on, hold on!" Pop said, scanning the remaining containers. "That's a fragging *elephant!* And a tiger! What the hell! I won't have anything to do with this. I didn't know you were a thief, Shona Taylor. At least you're going out on a grand scale."

Shona's heart sank. She grabbed his hand in both of hers. He started to pull it away, but she held on. "I'm not a thief, Pop. I swear by the Blue Star, I'm not. These creatures are all hot, every one of them. Please. I am a merchant's wife. I know what I'm saying. I can't leave them here. They're drugged all the time, and they're slowly being poisoned by the environment. Not one of them can roam outdoors the way they were meant to. I have got to get them back to where they belong. Please help me. I've been planning this for weeks, ever since I got your message. There's no time. We've got to hurry."

Pop's eyebrows lifted and his eyes left Shona's to meet his wife's. "Stolen, huh? Did you send messages?"

"Yes, I did," Shona said. "Time-stamped and sealed. You can see them later. I'll split the reward with you, but we have to hurry! If Chirwl and Saffie are found too soon, it's all over."

Mom's sculptured eyebrows rose as she conferred silently with her spouse. He nodded, and she turned to Shona. "All right, honey. We'd better get a move on. I can't wait to hear the rest of this, but it'll keep. Who goes in next?"

"LOOK there, my friend," Chirwl said for the hundredth time or more since early that morning. He leaned over in the pouch on Saffie's back to point. "See there? A fine specimen of an Earth-species beech tree. It is well-grown for not living on the world of its birth. Though the crown curls unhappily. It may lack sufficient water. The season has been hot."

Saffie did not appreciate his cheery discourse. This was unsurprising to Chirwl. The dog must be footsore from being on the trot all day long. The road was good, made as it was of crushed and compressed limestone chips, but it was still hard. He reached out to pat the dog on the head. Saffie looked back at him and whined.

"I am sorry, my friend Saffie." He glanced at the sun. "We do not have much longer to go before we may reverse ourselves."

He had not ridden on her back the entire journey. They followed this road because it ran alongside the main river in this part of the colony, the one that flowed down to the sea. He had swum in it a good deal of the way, taking the burden off the dog so she could run more freely, but he could not go all the distance in that manner, and he could not move fast along the ground. He regretted being a burden to her, though she was willing, as always. He admired her spirit.

The cart that had been running nearly silently behind them skipped over a stone. Both ottle and dog looked back at it longingly, but Chirwl knew his duty. He had promised Shona they would stay on foot until midafternoon. Saffie, though, had made no such promise. She turned and trotted toward it, making as if to jump up in the rear seat.

"No, no, Saffie!" Chirwl ordered, pulling back on her collar. "We need to remain on the ground so that your scent and footprints may be find by those who will surely be following us at this time. It is my apologies to you that you should be weary, and that I may be the cause of some of your tired, but all is for a purpose. Our friend Shona has asked this of us. I wish her the time to do what she needs to, and you would, if you comprehended the situation. We must not mount the cart yet, or your footprints will stop too soon. It is you that the others will seem to pursue."

Saffie whined again. She did not understand his explanation. She might be hungry and thirsty. He certainly was. He rummaged around in the other pannier.

"Come to a stop," he said. "Cart James, you stop, too."

Obediently, the cart halted. Saffie halted and dropped to her belly on the cool grass beside the white stone parkway. Chirwl clambered out and retrieved a folding bowl. He poured food in it for Saffie, then found his own provisions. The dog munched noisily. When the bowl was empty, Saffie looked at him.

"Hesitation to drink from this river," Chirwl told her, giving her the last water from the canteen. "I have drunk much, and not sweet of taste like rivers of my home." Saffie did not care, but lapped the water eagerly. "I myself will be thirsty until we return to the spaceport. It is a shame so much water is close, yet I will not trust it for you. Shona instructs that if any pollutants remain in this zone of the world the water will attract them. One day all will be changed, but not yet."

Chirwl marveled at how mere beings had caused the surface of a planet to change its state so thoroughly. The barrier, which he could hear easily no matter where in the colony he was, held back a most inhospitable climate. The Jardindorians had made springtime to suit themselves. He was glad that the humans had rules to govern which planets they did such things to, and that his planet was similar enough to their homeworld that it did not invite such treatment.

The smell of the air had been changing as they approached the ocean. It was fresher, but with a tangy smell not unlike the seas of Chirwl's own homeworld. Once Saffie had licked the last drops out of the bowl Chirwl folded it away, then trotted onward.

"Come, my friend! The last few kilometers!"

The dog lumbered awkwardly to her feet, but followed him gamely. Chirwl could see the little sign up ahead that marked the entrance to the house owned by Yelena and Rajid. A cart carrying their small shark in a tank back to Shona at the doctor's residence had passed Chirwl and Saffie some distance ago. Chirwl judged that they would make it to the drive just as it was time to turn around. Treading on the Kurows' ground would add a further scarlet fish to Shona's plan. With good fortune, the pursuers would follow the scent in, and go around the house a few times before they realized that they had lost it.

To keep from exhausting the dog further, Chirwl lolloped along on his own feet at Saffie's side. Every meter seemed longer than the ones before. The sun covered them with a blanket of yellow-white heat. It was never this hot on Poxt, nor did the many stars he could see through the portholes aboard the *Sibyl* ever bake him with this oppressiveness. Even the grass seemed to cut into his pads now, but he would not ride. He would share the discomfort with Saffie, who had borne him willingly for such a distance. He also hoped that his scent would excite the trackers even more.

The little sign came closer, then closer yet. One more step, Chirwl willed his heavy feet. Saffie was as tired as he. One more. Inside the gateway the road surface changed from compacted gravel to ornate swirls of mosaic tiles on the bridge as they crossed over the river into the Kurows' property. Chirwl was careful to scatter plenty of dust for Saffie to walk in, so her prints would be as clear as possible on the surface. Once over the bridge they turned off the drive onto the lawn.

The cart rolled in after them, then halted on Chirwl's command.

"Now," he said, and swarmed up the step into the seat. Saffie, forgetting how much her feet hurt, bounded into the rear seat in a single leap. "To the Sandses'," Chirwl ordered the cart, "via the minor track, at maximum speed."

Instead of going straight out onto the road, the cart took a right turn before it reached the bridge. A walking trail, little used by the Jardindorians, lay along the river on the bank opposite the road. It was kept mowed by the robot gardeners, Shona had observed on her last visit there, and would serve as a useful return loop so Chirwl and Saffie wouldn't run into the hunters behind them.

Like all paths on this planet, this was also smooth and even. Chirwl lay flat on the seat, thankfully, examining his pads for blisters. Saffie, on the other hand, sat bolt upright, leaning slightly forward, her ears flapping in the wind, tongue hanging out, a look of supreme bliss on her face. Chirwl eyed her with a pleased expression. "I need apologize to you no longer. You have your reward."

ThE Sandses' house was never so quiet. Usually it rang with the happy voices of its family, the two adults and three children. Of all the homes on this world, it was the most pleasant to visit. Chirwl was sorry. He knew Shona hated to leave these people. They were kind. No matter how great a hold technology had on humans, kindness was still the most powerful item in one's life.

The cart rolled up onto the grass, pulling alongside the pool house.

"Good gravy," Chirwl told the house. "Open this door." Chirwl and Saffie jumped down from the cart and lolloped inside. "Be on guard," he warned the dog. She settled on her belly with her chin resting on her paws, her eyes on the door.

Three-eet surfaced at the sound of the door opening, and walked on his tail on the surface of the water. "Greetings! Do you eat well?"

Chirwl slid into the pool with him. "My friend," he said, in gestures and squeaks. "We go back to the home ocean. The journey will be crowded and long, but home waters await you at the end."

The dolphin leaped completely out of the water for joy, diving in again nose first. Then he surfaced close to Chirwl, one large round eye on the ottle. "How do I believe you?"

"Believe," Chirwl urged him. "We must hurry. Go over there, and be prepared to move."

In Standard, he began giving instructions. Whirring and clanking arose as the house computer obeyed him. Part of the floor popped open, and a tank rose from it. A hose snaked out of it into the pool, and suction commenced, draining water from the pool into the tank. Robot arms fell from the ceiling toward the pool with a huge piece of cloth between them.

"No! No!" Three-eet shrieked. "Prison, pain, darkness!"

"Come, come," Chirwl said, swimming around to push the dolphin toward the litter, now ready to lift and crate him. "We must hurry!"

The dolphin continued to cry piteously, when footsteps on the marble floor and the sound of a dog barking made Chirwl dive deep in alarm. He surfaced, seeing Saffie and Lark circling each other happily, trying to sniff one another's tails. Chirwl looked up at the five humans, who stared down at him. He blinked.

"This is most unexpected," he said.

TWENTY-SEVEN

MIRACULOUSLY, Jamir had stopped growling as soon as they set him next to Lady Elaine, who, with her bales of hay, took up the entire wall of the lab near the bathroom. The tiger sniffed as best he could through the bars of his cage, then curled up contentedly, his tail tapping out a slow, steady rhythm.

"Whoa!" Pop said, fending off the little zebra. It seemed to have decided that his coverall's coloration made them family. It kept nuzzling against him, nipping at his sleeves. "How are we doing?"

Shona wiped her hair back out of her face. She'd had to have the small cages taken out to make room for the parrot, who squawked wildly when he was placed too close to Akeera. The eagle watched majestically but didn't move, even when Pop picked him up, perch and all, and carried him to a different part of the deck. Bock must have given him a hefty dose of sopophedrase that morning. Well, Shona vowed, that was going to end. They'd all had their last dose of that!

Having to separate the birds had ruined her initial floor

plan, but thankfully she was able to cut up her diagram and rearrange the sections without leaving anyone out. In a small, closed room the various musky, sharp, and downright malodorous smells was beginning to make her eyes water. She'd keep the module on house power as long as possible, but during the transit to the ship she'd have to cut back on ventilation. It was going to be a stinky ride.

"Almost there," she said. "We're waiting for the last two."

"You really have to take a parrot?" Pop asked. "There's thousands like him across the spaceways. I see one in nearly every bar I visit."

"Yes," Shona sighed. "He's a scarlet macaw, very rare. He was stolen from a conservation park on Earth, like the eagle and the dolphin. I matched his DNA."

Mom Meader came in with Jill, who'd fallen in love with her on sight. Mom had a gift with children and animals. "Honey, we're going to have to get a move on. The others will have to meet us at the spaceport. It's going to take us a little while to get there."

"We can't leave Saffie!" Jill cried. "I'll go look for her."

Shona and Mom Meader both grabbed for the little girl, who broke toward the door. Mom swept her up and cuddled her. "Now, you can't do that. Isn't Saffie the smartest dog in the galaxy?"

"Uh-huh," Jill admitted after a moment.

"Then you trust her to figure out how to find us. She knows where we're going to end up anyhow."

"Mama!" Alex shouted, running in. "The cart!"

Shona's shoulders relaxed. "Good! Now we won't have to worry."

But Saffie wasn't alone. To Shona's horror, there were two dogs on the cart along with the ottle: two dogs and two humans. Dwan, white-faced, rode in the front seat beside Chirwl. Ev rode behind them on a larger cart with his hand on a huge plastic box. Shona's heart thumped to a stop in her chest. The conveyances slowed to a stop. Shona stared in horror as Dwan dismounted and came to face her.

"I knew Lark could find them faster than anyone else, and she could outrun anybody, but when I told her to find them, she led me way out, then back again to the rear of my own house. Chirwl told me what's going on. He told me everything." The young woman swallowed. Shona noticed that her eyes were red, as though she'd been crying. "The others are still back running around Yelena's. I think you still have a little time." She tilted her head toward the cart. "Three-eet and Kajiro are both ready to go."

"Do you hate me?" Shona asked.

"No," Dwan said, taking Shona's hands in hers. "I hate myself. *I didn't know.* You have to understand that. Promise me you do."

"I do," Shona said, squeezing Dwan's long fingers. "I'm so sorry I couldn't tell you, but I was afraid . . ."

Dwan glanced over her shoulder in the direction of the Kurows' house. "I know. I haven't been honest with myself. Finoa's had all of us under her thumb. But not me, anymore!" She glanced at the module. "You're taking the reason away."

"Was that what she had, a lottery for the elephant's child?" Shona asked. She stopped. Everything she wanted to ask would take time, and there was none left. She leaned over and gave Dwan a big hug. "I had to leave so much behind, Dwan. Take what you want. Thank you for everything."

Alex whistled to Saffie. The dog, huddled up with Lark, gave him a reluctant look. "Come on, Saffie." He jumped up and grabbed her by the collar. Lark jumped down with her.

"C'mon, Lark, you're not going," Ev said. He took Shona's hand. "Good-bye, Shona." He picked Lark up around the chest and hauled her back up on the cart. Both dogs began to howl a frantic good-bye.

"Hush!" Dwan admonished her pet, then turned to Shona. "We'll go back and try to keep the others away from the spaceport for a while. Good-bye. I'll miss you."

"I'll miss you, too," Shona said. "I'll send a message—"

she stopped. Who knew when she could transmit freely again?

She ordered the mechanical arms to lift Three-eet's tank off the cart. Kajiro jumped from his master's breast to Lani's shoulder and began to play with her hair. Dwan couldn't look any longer. She started crying as the Sandses' cart rolled away.

"That's it," Mom said, slapping the door seal closed. "All the critters are in their seats, and the connections are off. Let's move it out." She gave Jill a piggyback ride up the ladder to the cab. Lani went behind Alex to make sure he wouldn't fall. He gave her a scornful look, but scooted up by himself. The big loader scooped up the module like a child picking up a rubber ball in its hand.

Pop gestured to Shona. "After you, little lady."

"Let's go, Chirwl," Shona said, turning her back so he could climb into his pack.

"I cannot go," Chirwl said.

"What?"

"I am not going without my cells. I must have the tissue back."

"Pick up the talking furry turtle and pack him!" Pop exclaimed. "We've got to move!"

"He's not a turtle," Shona said. "He's an ottle."

Pop's eyes brightened. "Really? You're his host. That's right, I knew that. But let's go. We've got a mob behind us, any minute."

"No," Chirwl said definitely, and Shona knew he was dead serious.

"Why?" she asked. "Why can't you let those cells stay here? You shed more cells than that normally over the course of a day."

"Because two reasons. I am entitled to my parts and what becomes of them. Also not to create children of me in the home of that human. What she does is evil and good as well, but without permission it is all wrong."

"Dammit, are you out of your mind?" Pop asked. "We could both lose our licenses."

"I'll take him," Shona said, making her decision. Chirwl was right, and she had to respect his beliefs. Besides, Alien Relations would have her head if they heard someone was cloning ottles and it was her fault. "I'll meet you at the spaceport."

The password "baggy pajamas" admitted Shona and Chirwl to the Malone house.

How silent it was in the darkened corridors. With Chirwl giving her directions Shona sprinted on her toes toward the lab. She'd only been in it once, but Chirwl insisted he would never forget it, no matter how many light-years they put between themselves and Jardindor.

The thick carpet muffled her footsteps. On the one hand, the lack of noise was comforting. It meant that no one could hear them wandering around. On the other, it meant they couldn't hear anyone coming up behind them. Shona kept glancing back over her shoulder in fear.

"Hurry," Chirwl said. "Care nothing for pursuit."

She palmed a door plate, and was momentarily blinded by the brilliant whiteness of the lab. Quiet humming of machinery and the soft shifting of animals in their cages were the only sounds they heard. On soft feet, Shona crept around the big room, looking for sample storage.

"Unless she's already using it, it'll most likely be frozen," Shona whispered.

"If a young one has been engendered, we must take it," Chirwl insisted.

But the incubators were empty. Dozens of small black-and-white rabbits watched them with twitching noses as Shona opened doors and drawers, seeking the kind of vial that was normally used for tissue samples.

Behind a panel in the wall she found the cold storage. Donning gloves and goggles, she checked labels.

"There are no names on these," Shona said. "Only dates and numbers. Wait, here's two from the day you visited her."

"Check them," Chirwl urged her.

Shona took the two containers to the nearest microscope. Using a probe she teased a few cells from each onto the plate, and turned on the viewer.

"This is it," Shona said, pointing at the first sample. She peered into the vial. The contents appeared to be the same amount that could have been abstracted from the cut on Chirwl's foreleg. The other tissue culture was Terran in origin, she had no time to find out from what animal. She had what she came for. She tossed the first vial in her pouch with Chirwl, slammed the other one back into the freezer, and ran for it.

NOt troubling to take the pack off her shoulders, she jumped into the cart and ordered it out onto the road.

"Top speed, James!" she insisted. "We have to hurry."

"Pursuit is imminent," Chirwl said.

Shona glanced back. "Can you see them?"

"No, but I can hear them. So can you."

Shona strained her ears. Ottle hearing was much more sensitive than human, but over the sound of wind in the trees she could hear voices shouting. They were still out of sight behind her, but advancing in her direction at speed. Shona held on to her seat as the little cart sped silently along the road and into the grand park that surrounded the spaceport. Ahead of her was the Meaders' transport shuttle *Ralegh,* a large craft about the same size as the *Sibyl.* The *Elizabeth R.,* their huge freighter, would be in orbit around the planet.

"There she is!" Alex shouted, as she came through the hazy barrier. He was standing on the loading ramp jumping up and down. Pop Meader stood beside him. The engines were belching steam around their feet. "Mama, hurry!"

Alex ran up the ramp and disappeared. The cart had almost reached the shuttle when Shona heard a yell behind her. She looked back to see Lewis in his flitter coming around the edge of the barrier. He was calling to the people behind him. Lewis pointed at them. He looked angry and shocked. Shadowy shapes were visible through the force field. She knew what that was: the rest of the population of Jardindor coming to reclaim their illicit possessions. Somewhere in that mob were Ev and Dwan. Shona hoped they wouldn't try any heroic actions to stop the others. They must not get hurt for her sake. They had to go on living here once she was gone.

She barely waited for the cart to come to a halt before she sprang off the bench seat, and scrambled awkwardly up the ramp. As she climbed it, it rose up. The second she was inside the cargo hold, she heard the hiss of pneumatic seals.

Pop Meader grabbed her around the waist and threw her into an emergency crash couch, ottle pouch and all. "Strap in, little Shona. You just made it. Go, honey!" he shouted.

He got himself fastened in just as the g-forces knocked them flat against the bulkhead.

"Crushed!" Chirwl choked out.

"Sorry," Shona croaked, trying to draw breath against the pressure. She grabbed the chest bar and tried to pull herself up so she wasn't crushing the ottle. She ended up with her spine arched and her cranium pressed into the cushions, but her back was not squishing Chirwl any longer. She squeezed her eyes shut and held on.

It felt as though she had been in that position for hours when the pressure eased.

"Come on, little Shona," Pop Meader said, holding his hand out to her. Effortlessly, the big man pulled the shock webbing and the chest bar away from her. "You're back in space, cupcake."

Space! Shona had missed being off-planet, but hadn't realized how much until that moment. She scrambled to her feet, eager to get to a port and see the velvet blackness pricked with diamonds.

"May I be out?" a plaintive voice at her back asked.

"Oh, of course!" Shona shrugged the pouch off and put

it down on the deck. Chirwl wobbled out, unsteady but triumphant.

"I have it," he said, holding up the vial of his flesh. "Which is the disposer?"

"Over here, friend," Pop said, leading him to a hatch in the wall. Chirwl swarmed up the tall man as if he was a tree, hooked open the small door, and pitched the container into the dark compartment.

"It is mine, and this is what I choose to do," Chirwl said.

Shona finally had a moment to look around her. The *Ralegh* was an old-style cargo shuttle, little more than a big box with an engine. They were in the vast cargo compartment. It was empty except for her lab module, which filled only a third of the area, looking like a large white mushroom cap sitting all by itself in the center, the loaders, small and large, and an insulated flitter car, suitable for transport on space stations or planetary surfaces up to several hundred degrees. The *Elizabeth R.* couldn't land through atmosphere. Not only wasn't it designed for it, but it was so old it would probably break up in reentry.

She had no time for more than a quick glimpse out at the thinning atmosphere giving way to darkness. It was time to check on her many charges. She dashed along the worn floor padding and unsealed the door of the module.

A cacophony assailed her ears, as every animal gave tongue to its displeasure at being crushed by gravity. Shona checked all of them, giving particular attention to the birds. Pepe sat in the tray of his cage, squawking avian profanity. As she watched, he beak-walked his way back up to his roost, glaring at her. Akeera had fallen to the platform below his perch, and sat on it looking dazed. Shona helped him up, and was rewarded with the beguiling chicklike peep. No bones seemed broken. He hadn't so much as shed a feather. She scratched him behind the neck as Laren had showed her how, and he closed his eyes with pleasure.

None of her charges seemed to have been harmed. She made sure they all had food and water. Some of the contents of several tanks had slopped over onto the floor. Shona hesitated to refill them, because the module was going to be moved again very soon. The dolphin in particular seemed very agitated. Shona knew he was very cramped in his tiny transport tank. She wished she could talk to him and tell him everything was going to be all right. Harry and Saffie yowled to be let out of their padded compartments. Shona didn't dare to let them loose yet, not until the shuttle had docked safely aboard the freighter.

"I'll be back," she promised them, then escaped to the fresher air of the cargo bay. She found Chirwl and brought him to the dolphin in the bathroom.

"Tell him we're getting him a bigger tub as soon as we can."

"That is not it," Chirwl told her, after watching the dolphin's antics. "He is upset because the striped killer is here with him."

Shona gasped, realizing how close to the bathing pool Jamir's cage had been placed. "I forgot about that! I'm so sorry! Tell him he has nothing to fear. See how placid he is? He's in a cage."

"The striped one's mind sleeps," Chirwl assured the dolphin. "And he is locked up."

"Take care he is kept that way," Three-eet shrieked. The tiger stirred at the sound, and looked around for its source. The dolphin leaped in the air and disappeared underneath the surface of the water. In a moment he reemerged, calmer. "Do not trust him. He kills. His mind must sleep."

"I will tell Shona to take care," Chirwl promised him. "He wishes you to always give the predator the drug," he told Shona.

Shona bit her lip. "I was going to stop the sopophedrase. These animals have suffered enough. They deserve to get their minds back."

"How can you?" Chirwl asked, reasonably. "They can have their minds restored when they reach home. Now is not home, is it?"

With a heavy sigh, Shona realized he was right. "No. Now is not home."

The children climbed out of their crash couches and ran to throw their arms around her. She held them tightly as she listened to the pilot chatter on the speakers set into the walls. The deck moved under their feet as the primary engines kicked in to help the shuttle catch up with the mother ship, in her orbit around the planet. Jill was talking excitedly about how she would see Papa soon. Alex had a lot of observations about the shuttle.

"It's a Mark 40," he said, in awe. "Those are over sixty years old! But they have the biggest capacity of any sublight cargo carrier in the galaxy."

Only Lani had nothing to say. Under her arm Shona could feel Lani's shoulders shaking silently. The girl's head was bent so her face was hidden. Shona had to duck down to look at her. She was weeping.

"What's wrong, darling?"

"I didn't get to say good-bye," Lani said, plaintively, her cheeks stained with tears. "Zolly and the others . . ."

Shona's heart went out to her. "I'm so sorry to take you away from your friends. They've been so good for you. I hated to do it, but we had to jump when the opportunity came. We couldn't let anyone know we were going."

Lani nodded, her eyes red.

"Well, they know now," Pop said, coming over to them. "Come on forward. You'd better hear this."

The Taylors followed the trader along the worn deck padding through the forward bulkhead to the cockpit. Mom Meader was at the helm with a communications screen pulled around. Governor Hethyr's scarlet face was on it. Shona wondered how she was able to send a message when she had blocked the system in everyone's house, then she realized Hethyr must be on one of the personal ships on the landing pad. Dina was beside her punching at controls with swift movements. Hethyr's angry voice rang out of the speakers overhead.

"I am the governor of this colony. I order you to halt where you are and return to Jardindor with our property. We are scrambling ships to escort you back. I don't know what that woman told you, but you are carrying precious and delicate cargo. Please do not endanger it. We will reward you very generously if you return it to us intact. If you do not turn around we will pursue you. You don't want to make enemies out of us, I promise you. We have influence all over the galaxy."

Shona clenched her fists. Pop put his arm around her. "Frag her," he said. "Turn it off."

"There's one for you, too," Mom said to Shona. "Marked 'personal.'" Shona leaned over and put in her code.

Hethyr glared out at her, looking even more furious than she did on the live transmission. "You viper. You thief. We will prosecute you in every court in the system. We trusted you! You are going to jail. You are going to lose your license and your family. I will see to all of it."

"Don't reply," Pop said.

"I won't," Shona assured him, briskly. "I don't want her knowing where we're going. How soon can you warp away from here?"

"We're pulling aboard the *Bessie* right now," Mom said. "Since we don't have to worry about landing too close to a planet, we can jump as soon as we're clear of the orbit." Shona looked at the forward vidtank. A glint above the night side of the planet grew larger and larger, coalescing into a cargo ship. As they approached, a hatch opened on the topside. Mom touched the controls lightly, and the shuttle's angle tilted to match the ship they were approaching. "Is everyone all right back there?"

"Yes," Shona said. "I mean, they're all healthy. Scared, though. So am I."

Mom reached behind her and took Shona's hand in

hers. "Don't you worry, darling. You're safe now. I promise."

Shona wished she felt that way. The stars disappeared around them, and the *Ralegh* bumped to a stop in the midst of blue and red lights. Mom shut down the controls with deft movements of her hands, and Pop tapped Shona on the shoulder.

"Let's go make our guests more comfortable."

TWENTY-EIGHT

"I'Ve got the kids filling up the suit-testing tank so your dolphin friend can stretch out a little," Pop said, leading the Taylors out the shuttle airlock and into the *Elizabeth R.*'s vast bay. "We're so glad you're safe. Gershom was so worried about you."

"Thank you. I want to send a message to him. Is that possible?"

"Don't do it now," Pop cautioned her. "Anything you transmit goes through this beacon. Wait until we've jumped. Besides, we need to talk."

"That's right," Shona said, sitting down and preparing to negotiate. "You've done Gershom and me a big favor by picking me up. A huge one in taking these animals back to their owners. You've got a right to part of the reward. No?" The trader was shaking his head.

"No. For something like this you can't pay me in money."

Shona's eyes went wide. "Oh, Pop, you're not going to take me back there? Or is this a citizen's arrest for grand theft?" Another horrible thought struck her. "I can't give

you any of the animals as payment. Now that I've sent af-
fidavits I have to bring them back to their owners."

"Shoot," Pop said, leaning back and putting his long
hands behind his head, the grin wider than ever. "You
haven't even thought about it, but the second I saw that zoo
in there I knew what I wanted. I want scat. Dung. They're
going to produce plenty of it. Do you know what *elephant
dung* would bring on the open market to gardeners?"

Shona remembered Finoa's astonishing flower beds.
Their luxuriance was probably due to input from Lady
Elaine. "I have to admit that I don't."

Pop looked smug. "About thirty credits per gram
dried."

Shona goggled. "Per *gram?*"

"Yup. Are you sure you just want to *give* me all of it,
just like that? Gershom would have seen the value in it."

"Well, Gershom doesn't have to shovel it. Yet. It's a
deal." Shona put out a hand, and Pop Meader shook it.

Red lights along the door frame and around the ceiling
came on and started to chase. "Uh-huh, there we go," he
said. "We're about to jump. Hang on."

Shona strapped herself to the seat and held on to the
sides of the table. In the screentank, the colored disk of
Jardindor wavered, shrank to a dot, and vanished. They
were away.

"FiSh is still frozen, Three-eet emotes," Chirwl said, sur-
facing just a split second after the offending food, which
popped up and floated stiffly on the surface. The dolphin
now occupied a portion of a huge tank in the engineering
section of the *Elizabeth R*. In normal circumstances it was
filled to find leaks in conduit or pressure suits. Now it was
segmented into three portions, two salt, for the use of the
dolphin and the reef shark, and one brackish, shared by the
platypus and the pigmy hippo.

"Holes!" Alex exclaimed, reaching for the fish. "I
didn't micro it enough. Hold the line." He popped it into

the heating unit that had been hastily brought aft from the break room. It came out floppy but not soft. "There we go." He threw it into the pool. Three-eet snapped it up before it hit the water.

"Much better," Chirwl translated.

Shona sighed. She had been planning the escape phase for weeks, but once faced with the mooing, growling, shrieking, rustling, and above all, smelling-to-high-heaven horde of animal life, she realized she had not really thought through what would come next.

Alex had researched everything, and created a table of how much food each of their charges needed to eat, and how often. He oversaw the doling out by his mother and the Meaders of meat to the predators, fish to Three-eet (and to Chirwl, who was acquiring a taste for it) and the shark, and mixed diets to the others. He knew the temperatures the tropical animals needed for comfort, and how to move the dead rats and rabbits the eagle ate to make it seem as though they were live prey. To Shona's surprise, Jill had shown no squeamishness about handling raw meat, and followed Alex's orders happily to help fill buckets, if only for the joy of playing keeper in "my zoo," as she called it. Saffie and Harry followed the crew of young people, and were quick to jump on morsels of food that fell from their hands. Chirwl continued to spend much of his time with Three-eet, conversing in squeaks and whistles.

"There is a learned paper in this," he insisted. "I shall be proud to study for it."

With the Meaders' help, they had moved the animals who didn't need tropical temperatures out of the module to make it easier to care for all of them. Most of the animals were not used to being cooped up in small cages, and were becoming more stressed as the day wore on. Shona knew she was going to have to continue to drug them. It broke her heart to realize it, but for the safety and health of them all, she had no choice.

Mom and Pop had been kind beyond words. From a seat-of-the-pants scramble off-planet, the trip away from

Jardindor was getting off to a better start than she'd dreamed. She was gratified that the dolphin was now in a pool where he could move around. When she'd left them, he and Chirwl were leaping and frolicking with the young crew. She hadn't a hope to avoid pursuit, but for now she could relax, though her bunk was a far cry from the luxury of Jardindor.

For the sake of the animals Pop had offered not to take the gravity generators down for the duration of their journey. It took an enormous expenditure of power, and Shona was grateful for his generosity. New fuel cells wouldn't come cheap, and as he'd said, he was officially running without a paying cargo. Shona wished they didn't need to keep the generator on; she missed the comforting feeling of weightlessness. Her body felt all too solid on the thin padding, and the bunknet made her feel as though she was trapped in a bag. She kicked it off the end of the bed and lay looking up at the darkness. That was better. Too exhausted to think any longer, Shona fell asleep.

Shrill voices woke her early in the next shift, and she went sleepily to check on her charges. The scoop of an immense front-loader had been filled with water for Peggy's amusement. The pigmy hippo, submerged to her nostrils in her wallow, wiggled her ears at Shona. The birds occupied an aviary with Earthstone, who stood on a pile of straw placidly chewing leaves. In the center of it all were Lady Elaine and Jamir. The tiger had been let out of his cage, and sat with his back against the elephant's leg. His tail lifted up in a slow curve and smacked down against the padded floor, over and over again. Lady Elaine's trunk dipped down to caress and coil around the tiger's chest, then lift up again to stroke him on the head. The tiger looked content, as though he was being fondled by a member of his own species. The moment Shona let herself into the enclosure Jamir was on his feet, blocking the humans from approaching Lady Elaine.

Shona picked up a hunk of meat and waved it, and the

tiger decided she wasn't much of a threat, and that he wouldn't mind a snack.

Shona went to pat the gray forehead that hung high above her head. Alex had informed her that at two and a half meters Lady Elaine was at the top end of the scale for elephants. She seemed to welcome the attention, but shifted her spine uncomfortably. Shona felt nervous about examining an animal of whom she had little experience, but she was responsible for the elephant's well-being for the next few weeks. She palpated the elephant's belly. Her hands were not strong enough to make out much detail of the womb through the thick hide. She put her ear to her side to listen to her heart. The booming pulse sounded strong. Shona thought she ought to bring in a stethoscope and a portable ultrasound and check on the pregnancy. It would be inexcusable if she endangered the elephant's fetus.

A streak of striped lightning interrupted her examination. Jamir finished his snack and came over to shove in between them. Shona backed off hastily. As soon as she was gone, Lady Elaine put her trunk around the tiger, rewarding her protector with a gentle hug. He settled down, watchful again. Shona felt her heart racing.

"There you are!" Pop said, gliding over to her. "Mom wants you. We're about to come out of the jump."

The ship was already beginning to shudder as it slid out of the fabric of jump space. Shona handed herself onto the bridge and slid onto a worn couch upholstered with lime-green fake fur. The pile molded itself to her body as she strapped in.

"Hey, honey," Mom Meader said, glancing at her briefly as her hands flew over the controls. The old ship responded to the slightest modification. Gradually, the screentank cleared from blackness of faster-than-light speed to the usual fabric of space. A reddish-yellow star burned fitfully in the distance. Shona counted three bright crescents that were planets or moons orbiting her. "Mission accomplished."

"Is that a beacon?" Shona asked, peering closely.

"It is. It's a regular relay on the communications web, but all it really serves is that mining colony in the asteroid belt there." Mom pointed at an artifact in the midst of the giant rock clusters. It showed an identification signal on the scope. "I wanted to get just clear of Jardindor space before I downloaded messages. Would you like your mail?"

"Oh, yes, please!"

SHONA went back to her module to use the console so she wouldn't drown out the Meaders' messages with her own. The lab seemed so small after the cargo bay, or even the shuttle. It was a miracle that she'd managed to get all the animals in it at all. Now the cobra reposed in splendid solitude in his terrarium, separate from the lizards and other desert creatures. The heat was so great Shona undid the collar of her tunic to cool herself even before she sat down. The platypus, who'd proved to have a temper, seemed to be better off here, with the bathing pool to himself. It'd be another adjustment when she had to pack everyone in again. She still felt as though if she stretched out her arms, she would bark her elbows on the bulkheads. For the moment, she was grateful for the relative privacy.

In the queue under her code number were several hundred sendings from Jardindor. Knowing they were probably threats and angry reprisals, she set them aside without listening to them. The only person she wanted to hear from was Gershom.

His worried brown eyes peered out at her when she activated the first message in the file. "Shona, you don't have to ask how concerned I am. I hope you don't mind that the Meaders were the ones to pick you up. You know how much I wanted to be there. Please let me know as soon as you're safe. I'll rendezvous with the *Elizabeth R.* as soon as I can. Love."

Whew! Shona thought, hitting the Reply key. *Where to begin?*

"Darling, we're all safe," she said. "You must have read my mind, because I know I only used our code for a minor problem, but the truth is I . . . Gershom, you won't believe what's been happening to us! We are all safe and well. The children have grown taller and smarter, and Lani is blossoming. Chirwl is fine. The animals are fine. All of them." That was the easy part. She stopped the recording for a moment.

"Gershom, do you remember when I asked you for the hot list?"

After a few false starts the whole story of her last several weeks began to pour out. She gave Gershom a full account of the whole situation: the animals, their drugged state, the attempts on her life, Finoa's research and her assault on Chirwl, and how she ended up with a hold full of rare beasts.

"I know you'll be upset that I didn't tell you any of this before, but my transmissions were being monitored. I didn't know whom I could trust. I think only a few people were involved in the animal-smuggling, but even those who are innocent had a stake in keeping the pipeline open. I don't even know whom we can trust out here. *Someone* had to obtain those animals. *Some* officials had to be looking the other way." She glanced at the return address of his last transmission. "We're not that far apart now. Can you make sure the hold is empty when you meet me? We'll need all the space we can get."

She signed off with love and sent the message, wondering how he was going to react. Perhaps she should have included video. No. Stranger things had happened in their lives.

Among the remaining messages were replies from the men and women who'd put notices of the animals' disappearances on the hot list.

"Dear lady, you're my angel!" cried Bohman Nehdi, the caretaker of Stripes the okapi. "These last few years I thought I'd go mad. The owners of the Associated Safari Protection Consortium of Alpha have blamed me. Now I am able to assure them he is safe. I look forward to meeting with you. I promise you that your reward is waiting! Sixteen hundred credits!"

Shona reflected glumly that a trip to Alpha would use up more than sixteen hundred credits' worth of fuel. But, a promise was a promise.

"Dr. Shona Taylor, don't I know your name from a tridee?" asked Steven Lopata. "I feel like I've walked into a video! Your image, and above all, the cellular scan, prove that you do have my tiger. He's alive! Is he well? Is he eating properly? Please, if you can send back to me and let me know when I can expect you, I would very much appreciate it."

Shona sent replies. She scanned over the list of the other messages she'd saved. No word from Susan. She sent an urgent message to get back to her. They could meet somewhere safe. For an exclusive story Susan would cross the void of space itself.

TWENTY-NINE

"This is the *Sibyl,* requesting docking instruction," Gershom said, as the little ship circled Far Cry Station. It was well-named, being at the far end of the frequently used spaceways, though nowhere near as far as Jardindor.

"Dock Sixty-Two," a bored voice said, after the usual time-delay. "Slow to sublight impulse, one-tenth power. Final approach of one hundred meters should be unpowered except for available reverse thrusters. Do not break vacuum and open hatches until your seals mesh with the station's. We will send a red-light signal that will change to a green-light signal when you sync up . . ."

"Phuh! Does he think we're in the Space Marines?" Kai protested.

"There are bureaucrats all over," Gershom said, and gave the order to proceed.

"Did I say Space Marines?" Kai asked, as the seals opened. Beyond them in the landing bay were a dozen men and women in uniform, all unsmiling.

"Captain Gershom Taylor?" asked the woman at their head, the officer who had given them directions.

"That's me," Gershom said, taking a step ahead of his men.

"We have orders to search your ship. Here is our warrant." She handed over a datacrystal, and Gershom stepped back inside to put it into a reader.

The other crew crowded around the little reader screen. "Contraband?" Ivo asked. "What in hell kind of contraband are you looking for?"

"Stolen livestock," the woman replied. "Where is Dr. Shona Taylor?"

"Not here," Gershom said. "The last time I heard from her she was still on assignment."

"May I ask where?"

"Jardindor."

The woman nodded. That obviously corresponded with what she'd been told.

"Have you seen or are you planning to see her?"

"Of course I am," Gershom said. "Her term of employment is six months. That'll be up in three more months."

"What are you doing here?" the woman asked.

"None of your damned business," Ivo said, coming to stick his chin out.

"Lieutenant," one of the guards interrupted, coming over to salute her. "The hold's back that way. Unlocked." He gestured toward the left turning in the corridor. The officer spun on her heel and marched along with him.

"You cretins had better not touch anything," Kai said, leaping to follow.

The guards were thorough. Gershom gave them credit for being in a hard place. Once an infrared scan revealed no other life-forms on board they really had no excuse to stay, but the lieutenant seemed determined to turn over every square centimeter of the ship. He couldn't remember being this angry, but he was not as mad as his crew, who blocked the doors of their cabins until forced out of the way.

"Keep calm," Gershom warned them.

He found it difficult to follow his own advice when they went through his cabin. They paged through his hanging clothes idly, but became more interested when they opened the compartments containing Shona's things.

"If you're looking for livestock," Gershom said bitingly, "nothing is going to be among my wife's lingerie unless you're looking for vermin, and I resent the implication." The guards backed off from the drawers immediately. The lieutenant told them to pull the drawers out and look in void spaces behind the containers. Nothing except a few alphabet blocks that Alex had probably shoved in there when he was a baby, and a small item that the guard who found it held as though he had the secret to cold fusion in his hands.

"Look, ma'am," he said, holding it out to her. The lieutenant held it up in triumph.

"Animal hair! And you tried to hide it from me."

"We have a lot of pets," Gershom began. "That's tan, so it's from our cat or one of our rabbits."

She shot him a pitying look. "Take it for analysis," she ordered one of the guards. The young woman took the clump of hair and ran out of the ship. "You'll do time for this, you and your wife."

"I'm telling you," Gershom said, more amused now than angry, stiff-arming his crew, who were about to do a pantomime demonstration with fists and feet describing what they thought of the lieutenant and guards, "that's probably cat hair. From an Abyssinian cat, a ruddy. Harry's belonged to us for several years. We bought him from a registered breeder."

"We'll see," the lieutenant said, leaning back against the bulkhead with her arms folded.

The guard returned much more slowly than she had left. In her hand was a plasheet, which she held out to her superior.

"Cat hair?" Gershom asked innocently. The officer

glared at him. Gershom and his men deliberately burst into loud laughter.

She threw the sheet on the ground and signed impatiently for her troop to assemble.

"This is not the end, Captain Taylor. If you see your wife, you'd better tell her there's nowhere she can hide. This bulletin was sent to fifty other ports. She had best turn herself in."

Gershom kept his face expressionless. "I'll tell her you said so."

The woman glared at him, but marched her force away.

"Whew!" Ivo said. "We dodged the business end of that weapon. What do we do now?"

"What we came here to do. Unload the hold, same as she asked us," Gershom said. "Fuel her up to the gills, and make ready to jump as soon as we possibly can. Then, we have one more connection to make."

SHONA was on her belly trying to hook bones out from the edge of Jamir's pen. She didn't want to upset the tiger more than she had to. Lady Elaine was pacing around and around their shared enclosure, trumpeting unhappily. Jamir, as always, picked up her mood, and was keeping in step with her, always maintaining the outer perimeter so all threats would have to go through him. The elephant seemed to be uncomfortable. Shona did everything she could for her, including trying to duplicate the shape of Finoa's garden so Lady Elaine would feel at home. None of it was working. And there were twelve more pens to muck out. And for some reason Saffie wouldn't stop barking. Maybe it was time for a shower after all.

EVEN a sonic shower felt sybaritic after spending hours shoveling dung. Shona let the full cycle run twice as her body vibrated itself clean. She put her hands close to the emitters to clear out the muck under her fingernails, and spread out her hair to let the waves strip away oil and dirt from every strand.

Saffie started barking again.

"Hush, Saffie!" Shona smacked the off button and reached for a robe from the clean stack above the booth door.

"Papa!" Jill shrieked. Honestly, everybody on board had gone crazy, Shona thought.

But Jill wasn't alone. Holding both her hands tight over her mouth to keep her from exploding again, Jill sat on the lap of a tall man lounging on the dressing room bench.

Gershom held out his free arm to his wife. Shona goggled for a moment, then threw herself into it as Saffie leaped up and down barking. Jill giggled with joy. Gershom's lips brushed gently across her cheek, then found her mouth for a long, passionate kiss that almost made up for the many weeks she'd had to do without him. When she finally drew back to take a breath, she smiled at his face, so loved, so familiar, so missed.

"And they all lived happily ever after," Jill said.

WHEN the two of them emerged from the cabin and joined the rest in the rec room, Shona was embarrassed by the pleased, indulgent smiles of her hosts, but she was so happy she didn't really care.

The *Sibyl*'s crew came over to hug her, three big men completely smothering her. She kissed them all, beaming with delight. "You look wonderful for someone who's been scooping poop nonstop for a week," Eblich said.

"We have a surprise for you," Gershom said, turning Shona around.

There was one more person in the room. Seated on the worn couch next to the coffeemaker with Chirwl curled happily on her lap was a long-legged woman who waved and batted long lashes over big blue eyes at her. Fair-haired and elegant, she was dressed in the latest silky blouse and trousers in tones of rich blue. Shona's mouth fell open.

"Susan!"

"Hey, twin," the other woman said, springing up to give Shona a warm hug. Chirwl hung over her shoulder like a shawl, happy as could be. He loved Shona's best friend.

Shona was overwhelmed with joy. "What are you doing here?"

Susan grinned. "Well, you kept on telling me that things were interesting. Are you kidding? This is the story of a lifetime!" She sketched headlines with her free hand. "Well-known medical heroine escapes from loony hatch with a zoo in tow. I'm going to record every minute of the rescue, from start to finish. It'll be one starblazing true-life docudrama."

Shona gasped. "You can't do that. They'll kill me."

"It has been tried twice at least," Chirwl put in.

"You innocents," Susan said, shaking her head. "I may not use it, or all of it, but you'd better have this whole adventure on vid somewhere in case you do need it later, though I doubt it. When Gershom told me what he had in mind . . ."

Shona turned to her husband. "And what do you have in mind?"

"In a little while," he said. "I'm starved, aren't you?"

"The ideal thing," Pop said, when they'd settled down after dinner to chat, "is to find a friendly planet and use it as a base. Get the cooperation of the authorites, maybe with a little sweetening, and have the owners come and meet you."

Gershom shook his head. "Impossible," he said. "If Far Cry Station is anything to judge by, there'll be few harbors where we can land safely without risking search and arrest." He told them what had happened, down to the tuft of cat hair behind the dresser drawer. Shona listened with a growing sense of dismay.

"So," Pop said. "Those rich people bought the cooperation of the authorities. Money doesn't just talk, it shouts and waves its arms. Don't worry. Us indies are used to running underneath the radar, as they used to say."

"That's what I intend," Gershom said. "We may not have official protection, but we've got something better."

Pop grinned. "You're reading my mind, son." When Shona looked puzzled, he explained. "The indies. They're family to us, and to you, too. They'll help."

"What can you do?" Susan asked, pulling an electronic notepad out of her belt pouch.

"Divide and conquer," Gershom said. "Find someone who's going toward Alpha, and let them take whatever animal lives there. Find someone who's going to Mars, and so on. I just have to arrange a meeting."

"Exactly!" Pop said. He looked a little sheepish. "I know you're already paying me off, but we'd be willing to take the shark home."

"All the way to Barnard's Star?" Gershom asked, unbelievingly.

"Active community out there," Pop said, sheepishly. "Plenty of manufacturing concerns. We can get a return load, no problem. I've always been crazy about sharks, ever since I saw them on school vids. The rest of the animals will still have to fit into *Sibyl*, though. Even if they don't have to ride there all the way home."

"Kai can do it," Shona said. "It's just going to be a headache."

Thirty

"Lead on, Shona. I must see the rest of them!" Susan surveyed the zoo with eyes wide.

Gershom and the crew of the *Sibyl* followed, with Pop pointing out their innovations in hasty but effective animal pen construction.

"This is gonna be a tight fit," Kai observed, sourly. "You've got ten times our space, Pop."

"I know," Shona said, glancing back over her shoulder. "Putting them all into the module seemed impossible at the time, but we did it. The thought of putting them back in again just makes me cringe."

At last, she brought them to the pen containing Jamir and Lady Elaine.

"What's this?" Susan asked.

"The pride of the collection," Shona said. "Voilà!"

She whisked aside the first cargo net. Behind it, the metal mesh and second net were translucent enough so that all of them could see Lady Elaine and Jamir pacing around and around the enclosure.

Susan shrieked. "Oh! Oh, Shona! I don't believe it! Is

that a tiger? Oh, my God. Oh, my Interplanetary Video Award! And an elephant!"

"She's pregnant," Shona said. "She won't be due for another year or more, alas."

"But still!" Susan exclaimed, furiously making notes. "Adding to the population of a nearly extinct species . . . it's too much. There's years' worth of video here. I'll be famous—you'll be famous."

"No," Gershom said. "Bad idea. She's already famous, and there's really no percentage in it."

"Sure there is," Susan said. "If you hadn't been well known, you wouldn't have gone you-know-where, and if you hadn't gone you-know-where, you wouldn't have been able to rescue all of these grand beasts. *Look* at them, Gershom."

"I've never seen anything so amazing," the tall man admitted, his face glowing with excitement. "Near-mythical creatures right before my eyes. I feel like a kid again."

With the Meaders' help, the transfer to the *Sibyl* was accomplished fairly swiftly. Three-eet didn't protest this time as he was loaded into his small box and carried back to the bathing pool in Shona's module.

"The next pool is home waters," he said, through Chirwl.

Lady Elaine decided she didn't want to be moved again, and waved her trunk dangerously at any of the humans who attempted to get close. Shona saw the whites of the pachyderm's eyes as she rolled them. Jamir threw himself at the curtains whenever he saw movement, making the monkeys scream and the zebra and okapi gallop around nervously.

"I'll have to give them extra sopophedrase so they won't hurt themselves," Shona said, after a good deal of soul-searching.

They threw a piece of beef liberally laced with the sedative into the enclosure, then left it alone. Soon, they returned. Jamir was sitting in the exact center of the pen with his paws crossed like a cat's.

By the time all the other beasts were in their new pens, Shona was able to lead Jamir to his new place. Lady Elaine, much calmer now that her roommate had relaxed, took his long striped tail in her trunk and followed him. Susan scooted here and there with her video, cackling to herself.

"I don't believe it," Gershom said, surveying the bay of the *Sibyl* with his hands on his hips. "There's actually a little room left. Kai, you're a puzzle wizard."

"Go safely and fly straight," Pop Meader advised Shona, giving her a last big hug. "On second thought, don't fly straight. Don't let those rich people find you."

Their good-byes were brief. The seals holding the two ships together hissed as the *Sibyl*'s airlock closed, and a boom echoed through the bulkheads as the *Elizabeth R.* nudged away from the side of the smaller ship.

"Now it's up to the indies," Gershom said. "Next stop, Unity Station. The others will be there waiting for us, and plenty curious."

LIKE Venturi Station, Alpha, and Earth itself, Unity was a major intersection point between several spaceways. It was nothing unusual for a group of ships to assemble off-station. Deals were made, passengers were exchanged, and meetings were accomplished in a kind of secrecy that was increasingly rare in the galaxy. Gershom's call for a meeting here sent a signal that something interesting was afoot, and any indie spacer who could make it would be there.

"So what's the deal, Taylor?" said Don Badowski, pilot of the indie ship *Space Stud*, and unofficial leader of the Interstellar Freight Carriers, the first to arrive on board. He looked over the array of goodies laid out on the long table in the common room, aware that the room would fill up quickly. He was a good-looking, athletic man in his thirties, self-conscious about the fact that though he was well-furnished with hair, none of it was on his head. "Hmm, potato chips. Is there any beer to go with them?"

"Of course," Shona said. With a smile she offered him a full mug and showed him to a seat, bringing the bowl and a selection of dips over within easy reach. She certainly had learned a lot about parties during her stint on Jardindor.

She had spent a lot of time making the room look nice, but made a point of dressing in an ordinary shipsuit for the conference. Gershom would have liked to see her wear something pretty, but agreed her instinct to appeal to the spacers as one of them, and not a sales representative of some kind, was sound.

"Well, well, how fancy you made this!" announced Ina Hariznova, a spare, dark-haired, dark-eyed woman, captain of the *Varna*. "This is bad—I don't see any chocolate."

"Do you think we'd forget it?" Shona asked her, pretending to be shocked.

"I don't know what you would do," Ina said. "You might want me to be disappointed."

"Never." Shona assured her.

"It's over here," Susan said, pointing to the end of the buffet where the desserts were. She was trying to be inconspicuous in a corner with her camera, but she wasn't fooling the indies. Peirce Richardson gave her a wink.

"Make sure you get my best side," Ina said, with a pointed glance at Susan's camera. She loaded up a plate with raw vegetables and sweets and plunked herself down near Don. Shona turned to greet Diana Unger, John Lartz, Benjamin Stocks, Kang Sun, Christine Dominick, and a couple dozen more pilots, all old friends and acquaintances.

The message Gershom had sent out, under Susan's address for the sake of security, had caught enough independents in between jobs or jumps to assemble a good-sized crowd. If half of them could help, it would be enough to largely empty out the hold. Shona was determined to take Akeera and Three-eet back to Earth herself, and Lopata was expecting his tiger to be brought there as well. Their biggest problem was Lady Elaine. Dan Patel, her owner, had not yet responded to Shona's query for a location to deliver her.

"Hey, Shona," Dave Potter said. Amey, his wife, came over to exchange kisses with Shona.

She turned and kissed Dave, too. "Thank you for forwarding those messages. You saved our lives."

"My pleasure," Dave said, with an embarrassed grin. "You know we all help each other."

Chirwl had asked to have his pouch placed on a hook in the break room. He hung halfway out, chatting with the guests as they arrived. Most of them knew Shona was hosting the ottle, but few of them had ever had a chance to meet him. The children made a brief appearance, at the request of the Potters, then were sent off to play in their quarters.

"Okay, I've got my pitcher, you've buttered us all up, what's going on?" asked Chris Karll, skipper of the *Lightning*, the fastest ship in ath IFC, hoisting a liter stein of beer.

Gershom scooted a chair into the midst of the group and sat down on it with his elbows on his knees. "Friends, I've got a proposition for you."

"Ahhh." Now, he was speaking their language.

"So we've got a hold full of animals. It would take us months to deliver all of them to their homes, and frankly, we're not set up for it. I wanted all of you to meet with us in person to ask you if you're going out toward any of the destinations, or passing through one, if you would take one of the beasts with you."

"This is all very interesting," Don said. "Before I leave this room or drive your lemur anywhere, we still have to work out one thing."

"What's that?" Gershom asked.

"There's money in here somewhere, isn't there?" He raised an eyebrow, daring the others to contradict him. "It's a long way to Alpha Centauri, and my ship doesn't run on pretty words."

"There's a substantial reward due for each animal," Gershom said. "They're all in the latest version of the hot list. Shona will get in touch with each owner and let them know you're delivering them instead. To cover the legal side she'll record an introductory message transferring her rights to you. If you bring the animal home, you can have the reward."

"I don't buy that," Chris said, skeptically. "You could take them all home. Why don't you? Why us?"

Gershom started to reply, but Shona got to her feet. "Because I've got to stay out of sight," she said. "We have to make one run, straight to Earth, because I promised to do that myself. Because they've already tried to kill me twice." Exclamations burst out of her listeners. "If we go to all the places we have to, sooner or later they will figure out where I'm going, and beat me there."

Diana nodded, her brown eyes thoughtful. "Now you've said something that makes sense. We look out for our own. I'm in."

"Me, too," said Tom Korzeniowski, a big man with an elaborate walrus mustache and a resonant voice. The others chorused agreement.

"Okay," Don said. "You've got yourself some bus drivers."

"Do we get to see the animals?" Amey Potter asked eagerly.

"Of course." Shona smiled. "Please, everyone, come this way."

BECAUSE of the tight squeeze the visitors could only go in a few at a time. Every single pilot wrinkled his or her nose at the smell, but the sight of the first rarity, Peggy, made them exclaim in amazement, and each subsequent revelation just added to their wonder and delight. Chirwl stationed himself on the edge of the dolphin tank, translating Three-eet's remarks to them, though Shona knew no one believed he really understood what the dolphin said.

Shona always saved the crowning glory of the collection for last: Jamir and Lady Elaine. Each time, she prefaced the display of a live tiger and elephant by saying she and Gershom were taking the special pair home to Earth themselves, and each time the visitors sighed.

THEY returned to the break room talking excitedly and comparing schedules and ships. To Gershom's and Shona's delight, a few arguments broke out over who got to take what animal home.

"I want to take the zebra. I'm going through the Cotton Consortium," offered Bob.

"Hey, the bearded monkey is cool," said Kang.

"I want to take the dolphin," said Ben.

"The tortoise is coming with me," said Don.

"No, I want to take it," Chris argued. "I'd enjoy the ironic contrast. *Lightning*? "Tortoise?"

Don's eyebrow went up. "Fine. Be that way. I'll take the platypus." No one challenged him, and he looked pleased. "It's a lot smaller."

"I've got a trip to Jury-Rig," said Tom. "I can take the cockatiel. Can it talk?"

Diana Unger looked over the list. "I can't take that okapi all the way to Glius in the Katana, but do you know Folie's Traveling Circus? I'm bringing them new tents. They've got a bunch of critters of their own. They know how to care for exotics. It's their bread and butter. One more will just blend right in. If you'll trust me as far as my rendezvous, I'll guarantee that he'll be fine after that. They'll do right by me, and I'll pass it on."

"I trust you, Diana," Shona said, making a note. Stripes had a ride. "Who's next?"

"The eagle," Christine said promptly. "He's cool. I'm on my way to Earth anyhow."

Almost reluctantly, Shona nodded. She had wanted to see through her promise to Laran, but the important thing was to get Akeeva home safely.

"Are there written instructions on feeding the beasts?" Don asked. "I'll want to read up."

By the time the discussion was over, none was left unspoken for. Shona let the indies copy all the animal care data she had, with links to databases where they could find more, and the connection numbers to branches of the GSPCA and other benevolent organizations along the way. She answered all their questions as best she could including, with great reluctance but an understanding of her responsibility for her charges' as well as her friends' safety, dosage information for sopophedrase."

Once the business was finished, the spacers of the IFC settled down to enjoy the party. They played with the kids, flirted with Lani, got into impenetrable discussions with Chirwl. Shona flitted from conversation to argument to bull session, enjoying it all more than she had ever enjoyed a gathering on Jardindor. Unlike her former employers the indies were open, honest, spontaneous, and made personal remarks because they had high regard and even affection for the ones they were teasing.

This is my *social group,* Shona thought, happily.

Thirty-one

"Shona, Shona, hurry," Ivo said, shaking her awake. "Gershom wants you. It's the elephant, she's kicking up a fuss." He waited while she shoved her feet into ship boots, and led the way back through the forest of cargo netting to the rear of the ship.

"What is it?" she asked. Gershom and Susan were peering through the thick tan coils. Gershom motioned her in front of him, then parted a fold of cloth so she could see.

Lady Elaine was walking up and back in between the bulkhead and the rear wall of the module. She would bump into one, then go back and bump into the other. She seemed to be doing it deliberately. Jamir obediently paced along with her. Shona let out an involuntary exclamation. Lady Elaine let out a trumpeting noise, and the tiger chimed in with a growl. His green eyes turned toward where the humans were hidden, as if he was ready to stalk and kill them for making his friend unhappy.

"Did you miss a dose of sedative?" Gershom asked.

"Heavens, no!" Shona said. "I gave her sopophedrase just last night, after dinner."

"Mama?" Alex's little voice came from the forest of netting. Jamir heard the sound and charged the side of the enclosure. Shona threw herself in between her son and the tiger, covering him with her own body. Gershom flung himself over both of them. Fortunately, the metal mesh sandwiched between the layers of rope net turned Jamir's claws aside. The tiger sniffed closely, then began to pace up and back on the side where the humans stood.

Shona extricated herself from the family sandwich and knelt down beside the boy, whose tousled hair stood up on his head. "What is it, Alex? You should be in bed."

"I heard something," he explained. "Is Lady Elaine okay?"

Shona exchanged glances with Gershom. "I don't know, honey. She seems restless."

"She has to roam for miles in the wild," Alex said, didactically. "This is too small for her. Even Ms. Finoa's garden was bigger."

Shona sighed. "We're doing the best we can, honey," she said. "When she gets back to her owner she'll have lots more room. This is only temporary. I wish we could get her to understand that." Lady Elaine moved unhappily from side to side, rocking on her big feet. It was clear she was uncomfortable. She began to bump against the barricades and the hull again. Jamir growled toward the humans, baring his teeth, blaming them for his friend's unhappiness.

Susan frowned. "Could you give her more sedative? I'm afraid she'll hurt herself."

"She's upsetting both of them. You'll have to drug her more heavily," Gershom said.

"I can't," Shona said. "I'd hesitate to use more than she's already getting, no matter how distressed she becomes. I won't endanger the fetus."

"What if the fetus is already in trouble?" Susan asked. "What if she's trying to tell you that?"

"Oh, no! I hope not. That would be horrible!" Shona looked at the huge creature warily. This was what she had feared more than any other problem: if any of the animals became ill or injured in her care. "I'm not a veterinarian," she said. "I don't even know what's where in there."

"I do, Mama!" Alex said. He ran out of the cargo bay.

He came back with a portable tri-dee unit, a present from Laren Shona had allowed him to keep. A trumpeting sound erupted from the speakers. Jamir snarled, doubling over on his feet to come and sniff the barrier near Alex. Shona dragged her son back out of reach.

"What is it?" she asked.

"*Natural Kingdom,*" Alex said. "This is the episode about elephants."

Shona didn't want to denigrate his contribution, he looked so eager, but she'd sat through all of these programs with him and Jill a dozen times, and the scripts were too general to be of any use. "Honey, this is a chidren's program," she said gently. "I've seen it. They just tell you about the animals when they used to live in their native habitat."

"No, they're not," Alex insisted. "They're interactive. They've got all sorts of stuff. Educational."

Susan examined the holographic advertisements on the box the crystal had come in. "He's right, Sho. Look at this! Anatomy."

Alex selected the entry. On the tri-dee screen, a long-legged, humpbacked quadrupedal skeleton appeared. Gradually it clothed itself with nerves, then veins and arteries, then muscle tissue, then the familiar gray skin, all in incredible detail with annotations. Shona looked at Alex with new respect.

"Can you enlarge the image?"

"Oh, yeah, this does everything!" Alex blew the image up until it was ten times larger, then twenty, until it was half the size of the real thing.

"Stop there," Shona said. "I can work with this." She glanced at the elephant, who was rocking from side to side. She was clearly in distress, picking up clumps of hay and throwing them across the pen, and letting out soft wails.

"We can't get her into my lab, but let's get her next to the door so I don't have to go so far for supplies."

Gershom eyed the tiger, who was leaping from side to side in response to his companion's distress. "We'll need help." He went for the other crewmen. They were wide awake after Shona explained to them what she wanted them to do.

"And be careful," Shona said. "Even under sopophedrase he's dangerous."

"You don't have to tell *us,*" Eblich said, eyeing the tiger's claws and teeth.

Using bribes of freshly thawed meat, Ivo and Eblich lured Jamir over to one side of the enclosure, then Kai and Gershom deliberately interposed themselves between the two beasts while Shona came in to lead Lady Elaine out. Behind her Susan pulled the triple curtain closed. Jamir tightened his haunches, then sprang right over the two men's heads. He hit the curtain, snagging it with his claws, and hung on to it, growling. He started to climb the netting.

"He's going to go nuts," Kai said. "Drug him!"

Shona moved in with a hypospray and stuck it through the mesh into the tiger's foreleg. He snarled and snapped at her. She jumped back. His fangs clicked on nothing. The crew started to lead the elephant toward the entrance to the module. Even though his head began to sag and his movements slowed, Jamir refused to give up. He threw himself at the netting, causing it to bell out.

"He'll hurt himself," Shona said. "There's no real need for me to take her out of his sight. I think that's what he is afraid of. I can examine her right here."

They brought her back to a clear area only an arm's reach from the tiger. He stopped trying to force his way through, and paced up and back. Gradually his pace slowed. He dropped to his belly, and with a huge sigh fell asleep, still with his eyes on Lady Elaine.

Using the diagrams in the text that accompanied the documentary show, Shona gave Lady Elaine an examination. Her eyes were clear and bright. It was difficult to examine her trunk, because that appendage was also trying to examine Shona at the same time. It snuffled up and down her body, tousling her hair.

"Are you sure she won't throw you?" Gershom asked anxiously.

"She knows I'm trying to help her."

And so it appeared. Whenever Shona stepped away for an instrument or to check her readings Lady Elaine started moaning and rocking again, but as soon as Shona touched her she held still. Shona kept going along the big body, using a stepladder and a stethoscope tuned up high to listen to breath sounds on either side of the big back. Lady Elaine obediently opened her mouth wide so Shona could look inside, and presented the end of her trunk for examination.

"I wish my other patients were as cooperative," Shona said. She felt down the massive forelegs, then in between them. "How many teats is an elephant supposed to have?"

"Two," Susan read in the much-enlarged text. "Between the forelegs, where you are."

"She has eight," Shona said, glancing over at the diagram. "How strange. Two big teats up where they're supposed to be, and six smaller ones about the size of the end of my thumb behind those. They're already engorged. So early?"

Susan's eyebrows went up. "Evolution?" she asked.

"Doubt it," Shona said. "Unless elephants have litters."

"One baby," Alex insisted. "One or maybe two. Elephants never have triplets."

"A freak of nature?" Gershom asked.

Shona pursed her lips. "Made, not born. I expect that this is something Finoa engineered."

"What for?"

"The baby, I expect. It's time we saw what's going on in there." Shona reached for the portable ultrasound unit from her module.

Following the diagram, Shona traced a pattern over the uterus from several angles. There was a mass within the womb, but it didn't look like a normal pregnancy according to *Natural Kingdom*'s researchers. Alex's tri-dee had a table showing the progress of an elephant fetus from conception to birth. A fully developed baby elephant weighed 120 kilograms. Lady Elaine had been pregnant only a few months. The size of the mass was too large for a three-months' fetus, and it should not be moving so much yet.

"Something is very wrong," Shona said. "The way it's moving the baby looks almost like it's in pieces. Big oval pieces."

"Is that the head?" Susan asked, pointing to a round feature in the scan.

"Yes . . . there's another one. And another." Shona counted six small heads. She glanced at the anatomy charts again. "These are not elephant calves."

"What are they?" Alex asked.

"Well," Shona said, thinking. "I'm not sure."

A red-brown blur jumped down from the top of the stack of hay bales and came to rub against Shona's legs with an interrogative noise. Shona glanced from Harry to the scan and back again. "They look like cats." Light dawned on her suddenly, and her eyes widened. "Not cats—tigers. She's carrying tiger cubs."

"But that's impossible," Susan said.

"Not at all," Shona replied. "Non-species animals have been made to act as host mothers before, though usually they're closer to the type of animal they're carrying. Finoa created six babies from Jamir's stem cells. No other animal on Jardindor was large enough to hold a litter like this. What's an elephant female but a huge, huge cow? Poor, hapless cattle, carrying a predatory species in her womb, like cuckoo eggs tipped into the nests of unsuspecting birds. So that's why she has six extra nipples. They're for these kittens."

"Will the nipples work, though?" Gershom asked.

"Yes. I forgot to tell you. Finoa is the scientist who perfected the Nentnor process for growing replacement organs. The way she tweaks and combines individual genes,

I bet if I tested that tissue I'd find it's part elephant and part tiger."

"So that's why Jamir likes Lady Elaine so much," Alex said wisely. "He's her husband."

Shona nodded, overwhelmed at her discovery. "Six of the most endangered of all species. This is what Finoa had over all her neighbors! I thought for a while it might be blackmail, but this would be the ultimate in an Animal Magnetism cuddly toy—the rarest creature in the galaxy. Do what I say, or no tiger for your collection."

"You say three months?" Susan asked.

"Or thereabout," Shona said, nodding.

"Alex, do you have the *Natural Kingdom* episode about tigers?"

"Big cats, episode two. I'll get it." His eyes shining, he dashed away.

"What about three months?" Shona asked.

"I did a program on zoo lions," Susan answered. "I have a half-memory that the gestation period isn't very long. I think these cubs are ready to come."

"Oh, no! I don't know anything about animal obstetrics."

"Looks like you're going to get a crash course, honey."

Alex came dashing back again, waving another datacrystal.

SHONA read through information on the life cycle of the tiger. Sure enough, three months was the period, and the little forms she could see in Lady Elaine's womb were fullsized and fully developed.

"This is probably going to be messy," she said, thoughtfully. "Alex, would you go back to your cabin?"

"No! I want to watch."

Shona looked at Gershom, who shrugged. "He's going to be a scientist. Let him. You decide if you've had enough," he warned his son.

"I'll be okay," Alex said bravely.

Shona took a look underneath Lady Elaine's tail. The way the elephant stood patiently with her legs astride and lowered her head in resignation told Shona she was ready.

Under the vaginal flap the cervix was squeezed tightly shut. She went into her module for a speculum, and laughed at how inadequately small they were. She brought out the largest and handed it over to Ivo. He paled, but agreed he could make an appropriately large duplicate in a short time.

"Well," Shona said, with an exhalation. "We're going to have some babies. It's not a sterile procedure, but I want this area as clean as possible. I don't want to risk infection to either the mother or the cubs. We'd better get moving before Lady Elaine tries to deliver them herself."

"Don't you dare!" Susan exclaimed, her blue eyes wide with horror.

"What? Why not?"

"Wait," Susan said, backing away toward the corridor. "Don't you dare deliver those cubs until I get my camera. I'll *never* forgive you if you don't!"

While Susan dashed out for her camera, Shona ordered the men to bring out the equipment she thought she'd need, plus bales of sterile bandage, disinfectant, and antibiotics. In the storage lockers under the floor she had an incubator in case she needed it for a premature baby. She had the men roll it out and set it up while she scrubbed. Once the makeshift operating room had been prepared and Shona was gowned and gloved, she dilated Lady Elaine.

"Are you going to use a drug to make her deliver?" Susan asked, with interest, her tri-dee camera held up against her gown.

"No! If I gave her pitocin or something like that she might push the cubs out, but they'd be crushed to death by her muscles. I've just got to go in and get them before she starts to have contractions. Finoa might have altered her system. Or she might have intended to do what I'm about to do."

It was a long reach for someone her size. Gershom held

the stepladder steady as she felt her way down the birth canal. She could feel the cubs writhing, each still in its little caul. Thankfully, the sopophedrase kept Lady Elaine relaxed enough.

"Get ready," Shona said, backing up with her hand around a bundle smaller than her head. "Here comes the first one!"

"This is a blessed event. It's a blessed event of an extreme size," Susan said happily, a few hours later. Six tiger cubs, each about a kilogram in weight, little striped sides heaving, little round ears folded close to their fuzzy skulls, paws too huge for them, little eyes blind, lay in the incubator. Once they were washed and rubbed clean Shona picked up and examined each one, then put it back into the basket on the heated blanket, where it rolled against its littermates, whimpering in surprisingly deep tones. A couple of the men retreated to the forward section before the very messy procedure was all over, but Alex, Gershom, Susan, and Harry made it through to the very end. The cat purred loudly through it all.

"He's happy because it's cats being born," Alex said.

Lady Elaine kept sending her trunk around to see what was going on. Shona wheeled the incubator over so she could see the cubs to whom she had given birth. The trunk sniffed all over them, overshooting the edges of the incubator several times because the babies were so small. She let out a pleased noise, and the lids of her eyes dropped contentedly.

"They're beautiful," Susan assured her.

"Three males and three females," Shona said with satisfaction. "I think we've added significantly to the population of living tigers. This is a great moment. Finoa created a miracle. It's too bad she didn't do it legitimately. I almost wish I could congratulate her."

They fitted a sling around Lady Elaine's massive middle and placed the babies into it. The cubs immediately smelled their way to the nipples, and started to suckle milk, their little pads visible against the cloth as they kneaded. Shona watched with pleasure as they nursed.

"Aw," Susan said, zooming in with her camera. "Aren't they cute?"

"You ought to get in touch with Jamir's owner," Gershom said. "Let him know his missing tiger has multiplied."

"That's true!" Shona exclaimed. "I'm going to wait, though, to make sure they live. It would be terrible to get his hopes up, then deliver bad news."

They heard a rattling sound behind them. Shona turned away from the slingful of cubs to see Jamir struggling to his feet. He sniffed the air, then started pawing at the metal curtain, idly at first, then more frantically.

"Let him out," Shona said. "I want to see what he does."

"Are you sure?"

"I've got a hypospray ready. Let's do it."

They pushed Alex and Harry hastily into the monkeys' pen so they'd be protected behind the metal curtain. Susan refused to budge. Carefully, Shona and Gershom got on either side of the opening, and Gershom jerked open the flap.

Jamir trotted out, in no kind of hurry. He rubbed against Lady Elaine's leg, his tail switching furiously all the while. He sniffed all along her length, as she stretched her trunk around to caress him. The sniffing became more intense when he came to the expanse of white cloth that mewled and squirmed. He let out an interrogative noise. The trunk lay quiescent on his back while he investigated it thoroughly, even sticking his head into the sling. Shona held her breath. He withdrew his head. A cub dangled from his jaws.

"Stop him," Gershom said. "He'll kill it."

"No, wait," Shona burst out, from years of experience of owning cats. "He won't hurt it. It's got his scent."

Jamir dropped to the ground with the cub between his paws, and began to wash it with huge swipes of his big pink tongue. A raspy exhalation like a purr erupted from his throat. The cub wriggled and protested vigorously, but not from fear. Susan looked up from her viewfinder, her eyes running with sentimental tears.

"That's the most beautiful thing I've ever seen."

"Congratulations," Alex said to Jamir. "You're a daddy."

SHONA had more confidence downloading her messages as the days went by and Earth came closer. She saved unread all the messages with beacon strings that led back to Jardindor. Hethyr and the others had gotten smart and started to attach homing pigeons, return receipt requests that would activate if Shona opened or deleted them, and would give them an entire string that would lead them to her last actual position. The mass of thousands of messages seethed like a volcano on her console's drive, but she didn't dare do anything about them until after the last animal was home and safe.

Not all the messages were good news.

Dan Patel's thin-lipped visage appeared on the screen. His gray-tan skin was pale, and his face was strained. "Dr. Taylor, I'm very glad you've found Lady Elaine. I thank you for all the trouble you've gone through, but I don't know what to do. I haven't been in touch because I've been going through personal bankruptcy. It's taken everything I had and more to search for her on my own, and I have just run out of resources. I even lost my job. I won't be able to pay your reward. I can't even afford to keep her if you bring her back to me. She's expensive to keep, as I'm sure you've discovered. I'm sorry, but I give you my permission to deal with her as you must. I only hope you'll let her live. I am so sorry. I miss her horribly, but what can I do?"

"Oh," Shona said, deflated. Suddenly it felt as though the 150 kilos of fodder a day that they had to feed the elephant had been strapped to her back.

"Clank," Gershom said, his personal noise for an empty cash drawer. "That just turned her reward into negative territory. But, just a moment—didn't your tiger man say he's stocking a pastoral planet?"

Shona's eyebrows went up. "Proxima 4. I've read about it in the nature science news."

"We're meeting him on Earth—would he like a *big* bonus?"

"He's already getting one: six cubs," Shona said, wryly. "But you're right. It's the obvious answer."

BECAUSE the *Sibyl* was so close to Earth they received the reply from Lopata by the next time they came out of a jump, and everyone—even Chirwl—gathered to hear it.

"An elephant? Really?" the thin-faced man said. "Well, I suppose . . . I'd be happy to take her in. We've got a huge tropical island, more of a subcontinent, you know, useless for anything except a wildlife preserve. She could have plenty of room to roam. You wouldn't know if she was old enough to breed, would you?"

Shona and Gershom laughed so hard she had to rewind the last part of the message to hear it again.

"The trouble is that all of us got into the program to preserve the big cats. We don't know anything about caring for elephants. But we can learn! Bring her. I'll clear the import with EarthGov and the Department of Natural Resources. Everything will be fine. Just get here!"

"Now, that is a win-win situation," Shona said with relief. The government agencies would protect them against pressure from agents of the angry Jardindorians. "And wonderful news for Mr. Patel, too." She put an arm around Gershom. "I guess we're on our way to Earth for real—there were times when I didn't think we would pull this one off."

"Nonsense," said Gershom. "We're the best. We deserve to visit Earth—we just have to decide what to see first. After we escort Lady Elaine and Jamir safely home with their brood, of course."

"Any suggestions?" said Shona, looking at her own brood.

"The ocean!" shouted Alex. "We can wave hi to Three-eet!"

"No, Doll World," insisted Jill.

Shona smiled. "Chirwl?"

Chirwl put his hand-paws together in thought. "I have a destination on Earth that has always interested me greatly," he said. "I think I would learn a great deal from a visit to where they make Crunchynut bars."